MW01088098

Written on the Mist
Dawn of Alaska

Naomi Rawlings

Praise for Written on the Mist

"Naomi Rawlings has crafted yet another series that delivers everything lovers of historical fiction will clamor for—a stunning setting, a big family that will make you want to be a part of it, women chasing their dreams, and men who know how to be both strong and loving. *Written on the Mist* will pull you in and make you glad it's just the first installment of the series, so that you can look forward to many more hours spent with these compelling characters!"—*Roseanna M. White, Bestselling and Christy-Award Winning Author*

"*Written on the Mist* by Naomi Rawlings will take you on a journey to Alaska from the comfort of your own home. You will experience history, adventure, mystery, romance and more as you peek into the lives of the Amos family of Juneau and Sitka. Get ready to experience the real scenery, the climate and more of Southeast Alaska without benefit of rain gear or cold weather gear."—*Susan Benton, Educator and Book Reviewer*

"Naomi Rawlings writes exciting novels that feature fresh, sharply drawn characters, fast-paced and fine-tuned adventure-romance plots, and gently pitched biblical themes. Her newest novel, *Written on the Mist,* is simply exceptional."—*Erin Healy, Multi-Published Author and Fiction Editor*

"An excellent storyteller with beautifully written characters and storylines. Her books shine."—*Jennifer Lonas, Editor and Book Reviewer*

"There were so many aspects to *Written on the Mist:* the love story, the historical perspective, the drama and adventure, the characters, the carefully woven messages against domestic violence and racial discrimination, it was an incredible read. I'm excited to see Naomi Rawlings has five more books planned in this series."—*Karen Hardick, Editor and Book Reviewer*

"Naomi Rawlings' writing style stirs emotions in an incredibly positive way. The characters come to life and in your mind and heart. You rejoice, cry, and laugh right along with them. *Written on the Mist* is one of my very top favorites."—*Keili Holmes, Book Reviewer*

Other Books by Naomi Rawlings

Dawn of Alaska Series

Written on the Mist

Texas Promise Series

Tomorrow's First Light

Tomorrow's Shining Dream

Tomorrow's Constant Hope

Tomorrow's Steadfast Prayer

Tomorrow's Lasting Joy

Eagle Harbor Series

Love's Unfading Light

Love's Every Whisper

Love's Sure Dawn

Love's Eternal Breath

Love's Christmas Hope

Love's Bright Tomorrow

Belanger Family Saga

The Lady's Refuge

The Widow's Secrets

The Reluctant Enemy

Written on the Mist

Published by **Naomi Rawlings LLC**

PO Box 134, South Range, MI 49963

All Scripture quotations are taken from The Holy Bible, King James Version.

The characters and events in this book are fictional, and any resemblance to actual persons or events is coincidental.

ISBN-13: **978-1-955356-18-3**

Copyright © 2023 by **Naomi Rawlings**

Cover art © 2023 by **Carpe Librum Book Design**

All rights reserved. No part of this book may be reproduced or transmitted in any form or by any means, electronic or mechanical, including photocopying and recording, or by any information storage and retrieval system, without permission in writing from the publisher.

Printed in the United States of America

2023—First Edition

To Nathanael, for your strength, bravery, and tender heart as you seek to follow God.

The Inside Passage near Juneau, Alaska; September, 1886

Never in his life had he been so cold. Jonas Redding hunkered deeper into his coat and stared out over the railing of the ship slowly chugging its way north. It wasn't just the air, which was cold enough to cause the tip of his nose to ache and the breath from his mouth to puff little plumes of white into the air. It was also the damp. There was a constant moisture that permeated the air. Even when it wasn't raining, it still felt like dampness was touching his skin.

But at the moment, there was no question it was raining. The heavy fog that the ship had been traveling through for most of the morning had turned into a light mist a half hour ago, and now that mist was turning into a steady rain that drove the handful of other passengers aboard the cargo vessel belowdecks.

But not him.

There was too much to take in about this new land that he

intended to call home—and too many memories to haunt him in the darkness of the ship's belly.

The wooden vessel chugged past the end of yet another island, with mountains climbing from the shores along the water into the thick layer of gray clouds above.

At least he thought they were mountains, but the mist was too thick for him to get more than an occasional glimpse of the dark green trees blanketing them. He had no idea how tall the mountains were, or if their tops were carpeted with trees or capped with jagged, rocky peaks.

Or if they were even mountains. They could be . . . Well, he couldn't quite think what they would be if not mountains. But—

"You can go belowdecks, mister." An older boy appeared at his side, rainwater plastering his long black hair against his head. "The rain's only looking to get worse."

Jonas glanced at the boy, who looked as if he belonged on the Cherokee reservation near where Jonas's sister lived in Oklahoma. Everything about his features was Native American, from the straight black hair that fell to his shoulders, to his high cheekbones, to his tan skin. Yet he spoke as though English was his first language, wore the clothes of a white boy, and seemed completely comfortable standing aboard the deck of the ship.

"How do you know the rain is going to get worse?"

The boy shrugged, but his dark eyes took in the surrounding scenery with a keen sense of understanding. "It always rains here. My brother says it's because of them mountains. See how they're on both sides of us right now? The mountains keep the clouds over the valley, and there ain't nothin' for the clouds to do but rain. When the valley widens, the clouds leave and get all misty-like. On a lucky day, you might even see the sun."

"On a lucky day?" He almost choked.

"Yes, sir." A smile lit the boy's face. "This here's the most beautiful place in the world when it's sunny."

Jonas tilted his gaze up toward the tiny, drizzling drops leaking from the dark clouds above and the endless mist that didn't allow a man to see much of anything.

The boy yammered on. He talked about how the trees were the richest green under the bright rays of the sun, and the water the deepest turquoise. How it never got too hot no matter how bright the sun was, and how in the summer whales congregated offshore along one of the islands.

Here Jonas had spent the better part of the year on assignment in the Texan desert, where the sun scorched the earth until the rocky terrain turned yellow, and the cacti were as brown as they were green. And he'd somehow ended up in a place where a glimpse of the sun was considered lucky?

"I sure do hope you get to see some sun while you're in Juneau," the boy continued, almost as though he didn't know how to stop his tongue from forming words. "Like I said, when that happens, this is the prettiest place the whole world over. Just ask my sister if ya' don't believe me."

"Then I hope I get to see some sun too."

And he did, but more because he wasn't sure that his Texan-born body could tolerate being in a place without sun for more than a couple weeks than because he was convinced the murky gloom of his surroundings would somehow morph into the most beautiful place on earth.

His comment made the boy smile again nonetheless, his face filling with an optimistic sort of hope.

What was it that made the boy so hopeful? So happy that something as simple as the possibility of sunshine could brighten his entire day?

The boy had already been on the ship when Jonas had

switched vessels in Bellingham, Washington, and nothing about his life seemed fun or optimistic. He'd spent the past two days mopping the deck, running errands for the captain, and fetching items for the other passengers traveling north.

It certainly wasn't the type of job that should inspire bright smiles and an outrageous sort of cheerfulness, especially considering the Indian boy couldn't seem more out of place, even with all his hard work.

"So are you going to go belowdecks?" the boy asked. "Your coat is awful wet."

"No." Though he probably should. The cold and wet only seemed to seep deeper into his bones the longer he stood on deck.

"It's the sea, isn't it? Don't worry, you're not the only one the sea makes sick. Lots of passengers lose their innards into the sea because of it. My brother says they're landlubbers, and they can't take the ship always moving so."

If only the sea was what kept him from going belowdecks, not the memories that haunted him the second he found himself inside the dark, stifling hull.

The boy kept looking at him, as though expecting him to admit to feeling nauseous because of the waves.

Jonas turned toward one of the islands they were passing and settled his arms on the railing of the ship. "How much longer until we dock?"

"Not long. But you still better go dry off, or you'll catch your death of pneumonia. Leastways, that's what my sister always says."

"Pneumonia?" Even saying the word gave him the sudden desire to cough. The air in this place was so thick and dense, it made his lungs feel heavy each time he drew breath. The doctors in Juneau probably earned a living wage from treating pneumonia patients alone. "And what would this sister of yours say about you standing there with no hat and your slicker unbuttoned?"

The boy shrugged. "That I'll catch my death for sure and for certain. But I won't. I'm used to the rain."

He certainly seemed to be. Just as the boy had predicted, the rain had picked up more since they'd started talking, but he seemed completely immune to the wet.

"So is Juneau located between mountains like this, where the clouds will get trapped and the sun never shines, or is it in one of the open spaces that's just misty?"

"It's got mountains, and it's always rainy in Juneau. Didn't no one tell ya?"

"No. I don't suppose they did." More to the point, he hadn't bothered to ask. He'd known it would be cold in Alaska, so he bought as warm a coat as he could find before boarding the steamship in San Diego that had taken him up the coast to Bellingham.

But considering the temperature in San Diego wasn't much different from that of Texas, the coat he had thought was thick and warm was proving useless.

The other passengers on the ship and the crew had at least known what kind of coat to bring. They all wore oilskin slickers and hats that allowed the rainwater to drip from the brim down their slickers while keeping the person beneath them perfectly dry.

Then there were the handful of men who didn't even seem to notice the rain. Like the boy beside him, or the tall man headed down the stairs from the upper deck. His slicker was unbuttoned too, and he didn't wear a hat.

"Looks like I'll need to buy myself a slicker once we dock," he muttered.

"You should get one from the Sitka Trading Company here

in Juneau. It's right across from the wharf. They'll have everything you need."

"Will they now?"

"Sure will. They've got otter-pelt coats too, iffin you're
staying for the winter. Then after you stop by there, you'll want
to . . ." The boy's brow scrunched. "Wait. Where are you
headed? You never said."

"Ilya." The man from the stairs strode toward them. "It's
nearly time to dock. Captain White needs you."

"Uh-oh." Ilya's eyes grew wide, then his teeth sank into his
bottom lip. "I forgot to bring the map the captain wanted from
his cabin. Sorry, sir. I've got to go."

And the boy scampered off, his feet racing across the rain-
slickened deck as though he hadn't the slightest fear of slipping.

"I'm sorry." The man came up to the railing. "He's been
instructed not to bother the passengers, but this is only his third
voyage. I'm afraid Ilya has much to learn yet."

Ilya. There was that name again. It was smooth and flow-
ing, rolling easily off the tongue, but certainly not the type of
name he expected for a native boy. Dark Hawk or Cheerful
Owl or Light Foot, he could understand. But Ilya?

"Thanks for being friendly to him."

An unsettled feeling lodged in his stomach. Just how long
had this man been watching him and Ilya? And where had he
been watching from? The upper deck? Jonas glanced in the
direction of the deck, the hairs on the back of his neck growing
prickly. He should have been more aware of his surroundings.
He couldn't let his guard down simply because he was in
Alaska. Yet he'd had no idea someone was paying that much
attention to him and the boy.

Not that there was anything about the man that seemed
menacing. He was serious and tall, with dark hair, a
pronounced nose and cheekbones, and prominent eyebrows

that slashed in harsh lines above his eyes. Nothing about how he carried himself seemed dishonest or threatening.

On the contrary, he seemed like a man who knew what he wanted and wasn't afraid to get it. He also seemed displeased with Ilya for talking to him.

"I didn't mind the chat," Jonas said. If anything, he almost felt like thanking the boy. The few minutes of conversation had distracted him from the memories that couldn't seem to leave him alone.

It had been two months, and still they were there, every time he looked into the mist, every time he closed his eyes at night. Every time he drew breath.

But Alaska was going to fix that. He'd bury himself in a dark mineshaft and . . .

What?

Would visions of Harriet and his mother haunt him there the way they had in the belly of the ship?

No. He'd work himself hard and fast, until his mind was too tired to form a coherent thought, let alone remember what had happened back in Austin. Then he'd eat a few bites of dinner, stumble into bed, and sleep until his next shift started. Six days a week, twelve hours a day. That's what the advertisement for workers had said in the paper.

It sounded like the perfect kind of job to purge a man of his memories.

"I'm Alexei Amos."

Jonas blinked, bringing the man beside him back into focus.

Because there was still a man standing beside him. He hadn't walked off while Jonas had gotten lost in his memories, and he was extending his palm toward him for a handshake.

A faint thrumming had started as well. It wasn't overly loud, but it was constant, almost as though the crew had fired up a second steam engine belowdecks, except the noise wasn't loud enough for it to come from anything on the ship.

"Jonas Darrow." Jonas gave Alexei the name he'd decided on back in Oklahoma, before he'd said good-bye to his sister. Then he reached out and shook the man's hand.

"What brings you to Juneau, Jonas?" Alexei asked.

"Gold."

A small smile turned the corners of the man's mouth. "You and every other unmarried man on the Pacific Coast."

Jonas let the comment slide past him. Better to let the man think he came from California or Oregon rather than Texas. "I saw an ad for jobs at the Treadwell Mine, and there was nothing holding me to where I was living. So I figured, why not?"

Alexei raised one of his eyebrows. "You've a mind to work for the Treadwell? I didn't peg you for that type of a miner."

"Well, I am." Or he would be by this time tomorrow. How hard could it be to haul gold and rock out of the belly of the earth? "What's that sound?"

It was growing louder, and there was a pulsing thrum to it.

The faint smile crept back onto Alexei's mouth, adding the smallest hint of friendliness to the serious man's face. "That, my friend, is the Treadwell Mine. Your new place of employment."

"That's the Treadwell?" He scanned the mountains through the rain, but he spotted nothing against the landscape that could possibly make such a racket. "Where is it?"

"You hear the Treadwell long before you see it, I'm afraid."

The noise from the mine was already loud, and they weren't even close enough to see it?

"You smell it too." Alexei sniffed the air, then scrunched his nose.

Jonas could smell a faint chemical scent now. It fought its way through the thick, dank air.

"See here, we're traveling up the Gastineau Channel." Alexei gestured toward the front of the ship, then extended his hand to the left. "That's Douglas Island to our left, and the mainland to our right."

"The Treadwell Mine is on Douglas Island." Jonas remembered that from the ad and the few articles he'd been able to scrounge up about the mine before purchasing his passage north.

"It is indeed." The pulsing noise grew louder, and Alexei had to raise his voice to be heard above it. "Give it about ninety seconds, and you'll be able to see it."

Just as Alexei said, the thrumming increased as the ship made its way down the narrow strip of water wedged between mist-shrouded mountains on either side.

And just as Ilya said, the closer the mountains were, the thicker the mist became and the heavier the patter of rain.

Along the island shore a series of buildings appeared, some made of wood and others of concrete, all crammed together into one small stretch of beach and patch of hillside. Jonas felt claustrophobic just looking at it. Was there any space between the houses behind the industrial buildings? Because it looked as though they had been built one on top of the other. Each one with identical rooflines and windows, rolled out as though the houses had been manufactured in some sort of factory that yielded countless copies of the same exact house.

As the ship drew nearer the buildings, the chemical stench increased, clinging to the dampness and rain as though the two were somehow inseparable.

"What's making all the noise?" The pounding of the machinery made it so loud he had to shout lest his words be swallowed.

"That would be the one-hundred-and-twenty-stamp mill," Alexei shouted back.

"Stamp mill?"

"It crushes the rock hauled from the mine so the gold can be extracted. And if you think this is loud, just wait until they finish construction on the other one hundred and twenty stamps they're adding next year. The noise will be twice as loud."

Twice as loud, and he already wanted to cover his ears.

"And the smell?" he yelled, nearly gagging on the foul air he dragged into his lungs.

"The chlorination plant. Yet another step in extracting gold from rock." Alexei nodded toward the mine. "I'm told you get used to both the noise and the stench."

Jonas didn't believe it. He'd handled his share of dead bodies over the years and was all too familiar with the stench of decomposing flesh, but the burning sensation from the chlorination plant was something else entirely.

"What happened to the trees?" He surveyed the mountain-side again, packed with buildings of all shapes and sizes. There weren't many trees, but the ones present appeared to be dying, their branches bare and brittle, with nary a pine needle to be found.

"You can thank the chlorination plant for that too. The mine had some kind of fancy scientist out here from the Department of the Interior to figure out why the spruce were losing their needles earlier this year. He determined it's due to the gases the chlorination plant releases into the air. Evidently they are toxic to trees."

Were the gases toxic to people too? It certainly seemed like they should be. Jonas drew a handkerchief out of his pocket, sodden as it was, and pressed it to his nose. "If the gases are toxic, why don't they shut the mine down?"

"Because gold is more valuable than trees, of course."

"Of course." He surveyed the buildings again. The entire complex looked like something one might find in Austin's industrial district or beside the wharves in Houston.

It was one thing to lose himself in the dark quiet of a mine tunnel somewhere, but another thing entirely to plant himself in the middle of the noisy, stinking hub of activity that was the Treadwell Mine.

When he'd pictured himself coming north to Alaska, he'd imagined a vast expanse of rugged wilderness where a man could lose himself.

And he'd been right. The *Alliance* had passed nothing other than wild, desolate wilderness ever since leaving port.

He might not have realized just how much rain and gloom would accompany the untamed land, but it was still a place where a man could get lost and never be found again—if that's what he chose.

Then there was the Treadwell Mine.

"I won't be working there."

"No?" Alexei arched an eyebrow, then ran his gaze down him. "Few men start out there, but the Treadwell is the only mine that operates year-round. Come November, you'll find yourself working there right along with everyone else."

He wouldn't, but he wasn't about to argue the point with a man he'd just met.

Maybe he didn't need to mine at all but could build a cabin, hole up on one of the mountains, and allow himself to be snowed in all winter while he tried his hand at trapping.

Except that seemed like the kind of living that would allow a man's memories to plague him, and he needed something that would erase them.

But it was only September. He still had two months to figure out what he'd do over the winter.

Someone shouted from the upper deck, and Alexei straightened, then gave him a slap on the back. "I wish you well, Jonas Darrow, wherever you end up working. Now if you'll excuse me, we're about ready to dock."

And with that, the man was off, calling something to a couple of crew members before stalking to the opposite side of the ship and grabbing one of the thick ropes that was almost as large in diameter as Alexei's forearm. He moved with the utmost confidence, almost as though he owned everything he touched.

But that couldn't be. Jonas had figured out who the captain was within the first hour of leaving Bellingham, and the captain was currently in the wheelhouse, slowly guiding the ship toward the wharf that grew ever closer.

The Treadwell Mine had disappeared into the mist, and dark green trees now covered the mountains of Douglas Island. But the mountains and trees and island altogether became less visible as the ship edged away from the middle of the channel toward the mainland.

Just like how he wanted his former life to slip from his memory. Would living in Alaska make his past disappear as easily as the mist made Douglas Island vanish from sight?

Dear God . . .

But the words wouldn't come. They hadn't been able to come for months.

So he stood on the deck, watching until the fog and gloom engulfed the mountains on the other side of the channel, and hoping the gloom just might find a way to shroud his heart from the memories that ravaged it.

2

By the time the ship docked in Juneau, the chemical scent had dissipated, but a low rumble could still be heard from the stamp mill across the channel. Never mind that the fog was too thick for Jonas to see any part of Douglas Island, let alone see a few miles south to the Treadwell.

Jonas took his time disembarking the ship. After all, now that he had no intention of working for the Treadwell Mine, it wasn't as though he had any place he needed to be.

He waited until the other passengers had grabbed their things from belowdecks before descending into the bowels of the ship, where he grabbed the carpetbag and satchel he'd brought with him. If anything good could be said about a man having his home destroyed in a fire, it was that he didn't have trunks full of possessions to bring on his journey north.

When Jonas arrived back on deck, only the crew and Alexei remained, and they were preparing to haul cargo from the hold.

Jonas lifted his bags and walked down the gangway toward the busy wharf.

For a town that could only be reached after days of traveling past uninhabited wilderness, Juneau was teaming with people. Some were already striding along the wharf with handcarts, likely ready to unload the *Alliance*. Others had clearly come to watch the ship dock and were gathering across the street. Perhaps they'd ordered goods or knew some of the passengers.

Or perhaps they simply wanted food.

Before the *Alliance* left Bellingham, a staggering amount of flour, sugar, potatoes, carrots, and other foodstuffs had been loaded onto the ship. It had seemed a bit odd. Was no one in Juneau enterprising enough to open a grain mill so that flour didn't have to be shipped two days north?

But after what he'd seen, Jonas wasn't sure wheat or corn or any other kind of grain could grow in such a damp and sunless environment.

"Excuse me, sir. I need to get up there."

Jonas looked around, only to realize he'd stopped right at the bottom of the gangway, blocking access to the ship for the stevedores.

"Sorry." He moved to the side, letting a group of men pass as his eyes scanned the buildings surrounding him.

Every one of them was made of rough-hewn logs, almost as though the people building the town hadn't had time to sand them smooth or cut the logs into boards or bother with any of the normal things that went into constructing a house or building. It was yet another oddity about Juneau, Alaska.

But now that he was off the ship, his first order of business was to buy clothes that would keep him dry, and that meant finding the Sitka Trading Company.

Hadn't the boy—Ilya—said it was near the wharf? The row of buildings closest to the wharf all looked to be warehouses, but across the street was a two-story log building that had some type of sign in front of it. He was too far away to read the words, but it looked as if it could be a trading post.

He started down the wharf as more workers arrived, wheeling handcarts up the gangway. Perhaps if he got directly across from the building, he could read the sign.

But a group of passengers had gathered at the edge of the walkway, blocking the part of the dock that the stevedores weren't using.

"He stole it, I tell ya," one of the men snarled. "It had to be him."

"Yeah. Weren't anyone else on the ship who looked like a thief."

Jonas pushed himself up onto his toes and craned his head, trying to see what was causing the commotion.

"I didn't take anything," a young voice pronounced from the middle of the crowd.

Ilya. Jonas dropped his carpetbag and satchel and shoved his way into the circle, only to find a man—Simon, if he recalled from his time aboard ship—holding Ilya by the collar of his shirt.

"You got two seconds to give me my money, or I'll beat the truth outta ya."

"Beat him," one of the men jeered. "That's the only way to teach a dirty In'jun like him."

Jonas scanned the crowd. There were seven men, all of them with bloodshot eyes and the stench of liquor sour on their breath.

And nearly all of them had their gazes narrowed on Ilya.

All but one of the men. He stood near the back of the crowd and seemed to be paying far more attention to the men around him than to Ilya.

Jonas studied the man from the side of his gaze. Long hair tied back into a ponytail, an unshaven face, a red shirt that peeked out from beneath the collar of his slicker. And most importantly, a bulge in the left pocket of his coat. The bulge could be anything. A gun, a stack of letters, money of his own.

But the nervous manner in which the man looked around and kept taking small steps away from the others gave him away.

"Please, Mr. Volker. I didn't take the money. You know I didn't. Alexei would tan my hide. You're just drunk is all, and you need to let me go."

"I don't believe ya." Volker's grip on Ilya's collar tightened, and he yanked the boy forward.

"Do you have any evidence Ilya took the money?" Jonas stepped forward.

Bloodshot eyes met his gaze. "This ain't none of your business, mister. Best just pass on by."

And turn a blind eye while Ilya was beaten by a drunkard? Jonas stiffened. "If you're going to search someone, it should be your friend there."

He pointed toward the man with the long gray ponytail, only to find his finger directed at nothing but air. Sometime in the last half second, the man had disappeared.

Jonas pressed up onto his toes and tried to see where the man had gone, but there were too many people on the wharf, nearly all of them wearing black slickers and wide-brimmed hats that looked exactly the same from the back.

"Maybe you're the one I should search," Simon snarled.

Jonas drew in a breath. Calm. He needed to find a way to defuse the situation before someone ended up hurt. "I didn't take your money any more than Ilya. Like I said, it was the friend you brought along with you. The one in the red shirt."

Volker didn't even look around for his friend. Instead, he released Ilya and took a step closer to Jonas, his bloodshot eyes burning. "That was *my* two hundred dollars. *My* grubstake. Do you know how long it took me to save up for it?"

"I . . . no." Jonas swallowed. Two hundred dollars? No wonder the man was angry. That was half a year's wage. "But that still doesn't mean Ilya took it. Like I said, you're much better off—"

A fist connected with the side of his jaw. Jonas hadn't seen it coming. He'd been too busy watching Ilya, who had sidled between the edge of the wharf and the water the second Simon released him.

"Now look what you did." One of the men pointed to where Ilya was racing up the gangway toward the *Alliance*. "The boy got away."

"You got two hundred dollars on ya?" Volker reached to his belt and pulled a knife out of its sheath.

Sweat slicked Jonas's hands. He had a knife of his own strapped to his belt, but reaching for it when he was already surrounded by six men would only mean trouble.

"Well? Do you got two hundred dollars or not?" One of the men behind Volker drawled, his words slurring together. "Because that's what you owe Simon after letting the thief escape."

He did have two hundred dollars, but that was his savings, all that he had to give himself a fresh start in Alaska. He'd be hanged if he was going to give it to a group of drunkards who would take it down to the nearest saloon and see how much of it they could spend before dusk.

"I keep telling you, Ilya isn't a thief." The lot of them would realize that the second they sobered up. "I'm fairly certain your money was stolen by your other friend who was just here. But no matter who took it, your first order of business should be to visit the sheriff, not to take matters into your own hands."

A coarse laughter erupted from the group.

"The sheriff. Ya hear that? He thinks there's a sheriff."

"Someone better tell him he's in Alaska now, not San Francisco."

Simon's angry gaze narrowed into two thin slits. "There ain't no sheriff in Juneau, as you're about to find out. He pointed the blade of the knife in Jonas's direction. Now you give me that two hundred dollars, or I'll knife ya."

Jonas's hand slid to his side, not for his knife, but for his pistol. He was a quick draw, and he could have the nose of his Colt pointed at Simon Volker's chest before the man had time to stab him.

But his hand closed around fabric where his holster used to be.

Because he wasn't carrying a gun on his person anymore.

Because he'd put that part of his life behind him.

And because holding a gun made his hands shake and his stomach roil until he felt like retching.

So his gun was buried in a hidden compartment of his carpetbag.

"I didn't take your money any more than Ilya did." He slowly put his hands up, trying to show he only wanted peace— and to help find the man who'd stolen the two hundred dollars. "The second you're sober, you'll realize that."

"I vote we search his things." One of the men kicked at his carpetbag. "Never know. We just might find your money hiding somewhere in there."

"No!" Jonas tried to lunge for the bag, but one of the men caught his arm, which gave Volker a chance to land a second punch to his jaw.

Jonas would have stumbled backward with the blow, but the assailant who was holding him kept him upright just enough for him to glimpse Volker swinging the sliver blade of a knife toward him.

He tried to wrench away, but there was nowhere for him to move.

The blade plunged between two of his ribs just beneath his collarbone, and fire sliced through his shoulder. He sucked in a breath, gasping against the pain.

A shout sounded from somewhere in the direction of the ship, and the man who had been holding him let go. Ignoring the pain in his chest, he lunged for the knife, attempting to twist it out of Volker's grip.

No sooner had his palm clasped the clenched fist of his attacker, than he found himself being pushed backward. He scrambled for purchase on the rain-slicked boards of the wharf, then took a step back, only to find nothing under his foot save air.

Another punch landed against his temple, causing his head to scream and the edges of his vision to blur as hands shoved him again.

He felt himself falling backward, tumbling through the air as pain tore through his head and his lungs burned. Then he hit the cold, deep water of the channel—and his world went black.

***

"Let him go!" Alexei shouted from the gangway, where he and the first mate, Dobbins, had been threading their way through the workers toward Simon Volker and his drunken friends on the wharf. If someone had stolen two hundred dollars from one of his passengers aboard ship, then he'd get to the bottom of it. He didn't tolerate thieves, sheriff or not.

But the commotion on the dock swallowed his shout, and Alexei could only watch as Volker reared back and punched Darrow while one of his friends held him still and another rummaged through his carpetbag.

Then he saw the glint of a blade in Volker's hand, and his heartbeat ratcheted up. Surely the fool wasn't going to stab Darrow. Drunk or not—and Simon Volker was always drunk—that would land him in a jail cell for more than a night.

The moment they'd docked, Ilya had begged to get off the ship and go visit Scott at the trading post. Even though most cabin boys would be expected to stay on the ship until it was unloaded and then take leave with the rest of the crew, Alexei hadn't been able to resist the excitement in his brother's eyes as he'd asked to leave.

But Ilya had returned to the ship only a few minutes later, racing back aboard with words tumbling from his mouth about Mr. Volker accusing him of stealing money and Mr. Darrow stepping in to protect him.

Ilya hadn't mentioned anything about a knife, but sure enough, that's what Simon Volker was holding. Alexei lengthened his stride, racing down the gangway with Dobbins before the drunkard decided to use it.

But he wasn't fast enough, and the drunkard drove the blade straight into Jonas Darrow's ribs.

"Help!" Alexei called. This time his shout stopped the activity on the gangway and wharf. He thrust his finger at Simon Volker and his friends. "There's been a stabbing. Stop those men."

The dockworkers looked around, as though trying to make sense of his words and figure out who in the throng of people had just been stabbed.

From his position on the elevated gangway, Alexei could see everything unfolding, but he wasn't close enough to stop any of it. A dark patch of red was spreading across Darrow's chest, and Volker shoved him backward.

Then the largest man of the group lunged forward and slammed a fist into Darrow's temple.

A sickening crack filled the air, Darrow's head jerked to the side, and Volker pushed him backward, Darrow's body nothing more than a limp rag as he splashed into the water below.

"Man in the channel," he shouted. Then he turned back toward the *Alliance* to see Captain White standing at the rail with Ilya and a handful of crew members. "Lower the dinghy."

The water was deep at the edge of the wharf. It had to be for ships to dock there. And the only thing worse than a man being shoved into water that deep was an unconscious man being shoved into it.

"Faster, Alexei!" Ilya called from the ship. "He's going to drown."

Alexei ripped off his slicker, unholstered his pistol, and shoved the gun at Dobbins. Then he dove into the murky water of the Gastineau Channel.

The coldness of the water stole his breath, but he forced his legs to kick as he surged forward through the water. If only the sun were shining. Then maybe he would have had a hope of finding Darrow. But between the salt of the ocean water stinging his eyes and the dark clouds that turned the water a gloomy gray, he could hardly see his hand in front of his face, let alone Darrow's unconscious body.

He surfaced and raked in a breath, turning wildly in the water for any clue of where Darrow might be.

"Over there, Alexei," Ilya called.

He glanced over his shoulder to find the crew had listened when he'd told them to lower the dinghy. Captain White, Ilya, and Jethro were rowing toward a series of circular ripples in the water that broke the pattern of lapping waves.

Alexei surged forward, the muscles of his arms straining as he swam through the water with large, determined strokes.

Then a head broke through the surface, the red of Darrow's hair plastered against his head. Maybe the cold water had woken him out of his unconsciousness, but the man obviously didn't know how to swim. He flailed about, splashing the water so wildly he had little hope of staying afloat.

"Help!"

"I'm coming." Only about twenty feet separated him from Darrow, but the man went down again before clambering back to the surface. Given the thick, sodden coat the man was wearing, he wouldn't be afloat for much longer.

Sure enough, Darrow's head slipped beneath the waves once more, but Alexei had a pretty good idea just how quickly the man would sink.

He dove, forcing his eyes open despite the stinging salt and angling his body to intercept the drowning man.

A moment later, a shadow of black appeared against the murky water, accompanied by the flash of a white, panicked face as Darrow struggled toward the surface.

Alexei gave his legs a final kick, cutting through the water with the skill of someone who'd spent all thirty years of his life swimming in the shallows of Alaskan islands. The water nearly parted for him as he glided forward, then wrapped his arms beneath Darrow's own arms and kicked upward until they broke the surface.

Darrow gasped, dragging air into his lungs while fighting to stay afloat.

"Don't. Be still or you'll drag us both down. See, the boat's right there." He nodded toward where Captain White, Horace, and Ilya rowed toward them.

The sight of the boat seemed to calm Darrow, his body growing limp in Alexei's hold. "Thank you," he rasped.

Alexei swallowed. What did he say in response to that? *No, thank you for saving my brother's life?*

Why would a stranger have involved himself in a drunken brawl to protect a boy he hadn't even known for half a week?

Fortunately, he didn't have to figure out what to say, because Captain White glided the dinghy to a stop beside them. Horace and Ilya both reached down and helped pull Darrow aboard, and a chorus of clapping sounded from the wharf, where Alexei turned to find a crowd had gathered to watch the rescue.

Alexei hauled himself aboard the dinghy, then frowned when he saw how quickly blood was seeping into Darrow's shirt. "Get us to the wharf, then go for the doctor at the Treadwell."

White and Horace looked at each other. "You want us to go clear over to Treadwell for the doc?"

"Yes. Darrow needs more than just a nurse. He's got to have an actual doctor if he's going to survive that knife wound."

"We know." The captain dug the oar into the water, propelling them right alongside the wharf, where hands reached down to haul Darrow up. "But what's wrong with your sister?"

Alexei had clasped one of the men's hands from the wharf that sat about three feet above where the small boat bobbed in the water. He was about to climb out of the boat when the Captain's words settled into his brain. He released the hand above him and turned back to Captain White. "My sister? She's in Sitka."

"No, she ain't," the familiar voice of Grover Hanover called from the wharf. "Kate's here."

Alexei felt his entire body go cold. "She is?"

He grabbed the hand above him once more and scrambled onto the wharf, then stood to face Grover, the town grocer to whom the *Alliance* delivered supplies twice a month.

"Sure is. Been here for the better part of two months, patching up the town." Grover scratched behind his ear. "Don't say you didn't know?"

He didn't have a clue. He left Sitka on a business trip to Washington Territory and California exactly two months ago. What had Kate done? Up and left for Juneau the day after him?

He was going to throttle her.

Alexei stalked forward, trailing the men who were rushing the litter with an unconscious Darrow toward the trading post, which was the mostly likely place for Kate to have set up shop.

Grover rushed up beside him, his chest heaving as he struggled to keep pace. "I'm sorry. I thought you knew."

"Who's with her?" Alexei pinched the bridge of his nose. "Please tell me she hasn't been in Juneau by herself for all this time."

"'Course not. She brought her sisters with her."

Alexei waited to hear which of his brothers had come too. Maybe Mikhail had returned from his expedition and had business in Juneau, or Sacha had returned early from his voyage to the arctic, or Yuri had come for no better reason than to stay with his sisters—at least one of which had to have the common sense not to move to a town that amounted to little more than a glorified mining camp, completely unprotected.

But Grover kept right on walking, leaving his words hanging in the air between them. As though . . .

As though *only* his sisters had come to Juneau, and no one else.

"Which of my brothers is here with them?" he rasped, a headache starting to form at his temples.

Grover looked over at him and blinked. "None of them. It's just your sisters, like I said. All three of them. Sorry, Alexei. I figured someone would have written ya."

"No one wrote me anything." Except that wasn't true. All three of his sisters had written to him while he'd been in San Francisco. Each of their letters had been painfully boring, filled with normal, everyday things like what they'd eaten for dinner or what other letters they'd penned that day. Evelina had talked about how Inessa's schooling was going, and Kate might have mentioned treating a patient or two.

But none of them had said a lick about moving to Juneau.

This had Kate written all over it. She was the only one headstrong enough to up and move to another town and convince her sisters not to send him word.

Alexei burst through the entrance of the trading post. He was going to lock his oldest sister in a tower and throw away the key.

Right after she saved Jonas Darrow's life, that is.

3

"No, these two letters together, they say 'oh' like in *oats*. They don't say 'aaaaaaa.' Only an *a* says that."

Shunaa bent his head over the primer, his dark eyes studying the letters on the page before him. But the puckered lines on his forehead told Evelina the young boy was just as confused as he'd been at the top of the hour, when they'd started their reading lesson.

She sighed, glancing around the dark log walls of the storeroom she'd converted into a makeshift school. How many times had she tried explaining English vowel sounds to Shunaa? But the child simply couldn't seem to understand anything other than the five basic short vowel sounds they'd covered six weeks ago.

One of the other students started talking, but not in English. Instead, he spoke in his own Tlingit language. Evelina tried to pick out a bit of what he was saying, but the guttural words rolled off his tongue in a rush.

Shunaa answered in his own tongue, but the grooves in his brow only grew deeper.

"Ah, Gajaa Héen," she interrupted the ten-year-old. "Remember to raise your hand before you speak."

The boy instantly straightened and raised his hand.

Evelina smiled. Not all of the students who came to the informal classes she'd been holding at the back of the trading post wanted to be here. There was no question their parents had forced some of them to attend.

But Gajaa Héen was always earnest in his studies and eager to behave well in her classroom. "And please try to use as much English as you can when you answer."

"I thought an *o* and a *w* together said 'ou,'" The boy spoke slowly. English was as foreign and unnatural to him as Tlingit was to her. "Like the word *out*."

She couldn't quite hide her wince. "Well, yes, an *o* and a *w* together can say both 'oh' and 'ou,' like in *bow*. But also remember, an *o* and a *u* can also say 'ou,' and that is how you spell *out*. With an *o* and *u*, not an *o* and *w*."

She moved to the chalkboard and wrote the words, trying to illustrate the difference to her students. "See there? It all depends on the word."

"I hate English," one of the boys grumbled in his native tongue.

Evelina knew enough Tlingit to understand at least that much, but she didn't quite recognize all of the words of agreement the other students started muttering.

She pressed a hand to her head. Maybe this was all a mistake. Maybe she needed to close her little half-day school and let the Tlingit parents decide whether they wanted to send their children off to one of the boarding schools, maybe even the one on Douglas Island, or let them attend the day school run by the Department of Education.

These half-day classes not only enabled students to help their parents in the morning and then come to school after lunch but also allowed them to speak in their own language during class instead of getting their hands rapped with a ruler if they forgot. And seeing how the Tlingit village was located directly across the channel on Douglas Island, it only took a handful of minutes for the students to canoe over to their classes each day.

But maybe this makeshift school was just the latest in a long string of her failures.

Just like her decision to drop out of teaching school.

"Remember, there are thirteen vowel sounds in the English language, but only five letters represent these sounds." She raised her voice over the chatter. "That means we often need to combine two vowels together to get the desired sound we want in a word."

"Why do we need to learn to read at all?"

Evelina glanced up, searching for the speaker, only to find Aashein staring back at her. True to the meaning of her name—"daylight"—Aashein was one of the brightest students in her class. She could learn anything she set her mind to, and in half the time it would take Evelina to learn something new herself.

"I have learned to speak English," Aashein continued, the other students quieting as she spoke. "I can go into your trading post and purchase anything I choose or have a conversation with any of the women I see around Juneau. I am getting better at it every day. But this reading, I don't understand why we need it. Why do I need to know whether *out* is spelled with an *o* and *u*, or an *o* and *w*? Being able to speak English should be enough. It is enough for the Tlingit."

Evelina tried not to sigh, truly she did. But how many times would she need to answer this question? Though this was the first time a student had asked her to explain the importance of having a written language. Usually she was explaining this to Tlingit adults.

And they didn't teach how to answer such a question in teaching school. She might not have attended long enough to get her certificate, but she'd never once heard any of her instructors address why there was a need for a written language. Everyone just accepted there was.

But Tlingit was an oral language only. There was no alphabet to represent its letters, no books that recorded historical events, nothing but artistic drawings and oral stories to preserve any part of the Tlingit people's past, or even to record something as simple as a business contract.

"Do you have an answer, Miss Amos?" Aashein asked, her gaze genuinely curious.

"Ah . . ."

"Doc Amos!" A door slammed from somewhere in the trading post, followed by a cacophony of male voices, each seeming determined to shout something louder than the last.

"Come quick!" one of the voices echoed above the others. "Someone's been stabbed."

Stabbed? Evelina rushed to the door that connected the storeroom to the main part of the trading post and cracked it open.

Sure enough, a man was being carried in on a litter, and Kate was directing the men toward the room where she'd set up her doctor's office, which was right next to the schoolroom.

Dear heavens, what had happened?

"Was someone really stabbed?" one of the students asked from behind her.

Evelina turned back to find every last eye in the room pinned to her. "I'm afraid so."

And her twin sister would likely need her to act as a nurse. Voices were already filtering through the thick log walls that separated the schoolroom from Kate's examination room. Kate asking what happened, and one of the men saying the man on the litter had been stabbed on the wharf, then shoved into the channel.

"School is out for the day," she announced. "Go straight home to your parents. Until we know who did the stabbing and why, it is imperative that each of you remain somewhere safe."

The students scrambled to collect their things, their eyes alive with excitement, probably more so over news of the stabbing than the fact they were being released from school half an hour early. Either way, it took only a matter of seconds for all fourteen of them to rush from the room.

Evelina closed the door behind them, watching to make sure they all left the trading post before she went to assist Kate. She had little cause to be concerned. Her students were practically fighting over who got to go out the door first, each one anxious to be the first to announce the stabbing to their village.

But the door never closed behind the last child. Instead, it flew the rest of the way open, banging against the wall. Then her oldest brother, Alexei, stepped inside, his eyes dark and serious.

Their eyes met across the wide space of the store, and Alexei's jaw hardened.

"You." He shoved a finger in her direction. "You owe me an explanation. But first I need you to help save Jonas Darrow, because the man just got himself stabbed in Ilya's stead."

"He saved Ilya?" The words rushed out of her.

"Evelina!" Kate shouted from the examination room. "Someone get me Evelina!"

"Coming," she called, then turned her back on the brother she hadn't seen for two months and raced through the doorway —only to find her sister elbow deep in a pool of blood.

4

P ain seared Jonas's head as though someone had stabbed
his temple with a knife. Or maybe the stabbing sensation
was in his shoulder, not his head, because that felt like it was on
fire, almost as if someone had torn it open and inserted smoldering embers beneath his skin.

He turned, trying to relieve the pain, but that only caused
the embers burning in his shoulder to flame into a blaze. He
groaned, the sound low and guttural, then tried moving again,
but his entire body felt heavy, as though it had been weighed
down with rocks.

"What's happening?" a man said from somewhere above
him, his voice sharp and commanding. "Is he waking up?"

"I don't know," a woman answered, then a warm, slender
hand gripped his. "Mr. Darrow, can you hear me? Can you try
opening your eyes?"

Her voice was soft and kind, and her hand so warm against
his palm that he couldn't help but obey. He wanted to see the
woman with the voice of an angel.

But his eyelids felt just as heavy as his arm, refusing to open even a sliver.

He groaned and tried moving once more, then his body started moving on its own, and he could control it no more than he could the waves in the sea.

"He's convulsing," another woman said, her voice brisk and sharp. "Help me hold him down. I can't risk him reopening his wound."

Hands gripped his upper arms and ankles, causing even more pain to tear through the shoulder that was on fire. He tried to fight, to move, to free himself. He might not know where he was, but he knew he didn't want to be there, in a strange place with strange voices and strange people holding him captive.

But the more he fought, the more his head pounded and his shoulder burned and his body shook.

And then it was over. His body was limp once again, his arms and legs and eyelids all as heavy as boulders.

"Is he going to be all right?" Another voice drifted through the pain, this one younger and familiar. Almost as though he should know it somehow.

He tried to think back, to recall the last time he'd heard the voice, but thinking only caused the pounding in his head to worsen.

"We should give him more laudanum." It was the angel woman again, a note of worry threading through the kindness in her words.

"No," came the man's reply, just as sharp and cutting as before. "We need him awake and coherent. One of the men from the wharf is missing. Ilya can't provide any details about him, but maybe Mr. Darrow can."

A hand landed on his forehead, slender like a woman's, but

it didn't belong to the angel who had held his hand earlier. This touch was brisk and efficient, clinical.

"He doesn't have a fever," she answered, her voice just as formal as her touch. "My guess is he's coming around enough to feel pain, but he's not yet conscious enough to wake."

"And you'd normally give a man in his condition laudanum," the angel woman said.

"See if you can get him to drink some willow bark tea." Impatience laced the man's voice. "That might help."

"For a knife wound? It's not nearly strong enough. He needs laudanum." The angel woman was touching him again, sliding her hand back into his.

The contact caused a ripple of warmth to travel up his arm —until it reached the burning in his shoulder.

"I said to hold off," the man growled. "We need to know who that seventh man was, and the others in the jail are too drunk to remember anything useful."

"Kate, talk some sense into him." It was the soft-spoken woman. "Shouldn't we be giving him laudanum for the pain? Surely he can wait a few hours to answer Alexei's questions."

More words drifted around him, continuing the debate over whether he needed medication, but they faded farther and farther away, until nothing but quiet and darkness surrounded him.

"WELL, THAT'S NOT VERY HELPFUL." Alexei narrowed his eyes at Jonas Darrow, who seemed to have slipped back into unconsciousness without so much as a lick of the medicine Evelina wanted to give him. "Any idea how long it will take him to wake this time?"

"He lost a lot of blood, which certainly wasn't helped by taking a dunk in the channel." Kate didn't bother to look up from where she stood by the hutch, methodically washing the surgical instruments that she had used to save Darrow's life. "And I can only guess what kind of bacteria might be living in that water. Infection could be setting into his shoulder even now."

"No." Evelina stiffened where she stood beside Darrow, placing a cool cloth on his head. "You mustn't say such a thing. We can't let him get an infection, not after he saved Ilya."

"I'm not God. I can't control whether there's an infection. I can only try to prevent one." Kate shrugged, her voice flat, never mind that she'd fought for over an hour to control the blood seeping from Darrow's chest.

Alexei glanced between his twin sisters. They looked identical, both with green eyes and high cheekbones and rich brown hair that held the faintest hints of red. Most people in Sitka had never been able to tell Ekaterina and Evelina apart.

Until they opened their mouths.

Kate had always been brisk and efficient, ready to embark on an adventure at a moment's notice. And Evelina was soft and kind, a type of mother to their giant, sprawling family long before their actual mother died.

Kate set the last of her cleaned instruments inside the drawer of the hutch—the hutch that hadn't even been in his office the last time he'd been in Juneau. Somehow she'd managed to have the monstrosity moved in here and was using it to store her medical equipment and supplies. She'd also had his desk moved from his office and replaced it with a sickbed. And the space along the far wall that a series of filing cabinets once claimed now held the table she had pulled into the center of the room and used for surgery.

"Maybe we can try to wake Mr. Darrow with some

smelling salts," Inessa suggested from where she and Ilya were washing down the operating table.

"Just let him rest," Kate huffed. "He'll wake in his own time, and hopefully he'll be conscious enough to answer Alexei's questions."

If Kate and Evelina looked identical, then his youngest sister, Inessa, couldn't look more different, with her straight dark hair and tan skin and native features. Most people blinked when they learned that she was a member of the Amos family, just like they did with Ilya.

Alexei turned back to Darrow, lying as still as death on the bed, with nothing but the shallow rise and fall of his chest to indicate he lived. "Are you sure there's not a way we can wake him?"

"Mr. Darrow's life is more important than whatever interrogation you have planned." Kate crossed her arms over her chest, eyes flashing. "You'll have to be patient."

"Patient?" Inessa smirked. "I don't think he knows how."

He narrowed his eyes at his youngest sister. "Fine. If Darrow's not going to wake anytime soon, then I want to see the lot of you next door."

Kate plastered a sickeningly sweet smile across her lips. "Whatever for, dearest brother?"

"An explanation."

"Can't we talk here?" Inessa went back to scrubbing the table. "There's still cleaning to be done, and it's not as though Mr. Darrow can hear us."

Alexei scowled. "I'm not of a mind to discuss family business in front of an audience—conscious or not. Now I want everyone in the storeroom."

As soon as Kate had managed to stanch the flow of blood from below Darrow's shoulder and proclaimed the knife hadn't damaged his lungs, Alexei had gone off with Grover Hanover to make sure Simon Volker and his friends ended up behind bars and the items in Darrow's carpetbag that the ruffians had been tearing through were all returned to him.

Now the drunkards were all locked up and had given statements to a couple of men on the Committee of Public Safety—one of whom was Grover. But there was still a question of who had stolen two hundred dollars from Simon, because it appeared the man actually had managed to save that much. Either that or Volker had gotten a loan from his wealthy brother in Seattle, which may have been the reason he and his friends had left Juneau in the middle of the summer prospecting months and booked passage to Seattle and back.

Unfortunately, any useful information Darrow might have was going to stay buried until the man regained consciousness.

And Inessa was right. Alexei raked a hand through his hair. He'd never been a patient man.

"I said the storeroom." He glared at his siblings. "Now."

"Suppose we better get this over with." Kate set down the rag she'd been using to clean the hutch and headed toward the door.

"Is he going to make us go back to Sitka?" Inessa asked.

Kate rolled her eyes. "Of course he is. Don't worry. We'll come back the next time he leaves."

Alexei ground his teeth together. "You realize I can hear you."

Kate sent him an innocent blink. "Oh dear. Maybe you should just relent and let us stay here with your blessing, then."

"Next door," he growled.

"Surely you don't want all of us to leave?" Evelina was still standing at the head of Mr. Darrow's sickbed, exchanging the cool rag on his head with a new one every few minutes.

"If something goes wrong, we'll be able to hear it through the wall." Kate strode through the doorway, her gait strong and determined, as though she was headed off to find the man who'd knifed Darrow, not wedging herself into a cramped storeroom stuffed with furs and blankets and prospecting supplies.

Inessa frowned after Kate, then put her rag back into the bucket. "Come on, Ilya. Best to get this over with." She took his hand and tugged him out the door, her face just as indignant as Kate's.

That left Evelina, who had yet to move from the sickbed. "I still don't like leaving him alone. He was just stabbed. And for Ilya's sake."

Alexei sighed, the stiffness melting from his shoulders. "It'll only be for a few minutes. And like Kate said, you'll be able to hear if he needs anything."

"That only makes me certain I'll be able to hear whatever you say next door if I stay here, especially since you're planning to yell."

"I'm not planning to yell."

But he would end up yelling, because how could he not? When he'd left for San Francisco two months ago, Ekaterina, Evelina, and Inessa had all been in Sitka, where they had seemed content enough.

Sure, Ekaterina—or Kate, since she insisted on going by an American version of her name—was fuming that she only had a handful of patients, all of them women. But she'd been fuming about that since she'd come back from Boston with her medical degree two years ago. That was no reason for her to up and leave the island she'd grown up on.

And Evelina had seemed perfectly content doing . . . well, whatever she found to do. Helping Kate or schooling Inessa or poring over various government reports related to the running of Alaska now that it belonged to America. His second sister was never idle, even if she didn't have the drive that Kate did. If anything, Evelina was the mother that held their family together.

Which meant she belonged in Sitka—as did the rest of the family.

"Next door, Evelina." He pushed the door open farther. "You're keeping everyone else waiting."

She sighed, her shoulders slumping as she left her place beside Mr. Darrow's head and slowly crossed the room.

"Thank you." Alexei pulled the door shut behind her and followed her the few steps into the storeroom. Or rather, what should have been the storeroom.

"What in the devil . . .?" He sucked a breath in through his nose as he looked at the dozen or so desks that had been situated into neat rows, all of which faced a larger desk and a chalkboard at the front of the room.

First his office had been turned into a medical exam room for Kate, and now the storeroom was . . . a school?

"Evelina's started a Tlingit school." Inessa yawned, as though she somehow found that little tidbit of information boring.

Alexei narrowed his eyes at Evelina. Had he just been thinking she was innocent? "There's already a Tlingit day school in Juneau. And a boarding school across the channel on Douglas Island."

Evelina ducked her head, not offering a single word in her defense.

Kate, on the other hand, was looking at him with a smug smile on her face.

He could almost hear what she was thinking. *See? I'm not the only one who can cause a ruckus.*

"No one wants to go to Miss Thompson's school." Inessa crossed her arms over her chest. "It's dreadful. And the boarding school is full—not that I would go there if they had room."

Alexei looked back at Evelina, but she was still staring down at her feet, her tongue peeking out to wet her lips.

"The Department of Education is going to be furious," he prodded. Never mind that *furious* was far too mild a word to describe what the Minister of Education himself would do when he found out.

"Janice Thompson is a terrible teacher." Evelina finally peeked up at him. "She insists the children arrive by eight every morning, never mind that most of them are out gathering seaweed and clams at that time. And she won't let them speak a word of Tlingit, which means none of the younger ones can understand what she's saying. Even worse, she's overly fond of her ruler, and not for measuring things."

"I went for a week." Inessa shoved a lock of long black hair behind her ear. "It was a disaster, and that's when Evelina said she'd teach me in the afternoons. I invited a few of the other students to my lessons, and, well . . ."—she shrugged and looked around the classroom—"you can figure out the rest."

"Indeed." His temples began to throb. He didn't know how his father had done it. The man had had nine children and ran both a trading company and a shipyard. Yet nothing about his childhood had ever felt crazy or uncontrolled.

But now that he was running the family? Alexei raked a hand through his hair. Chaos. It was nothing but chaos.

"I only teach for four hours in the afternoon." Evelina twisted her hands together in front of her. "That way the children can help their mothers in the mornings. A couple of the older boys even go to work on the canal and then come here after lunch, so they have a way to earn money for their families but still learn."

"And yet you dropped out of teaching school," he muttered.

Evelina's face went white, and he instantly regretted the words. "I'm sorry. That was a cruel thing to say."

She shook her head as the last hint of rosiness faded from her cheeks. "No. It's not cruel; it's true. I don't have a teacher's certificate, and yet here I am teaching instead of . . ."

She didn't finish, but they all knew what she was going to say. There was one thing she'd decided she wasn't going to do anymore, which was probably why she'd started a school—not because she loved teaching, but because she'd never met a person she hadn't wanted to help. And because she had the kindest, sweetest heart in all of Alaska.

And the thing she'd gone to school for, that she'd studied for and passed exams in and received a degree for as one of the only women in a college full of men?

She seemed just as determined to leave that in the dust as she'd been last spring, when her world had come crashing down.

"All right, enough about the school," Alexei croaked, his throat suddenly raspy. "Why are the three of you here? And more importantly, why are you by yourselves?"

Kate shrugged. "There wasn't anyone else to run the trading post."

"Rev. Jackson wants to marry Evelina, and she doesn't know how to tell him no." This from Inessa, who earned a glare from Evelina, but his youngest sister only shrugged. "What? It's true."

Alexei raised an eyebrow at Evelina. "The Minister of Education proposed?"

"No." She twisted her hands in front of her. "At least not yet."

"But it's coming," Inessa said. "No one will be surprised when he asks."

"And you came to Juneau and started a school behind his

back? One that is sure to be pulling students away from the official school he started just last year?" Had his sister no sense?

Evelina threw up her hands. "I didn't know I was going to start a school when I came."

"You must not want to marry him that badly either," he muttered.

"I don't. I don't even want him to ask. You have to understand why."

Alexei rubbed the back of his neck. Sheldon Jackson had a good heart. No one would argue that. But his method of educating the native children of Alaska was nothing short of misguided—and that was putting it kindly.

Still, tell that to anyone outside of Alaska, and they would look at you as though you'd lost your mind. He knew because he'd tried. The papers from California to Washington, DC were full of his successes. "Jackson's rather popular in California."

"And very good at raising mission money for the native schools so that the federal government doesn't have to pay for them." Evelina quipped.

That too.

"He fancies himself in love with Lina," Inessa added. "He writes her letters every week, but she never writes him back."

Alexei pressed his eyes shut. "Seriously, Lina? Write the man and let him know you're not interested in any type of a relationship with him."

She shifted her weight from one foot to the other. "I'm not sure what to say."

"Figure it out." He sucked in a breath, then turned to Kate. Calm. He needed to stay calm. And discussing Rev. Jackson with Evelina any further was only going to make his blood boil. "What's the rest of the story? How did you end up here, and where on earth is the stock for the storeroom?"

"We partitioned off a section of the company warehouse across the street to use for storage." Kate shrugged. "It's not terribly far to bring new stock over."

No, it wasn't. If a person was of a mind to cram a trading post, doctor's office, and school into one building, his sisters had found the best possible way to do it. Though this had to be the only building in the world to house all three.

"I'm assuming you moved the contents of my office to one of the rooms upstairs?"

"We did."

He nodded, then looked around. "That leaves me with only one question . . ." A question he probably knew the answer to but had to ask nonetheless. "Where is Scott Paddington?"

Kate rolled her eyes. "He got gold fever and sent Yuri a note saying he was headed off to the Yukon. Half the prospectors are convinced there's gold somewhere up by where the river turns south, and a group of men came through town by way of San Francisco, offering to pay handsomely for his guiding services."

Alexei resisted the urge to groan, but barely. If he could change one thing about the entirety of Alaska, it would be the existence of gold.

For thirteen years, no one had cared that America owned Alaska. But now that the Juneau Gold Belt had been discovered, he couldn't keep an employee around to save his life. Any frontiersman who could survive a week in the wilds of Alaska got offered a job, and usually by some highfalutin citified man who could afford to pay three times what the trading company did.

Never mind that he needed someone familiar with prospecting and the ways of the frontier to run the trading post. Otherwise there would be no one to direct customers to the right kind of gear they would need for whatever gold-driven adventure they were about to embark on.

Alexei rubbed his temple, where his headache was only worsening. "Let me guess, you were the only ones in Sitka who could come to Juneau."

"It was only supposed to be for a week or two," Evelina said. "Until Yuri could find someone to replace Scott."

"But now that we're here, we're not leaving. Or at least I'm not. I can doctor here, Alexei!" Kate's eyes lit with excitement, her face coming alive at the mere mention of getting to use her medical training. "There's only one other doctor in all of Juneau, Axel Prichard, and you visit the trading post here often enough to know that he's drunk more than he's sober. So people are coming to me. Miners, townsfolk, everyone. If they don't have time enough to travel to the Treadwell and see the mine doc across the channel, they're coming here. Jonas is the fourth person I've treated this week."

Alexei pressed his lips together. How long had Kate wanted to be a doctor? Since she was six, maybe, or seven? She'd saved every newspaper article she could find about female doctors and medical schools for women.

But after she'd returned home to Sitka with her medical degree, she'd been treated as little more than a nurse.

Unlike Sitka, which was filled with bureaucrats determined to make a muck of running Alaska, Juneau was rough and tumble, full of fights and squabbles and people who would get nervous talking to a sheriff.

But at the end of the day, he could do nothing that would strip the smile from Kate's face, just like he couldn't bring himself to tell Evelina to start moving the desks out of her schoolroom and convert it back into a storeroom.

"All right. You can stay."

A cheer went up from his sisters.

"But not by yourselves. I'll send for Yuri as soon as Sacha returns and can take over the shipyard. And don't tell me you're fine on your own. I might believe it in Sitka, but not Juneau. If not for Mr. Darrow, Ilya could have been stabbed today."

"Thank you!" Kate pressed up onto her heels, excitement still radiating from her face. "Thank you, thank you, thank you!"

Inessa sprang forward and gave him a hug, and even Evelina managed to smile.

He couldn't help but smile back. Heaven help him, he'd just made his life harder, but if his sisters were happy, it might be worth it.

5

"Mr. Darrow. Mr. Darrow."

A hammer pounded against his skull, fierce and unrelenting. Jonas groaned, but that only seemed to unleash a fire where his shoulder and chest met.

"Mr. Darrow. You gotta wake up. Alexei is worried somethin' fierce. Please, Mr. Darrow. Can you hear me? I didn't mean for you to get hurt. I promise."

A hand, small and clammy, wrapped around his.

"Can you open your eyes? Just once? It would make everyone so happy."

Jonas turned his head toward the voice and tried to do what was asked. But his eyes only fluttered open for a fraction of a second before he slammed them shut.

"Too bright." The small bit of light caused the pounding sensation in his head to strengthen, hammering away at his temples.

"Do you want me to turn the lamp down? I can draw the curtains too. It's not quite dark out yet."

The small hand left his, and the sound of curtains sliding against their rod filled the room.

A moment later, the hand was back, gripping his palm in a fierce hold. "Is that better? Can you open your eyes now?"

Jonas cracked one eye open. The light didn't assault him, so he opened the other eye into a narrow slit, squinting at the log-hewn ceiling above, where the dim light from a lamp cast a pattern of orange flickers against the wood.

"Where . . . where am I?" His voice sounded gritty, as though he'd swallowed a mouthful of sand before attempting to speak.

"You're in Juneau, remember?" the voice said from beside him. "You came here on the *Alliance*. And then you got into the middle of that fight and ended up stabbed, all because of me."

Jonas turned his head toward the voice, only to find the familiar face of the cabin boy from the ship peering down at him. What had he said his name was?

"You shouldn'a tried to help me. They wouldn't have used a knife on a boy."

A knife. The words caused pain to slice through his chest anew, and with it came the memories. Ilya standing on the wharf surrounded by six drunken, angry men, him stepping in to try to calm the situation, the man who'd been making the accusations pulling out a knife.

The pounding in his head ratcheted up, and Jonas looked down to find he'd been stripped of his shirt and a bandage wrapped the skin from the top of his shoulder to beneath his arm. Unfortunately, the clean linen did little to stop the pain searing the ribs beneath his collarbone.

"I know they were talkin' mean-like, but Simon Volker always talks mean when he's drunk. He wouldn't have hurt me.

Besides, Alexei would have figured out what was going on right soon, and he would have come to help."

"I . . ." How did he even respond to that? The boy had been surrounded by cruel, drunk ruffians threatening to beat him. He'd done what any man would have done . . .

Hadn't he?

"But then Mr. Volker up and stabbed you, and now the town's in an uproar over it. And what's worse, someone really did take his two hundred dollars, and no one knows—"

"Ilya?" A woman's voice sounded from the opposite side of the room. "What are you doing disturbing Mr. Darrow?"

Ilya turned, his eyes bright and a wide smile plastered across his face. "I didn't disturb him. I got him to wake up, see?"

There was something familiar about the kindness in the woman's voice, as though maybe he'd heard it before. Jonas tried to shift himself to get a glimpse of her, but when he put weight on his left arm, a burst of pain tore through his ribs, and he collapsed back onto the mattress.

"What is it you're trying to do?" Footsteps sounded against the floor, and the voice grew closer. "Do you want to sit up?"

"Yes. I think if I . . ." He planted his hands beside him on the bed yet again and tried to shift himself up, but just like last time, another jolt of pain knifed through him when he put the slightest bit of weight on his arm.

"Let me help you." The woman was by his side a moment later, almost as though she'd flown across the room rather than walked.

Heat crept onto his neck. It wasn't that this was his first injury. Getting injured had almost been a requirement in his former line of work. But last time, his ma had been alive to care for him. And the time before that too. It was embarrassing to ask for help from a stranger, especially when the stranger looked so lovely.

Because the woman beside him was certainly lovely. Her thick mane of hair hung loose, cascading about her face and shoulders in a wavy mass of brown and red that looked richer than a sea-otter pelt. Her eyes were wide and round, her lips soft and full, her skin the color of fresh cream, and she smelled like wildflowers on a spring day.

And here he couldn't even sit up on his own.

"Let's do this together." Her hand slid beneath his back, the bare skin of her palm warm against his spine. "If you can put weight on your right side, I'll help support the left."

She placed her other hand on his chest, smack over his sternum and well away from his injury.

The heat from his neck crept onto his face. Did she realize he was shirtless? That it wasn't appropriate for her to touch him in such a way, nurse or not?

He glanced up at her, but she didn't seem bothered by the touch. "On the count of three now. One, two . . ."

He positioned his right elbow on the bed, and leaned against it, shifting as much of his weight to his right side as he could.

"Three . . ."

She lifted his left side while he pushed on his right arm. A fresh round of pain ignited in his wound, but it wasn't so bad that he had to stop moving. Ilya grabbed the pillow he'd been lying on, plus an extra pillow from a nearby chair and stuffed them behind his back.

"Thank you." He clasped a hand over his bandage. It was a mistake. The slight bit of pressure only worsened the fiery pain beneath him, and he yanked his hand away.

"Ilya, fetch Kate," the woman said. "And Alexei, if you can find him. They'll both want to see Mr. Darrow."

"No," he blurted.

The woman looked at him, her brow furrowed with

concern. "Is something wrong, Mr. Darrow? Do you have pain somewhere?"

Yes, he had pain, but that wasn't why he wanted Ilya to stay. Surely the two of them couldn't be alone together. It wasn't proper, not with his shirt off and her looking so lovely and . . .

Hang it all. Had getting punched in the head made him go daft?

Of course the two of them could be alone. She was his nurse and nothing more, which she proved by reaching out and touching her hand to his head. "You don't seem feverish. Do you need Ilya to fetch something for you?"

The boy moved closer to him, his eyes wide with concern.

"No. I'm fine. I mean, my shoulder and head hurt, but that's to be expected, right?"

"It is, unfortunately, but Kate might be able to give you something for the pain after she gets here."

"That sounds nice."

"So Ilya can go get Kate?"

"Yes," he mumbled. It wasn't as though he could give another answer without looking like an idiot.

As the boy scampered out of the room, the woman turned to the small stand beside the bed and poured water from the pitcher into a glass. "You should drink water. Can you manage the glass on your own, or do you need me to help?"

What did she think he was, an invalid? He held out a hand for the glass. "I can do it myself."

She handed the cup to him, again watching him with that concerned expression, as though she expected he might keel over and die from the exertion of taking a drink.

He took a few sips, then tried to reach across his chest to set the cup back on the bedside table, but when he twisted his body, pain flashed through his upper ribs.

She took the glass from him and set it down. "I'm sure it must be hard to wake up confined to a bed, but your recovery will go much faster if you let your shoulder rest."

"Right. I just didn't expect it to hurt so much."

"Would you like a cloth for your forehead?" She turned and began wringing one out in the basin that sat atop the bedside table.

"I'd like to know your name, actually."

She turned back to him with the cloth. "Evelina."

"And you're a nurse here in Juneau?"

"I'm a . . ." She blushed. "Yes, I suppose you could say that. What brings you to Juneau, Mr. Darrow?"

Mr. Darrow. He blinked for a moment, the name strange to his ears. But it was the name he had given that Amos fellow on the ship. Mr. Amos must have told others it was his name while he was unconscious.

And why wouldn't he? There was no reason for anyone but him to know that Darrow wasn't his true surname.

"Well?" Evelina wrung the last bit of water out of the rag in her hands, the sound of splashing water filling the room. "Should I assume gold brought you north? The same as it does for everyone else on the Pacific Coast?"

The way she said the word *gold* made it sound almost dirty, as though there was something wrong with a man wanting to find gold and make a better life for himself. "I needed a new job and saw an ad for work at the Treadwell Mine. So I came up thinking I'd work there—right up until we passed it."

She smiled. "I don't blame you for that. The stench of the chlorination plant is horrible. But good luck finding a job elsewhere during the winter months." She reached out and touched the rag to his forehead.

He jumped. First placing her hands on his chest and back, then checking to see if he had a fever, and now touching the rag to his forehead—was it just him, or was the woman constantly finding a reason to touch him?

"Is it too cold?"

"No, I . . ." How to explain it was her hand against his skin he was opposed to, not the rag? "It's nothing. Just not feeling myself is all."

"Mr. Darrow," a voice sounded from the doorway. In some ways, it sounded like Evelina, but there was a certain briskness to it that Evelina didn't have. "My brother will be pleased to see you're awake."

He peered around Evelina to see another woman bustle into the room. He stared. He couldn't help himself. The woman's hair was pulled back into a loose bun rather than hanging free, and she wore a shirtwaist that was tucked primly into a serviceable blue skirt. But other than that, the two women were identical. They shared the same wide forehead and green eyes, the same full lips and red highlights peeking out from their rich brown hair.

"You're twins?"

"Don't act as though you've never seen twins before." The second woman, whom he assumed to be Kate, strode to the hutch on the far side of the log-hewn room and washed her hands in a dark sort of liquid, then dried them on a towel before turning his direction. "Now tell me, where is the pain greatest? In your head or your chest?"

"My chest. Definitely my chest."

"Do you need me in here?" Another woman entered the room.

Or no, she wasn't a woman, even though she was tall. She was more like a girl caught in that awkward stage where she was starting to become a woman, but still five years or so away from a marriageable age. She had the trademark black hair, high cheekbones, and tan skin that pronounced her a native, even though she wore a dress similar to Evelina's and spoke without an accent.

"Sure. Let's see what we find when we examine Mr. Darrow." Kate pulled a stethoscope out of one of the drawers and approached.

Jonas scooted a little higher on the bed and glanced toward the door. "Ah, maybe we should wait until the doctor arrives?"

Evelina frowned at him. "Whatever do you mean?"

"I mean the fellow who patched me up. Shouldn't we wait until he returns to start the examination?"

The room turned suddenly quiet, the eyes of all three women boring into him.

Jonas swallowed. Was he somehow being too demanding by asking for the doctor? Every other time he'd suffered a life-threatening injury, he'd dealt with a doctor.

Were things different in Alaska?

He opened his mouth to ask, but just then the door to the room banged open, and Ilya scampered back inside, his eyes bright and chest heaving, as though he'd just run three laps around the town—and enjoyed it.

"Alexei will be here in a minute." He looked around the room. "Wait. What's wrong? Is it something with Mr. Darrow?"

"I'm the fellow who patched you up." Kate set the stethoscope against his chest, and he jumped, the metal cool against the skin usually covered with a shirt.

"But . . ." He looked around. "Did no one send for a doctor?"

"I *am* a doctor." Kate's voice was hard enough it just might crush rock right alongside the stamps down at the stamp mill. "Now take a deep breath in."

"But you're a woman."

She pressed the stethoscope even harder against his chest and narrowed her eyes. "I said to breathe in."

He did as instructed, and she moved the stethoscope to another position on his chest. "Again."

"Why do people always say that 'bout Kate?" Ilya whispered to the native girl beside him.

"It's not normal for a woman to be a doctor," she whispered back.

Not normal? It wasn't something he'd even heard of. He eyed the woman with the stethoscope. "You sure you're a doctor, not just a nurse who's had a bit of extra training?"

The woman stiffened. "Would you like me to show you my diploma from the New England Female Medical College?"

"Ah . . . yes, please."

Ilya's eyes widened, and he exchanged another look with the girl beside him. Meanwhile, Evelina was looking straight at him, giving her head a subtle shake.

What was so wrong with asking to see this Kate woman's diploma?

And since when were they letting women into medical schools alongside men?

Or did women go to their own schools for medicine? He didn't know, because never before in any of the myriad places his former job had taken him, in all the visits to doctors' offices and hospitals he'd made, had he met a woman who claimed to be a doctor.

"I'd be happy to show you my diploma." Kate smiled at him, but there was nothing kind about the stiff curve of her lips. "Right after I tear out your stitches and reopen your wound. Maybe you'd prefer to bleed out on my exam table while you wait for the male doctor to arrive from the Treadwell . . ."

The girl with the long black hair let out a loud sigh. Ilya

mumbled something that sounded an awful lot like "Not this again." And Evelina buried her head in her hands.

". . . Because mark my words, Mr. Darrow"—Kate sneered —"if I hadn't been here when you were dragged out of the channel, you'd be—"

"Kate!" A sharp voice from the doorway cut her off, and Alexei Amos strode inside, his eyes narrowed into two slits at the woman claiming to be a doctor. "Good heavens, have you no manners? And after Darrow here saved our brother's life?"

Our *brother?* Jonas blinked at Ilya, then looked around the room.

Evelina hadn't given him her last name, but he could see the resemblance between Evelina, Kate, and Alexei. The three of them being siblings wasn't so hard to believe.

But unless he'd been walloped in the head harder than he remembered, he'd only saved one person's life this afternoon. "Ilya's your brother?"

"He is." Kate planted her hands on her hips. "Why? Are you going to start running your mouth about that? Maybe you want me to produce both of our birth certificates, proving we have the same father?"

"Kate!" Alexei clenched his jaw. "I said enough."

"Ilya and Inessa are our half siblings." Evelina reached a hand toward Ilya, and he took it, burying himself in her side for a hug. "Our father remarried an Aleut chieftain's daughter after our mother died."

Aleut? He'd never heard the word before.

"So you're all siblings." His gaze drifted over the people in the room once more. Kate, Evelina, Ilya and . . . he believed someone had called the girl Inessa. His eyes finally stopped on Alexei. "I had no idea."

"Had I realized I'd have cause to introduce my family to you, I would have told you about them aboard the *Alliance*," the man said, his eyes moving to Ilya. "But I'd much prefer my youngest brother learn to sail the way I did, without being given an ounce of special treatment because he's related to the ship's owner."

"You own the *Alliance?*" Somehow he missed that part on the ship as well. But it made sense now that he thought back to the commanding way Alexei had strode about the deck, issuing orders that were followed immediately, even though it was clear he wasn't the captain.

"It's not just the *Alliance*. We own the *Aurora*, the *Serenity*, the *Halcyon*, and the *Orion*." Ilya stepped away from his sister and came to the bed as he rattled off the list of names. As though it was somehow normal for a man to own five ships the size of the *Alliance*. "Oh, and the Sitka Trading Company. The Amos family owns that too, which means we got trading posts all over Alaska, even in places that take a year to get to and where there's no sun all winter long. And I'm an Amos, so it ain't just Alexei who owns everything, even though he acts like he owns the world. I own some of it too, right along with Kate, Evelina, Inessa, Yuri, Sacha, and Mikhail. But Alexei is still in charge of running—"

"Ilya," Alexei barked, his jaw clenched. "Please go fetch Mr. Hemmings and Mr. Hanover so they can take Mr. Darrow's statement about his stabbing."

Ilya straightened. "Yes, sir."

And then he was off, darting from the room as though his previous run through Juneau hadn't provided him with nearly enough exercise.

"Mr. Darrow." Alexei stepped to the bed. "Please accept my sincere condolences for your injuries. I am quite aware that you received them while protecting my brother, and I am in your debt. You have my deepest gratitude for what you did today, but if there's any other way in which I can repay you, please don't hesitate to ask—for anything. And I do mean that."

Jonas looked up into the dark eyes of the man who, as Ilya had put it, seemed to own the entire world. He was well dressed, with perfect posture and impeccable manners and a face that was likely trained not to give away even a hint of emotion.

And yet emotion was there, in the depths of his brown eyes and the lines that creased the sides of his mouth.

This was a man who loved his brother deeply, and probably his other siblings as well. "I don't have need of anything, but thank you for offering."

"Please know that the Marshal has already been sent for."

"There's a Marshal?" Jonas stilled. Those weren't words he'd expected to hear. Simon Volker needed to answer for his crimes, yes, but that didn't mean a Marshal needed to oversee the case.

"Don't get too excited." Alexei's voice turned dry. "He's clear over in Sitka."

Right. "And just how far away is Sitka?"

Alexei looked at him as though he was daft. "Do you know nothing of Alaska?"

Jonas shrugged his good shoulder. He'd assumed he'd be working underground, spending twelve hours a day hauling rock out of the earth. He hadn't paid too much attention to anything other than the path he would need to follow from his sister's home in Oklahoma up to Juneau. He'd just wanted to be away from Austin and the memories, from the guilt that had chased him throughout the entire state of Texas.

But judging from the look on Alexei's face, maybe he should have planned a little better.

"Sitka is a two-day journey by sea," Evelina said, her voice soft against the quietness of the room.

"How long does it take by train?"

Her brows pinched together, then she gave a slow shake of her head. "There is no train. Sitka is on Baranof Island. It's the capital of the district."

He sat back. "The capital of Alaska is on an island?" Why had no one told him?

"There are no roads in Alaska, or railroads, or any of the other things a man might use to travel overland from one place to another. There is only the sea." Alexei pressed his eyes closed and rubbed the back of his neck, his voice strained, almost as though giving the explanation drew on his last bit of patience.

And maybe it did. Taking care of Ilya couldn't be the easiest job in the world, and on top of that, the man ran five ships and a trading company.

"As I was saying," Alexei continued, "it will take at least two days to send for the Marshal, then another two him to travel here, and that's if he leaves right away. It will likely be close to a week before he arrives to investigate what happened, and that's if he's in Sitka to begin with. If he's in the Aleutians or Wrangell or somewhere else, who knows how long it will take for him to arrive."

"And there's no road to Wrangell or the Aleutians?" he asked. "Or anywhere else?"

Alexei raised a brow at him. "The Aleutians are another chain of islands, located about a thousand miles north of here and extending across the Bering Sea toward Russia. It's where the Aleut people, including Inessa and Ilya's mother, are from."

"And Wrangell? Is that on an island too?"

"It is. We passed it on the voyage here. The only roads that exist in Alaska are the small streets in towns."

"I see." Except he didn't. Texas was wide and open, mostly flat, and connected by roads and railroads running east and west, north and south. There were only a handful of rivers throughout the state, and none of them were large enough to take more than a rowboat down them. Only the Gulf of Mexico, on the southeast side of the state, provided any access to water or shipping or the maritime trade.

But while Alaska was a large, vast land—he'd at least known that before embarking on his journey—it seemed the only places that had been settled were on the water.

That explained why the Amos family owned five ships, if nothing else.

And hopefully the Marshal was in the Aleutians or Wrangell or another place far away. Because the last person he wanted to interview him was a Marshal. "Just let me talk to the sheriff. Is he here now? I should be able to answer at least a few questions."

Alexei gave his head a small shake. "You're on the frontier. The only lawman is a Marshal who oversees all of Alaska."

His assailants had said something about that on the wharf, hadn't they? Right before they stabbed him.

But he hadn't quite believed it. After all, he'd passed a mine teeming with people, and Juneau itself looked large enough to need a lawman. "How can there not be a sheriff?"

Alexei sucked in a breath, as though this conversation was using every last drop of his patience. "Mr. Darrow—or Jonas, if I may. I'm afraid this isn't like California or any other state where you may have lived. Because Alaska is not a state at all. In fact, it's not even a territory, which would at least have its own government. We are a district, which means we are controlled by the Department of the Interior. And that makes Alaska the most poorly organized, poorly managed five hundred and eighty thousand square miles of land in the entire world. I'm sorry to tell you, but there is no sheriff in Juneau, because there is no official town to hire a sheriff or collect taxes or plot growth. The officials in charge of maintaining law and order in Alaska are all appointed by the Department of the Interior, and they all live in Sitka. And to give you an inkling of just how well that is working, Alaska has been through three governors in the last two years."

Jonas rubbed his temple, the pain growing with each moment this conversation dragged on. "So there's no chance the man who stabbed me will be held accountable for his actions? What about the man who stole the two hundred dollars? Who is going to track him down?"

Alexei's shoulders rose and fell on a sigh. "Juneau has a committee of public safety that makes arrests when a crime occurs and keeps men jailed until the Marshal and district judge arrive for trial. Simon Volker—the man who stabbed you —is sitting in the town jail, right along with his friends. Your carpetbag and the satchel they were searching are in the corner there." He pointed to a space behind Jonas. "After Kate examines you, please inspect your belongings and make sure nothing is missing. We believe we recovered everything, including your pistol and the money sewn into the seam of the bag, but we can't be sure."

This sounded like chaos. Absolute, complete chaos.

He'd been thinking Alaska might give him a fresh start, but perhaps he'd be better off making a home for himself in the mountains of Idaho or Montana. At least those places were allowed to form towns with mayors and sheriffs and anything else that might be needed.

"How long?" he asked, the pounding in his temple increasing, and not because he'd been punched in the head three times.

"Until what?" The woman doctor stepped forward and wrinkled her brow.

"Until I'm recovered enough to be on my way."

"Are you going to prospect?" Evelina asked.

"Where are you headed?" This from Alexei, who already knew of his plans to work at the Treadwell Mine.

If only he knew how to answer that question. Did he really want to leave Alaska without even trying to find a job? "Is there another mine where I can work? Something not as big as the Treadwell?"

"Not with your injury, at least not before the snow comes." Kate crossed her arms over her chest, her gaze narrowed at his bandage. "It will take six weeks or better before you make a full recovery, and that will put us into late October, when the Treadwell will be the only mine open."

"As soon as the rivers freeze, the smaller mines shut down," Evelina said, seeming to understand he'd need more of an explanation. "They're unable to extract any ore without water."

"But even then, you ought not do anything that requires heavy lifting." Kate's lips pinched together. "Too much strain on your wound could reopen it."

So he was stuck here for the next six weeks? In a spartan log room that would provide nothing but time for memories to haunt him?

So much for the notion that Alaska would heal him.

6

He was sleeping like a baby.

Evelina sighed as she stared at Mr. Darrow's peacefully slumbering form. And here she'd been certain something was wrong, that she needed to check on him just one more time before allowing herself to drift off to sleep.

Never mind that it was past midnight, and she'd heard no sound coming from downstairs. Still, she'd gotten out of bed, pulled on her wrapper, and traipsed down to the examination room.

And all for nothing. Because he clearly had no need of her.

But that didn't change the fact that staying upstairs, so far away from him, somehow seemed wrong. Kate had assured her Mr. Darrow was stable, and nothing would happen during the night.

But what if Kate was mistaken? What if something happened, and he called for one of them?

Evelina tightened the sash about her wrapper, just to make sure her nightdress was fully covered, then crept closer to the bed.

He slept soundly, as though nothing in the universe could wake him from his slumber. And seeing as how Kate had given him laudanum earlier, perhaps she shouldn't be surprised. But that still didn't change the fact that if something did happen, no one would be able to hear him.

She had half a mind to make up a pallet and sleep down here, just to put her mind to rest. Yes, that's what she would do. After all, it wasn't as though she'd be able to sleep if she carted herself back upstairs. She'd simply lie awake wondering if Mr. Darrow was all right.

She wouldn't stay in the same room as him, though. That would hardly be proper, but if she made up a bed in the schoolroom, she could hear any noise he might make through the wall.

"I'll be back in a few minutes," she said. "And I'll be just on the other side of that wall there if you need anything."

He gave no acknowledgment that he'd heard her, but his long, steady breaths filled the room, their cadence so rhythmic she could probably time the rise and fall of his chest with a watch.

She couldn't seem to take her eyes away from him. Because he'd saved her brother, of course. Because her entire family owed him a debt she wasn't sure they'd ever be able to repay.

Not because he was handsome. That had nothing to do with it.

Yet even lying in a sickbed with his face pale from pain, she couldn't deny how attractive he was. His short red hair tried to form curls atop his head, though it wasn't quite long enough for any of the strands to curl fully. His jaw was covered in that same reddish hue of stubble, but the bones of his face were firm and strong beneath the scruff. The rest of him was solidly built, with a chest almost broader than her brother Mikhail's, and legs as thick as tree trunks.

He was the type of man most others would think twice

about before picking a fight. Had Simon Volker not been drunk, he probably would have taken one look at Mr. Darrow and then walked away.

And here she was, gawking at a sleeping man like some sort of wanton woman. Her cheeks heated. She needed to leave before her thoughts ran even further afield. "I'll be back in a few minutes."

She forced herself to turn and walk through the doorway, pulling the door shut behind her with a soft click before padding her way up the stairs.

But rather than finding everyone sleeping when she reached the top, lamplight shone through a narrow crack in the first door.

She frowned. That was the room where they'd moved the contents of Alexei's office so they could create an exam room for Kate. Had the lamp been lit when she passed by on her way downstairs a few minutes earlier?

"Alexei?" She knocked softly on the door, the gentle pressure causing it to open further.

Her brother turned from where he stood at the window looking out onto the street below, and beyond that, to the channel where the *Alliance* was docked.

"Evelina." He frowned. "What are you doing up?"

She stepped inside. "I should ask you the same thing."

He shoved his fingers into his hair, his shoulders rising and falling on a sigh. "I've been gone for two months. You have no idea how behind I am, especially with Scott leaving so long ago. The records are a mess."

"We've been filling out the ledgers. The most recent ones are still downstairs by the counter."

"That doesn't tell me what shipments came in while I was gone, only what went out." He looked around the disorganized room. The haphazard stacks of papers randomly piled on his desk were probably enough to give her order-loving brother a rash, not to mention she wasn't sure they'd managed to put the drawers to the filing cabinets back in the right order after moving them—something he'd discover eventually.

"I can help you sort things in the morning."

"I was planning to go to Sitka in the morning."

"But you only just arrived."

They stood there for a moment, the two of them looking at each other across the cramped space. Alexei's shoulders were tight and his back stiff, but when were they ever relaxed?

Yet for all his complaining about his messy office, he hadn't been hectically trying to organize things when she'd entered the room. He'd been staring out the window.

"What is it?" she asked. "Did your time in San Francisco go poorly?"

He shoved his hand through his hair again. "It went about how I expected. In twenty more years, our ships will be obsolete, replaced by large iron- and steel-hulled monsters built and owned by giant corporations. No one wants wooden ships built, and no one wants to secure shipping contracts with companies who own them."

"That can't be right. Those giant ships aren't interested in stopping at the native villages on the coast."

"No."

"So who will bring supplies to the Aleuts and Inupiat?" While their family might own five ships, two of them were dedicated solely to routes that supplied Alaskan villages and towns. Most large shipping companies wouldn't bother with such routes, claiming the villages were too remote and the goods that the natives brought to trade weren't lucrative enough to be worth the trip.

"I don't know who will replace us," Alexei answered. "For now, our ships are seaworthy. That's all I can tell you."

"But you keep losing shipping contracts to the big corporations with the giant ships. And without the more lucrative contracts, the ones that pay the bills, how will we be able to run the remote routes?"

"We'll find a way. It's not as though the family coffers are empty. When one door closes, another often opens. It's how economies work. Just look at what has happened to shipping in America. As railroads have grown, shipping has decreased. Ships are used to transport goods across the Atlantic and Pacific, but there is no need to take a ship from San Francisco through the Panama Canal and the Gulf of Mexico, up the Eastern Seaboard, down the Saint Lawrence River, and through four of the Great Lakes to Duluth for transport to North Dakota, when a railroad can reach Bismarck from San Francisco in two days' time."

"That's why the smart shipping-company owners bought stock in railroad companies several decades ago, like you asked Father to do before he died." She could still remember standing in their house in Sitka, hearing the discussion between her brother and father as her brother prepared to leave for school in San Francisco.

Alexei drew in a breath, and he didn't need to answer her for her to know the sudden creases in his brow were lines of regret.

If Papa had listened and invested something in the railroads, would they have been in a different position now? Better set to face the future if it meant a decline in the shipping industry?

"At least we still have the Treadwell contract. That alone should provide enough profit to. . ."

A dark look crossed Alexei's face, and her words trailed off.

"Treadwell did renew our contract, right?" It was all Alexei had been working on last spring before he left for San Francisco.

"No." The single word dropped like a boulder into the room. "They're going with a corporation out of Seattle, one that has a fleet of iron-hulled ships, all of which are larger than ours."

"That can't be right." She stared at him for a moment, waiting for the words to settle, for her mind to make sense of them. "We knew Joe Juneau and John Treadwell in Sitka before either of them discovered gold here. Surely the Treadwell Mine, of all places, would want to partner with us."

Alexei crossed his arms over his chest. "John Treadwell sold his mine five years ago to a corporation full of rich investors on the Eastern Seaboard, and they have no interest in propping up a dying shipping company with such a lucrative contract."

Her eyes burned. She couldn't help it. The Treadwell Mine was a dream for any shipping company owner, because nearly all food and supplies had to be brought in by ship, and the cargo hold was then filled with gold on the return voyage. How could they have lost the contract?

And how could her brother appear so calm about it?

"Lina," Alexei sighed. "Please don't fret. I received this news over a month ago. I'm already working on a solution."

"But what can possibly replace the Treadwell contract?" She braced herself against the desk. For three centuries, the English part of the Amos family had built and owned ships, first in England in the 1500s, then in Maine when it was a British colony, and finally, for the past ninety years, in Sitka, where three full generations of Amoses had been born and buried.

Were the days of a man being able to own his own ship truly fading? What would their family do?

"I . . ." She sniffled and swiped at her cheek. "I want to say there will be another contract that comes around, bigger and better than the Treadwell contract. But . . ."

"There won't. And there's no use trying to sugarcoat it."

She drew in a breath and looked at her brother, with his towering height and wide shoulders and stoic face. He looked so strong and determined, ready to take on the world. But it couldn't be an easy job running a family business that grew more difficult to manage every year while keeping track of all his siblings.

Because even though everyone but Inessa and Ilya was grown, they still made work for him. All of them still called the large white house on Sitka Sound home. All still relied on the Sitka Trading Company and Amos Family Shipbuilders to pay their bills.

"Most of the time I can come up with a plan, a series of action steps, something I can do next. But sometimes . . ." Alexei slumped into the chair behind his desk. "Sometimes I feel like the world is changing too fast for me to keep up with it."

Evelina reached out and settled her hand atop his. "At least we still have each other."

"Do we really?"

"What's that supposed to mean?"

"It means that Ilya could have been stabbed earlier." Alexei tugged his hand away from her and scrubbed it over his face. "If not for Darrow stepping in, I hate to think what might have happened to Ilya."

"Do you really think Simon Volker would have pulled a knife on a child? I bet he only reached for it because he found Mr. Darrow so . . . so . . ." How exactly should she describe Jonas Darrow? Handsome was hardly the effect she was going for, even if it was the first word that sprang to mind. "Imposing."

Alexei sighed. "You might be right about the knife, but Volker still would have accused Ilya of stealing the money, and all because he's half Aleut."

She couldn't argue. Though the Aleut people lived on the Aleutian Islands and mainland coast nearly a thousand miles north of Sitka, in Russian America, it had been quite common for Russian men to marry Aleut women. Especially when those women were from powerful families that could help foster trade.

But now that Alaska was part of the United States? Marrying a native woman was unheard of, and the more Americanized Alaska became, the more the large, sprawling Amos family didn't seem to belong.

People took one look at their Creole siblings and assumed things that never would have been assumed when Alaska belonged to Russia.

Like assuming that Inessa and Ilya were illegitimate.

Or couldn't learn alongside white children in white schools.

Or were thieves.

"What about Inessa?" Alexei asked, almost as though sensing her thoughts. "I know you and Kate like it in Juneau, but how is Inessa doing here?"

Now it was her turn to sigh. "Much the same as she did in Sitka."

"So the Tlingit girls her age . . .?"

Evelina pressed her lips together. She knew what Alexei wanted to hear. That Inessa had made friends, that the Tlingit here were more accepting of her than the Tlingit in Sitka had been.

But it simply wasn't true. "A few of the girls are kind to her, but it's unrealistic to expect the Tlingit will ever accept her or Ilya the way they do their own people."

The Tlingit and Aleut tribes had spent centuries fighting each other. But even more than that, the Aleuts had allied themselves with the Russians when the Russians had first arrived in the early 1700s, and that alliance had held for the entire time that Russian America had existed.

While the alliance might have made a Russian-American man like their father more inclined to marry an Aleut woman, it had also meant the Aleuts were at odds with every other tribe in Alaska.

In some ways it didn't matter that the Russians and Aleuts had always accepted mixed-raced children, because the other tribes often saw them as enemies.

"Sometimes I wonder . . ." Alexei looked down and fiddled with the edge of a sheet of paper on the desk. "Sometimes I wonder if Ilya and Inessa would be better off in Unalaska, with their mother's family."

Evelina's heart nearly stopped in her chest. "How can you say such a thing? They are our siblings, part of our family. They know no one in Unalaska!"

"But they would be accepted."

"Would they?" A knot formed in her stomach. "Or would they be carted off to a boarding school like the one across the channel or the one in Sitka? You were right about the world changing, about there not being a place for Inessa or Ilya like there would have been thirty years ago. But you're wrong to think that taking them back to their mother's people would solve anything, especially with how the Americans treat the natives."

"Perhaps you're right. I just . . ." Alexei swallowed, worried grooves forming more lines around his mouth and eyes than a man of thirty should have. "When I think of what could have happened to Ilya today, or how Inessa has no friends . . ."

"But nothing did happen." She came around the desk and

wrapped her arms around her brother from behind, resting her cheek atop his head. "Because there are still decent people living in Alaska, just like there were decent people living in this place when it was Russian America. The Department of the Interior might decide to send a horde of nincompoops to Sitka to run things, but that doesn't mean all the people here are bad."

A breath rushed out of him. She felt it more than heard it, since her arms were still wrapped around his chest.

"I hope you're right," he whispered.

She hoped so too.

Their family had already suffered enough by losing first their mother, then their father and stepmother, and finally their brother, Ivan.

She couldn't imagine how much more they might suffer if what remained of their family was broken apart.

7

"Mr. Darrow? Are you awake?"

Jonas blinked at the light coming through the doorway, a groan falling from his lips. His head. Was it ever going to stop pounding?

The shadowed form of a woman entered the room, then the door fell shut behind her and cast him in darkness once more. But he didn't need light to know which of the Amos sisters had entered. It was Evelina, the one with the soft footsteps and kind smile.

"You slept through dinner last night and breakfast this morning." She set a tray with some toast and oatmeal down on the small table beside his bed, then reached out and held a hand to his brow.

Did her skin always have to feel so soft and warm?

"Where's the doctor?" he rasped. There was no danger of her touch feeling soft. She had the bedside manner of a rabid cat. "Shouldn't she be the one checking on me?"

"Kate got called away." Evelina pulled her hand away.

"There was an accident up in Silver Bow Basin, but she tasked me with checking your wound and making sure you eat."

"Not hungry." He just wanted the pounding in his head to go away and his shoulder to not feel like it had been seared with a branding iron.

"I'm afraid you'll need to eat at least a few bites. It's important to keep your strength up. Kate says it helps stave off infection."

"My wound's not infected."

"How do you know?" She cocked her head to the side, then reached out and covered the bandage with her hand.

The pressure was slight, but he still couldn't stop himself from hissing in pain. "I know because . . . it doesn't feel like it's burning . . . even if it hurts."

"I need to check your wound all the same. Kate will have my hide if I don't."

"I believe that. Your sister doesn't have the kindest bedside manner."

She laughed, the sound light and tinkling, like how he might imagine an angel would sound laughing. "Kate can be a little bullish at times, especially when she feels someone is questioning her doctoring."

"I hadn't noticed."

Another laugh escaped her lips, light and airy and filled with hope. "Just don't let on that you're cross with her when she returns. I don't think that will help overmuch."

"Thanks for the advice."

A smile spread across her face. "Can I open the curtains? I need a bit of light to continue."

He groaned and turned his head away from the window. "The light hurts my head."

"It's either the curtains or the lamp. I'm serious about

checking your wound, Mr. Darrow. I need to make sure there's no sign of infection."

"Then do whichever will help you the most. Either way, my head will hurt."

She slid the curtains halfway open along the window, but it wasn't as bright as he'd expected. Clouds hung low in the sky, casting the world in a dark, dreary gray.

"After I'm finished, I'll brew some willow bark tea for your head."

He groaned a second time. He couldn't help himself. "Have you ever tasted willow bark tea? It's horrendous."

"But will it be worse than the pain? Kate is careful with how much laudanum she doles out, and you already had some this morning."

"The pain reminds me I'm still alive. Things could be worse."

"Yes. I suppose they could." Evelina Amos really was quite lovely to look at, with her creamy skin, green eyes, and full lips. Yesterday she'd worn only a dress, but today she wore a shawl over her dress. The thin material didn't look as though it would do much to keep her warm, but it hugged her shoulders in a flowery pattern of blues and purples and reds that looked lovely against her reddish-brown hair.

"I know Alexei thanked you yesterday." She swallowed. "But I owe you thanks as well. You barely knew Ilya, and yet you protected him from a gang of drunkards."

Jonas's throat closed, and he turned his head away. "It was nothing. Any man would have stepped in to protect your brother."

"I beg to differ." Her hand reached down and found his lying atop the quilt, and she gave it a gentle squeeze. "Most of the men on the wharf were more interested in attacking him than protecting him, if you remember."

He untangled his hand from hers. "How long until my head stops pounding?"

Her brow furrowed, and she shifted to study his eyes. The movement brought her close enough for him to catch a whiff of flowers and rain. The rain was probably from outside, but the flowers reminded him of a field on a spring day. Light and airy, and in direct contrast with the gloomy sky outside.

"What are you doing?" he whispered.

"Looking at your pupils." Her eyes were focused directly on his own. "You asked about your headaches, but their length and severity will depend on the severity of your concussion."

So there was a medical reason for her to be this near him, just like there was a medical reason for her to touch his forehead when checking his temperature. And in a few minutes, when she looked at his wound, there would be a medical reason for her to touch his chest.

In fact, the only time she'd touched him without a medical reason had been when she'd taken his hand earlier and yesterday, and considering he was lying abed in an immense amount of pain, those touches weren't inappropriate.

Maybe he'd been punched harder than he realized, and he was construing Miss Amos's every movement to mean something more than it did.

She leaned a bit closer. "Your pupils appear to be dilating."

Her breath brushed his chin as she spoke, and heaven help him, even that was warm and sweet.

She pulled back, but he had an inane desire to ask her to check his pupils again, just so he could smell the scents of rain and wildflowers, to feel her breath on his face.

Maybe he'd even be able to sneak a hand up and see if her hair felt as soft as it looked.

He pressed his eyes shut. Yes, he'd definitely been hit in the head harder than he'd realized. Otherwise he wouldn't be fawning over a nurse who was in his room for the sole purpose of doing her job and nothing more.

"Your pupils dilated yesterday too," she said. "So Kate wasn't overly concerned about the punches you took to your head. But you did lose consciousness for quite a while after you were pulled from the water. Kate had thought that was due to loss of blood, but now I'm wondering if your concussion is worse than my sister realized."

She took a step away from the bed. "I'll ask Kate about your headaches after she returns. Otherwise, I'm afraid there's nothing more I can do for them other than offer you willow bark tea."

"I'll take it." Never mind that he might well have to plug his nose and force the bitter liquid down his throat. He had to find a way to get some sense back. Fast. The last thing he needed was to make a fool of himself when he was going to be stuck with Kate and Evelina Amos as his doctor and nurse for the next six weeks.

"Can you roll onto your side now, please? I'd like to check your wound before I brew the tea, and it will be easiest to unwrap the bandage with you on your side."

He chanced a glance up at her. It was yet another mistake, because she was looking at him with so much kindness and concern that it was nearly impossible to tell her no. Never mind that moving was sure to hurt like the dickens.

Was Evelina Amos this kind to everyone? Or was she being especially kind to him because he'd rescued her brother?

He rolled onto his uninjured side, which allowed him to face away from her soft green eyes and the concerned lines etched across her forehead.

"Does your wound hurt more today than it did yesterday?" She asked as she unwound the bandage.

How was he supposed to answer that? "I don't know. My head hurts too much to try figuring it out."

The last of the bandage left his skin, and a flood of cool air rushed in.

"You can roll onto your back now."

He did as instructed, and she turned and lit the lamp beside the bed. "I'm sorry if this is too much light, but it's imperative that I see the wound clearly."

"I understand." His eyes had already adjusted to the brightness from the window. Hopefully his headache would calm again once his eyes adjusted to the new light from the lamp.

She leaned close over his chest, her eyes studying the skin around his stitches. It looked clean. Sore, but not infected.

She pressed against the edge of the wound, and he sucked in a breath, but no blood or fluid leaked from the angry seam.

"Satisfied?" he asked.

"It looks . . . You were shot before. At least a year ago, it appears." Her hand moved from his wound to the puckered skin just below his clavicle. "How long ago did this happen?"

He shifted. "A few years back. The bullet went straight through and exited the other side. The doc said I was lucky it didn't hit any bone."

"You certainly were."

He gave her a one-sided shrug with his good shoulder. "It took me a few weeks to recover, but I was good as new after that. Didn't get a concussion with it either."

He expected her to smile, but she didn't. Instead, her eyes were narrowed on the old scar. "Who shot you?"

"Doesn't matter."

"Was it some kind of accident?"

"Miss Amos." He reached down and clasped her wrist, pulling her fingers away from his chest. "It's time to put the bandage back on."

"But someone tried to kill you."

"Nothing as exciting as that. I was a bit too careless while cleaning my pistol and accidentally discharged a round." It was a lie, because someone had tried to kill him—more than once. But he had no intention of allowing any part of his life from Texas to follow him to Alaska.

Especially not a man by the name of Lucas Crowe.

Which was why he'd changed his name. Hopefully that would be enough to conceal his identity.

But if Crowe truly set his mind to finding him, just how traceable was the path he'd taken from Austin to Oklahoma to Juneau?

Jonas shifted again, suddenly uncomfortable on the bed. "Are you going to put a fresh bandage on my wound or use the old one?"

"Fresh, of course. Soiled bandages breed infection." She moved across the room to the hutch where the medical supplies were stored.

Her steps were swift and graceful, almost as though she glided rather than walked there and back. But once she returned, she frowned at him again. This time when she reached out, her fingers grazed his stomach.

It tickled, even with the pain in his shoulder, and he gasped out a laugh.

But she wasn't smiling. "You have another scar."

He looked down to find her tracing the scar from the knife wound that had almost ended his life. Somehow the blade that had been thrust just beneath his ribs had missed all his internal organs. The doctor had called it a miracle.

She leaned closer to stare at the old injury, two wide pools of green trying to make sense of the scars on his body.

This woman was going to be the death of him.

"The bandage, Miss Amos." He rolled onto his side and raised his arm, giving her access to rewrap his wound.

"There's another scar on your back." Again, her fingers flitted over the puckered skin on the small of his back, then another up by his shoulder blade. "What happened to you?"

"I got caught in a knife fight a few years back," he snapped. "As you can see, I recovered. Now are you going to assist me with the bandage, or do I need to do it myself?"

"But how did you get caught in a knife fight?"

He rolled onto his back, only to find that she hadn't even picked up the bandage. "Why aren't you married?"

She frowned. "Excuse me?"

"If you're going to start asking personal questions, then it's only fair I ask you questions in return. You're pretty enough that someone must have asked for your hand, especially in a place with few women."

She looked away. "I've only been in Juneau for two months."

"So no one has asked for your hand in marriage?"

"I didn't say that."

"Then share the story, please."

He could see her ire rising in the way her eyes lit with fire and her breaths turned quick and brisk, could feel it in the coldness that descended upon the room.

Good. Evelina Amos might be lovely, but he had no desire to get close to her, to feel her hand against his skin or her hair on his chest. No desire to even look her in the eyes. The more she disliked him, the easier it would be to leave when the time came.

"You haven't answered me." His voice sounded harsh even to his own ears, but he wasn't about to apologize. "Who asked you to marry him, and why did you turn him down? I can tell by the look on your face that there's a tale to accompany your reason for spinsterhood."

He spat the last word as though it were poison.

"I see your point, Mr. Darrow." She took a step back from him. "These are hardly appropriate conversations for two people who barely know each other."

"Indeed. Just because my shirt is off so I can receive medical care does not mean I invite questions about any old injuries you might happen to discover. If any of them prove relevant to my current recovery, I'll mention them to your sister, the doctor. Am I clear?"

"Perfectly. Now if you'll excuse me, I'm needed in the trading post. I'll be back in a few minutes to replace your bandage."

There was nothing light and graceful about how she moved across the room this time. No. She strode across the floor with strong, determined steps.

Only then did he notice the rising voices coming from the other side of the wall. It wasn't just one man but several, and they didn't sound pleased.

He expected her to fling the door open, stride through it, then slam it shut behind her.

But instead, she paused inside the room, jerking her shawl up over her hair and wrapping it about her neck once. A colorful pattern of red and purple flowers exploded against the rich blue background, and he could only stare as she slipped through the doorway, then banged it shut behind her.

Perhaps the shawl wasn't a shawl at all but a scarf, and it was likely her version of concealing her hair in public.

And even though she was gone, he still couldn't clear from his mind the image of the brightly-patterned scarf draped over her hair and slender shoulders.

Nor could he wipe away the hurt he'd seen in her eyes when he'd started asking why she wasn't married.

———————

EVELINA SLAMMED the door behind her louder than was necessary. She should probably feel bad about it. After all, Mr. Darrow had a severe headache, and loud noises were certain to make it worse. But she couldn't bring herself to care, not after the callous way he'd insisted on knowing personal things he had no reason to ask.

But hadn't she done the same to him when she'd asked about his scars?

Perhaps, but they were so plain and obvious, it was only natural to be curious. Wherever Mr. Darrow had come from and whatever he'd done before, the man hadn't had an easy life.

"There ain't no way it cost that much, ya little cheat." A voice rose from the front of the store, loud and irate. "Now tell me what I owe ya for real."

Evelina started for the counter near the door, where four large men had gathered around the cash register.

"I'm not cheating you," Inessa answered calmly from where she stood hidden by the group. "This is the correct price."

"There ain't no way a gold pan and screen cost twenty dollars. That's an entire month of wages!"

Evelina slid behind the counter next to Inessa, who had been running the store while she tended to Mr. Darrow. A quick glance at the items on the counter told her the price was, in fact, correct.

"Hello, I'm Miss Amos, co-owner of the Sitka Trading Company." She attempted to give the men her kindest smile. "Is there a problem?"

"Well, well, aren't you a pretty one?" one of the men

muttered. "What's a little lady like you doing in a place like this?"

The smile dropped from her lips. "Running my family's store. Now how can I help you?"

The man in front of the register leaned over the counter, close enough for her to see bits of dirt and old food tangled in his beard. "The In'jun who works for you is a cheat. She's running up your prices, probably trying to pocket the extra without you knowing it."

Evelina met the man's gaze. "The In'jun who works for me is my sister and will be co-owner of this store along with me when she turns eighteen. Furthermore, the price she gave for your items is accurate. It's ten dollars for the gold pan, screen, and shovel, then another four dollars for the tent. The bedroll is two, and your dried goods and the bear pelt make up the last four dollars."

"Those prices are outrageous!" the man exploded, foul breath wafting into her face.

"You are not in San Francisco anymore, or Seattle, or wherever you came from. The bear pelt is the only item from Alaska on the counter. Everything else was imported via ship, causing our own cost on each item to be higher than what you might expect in California."

"It's robbery," one of the other men drawled, his haggard face creased with lines from a life spent out of doors.

"It's the cost of doing business. Now do you want to purchase the goods or not?"

"It's cheaper here than the store at the other end of the wharf," another man said.

Indeed, it was. The Sitka Trading Company offered the best prices around, but mainly because they owned the ships that brought the goods up the coast. If they had to pay shipping costs, their prices would be similar to the other stores in Juneau.

The man with the long beard gave a tug on it, his eyes running down Inessa before he wrinkled his nose. "Maybe the store down the way is more expensive, but they don't have an In'jun working for them. And you say she's your sister?"

"My half sister. My father's second wife was Aleut."

"Filthy In'jun lover." The man stalked off, leaving the items on the counter. His three friends followed, muttering things that Evelina had no intention of trying to make out.

The moment the door closed behind him, she slammed her hand on the counter, her teeth clenching together until her jaw ached.

"Don't, Evelina." Inessa laid a hand atop hers. "It's simply best if I don't work the cash register. It causes problems every time. I can bring over stock from the warehouse or fill out the ledger and keep the books, but no one in Juneau trusts me with money."

"That's not true."

Inessa met her gaze, her younger sister's brown eyes calm and even. "It's the way of things. You can't fight it."

But she wanted to. Did everyone in Juneau have to be so prejudiced?

Was there a single man from America who looked at Inessa and Ilya without forming an instant judgment against either of them?

The clock chimed behind her, and she sighed.

"School starts in a half hour, and I have yet to feed Mr. Darrow." She swept out from behind the counter. "We'll discuss this more later. But for right now, get me if another customer arrives."

Inessa merely shrugged. "Don't let it bother you overmuch. The Americans are the ones at fault. They see a Tlingit or Aleut or Inupiat, and they're the ones who assume we are liars and cheats. That speaks more poorly of them than it does of us."

Her sister was right. It did speak more poorly of the Americans than of the Alaskan natives or Russians—what few of them were left. The American's didn't even call the Inupiat and Yupik by their actual name. They just called the natives who lived north of the Arctic Circle Eskimos and expected everyone to accept it.

The situation was infuriating.

How was it that Inessa let it all roll off her so easily?

Evelina stomped back into the sickroom, wrenched open the door, then narrowed her eyes at Mr. Darrow. "You tried moving."

He winced. "Had a mind to try feeding myself, but I got stuck."

"I can see that." He'd moved himself to a partial sitting position, but he hadn't been able to maneuver his body all the way up, which meant he sat in a low, awkward slump against the pillow behind him, lines of pain wreathing his face.

"You should have waited for help." She stalked to his bed.

"The point was to see if I could do it on my own."

"Must all men be fools?"

Mr. Darrow sent her a slow blink. "I'm sorry, you look like Evelina Amos. You're certainly wearing the scarf and dress that she had on when she checked my wound a few minutes ago. But I'm starting to wonder if you're really the doctor-sister, because there's been a rather profound change in your bedside manner."

She snorted, unable to help the small smile that tugged at the edges of her mouth. "I'm not Kate."

She slid a hand beneath the lower section of Mr. Darrow's ribs on both his back and front. "All right, let's do what we did yesterday. You raise yourself up on your right side, and I'll guide your left. On the count of three."

She counted, then he pushed his right side up while she guided his left. He slid easily into an upright position on the bed. "Excellent, now lean forward and raise your arm a bit. I need to reapply your bandage."

He did as instructed, and she made quick work of wrapping the clean material around his upper chest and shoulder, careful to not let her eyes wander to the obvious bullet scar above his recent knife wound—or any of the other scars on his torso.

"Which do you want first?" She pinned the edge of the bandage to a thick swatch of fabric. "Your toast or oatmeal?"

He scowled. "I'm twenty-seven years old. I should be able to eat without—"

"I'm sure you will, once you've recovered. Don't tell me you ate without assistance when you were recovering from that previous knife attack."

"Those aren't days I prefer to dwell on."

Of course not, and it had been careless of her to bring up the attack, especially when he'd already asked her to let the issue rest. "Forgive me."

She turned to the tray and picked up the bowl of oatmeal.

"I think I'm the one who owes you an apology. I can see you're still upset about earlier. I truly am sorry. Your suitors and marital status are none of my business."

She stilled, her hand pausing on the spoon. "You were right about my questions being too personal. What matters is that your other injuries are healed, and one day the wound beneath your collarbone will turn into a scar to match the others. That's all there is to it."

He repositioned himself on the bed, tugging on one of the pillows behind him until he got it into a different spot. "If you're not cross with me, what has you so upset?"

Was she really acting that upset? She stirred the congealed oatmeal. She must be if her patient with a pounding headache was commenting on her mood. "It has nothing to do with you or your questions earlier. The men in the trading post put me in a foul mood."

"What happened?"

"Nothing unusual, I'm afraid." But that was the problem. She plopped herself onto the chair by the bed and scooted it closer. "Tell me, Mr. Darrow, why do Americans take one look at Inessa and Ilya and assume the worst?"

He grew still for a moment, the brown hue of his eyes turning suddenly serious. "It's probably because people are often distrustful of those who are different from them. It was the same way where I lived before."

"That doesn't make it right." She jabbed the spoon into the oatmeal and held out a bite. "Oh, why did Russia have to sell its colony to America? Russia was actually interested in maintaining good relations with the native tribes. Or most of them, at least. But Americans assume every Indian is a thief, some other kind of criminal, or illegitimate."

"Surely not *all* Americans are that way." He spoke around his mouthful of oatmeal.

"Oh yes they are. Just ask Inessa if you don't believe me. Americans are rough and coarse and unrefined."

He raised an eyebrow. "Careful there. You're an American."

"I'm a *Russian* American. Who was born in *Russian* America, not the United States. There's a difference."

"Ah, so that's what your family is—Russian." He spoke as though he'd just been given the giant clue to a puzzle she didn't even know he'd been trying to solve.

"Don't tell me you didn't know?"

He rubbed his head. "That you were Russian? No, it never

occurred to me. But it makes sense. And for some reason—your family business, I assume—you didn't leave after Russia sold Alaska."

"Of course we didn't leave. This is our home." She dropped the spoon back into the oatmeal and gestured toward the window. "Or rather, Sitka is our home, but the islands and channels surrounding it are our home too. We've moved between them almost as much as the Tlingit over the past ninety years."

"That's how long your family has been in Alaska? Ninety years?"

"It wasn't Alaska then," she gritted. "It was Russian America."

"And in Russian America, it was common for white men to marry native women?"

"Yes."

"And the children who resulted from such marriages . . ."

"Creole. We call them Creole, and both the Russians and the natives accepted them."

"But not the Americans."

She sighed. Why were they talking about this? Alexei was right about times changing. Sometimes she felt as though the world was changing too fast for her to keep up. But Mr. Darrow certainly didn't have the ability to stop any of it from changing. And at the moment, he didn't even have the ability to eat by himself.

"We best finish this oatmeal. I need to go s—"

"Mr. Darrow!" The door to the room burst open, and Ilya bounded inside. "Oh, good. You're awake!"

"After an entrance like that, I daresay I'd be awake now, even if I'd been sleeping," he muttered. But he wasn't scowling at Ilya. If anything, his face held a bit of softness.

"I brought you books!" Ilya rushed to the bedside, all youthful energy and boundless enthusiasm. "See?"

A smile twitched at the corner of Mr. Darrow's lips as he surveyed the stack of thick books piled clear up to Ilya's chin. "Not sure I could miss it. But I'm afraid my head's not up for any reading."

"That's all right. I can read the books to you or tell you anything you need to know. I have all the important parts memorized."

Mr. Darrow scratched the side of his head. "Anything I want to know about what?"

"Panning for gold! Last night you said that's what you're going to do, didn't you? It's what I would do too. Why work in a boring tunnel when you can strike off and find gold on your own?" Ilya grinned as though he could sense piles and piles of gold just sitting on the ground waiting for him to come along and find them.

"Ilya . . ." Evelina reached out, placing a hand on her brother's shoulder and pulling him back from the edge of the bed. "Mr. Darrow needs to finish eating and rest, not learn about prospecting."

Ilya frowned. "But he rested for most of the morning."

"He did, yes, but he needs more, and you need to eat lunch before class starts. You only have about fifteen minutes."

His frown turned into an all-out scowl, and he dug the toe of his shoe into a crack in floor. "Do I gotta go to school?"

"You do. That was the deal you struck with Alexei, remember? You're going to stay here for the fall and winter and go to school rather than sail with the *Alliance* again."

He let out a long, giant huff. "I suppose school is better than sailing."

"You don't like sailing?" Mr. Darrow asked.

Ilya rolled his eyes. "Why would I want to be at sea when I can be looking for gold?"

Evelina tucked a strand of hair behind her ear. "Ilya comes from a long line of fearless seafarers on the Aleutians, nearly a thousand miles north of here. His grandfather led more successful whale hunts than any other man in his village, and his uncles are expert sealers to this day. And that's just on his mother's side. On our father's side, he comes from a long line of shipbuilders, going back clear to the sixteenth century."

Mr. Darrow quirked a brow at the boy. "Yet you don't like sailing?"

Ilya crossed his arms over his chest defiantly. "I like the land, like Mikhail and Father. There's so much to explore, areas where water will never touch. Why limit yourself to the sea?"

"Uh . . ." Mr. Darrow looked between the two of them. "Who's Mikhail?"

"One of our older brothers," Evelina answered. "He's currently leading an expedition up the Taku River. There are some who feel it might connect with the Yukon, and establishing a water route between the Yukon and Southeast Alaska would provide invaluable access to the wilderness of the interior."

"He said I was too young to go." Ilya stomped his foot on the floor, his lips scrunched into a frown. "And then Alexei said I had to work on the *Alliance* over the summer. But I won't be ten forever. One day I'll be able to guide my own expedition."

"And look for gold along the way." A bit of a drawl crept into Mr. Darrow's voice.

"There's nothing wrong with prospecting." A faint hint of red colored Ilya's cheeks.

"I never said there was. Thank you for the books. I'm sure they'll be useful once the pounding in my head subsides."

Voices sounded outside the room, followed by the pitter-patter of children's footsteps and the opening and closing of the schoolroom door. The voices drifted closer, now beside Mr. Darrow's bed.

"Ilya, you've talked so long, you'll have to miss lunch now." Evelina tried to nudge her brother toward the door. "Quick, go grab a slice of bread and some grapes from the kitchen so you're not cross during class."

Ilya cocked his head to the side, a scheming look in his eyes. "I don't know, Lina. Maybe you should cancel school for the day. Mr. Darrow here just said his head is pounding something fierce. Bet he needs peace and quiet if that's gonna get better, and he won't have that if he's gotta listen to you lecture us for the next four hours."

A soft chuckle escaped Mr. Darrow's lips. "What makes you think the sound of your sister's voice will keep me awake? It's so soft and kind, it just might put me to sleep."

He thought her voice was soft and kind? Heat climbed onto her cheeks. Mr. Darrow probably didn't mean it, of course. He was just trying to get Ilya out the door.

"There, see?" She turned to her brother. "School won't be any trouble at all, unless you and the others get overly loud. Now get moving."

"I'm going, I'm going." Ilya turned and scurried off without further prompting, likely driven by the thought of enduring school on an empty stomach.

Evelina looked back at Mr. Darrow, whose eyelids were already drifting shut, never mind that he'd barely had any oatmeal. "Is there anything I can get you before I teach?"

"Don't suppose there's any chance of me getting that willow bark tea?"

"The tea." She pressed a hand to her cheek. How could she have forgotten, especially when Mr. Darrow was feeling so poorly?

Though his eyes were half closed, the corners of his mouth turned up into a smile. "It's no bother. Just bring me some when you have time after school."

"If Kate returns before school has finished—"

"I'll be sure to ask her for it."

"I'm truly sorry."

He settled further into the bed, his eyelids heavy with sleep.

And just like last night, she couldn't stop herself from watching him for a moment, taking in the strong form made weak in an attempt to rescue her brother.

But he wouldn't be weak for long. In a month or better, he'd be hail and hardy, standing to his full height and walking around town with his curly red hair and broad shoulders and imposing chest. His shirt would conceal his muscles then, but she'd still know what they looked like underneath, sculpted and taut and well-defined. She didn't think she'd ever be able to forget.

Just like she wouldn't be able to forget his scars—or the questions she now had about how he'd gotten them . . .

And what had brought him to Juneau.

8

Sitka, Alaska, Two Days Later

Home. Alexei leaned over the side of the sharpie, the sail above him filled with wind as he guided the vessel between the two rocks marking the entrance to Sitka Sound. The town sat straight ahead, a series of white clapboard buildings with the dome and two spires of the Russian Orthodox church, St. Michael's Cathedral, rising above them.

To his left sat Castle Hill and the governor's mansion atop it, though it was more of an administrative building and less of a mansion these days. But when Sitka had been part of Russian America, it had been a grand house, built with the finest Sitka spruce and filled with furs from the island, along with silks and porcelain from trade with China and Japan.

Behind the town the mountains rose straight from the water. There were no sandy strips of beach or gentle, rolling hills. Just mountains guarding the calm, clear water of the sound like sentinels sent by God. Some of them were snow-capped, and others were covered in a lush carpet of green, each one doing its job of sheltering and protecting Sitka from the open waters of the Pacific Ocean.

Alexei angled his boat straight toward where the warehouse and shipyard sat to the right of a big white house sitting on the rocky promontory jutting into the harbor. Just the sight of it caused a feeling of warmth to swell in his chest and memories to rise in his mind. His mother wrapping her arms around him and whispering kind words into his ears as a boy. His twin sisters playing with dolls and shooing him out of their room before he swiped one of their toys. His father, sitting in the study with a map spread across his desk and charting new routes into the interior where they could trade with the Athabaskans. His closest brother Ivan showing him business plans and projections, dreaming with him from a bed on the opposite side of the room they'd shared.

Alexei drew in a breath of air and adjusted the sail, pointing the nose of the boat not directly at the house but toward the warehouse and shipyard sitting just to the north. He might have been gone for two months, but he had business to discuss, and at this time of day, Yuri should be in the warehouse office.

A quick glance around the shipyard showed him a revenue cutter was in the dry dock being repaired and a small fishing yawl was being built.

Alexei lowered the sails as the boat glided across the distance separating it from the small dock in front of the shipyard. Once he'd docked, he tied off the boat and climbed onto the wharf.

A handful of workers in the shipyard stopped what they were doing and looked over at him, but he waved at them to continue before heading toward the warehouse. The large building acted as both storage for their trade goods on the first floor and an office for the trading company and the shipyard on the second floor.

He pushed open the heavy door, only to find the sound of a woman's giggle filling the stairwell.

No, not a woman's giggle. Several women's giggles.

Yuri muttered something in response, though Alexei couldn't quite make out the words as he climbed the stairs to the office on the second floor. A moment later, the front desk came into view above the half wall that lined the stairway.

Or rather, what *should* have been the front desk, which *should* have had his brother sitting behind it. Instead, the four women and one girl standing in front of the desk blocked both the desk itself and Yuri from view.

"Well, now, don't you worry about that, Jane." Yuri's voice sounded from behind the wall of feminine ruffles and flounces. "There'll be plenty of men waiting to dance with you at the ball. I'm sure you won't have any trouble filling your dance card."

"Yes, but will *you* dance with me?" Jane leaned over the desk, a look of concern on her face, as though she was almost afraid Yuri wouldn't dance with her.

"Of course I will."

Alexei swore he could actually hear a smile in Yuri's voice. He shook his head and leaned against the half wall, unable to stop the corners of his mouth from tilting up into a smile. Never mind that he should probably be frowning and telling the women that Yuri needed to get back to work.

"I'll dance with Freya here too, and Millie, and maybe even Rosalind," Yuri continued.

Rosalind? As in Rosalind Caldwell? Alexei surveyed the women a little more closely. Sure enough, Rosalind Caldwell—daughter of Preston Caldwell—stood to the side of the desk, her posture somehow both proper and graceful.

What was she doing in their office?

Alexei's heart gave a single heavy thump. Did Yuri have any important papers sitting out? Anything that might tip the Caldwells off to their shipping contracts or work they had lined up at the shipyard?

He pressed the heel of his palm to his chest, which had suddenly started to burn. But he must have made some other sort of sound as well, because all four of the women turned to him at once.

"Mr. Amos! You're back!" Ingrid Eriksson rushed toward him, her two blond braids flying out from behind her as she opened her arms for a hug.

The girl was a few years younger than Inessa, and certainly small enough that he didn't need to feel awkward hugging her back. She must have come to the office with her sister, Freya.

"Well, well, look what the pretty weather dragged in." Yuri came around the desk, a smile plastered across his face.

Alexei wrapped his arms around his brother and clapped him on the back. At nineteen, Yuri was the youngest of his full-blooded siblings, but he was hardly the smallest. Yet his tall stature never made him look all that intimidating, probably because he couldn't keep a smile off his face for more than a handful of seconds.

"Did you get taller while I was away?" It seemed his brother had grown an inch each month he'd been gone. "I swear you're going to outgrow every last one of us one day, maybe even Mikhail."

Yuri laughed, the sound full and throaty. "Seems like I'm on track to outgrow you, at least."

"I see you've been working hard in my absence." Alexei glanced at the women, all of whom were watching them.

The smile on Yuri's face only grew wider. "Are you jealous I'm the one having all the fun while you're away? Don't worry, brother. There's a dance in two weeks, and you might even enjoy the festivities enough that you'll find it in your heart to smile a time or two."

The older women giggled, but Ingrid stepped forward, her blue eyes round and sincere. "I'll dance with you, Mr. Amos. Even if no one else wants to."

The back of his neck turned suddenly warm, and another round of laughter filled the office. Or rather, everyone but Ingrid laughed.

The girl just looked at him with a mortified expression. "Did I say something wrong?"

"Come on, Ingrid." Freya stepped forward and gripped her younger sister's hand. "I'm sure Mr. Amos has things to discuss with Yuri, which means we best go."

"Why do we call one of them Mr. Amos and the other one Yuri when they're brothers?" The girl blinked up at her sister, her wide blue eyes full of innocence. "Shouldn't they both be Mr. Amos?"

"Because Mr. Amos is more . . ." Freya glanced at him, then back down at her sister. "He's just not the type of man who invites a woman to use his first name. Now let's go."

Freya dragged her sister toward the stairs before the girl could ask any more questions. Jane, Millicent, and Rosalind followed the sisters out, not a single one of the women stopping to ask if he'd fill a slot on their dance card.

As it should be. It wasn't exactly proper for a woman to ask a man to dance.

And yet Yuri hadn't had just one woman ask him to dance but four.

"Am I really that . . ." What was the word he was looking for? Terrifying? Intimidating? "Unapproachable?"

"Unapproachable. Severe. Serious. The antithesis of fun."

His younger brother patted his shoulder. "That sounds like an excellent way for you to describe yourself."

"Perhaps that's a blessing if it means I'm not constantly interrupted by a gaggle of women when I'm trying to work." Alexei headed toward the desk, where he picked up the ledger and opened it. "How has the company been while I was away?"

"And you wonder why no one wants to dance with you."

Alexei studied the ledger. A load of beaver pelts from the interior had been delivered, and the lumber beside the warehouse was waiting to be transported to Japan.

"It's been busy here at the office for the past two months. You'll find these of interest, but not in a good way." Yuri handed him three separate envelopes, his face suddenly serious. "I'm sorry."

"Sorry about what?" Alexei slid the first letter out of the already-opened envelope and skimmed it, a lead ball forming in his stomach. "The cannery north of here is terminating our shipping contract?"

Why? The contract was good for two more years.

"It says at the bottom of the letter that they are going with a different shipping company." Yuri pointed to the last line of the letter. "One that can arrive on a two-week schedule during canning season, and for a better price."

"What company?" There were precious few companies that ran shipping routes to the tiny villages and canneries scattered along the Alaskan coast. While the Bering Sea was filled with ships, the money was in whaling and sealing, not in actual trade routes.

"I don't know. All I can think of is that there must be another shipping company starting, because this isn't the only letter."

Alexei tore open the second letter, then the third. They were all from canneries located on the various islands and inlets that made up Southeast Alaska, and they all said the exact same thing. They were terminating their shipping contracts early and wouldn't need the Sitka Trading Company's services next year. It seemed there really was some kind of new shipping company starting up, or at the very least, one of the companies from Seattle was opening a new route.

One that would run every two weeks during fishing season.

Did that mean he could expect more letters from other canneries?

The canneries would owe him a fee for canceling the contract before it was up, but not a big enough fee to replace the revenue their family would lose.

"You can't blame yourself for this, Alexei." Yuri's hand landed on his shoulder. "Other companies are allowed to send ships up here."

Yes, but it was nearly impossible to do so and make money. The villages were too spread out, and most didn't either yield or need enough cargo to fill a ship on an eight-week schedule. But canning season was different. The canneries brought workers in during the height of fishing season and were operational for only two to three months every summer. During that time there was plenty of cargo. It was one of the only things that kept his Alaskan trade routes from hemorrhaging money over the course of the year. But if another company was moving in and servicing canneries only for the few months it was possible to make a good profit off the shipping route, where would that leave the Sitka Trading Company—and his family's bank account?

"I think I feel sick," he whispered.

"Don't be as maudlin as all that." Yuri started shuffling through the papers on the desk. "There's some good news too."

"I don't suppose you're going to tell me some of the companies got back to me about the shipping contracts I offered them

while I was in Washington and California?" Most of those businesses had been contracted with far larger companies than the
Sitka Trading Company. He'd been hoping to drum up enough
business that the *Alliance* or *Aurora* could dock somewhere
like Seattle and run an entire load of cargo to Japan, but it had
quickly become apparent that the massive iron- and steel-
hulled ships were ruling the markets at the larger ports—and
evidently at the Treadwell Mine too.

Now that he was home, he'd been hoping to spend a few
days with the trade-route maps laid out in front of him, figuring
out where they might be able to add more stops at smaller ports
that the giant barges overlooked.

The last thing he'd expected was to find that three
canneries no longer needed his services.

"No, we didn't have any requests for shipping contracts
come in, but we did get a request for a ship last week." Yuri
handed him the piece of paper he'd been searching for on the
desk. "A clipper from a company out of Bellingham."

"Somone wants us to build a clipper?" That was unexpected. Alexei took the paper and studied the diagram.
Building the clipper would pay well—better than the three
shipping contracts he'd just lost, in fact.

"The letter says they met with you down in Bellingham
over the summer." Yuri crossed one foot over the other and
leaned against the desk in a boyish and carefree way. "They
were impressed with the number of years we've been building
ships to sail in the Arctic, and they're particularly impressed
with the *Aurora*. They want something that can break through
ice, and they're not of the opinion that any shipbuilders in California or Maine or even Australia can build such a vessel."

It was true, the shipyards from California up through
Washington Territory were much better at building vessels for
regular seas than they were for building anything that could

spear its way through a layer of ice. And there was always ice north of the Arctic Circle, even in the warm months.

He blew out a breath he hadn't realized he'd been holding. "When do we start?"

"A couple weeks." Yuri jutted his chin toward the windows overlooking the shipyard. "As soon as we get the revenue cutter repaired and out of drydock."

There was a time when they'd have been able to start on the ship immediately, but their current staff would struggle to build the clipper, plus keep up with the smaller boats on order. "Maybe Sacha can stay in port after he returns. He's got a knack for shipbuilding, and we can send Tavish to Japan as captain of the *Aurora*."

"First Sacha has to come back from the Arctic," Yuri said. "In either case, good luck convincing our brother his feet belong on land for more than two days at a time."

Alexei stared at Yuri. "Sacha hasn't already come and gone? I assumed he was on his way to San Fransisco by now."

Yuri shook his head.

It wasn't a reason to get nervous, per se. Any manner of things could delay a ship. But still, he'd rather one of the ships be delayed that was *not* captained by their brother.

Alexei snapped the ledger closed. "I'll ask around the wharf for a possible explanation. Maybe some of the seamen have seen the *Aurora*."

"I already did. One of the ships that was in port last week saw her two weeks ago in Unalaska. They said she was headed up to Barrow."

Alexei rubbed the back of his neck. "Sacha was in Unalaska only two weeks ago?" Their brother must have been delayed sometime before that on his route, and two weeks wasn't enough time for him to sail from Unalaska to Barrow and back to Sitka.

But it could be worse. At least the *Aurora* had been spotted, and they knew a general time when they could expect Sacha. It was better than spending the next week or better fearing another member of their family had been lost.

"Don't worry." Yuri slung an arm around his shoulder. "Sacha has plenty of time to make it back here for the dance."

Alexei rolled his eyes. "You realize that most adult men don't plan their calendars around dances?"

"Then most adult men don't know what they're missing. The entire town will be there, every woman dressed in her finest, spending hours on her hair and wearing her best jewelry. And every man in town can go there and be surrounded by beautiful women until the wee hours of the morning. What's not to love?"

"You realize that most adult men choose one of those beautiful women and marry them, right? They don't just dance with them a couple times a year."

Yuri let out a big bellowing laugh. "Why, brother, is that your way of telling me you plan to propose to one of the women at the dance?"

Alexei shook off his brother's arm. "No."

"'You realize that most adult men choose one of those beautiful women and marry them, right?'" Yuri deepened his voice until it sounded startlingly close to the timbre of Alexei's.

Alexei sent his brother a dark look. "Don't suppose I'm like most men."

"Neither am I. Maybe I can convince Sacha to propose at the dance."

Alexei raised his eyebrow. "If you're of a mind to hear wedding bells, then you're the one who should do the proposing."

Yuri winked. "Maybe I will."

He wouldn't. Yuri had always been a bit of a charmer, but

the last time he'd been serious about a woman was . . . never. It was all he could do to get the man to be serious about the trading company and shipyard.

"While we're on the topic of the dance . . ." Alexei narrowed his eyes at Yuri. "You know better than to dance with Rosalind Caldwell, right?"

The smile dropped from Yuri's lips. "She needs her dance card filled the same as Freya and Millie."

"There will be plenty of men to fill her card. Your name won't be on the list. Do you understand?"

Yuri's lips pressed into a flat line.

"Answer me, Yuri. We're in no position to play games with the Caldwells."

"She's not like her father."

"It doesn't matter. Having her here, in this office, is a danger, and dancing with her in front of all of Sitka would be doubly dangerous."

His younger brother rubbed his hand over his stubbly jaw, his shoulders deflating on a large sigh. "Fine. I promise not to dance with Rosalind."

"Good." Alexei turned back toward the order for the ship. "Now let's take a closer look at the materials we'll need to build this clipper."

He needed to be smart about building this ship, smart enough that they would make up the money they were losing from the canceled shipping contracts at the Treadwell and the canneries.

He didn't want to think about what might happen if he couldn't manage to do that.

9

Juneau, Seven Days Later

Ilya tapped the map he was holding in front of them, singling out the place where a creek dumped into the channel. "Like I said, all of Gold Creek has been claimed and is being worked by placer miners, but if you go south down to Sheep Creek, you can still find some gold."

"And you think there's gold there?" Jonas slanted a glance at the boy beside him.

Ilya looked up, excitement dancing in his eyes. "That's just it. There could be gold in any of the creeks around here, or there might be none. No one knows until they go searching for it."

Jonas leaned back against the headboard, causing it to creak with his weight. The sky outside was gray and dreary, the mist especially thick.

Was it just him, or did the ceiling seem to hang extra low today, and the room seem smaller and more cramped than usual?

"Have you been down to Sheep Creek?" he asked Ilya, more to distract himself from the oppressiveness surrounding him than because he had an interest in panning for gold.

The boy blushed, then glanced around, as though afraid someone might overhear them. "Don't tell Alexei. He doesn't like me venturing off by myself."

"I take it you didn't find anything." Because while he could envision Ilya sneaking off when his brother was gone or too busy to notice, he couldn't imagine Ilya finding gold and keeping quiet about it.

"Oh, and there's a creek north of town too." Ilya scooted closer to him on the bed, the scent of rain on his hair wafting around them. He tapped his finger against the edge of the map. "It's not on here, but it's just north of this little outcropping. You'll need to go at high tide, though. The channel is too shallow to take a boat up it otherwise."

"And I just take a pan and screen and scoop the silt out of the creek bed, then see if anything shiny is left in my screen after the water drains out?"

The boy gave a quick nod. "That's the easiest way to do it. Placer deposits can indicate hard rock veins too, but it's easiest to find the placer first."

Ilya leaned over and pulled the fattest book from the ever-growing stack that had been collecting on the chair beside his bed. "But if you want to look for veins rather than placer, you want rock that looks like this."

Jonas squinted at the grainy black-and-white image on the page. He didn't have the first clue how he was supposed to find rock that looked like that, because whatever he saw in the mountains would certainly have more color to it.

He had half a mind to tell Ilya this entire thing was ridiculous.

But Ilya's eyes were bright as he scanned the page of the

book that weighed half as much as he did, his brain soaking up every last bit of information.

Jonas had heard the term gold fever before, but he'd never understood it until he met Ilya Amos. The youth ate, slept, and dreamt about gold. Not because he wanted to be outrageously rich but because he was genuinely fascinated by its existence—what types of rock it was found in, how it was formed differently from copper or silver, how gold could often be extracted from copper ore and copper from zinc ore, and on the list went.

"When you go prospecting, remember the first thing you need to do is test the gold and make sure it's not pyrite," Ilya said.

"You mean fool's gold?"

Ilya sighed. "I keep telling you, it's got a scientific name, and it isn't fool's gold."

Jonas rubbed his chest, where the bandage was wrapped snuggly against his skin. Eventually he was going to have to tell the boy that he had no desire to prospect for gold. That he really just wanted to leave this room and go . . .

Well, he didn't know what he wanted to do, only that he'd been sitting abed for far too long. Surely after eleven days, he was strong enough to at least leave this room and get a breath of fresh air. "Do you think Kate will let me go for a walk today if I ask?"

Ilya shrugged, his head still bent over the book. "Kate likes to keep people cooped up extra long." His head popped up, and he narrowed his eyes. "Why? Has your chest stopped hurting? Are you ready to prospect?"

"I'm ready to be out of this room," he mumbled. His wound was hurting less than it had the first few days after the attack, and his headaches had mostly faded.

But if he had to spend so much as another hour staring at the same four walls and looking out the same dismal window, he just might pull his hair out. He swore he'd memorized every dip and crag in the rough-cut boards that made up the ceiling, every bump and crevice in the rounded logs of the walls.

If not for Ilya keeping him company in the mornings, and Evelina's teaching to fill his afternoons, he'd have gone mad days ago.

Almost as though he'd conjured up her students on cue, thumping and voices sounded in the room beside his.

He reached over and nudged Ilya. "That's your cue. It's time for school."

Ilya frowned. "I don't want to go today."

"You don't want to go any day, and I don't understand why." He patted the page of the book. "You obviously like learning."

"Yeah, about real things. Like rock formations or fish breeding habits or what causes the northern lights. Lina's teaching the class to read, and I've been reading since I was four." The boy plopped his head in his hands, a look of disdain on his face.

"Doesn't Inessa go to class with you?"

"She does, but it doesn't change the fact that everyone else in the school is behind us. I mean, Lina might tell Inessa and me to read *Treasure Island*, but we never get to talk about it, because no one else is reading it. We just read about it and write a report. And once we finish *Treasure Island*, Lina will find something else for us to read."

The boy had a point. He'd found school boring enough at ten, and he'd had a gang of friends studying the same things he was studying. But what else was Evelina to do with such wide learning gaps between her students?

"*Treasure Island* is a pretty fascinating book." He nudged Ilya's shoulder. "Don't you want to find out if Long John Silver finds the buried treasure?"

"I'd rather find my own gold than read about someone else searching for it." The boy straightened. "Wait. Mr. Darrow, do you think I can go with you when you leave? Just for a day or two. It would be a lot more fun than sitting around here and going to school and helping with the trading post."

"I thought you said helping with the trading post was more fun than being a cabin boy on the *Alliance*?"

"It is, but that doesn't mean it's as fun as prospecting."

Jonas couldn't stop his laugh. The poor boy had adventure in his blood, and it seemed that nothing short of being out in the wild was going to cure it.

"I wish Mikhail would have taken me with him. But no. 'It was a paid expedition,' he said." Ilya deepened his voice, likely in an approximation of this older brother Jonas had yet to meet. "'There will be scientists and cartographers, and I can't have you underfoot.' And then there was Evelina saying that I'd get behind in my schooling if I went, so Alexei said I had to learn to sail instead." Ilya crossed his arms over his chest, a look of pure torture on his face.

"You better go." Jonas tugged the map from Ilya's hands. Evelina's voice was drifting through the wall, and she was calling the class to order. "Don't want to see you get in trouble."

Ilya slid off the bed, his shoulders drooping. "If I go to school today, will you at least promise to take me prospecting? Just for a day or two? I can show you what to do just as well as any of the men in Juneau."

"I'll think about it," he said, even though he had no intention of doing so. If he couldn't manage to keep his mother and fiancée safe in his own home, he wasn't about to risk taking a boy off into the wilderness.

But his words had been enough to bring a smile back to Ilya's face. "You mean it, Mr. Darrow? I can really go with you?"

"I said I'd *think* about it." The boy was too charming by far, and if Jonas wasn't careful, he just might end up with a friend before he left the trading post.

But he hadn't come to Alaska to make friends.

The second the door closed behind Ilya, Jonas scooted to the side of the bed, then braced his hands on the mattress and swung his legs to the floor. The little bit of pressure he put on his left arm caused his chest to smart, but not as much as it had yesterday when he'd gotten out of bed.

He'd seen enough injuries to know that the longer a man stayed abed, the longer it took him to recover, and he wasn't about to let his legs grow weak as a babe's because he'd been stabbed in the chest.

Evelina's voice filtered through the wall beside his bed, calm and melodic as she worked on assigning letters to the sounds in the native language the children spoke.

She was proving to be quite the creative teacher. Not only did she hold classes in the afternoon, giving her students time to work at home in the mornings, but on his first full day confined to the sickbed, he'd listened through the walls as she'd made a bet with the students.

The Tlingit children had been quite adamant they didn't need to learn to read in English when they couldn't read in their own language to begin with. But if they'd been trying to get out of reading, it hadn't worked. Evelina had simply said they would assign letters to the sounds they used in the Tlingit language and learn to read in both languages.

So every day, the students worked on assigning letters to their native tongue, and then they worked on learning to both read and speak English. Finally they concluded with arithmetic before being dismissed for the afternoon.

And every day, Evelina's voice floated through the wall for four straight hours, all kindness and understanding.

Like Harriet. The two of them would have been fast friends, if only . . .

Jonas slammed his eyes shut, but that only brought the image of Harriet more fully into his mind, her blond hair and blue eyes, her kind smile, the way she'd pressed up onto her toes and kissed his cheek that final time—neither of them realizing this time together before the quick trip he needed to make back to the office would be the last time he saw her alive.

Or that he would be the reason for her death, right along with his mother's.

With a growl, he walked to the single window at the back of the room.

Kate—or Dr. Amos, as the townsfolk called her—would be furious if she saw him standing. But he wasn't going to lie abed all day while the memories assaulted him. Just like he wasn't going to stay here four or five more weeks. He wasn't even sure he could manage one more week at the moment.

But what would he do once he left? Ilya had been yammering on and on about all the places where gold might yet lie undiscovered. But he'd also said there was gold already being mined in the basin between the two mountains that sat behind Juneau. Those operations weren't as large as the Treadwell Mine, but they still might be large enough that he could get himself hired. Maybe if he was lucky, he could find a job that his injury could tolerate while he grew stronger.

It wasn't the fastest way to get rich, but just like he hadn't come to Alaska to make friends, he hadn't come to find gold either; he'd come to disappear.

And he'd come to forget—or maybe to find forgiveness. He wasn't sure which.

All he knew was that nothing was going as planned, and he couldn't quite tell if the pain in his chest as he walked across the room was from his stab wound or his memories.

10

Evelina glanced at the clock hanging on the wall. Only half an hour remained until she needed to dismiss her class. Would that be enough time to cover their lesson in mathematics? She gave her head a small shake. She shouldn't worry, not when the extra time she'd been spending on reading was paying off. Especially with Shunaa. She smiled at the child who stood next to her desk, softly reading the last sentence on the page of his primer.

"Very good." She gave his shoulder a gentle squeeze. "See? I knew you'd be able to figure out those vowel sounds."

The child beamed at her, then an explosion of excited words in his native tongue tumbled out. Evelina only understood a handful of them, but she didn't need to know every last one to read the pride in his eyes.

"Yes, you did well, didn't you? Now can you try saying some of that in English?"

"He said he's been practicing at home after—"

Evelina held up her hand, stopping the boy's older sister

from finishing. "I want Shunaa to tell me." She stroked the child's long, dark hair back from his face. "What did you say?"

"I've been . . . protesting . . . at home. After we eat."

"Practicing. You've been practicing. And I can tell you've improved a lot over the past week, both with your reading and your English."

Shunaa smiled at her, then released another burst of Tlingit. She understood the words *happy* and *help*, but that was all. She wasn't like her older brothers Mikhail and Sacha, both of whom had an ear for languages and could pick up enough of a foreign tongue to communicate any place their travels took them. Instead, she was relegated to picking out a word here and there and hoping that someday, if she was studious enough, she just might be able to carry on a conversation in Tlingit.

"Very good." She gave his shoulder another squeeze. "You can go back to your seat now and take out your arithmetic primer."

The boy scampered back to his desk, only to be greeted with another round of excited whispers from his older sister who sat beside him.

Evelina turned in her chair and reached for her mathematics book.

"Well, I see it's true," a stern voice rang through the classroom.

Evelina straightened, her hand dropping away from the spine of the book as she looked toward the back of the room.

Miss Thompson stood in the doorway, her hair pulled back into a severe bun, and a pinched expression on her face. "You've started a school behind my back."

"I . . . um . . ." Evelina pushed to her feet. "It's more of a tutoring session. I only teach in the afternoons for about four hours."

Janice Thompson took a few steps into the room, bringing

her even with the last row of students. "And you don't punish the students for speaking in their heathen tongues." She crossed her arms over her narrow chest, her eyebrows slashing downward.

"I . . ." Evelina glanced around to find every single student looking at either her or Miss Thompson.

"I wouldn't call their native language heathen, just different from English. It's what the children feel most comfortable with," she whispered, her mouth growing dry, never mind that they were discussing children speaking in the same language their ancestors had used for centuries. "I'm . . . I'm sure you understand."

"Understand?" Miss Thompson's back grew stiffer, which shouldn't have been possible given the way she was already standing as though she had a ship's mast for a spine. "Here's what I understand. You are luring my students away from me, a trained teacher who traveled thousands of miles to come to Juneau and teach the native children. And not only that, but you're spreading dangerous ideas. Are you truly suggesting the language these children speak is equal to English?"

"Why wouldn't it be?" Evelina took a step closer to the other woman. "Have you ever heard some of their stories? They have the most wonderful legends. Stories of battles and brave warriors, of ravens and wolves and whales. These things should all be preserved in some type of written record. Did you know the Russian bishop's school in Sitka was working on that very thing before Russia sold Alaska? The bishop was assigning Russian letters to the Tlingit language and recording—"

"There is no need to preserve a language that will soon become obsolete!" Miss Thompson stretched out her hand toward the window overlooking the street and harbor. "Who is filling the streets of this town and bringing ships full of passengers from San Francisco and Seattle? Who is working the mines and building houses and heading the Committee of Public Safety? Not the Tlingit. These children are growing up in a world far different from the one their parents knew, and I'm trying to prepare them for that world by teaching them math and reading, science and history. But here you are, feeding them lies, saying that their language is worth preserving and—"

"But it is. Their stories are beautiful. There's one about a bear that—"

"There is nothing beautiful about the Tlingit." Miss Thompson slapped her hand on one of the students' desks. "Just like there is nothing beautiful about the Cheyenne or the Cherokee or the Seminole. Do you know this is the third Indian school I have taught in? The third time that I've taken students who barely knew English and taught them to read and write? The students who excel in my day school will have the option of going on to an industrial school, where the boys can learn skills like carpentry, blacksmithing, and masonry, and the girls can learn sewing and cooking. That is progress, Miss Amos. What you are doing is not."

Evelina opened her mouth to respond, but her tongue felt as though it had been wrapped in freshly picked cotton.

Miss Thompson must have taken her silence as some kind of agreement, because she strode to the front of the classroom, then turned to face the students. "If any of you would like to learn those things, if any of you wish to advance and make a place for yourself in America, to learn the language that everyone in America speaks, then I suggest you arrive at my school tomorrow morning at eight o'clock sharp."

The children looked around, their eyes wide. Some of them began whispering to each other.

"Not to mention . . ." Miss Thompson turned to face her. "I

have it on good authority that Miss Amos doesn't even have a teaching certificate. Tell me, Miss Amos, is this true?"

"I . . ." Her entire body turned cold. How had Miss Thompson discovered that? She'd attended teaching school in Boston, nowhere near the wilds of Alaska, and her brief stint at the teaching academy wasn't common knowledge. It wasn't even something her family really spoke of.

"Is she right, Miss Amos?" Shunaa peeked up at her from where he sat in the front row. "Are you a real teacher?"

"I . . ." Again, that thick, cottony feeling wrapped itself around her tongue, and all she could do was look glumly around the classroom, where every student was now watching her, waiting for a response she couldn't seem to give.

Oh, why did she always have to get so tongue-tied when people confronted her? But she knew the answer, and she couldn't afford to think about the last time she had so many eyes pinned to her.

The last time there had been such a heavy silence in the room.

The last time so many people had waited for a response.

She was supposed to say something, supposed to calm down the situation. And yet, when it mattered most, not so much as a word would come.

Not then, and not now.

She swallowed slowly. She hadn't used to be this way, so frightened to say what she thought. But standing in front of Miss Thompson, with the other woman's eyes narrowed into two thin slits, it was almost as though her words didn't know how to come out.

"As I said"—Miss Thompson moved her gaze back to the class—"anyone interested in procuring a future can arrive at my school in the morning. Because that's what I will be providing you, a way to better your life and fit into the society of the country who owns the land on which you—"

"That's enough," a strong male voice said from the doorway.

Evelina looked up to find Mr. Darrow standing in the doorway, his chest bare save for the bandage covering his knife wound.

Miss Thompson's eyes went wide, her hand creeping up to her throat.

"Why I never! What is the meaning of this?" She thrust her hand toward Mr. Darrow and glared at her. "You . . . you allow nudity? In your classroom? You're no better than the natives with their longhouses!"

"I . . ."

"Can we be dismissed?" Inessa whispered from her place at her desk. "It seems like this might be the kind of conversation best had in private."

"Yes, of course. Children, you are dismissed for the day."

Not a single one of the students rose. Their gazes were either locked on her and Miss Thompson at the front of the room or on Mr. Darrow at the back.

"You heard your teacher. Class is dismissed." Mr. Darrow sent the students a stern look and opened the door. "Now."

All of a sudden, the students scrambled to their feet and dashed toward the opening, likely to see who could beat the others back to their village and tell their families about the confrontation.

Because that was what she needed—more stories about her spread around town.

"First you make yourself out to be a teacher when you're not adequately trained." Miss Thompson ignored the students and took a step closer, her face contorted into a mask of angry lines. "Then you go and poach my students right out from under me. And now you're allowing half-naked men into your classroom."

"He's my sister's patient. Surely you heard that he was stabbed last week, and—"

"I thought you were from a respectable family. When I moved here, I was told if I ever needed anything, I should go to the Sitka Trading Company. I was told that the family who owned it were good people who had a good relationship with natives and miners alike. But then I find out you have two half-breed siblings, and rather than return them to their mother's clan like a decent family, you bring them into your home and treat them as your equals."

Miss Thompson took another step closer. "After that, I learn you have a sister who went to school to be a doctor—of all things—as though that's somehow proper for a woman! And this sister of yours darts about town unchaperoned, not just treating female complaints, but treating men like him."

Miss Thompson ran her angry gaze down Mr. Darrow's naked chest. "Never in my life have I witnessed such improper behavior. Mark my words, Evelina Amos, there is nothing respectable about you or anyone else in your family. You are a blight on those who are trying to civilize Alaska, and tomorrow afternoon, if any of these students have the audacity to return here, I hope you do the right thing and direct them to my school, where they will—"

"You've made your position quite clear." Jonas stalked up the aisle, the bare muscles of his chest coiled into tight, sculpted lines. "Now it's best you take your leave and not return to any property owned by the Amos family. Ever."

"I wouldn't dream of it." Nostrils flaring, Miss Thompson swept past Mr. Darrow and stormed out of the room.

Evelina squeezed her eyes shut, not quite willing to meet Mr. Darrow's gaze.

Heat pricked the backs of her eyes. She thought she'd been helping, but was she somehow wrong for trying to teach the Tlingit when she didn't even have a teaching certificate? Was she doing something wrong by letting them use their own language and attend class for only a few hours in the afternoon?

Was she ruining their future as Janice Thompson had suggested?

"Don't." A hand landed on her shoulder, warm and strong.

She sniffled away a tear and peeked up to find Mr. Darrow towering above her, the muscles in his chest well-defined from years of hard work. Her gaze traveled up to his thick neck and strong jaw, covered in a faint red beard, seeing as how he hadn't shaved since arriving in town.

A small smile crept over his lips. Why, she didn't know. It wasn't as though—

Oh dear heavens! How long had she been staring at him? And all while he stood there shirtless! Perhaps she really was as wanton as Miss Thompson made her out to be. She forced her gaze away from him.

He only moved closer. "Nothing about what that woman said or did was kind. Please don't let her upset you."

Miss Thompson. Right. That's why he was standing so close to her. Not because there was anything romantic between them.

She sniffled again, another round of heat springing to her eyes. "But what if she's right?"

"She's not." He reached out and took her hand, clasping it in his large one. "And I see why you opened your school now. I wouldn't have wanted Miss Thompson teaching my sister either."

She tugged her hand away from him. "She's right about me not having a teaching certificate."

"Probably not because you weren't smart enough to get one.

I've been listening through the wall. You're a good teacher. Bet I would have learned twice as much had you been my teacher as a lad. I might have even been so busy learning that I wouldn't have had time to hide scorpions in my teacher's desk."

She reared back. "You did not!"

The mischievous glint in his eyes told her that he had, in fact, been the type of student to put scorpions in his teacher's desk, not the type that got to the schoolhouse early each morning to build a fire so the building was warm by the time everyone else arrived.

She cleared her throat, attempting to shove aside the image of the cute little boy with red hair that kept falling into his eyes and an impish smile on his face. "I went to teaching school in Boston while Kate was in medical school there. But the classes were all, well, like Miss Thompson's classroom. And the teachers were so stuffy, and every time I turned around I was . . ."

She clamped her mouth shut before she said anything else. Mr. Darrow didn't need to know about how miserable a time she'd had bringing her Alaskan manners and her Russian traditions to Boston.

Goodness, but what was it about this man that had her thoughts going wild places and her tongue running away on her? If they stayed here much longer, she just might end up telling him about Sophie Haliburton.

"You don't need to explain. I just wish you'd done a better job defending yourself. Miss Thompson made some rather cruel accusations, and everything except the bit about the teaching certificate is untrue."

"Sometimes when people get really upset with me, I . . . I have trouble knowing what to say, and . . ." She looked up at him, only to have her words die on her tongue as she yet again found herself staring at his bare chest. He really should put a shirt on if they were going to continue this conversation.

"Is what she said about Ilya and Inessa true?" Mr. Darrow asked. "Would most families have put them in the care of their native relations rather than raise them in polite society?"

She looked away, but not only because she didn't want to meet his gaze. The other part of her knew her tongue would never be able to find the words while he stood there shirtless.

"That's the American way of doing things, not the Russian way."

"And the comment about the longhouses? What did that mean?"

"The traditional Tlingit longhouses put an entire clan inside one giant living area. Men and women and children all share the same space, regardless of who is married to whom. There isn't much privacy for things like sleeping or changing clothes or . . . ah . . ."—her face grew warm—"conceiving children, or anything else, I'm afraid."

She cleared her throat, willing the warmth to leave her cheeks. "And I have to admit, even though I grew up around them, the longhouses are a bit much for me. But the Tlingit are slowly moving into regular houses. There's a village being built across the channel, all with regular houses so each family can have its own privacy."

Mr. Darrow looked down at his bare chest, the tips of his ears turning red. "Yes, I suppose this is a bit scandalous."

Evelina swallowed. Had the room suddenly grown hot? Because she had a rather unexplained urge to start fanning her face.

"I should go put a shirt on."

"Yes," she whispered. "You, ah, should probably keep one on now that the risk of infection has passed for your wound and you are up and about."

"I will." He reached out and brushed her shoulder, the touch quick and feather-light, but somehow comforting. "Just as long as you promise to speak up for yourself if something like that happens again."

She looked up at him. If only it were as easy as that. If only she could promise her tongue wouldn't grow thick and dry or her words wouldn't desert her. "I'll try. Now I best go start dinner."

"And I best go find a shirt." He stepped to the side so she could precede him down the aisle, then followed her out the door into a trading post that felt suddenly cold and empty—just like the inside of her classroom.

11

Of all the ridiculous, cruel, malicious things! Jonas stormed into the room he'd been confined to for several days too long, grabbed the shirt that had been laundered and was hanging on a hook by the door, and shoved his arms through it.

How could Evelina have stood there so calmly, as though she'd somehow deserved the public humiliation Miss Thompson had just put her through? As though every word of what that shrew said had been true?

What right did another teacher have to storm into the trading post, interrupt class, and make accusations? Jonas's hands balled into fists. Had Miss Thompson been a man, he would have knocked her out, just to stop her from running that cruel mouth.

Evelina might want to make dinner, but if he didn't head outside and find somewhere to go, something to do, he'd explode.

It shouldn't matter whether Evelina had a teaching certificate. The children were learning from her, and she was treating them in a far kinder and more gracious manner than Miss Thompson was.

Then the woman had said the Amos family wasn't respectable.

Why? Because Kate had taken off his shirt to save his life? Because she'd told him to keep it off to help prevent infection? Or because Alexei treated Inessa and Ilya as though they were his siblings rather than his inferiors?

If he never saw Miss Thompson again, it would be too soon.

Jonas shoved the bottom of his shirt into the waistband of his trousers and strode out the door.

"What are you doing?" Evelina had paused beside the stairs to refold a wool blanket that had gotten mussed at some point.

"I'm going for a walk." He nearly barked the words.

"But you can't." She dropped the blanket into a haphazard pile on the table. "You're injured."

He rubbed a hand over the bandage beneath his shirt. Being up and about did pull on his wound and cause his chest to smart, but that didn't mean he should be abed either. "Reckon if I can walk into your classroom and defend you from a crazy lady, then I can walk down the street. I have no intention of becoming a permanent invalid."

Worry creased the lines around her mouth, but rather than say something, she bit the side of her lip.

He had the most ridiculous urge to tell her to stop lest she bruise it. Instead, he turned and strode toward the door at the front of the trading post. Why should he care about whether her lip got bruised?

Because she's the sweetest, kindest person you've ever met, you dolt!

That, and the thought of her coming to any kind of injury, even one so small as a bruise, set his insides on fire.

"Don't go too far, Mr. Darrow," she called after him. "Your goal is to regain your strength, not make your injury worse."

He couldn't help but shake his head as he reached for the door handle. Had he ever met someone as wholly good as Evelina Amos? Someone always so concerned with the welfare of everyone else?

The only person she didn't demonstrate concern for was herself, it seemed.

"I'll keep that in mind." Then he opened the door and stepped into the sunlight.

Or rather, what was supposed to be sunlight. But he wasn't in Texas anymore. He was in southern Alaska, and it was raining. Again.

Puddles had formed on the road, creating a muddy mess that horses and wagons could get around only by moving to the far side of the street. And unfortunately, a series of soft, deep ruts had formed on the small part of the road that wasn't submerged in mud. By the end of the day, the section of road in front of the trading post might not even be passable.

Jonas picked his way around the large puddle taking up most of the road, but when he emerged on the other side, mud clung to his boots and coated the hem of his trousers.

Then a gust of wind swept down the channel, and he found himself shivering in the cold.

Because he'd forgotten to grab his coat.

Which he'd never needed to worry about in Texas.

He shoved a hand through his hair. All he'd wanted to do was step into the sunshine for a bit to lift his mood, but he'd only managed to get himself muddy and cold.

He looked back at the trading post. He could head back inside where it was warm, where Evelina was sure to talk to him if he followed her up to the kitchen.

Instead, he turned and continued past the wharf. He

dodged thick patches of mud and watery puddles whenever he could and ignored the increasing amount of mud caking his boots and trousers.

He hastened his pace, walking quickly enough to keep his body warm, never mind the air was so cold his breath formed little puffs of white. He had no idea where he was going as he strolled toward the center of town. Maybe he'd make his way to the jailhouse and see if the two hundred dollars that had been stolen from Simon Volker had ever been recovered. Or maybe he'd—

"Hey, that's mine. Give it back." A small girl's voice traveled down the road, followed by the sounds of taunting and laughter.

"I'll give it back if you can reach it."

Jonas looked down the street to find that two boys had cornered a smaller girl in front of a building. She was stretched up onto her toes, her scrawny arms trying desperately to reach the loaf of bread that one of the boys was holding over his head.

Jonas quickened his pace. "What's going on here?"

The boys spun toward him, smug smiles dropping from their faces.

"We're just having a bit of fun, sir." The boy with the bread lowered his arm, and the girl snatched the loaf away from him and tucked it against her chest.

She took Jonas in with a worried look—almost as though frightened he would try taking the bread from her next—then she turned and darted down the street as fast as her legs could carry her.

"Now look what you did." The boy who'd stolen the bread balled his hands into fists. "You done scared her off."

Jonas swung his gaze to the other boy, who was a bit shorter and had bangs hanging in his eyes, as if he hadn't had a haircut in months. He was shifting nervously from foot to foot, and his gaze kept darting down the road, as though he was looking for a place to escape.

But the taller boy was glaring at Jonas with a defiant look plastered across his face. A half-eaten doughnut lay forgotten on the ground by his feet.

"There might not be a sheriff in Juneau," he spoke loudly enough that his voice carried in the heavy air. "But I hear there's still a jailhouse, and a Marshal who comes 'round these parts from time to time to enforce the law. That true?"

"Yes, sir." The second boy, the one with unruly bangs that needed trimming, nodded.

"I also heard there's a public safety committee I can take you to, and after they learn I caught you trying to steal, they might be of such a mind to lock you up until the Marshal gets here." Jonas straightened himself to his full six-foot, one-inch height and stepped closer. "So here's what's going to happen. I'll give you a warning this time, but if I see you stealing bread— or anything else—from another person again, I'll report you."

"We didn't mean nothing by it," the taller boy said. "We was just having a bit of fun with Sally. We was always gonna give it back."

Jonas crossed his arms over his chest, never mind the way it pulled at his stitches. "You sound like every thief I've ever met. Planning to give something back after you take it won't keep you out of trouble with the law. You understand?"

The shorter boy nodded, causing his bangs to flop over his eyes.

But the taller boy curled his lips into a scowl, then turned and gave the other boy a shove. "Come on, Robbie. We don't got no time for this."

Jonas narrowed his eyes as the boys darted off in the same direction the girl had gone. If only he still had a tin star pinned to his chest. Then he would have marched the boys back home and told their parents what they'd been doing, maybe even seen to it that the boys spent a weekend picking up trash around town so they'd think twice before trying to steal again.

But did he really want that tin star? Did he want all the responsibilities that came with being a lawman?

He closed his eyes, trying to shove aside the pain that swelled inside him whenever memories of his mother and Harriet came.

"Is everything all right?"

Jonas opened his eyes to find a short Asian man poking his head out of the door to the building he was standing in front of.

"I thought I heard a commotion."

Scents of yeast and flour and sugar filled the air, enticing Jonas to drag in a breath. He must have stopped in front of a bakery, which made sense considering the girl had been holding bread and the older of the two boys had been eating a doughnut.

"Ah, was there a girl who just bought a loaf of bread from you?"

The man straightened, concern darkening the kindness in his eyes. "Are you talking about Sally? Don't tell me the Finch boys were giving her trouble again."

"Does one of them have dark hair with bangs that keep falling over his eyes?"

"Those two." The man looked down the road and scowled, seeming to know the direction they'd gone even though they'd already disappeared. "They know I give her day-old bread, and it doesn't matter what time she comes or what route she takes, they always hassle her. Some people think they can get away with anything."

"I'm told there's a Marshal?" The boys hadn't liked being threatened with the fact he would come to town—eventually.

"You ever heard of a Marshal that bothered with bullies?"

Jonas rubbed the back of his neck. "No."

"The Marshal hasn't even made it here yet, and you were stabbed well over a week ago."

Jonas's hand crept to the place on his chest where his wound still smarted. "How did you know that?"

The man narrowed his eyes at the bandage peeking out from the collar of his shirt. "I might be Chinese, but that doesn't make me dumb. It's good to see you out and about. Glad Simon Volker didn't do any lasting damage."

Clearly he had underestimated just how small of a town Juneau was. Either that, or just how famous he'd become thanks to his injury. "Thank you."

The man pushed the door to his bakery open farther. "Best come in. I've got a little something you can take back to Evelina for her students."

The man turned and walked back into his bakery, leaving Jonas to follow.

Like everything else in Juneau, the building was made of rough-hewn logs, chiseled and fit together like a puzzle with cracks and holes where someone had forced the pieces into place. Wooden shelves that were just as rough as the logs lined all four sides of the storefront, holding a variety of breads, muffins, pastries, and cookies.

The sweet, yeasty scents that had filtered into the street now hit him in force, and warmth emanated from a back room that clearly held the kitchen and oven.

"What did you say your name was?" Jonas asked.

"Joe. But you can call me China Joe if you like. Half the people in town do. I answer to both." He grabbed a sack from behind the counter, then sauntered over to the glass display case holding the cookies and started putting them into the sack. "You tell Evelina I said it's awful nice of her teaching the Tlingit like that, letting them speak their own language and all.

Sure wish there were a few more people in town who spoke Mandarin."

The image of Miss Thompson's stiff body and angry face popped into Jonas's mind, and he swallowed. "I'm sure Miss Amos will appreciate hearing that."

"Do you know how many children are going to that school of hers?"

"Ah . . ." He thought back, trying to remember how many bodies had been in the room when he'd barged in earlier. "Over a dozen. Maybe fourteen or fifteen?"

"Best take eighteen cookies, then, just to be sure." Joe finished putting the last few into the sack, then held it out to him. "Tell her these are for the students tomorrow."

"Thank you." He reached for the bag. "She'll appreciate it."

"And you tell her that if she's ever of a mind to teach the children in her school how to bake bread, she has only to let me know. I'd be glad to close the bakery for an afternoon and bring the children here for a lesson."

Jonas couldn't help but smile at the short, kindly man. At least not everyone in town shared the same opinion as Miss Thompson. "I'll be sure to pass that along."

"Good. And Mr. Darrow, thank you for helping Sally today."

He shrugged. "It was nothing."

The man shook his head, a knowing look in his eye. "I'm not sure I believe that. First you stopped Simon Volker from attacking Ilya, then you stopped the Finch boys from stealing bread. If you decide to stay in Juneau rather than head up into the hills, I'm sure we can find a job for you here, maybe as a sheriff."

The word caused Jonas to still. He hadn't been a sheriff back in Texas, but the Chinese man had made a fairly good guess as to what his job had once been.

Was his training and former line of work that obvious?

It didn't matter. Because becoming a lawman again—even just a sheriff—wouldn't just mean stopping the Finch boys from hassling a little girl. It would mean all the other things that went with being a lawman.

The guns. The injuries. The dead bodies.

Another image rose in his mind, this one of a tombstone marking the place where the woman who was to become his wife had been laid to rest.

A cold chill swept through him.

"You're mistaken," he whispered, his throat so thick he could barely speak. "I'm not the right man for a job like that."

At least, not anymore.

12

E velina stirred her bowl of chowder in front of her that she'd barely touched. A quick glance at the clock on the wall told her it was quarter past eleven. In forty-five minutes, she'd need to go down and call her class to order.

Would anyone other than Inessa and Ilya be there?

She bit her lip. She might prove to be an even bigger failure as a teacher than she was at the last thing she'd set her mind to —and she'd failed at that rather spectacularly.

"The soup isn't going to eat itself," a deep voice sounded from across the table.

She glanced up to find two brown eyes staring at her. The eyes held a hint of kindness, just like they always seemed to when they looked at her.

The trouble was, those were the *only* eyes staring at her. She frowned and looked around the room. Had Ilya, Inessa, and Kate all finished their lunch? They must have, because she and Mr. Darrow were the only two people still in the kitchen, and Mr. Darrow was far beyond his first helping of chowder.

"Is something not to your liking?" He used the spoon in his

hand to point at her bowl, then plunked the spoon back into his own bowl and scooped up a bite. "Because as far as I'm concerned, this is the best fish chowder I've ever tasted."

She gave him a faint smile. "Or perhaps this is only passable fish chowder, but regaining your strength makes you ravenous."

He raised an eyebrow at her. "And how would you know?"

She shifted on the chair. "I've nursed enough of my sister's patients over the years to have noticed a few things."

"Maybe you're right." He stuck the spoon into his mouth, then plunked it back into the bowl to scoop up another bite. "But Inessa, Ilya, and Kate all devoured their soup as well. Which tells me it really is excellent soup. And it also makes me wonder why you haven't tasted it."

She stared into the thick, creamy liquid. Was the soup really that good? She didn't even remember what she put into it that morning while the pot had been simmering on the stove. Her mind had been far more preoccupied with what would happen when she went downstairs and attempted to call her class to order at noon—if she had a class.

She pushed the bowl away without taking so much as a bite. "I'm not very hungry."

Mr. Darrow set his spoon on the table with a thunk. "Don't let what that shrew said yesterday bother you, because that's exactly what Janice Thompson is, a shrew of the worst sort, because she's self-righteous about it."

Evelina gripped her hands together in her lap. "But I don't have a teaching certificate. She was right about that."

"Do you need one to teach reading and ciphering?"

"Does it matter?" Heat pricked the backs of her eyes. "No one is going to show up today anyway."

"You don't know that." Mr. Darrow pushed himself up from the table. She expected him to take his bowl to the sink, but instead he moved around the table and sat in the seat beside her. "Let's say a couple students come today. Not many, but maybe two or three outside of your siblings. You can still teach them."

She sunk her teeth into the side of her lip. "I suppose, but it will feel like moving backward. Then when I think of the other students arriving at Miss Thompson's classroom, I feel like even more of a failure."

Mr. Darrow reached out and settled his hand atop her clenched ones on her lap.

His grip was strong and warm, and the feel of his skin against hers had her looking up.

It was a mistake, because his eyes held her there, trapped in a gaze she didn't want to pull away from. And even though only their hands were touching, she somehow felt as though he was wrapping her in a fluffy blanket, then pulling her into the comfort of his chest.

She blinked and drew her hands away from his. Goodness, but what had gotten into her? Janice Thompson made one comment about Mr. Darrow being shirtless—which he'd been for the entire time they'd been nursing him back to health—and suddenly she couldn't keep images of a shirtless Jonas from her mind.

"The students who go to Miss Thompson's class will be back by the end of the week," he said, his voice low and deep. "I have no doubt."

She took her bowl and moved to the sink. It was a terrible amount of food to waste, but she didn't see any help for it, since it had already been dished up. If her appetite hadn't returned by dinner, she just might skip the meal altogether rather than waste more food.

"Which direction is the jailhouse?"

"I beg your pardon?" Evelina turned, only to find Mr.

Darrow now standing straight behind her, his empty bowl in his hand.

When Kate had returned home yesterday to find he'd gotten out of bed, interrupted her conversation with Miss Thompson, and then walked to the bakery in the rain, she'd said it was clear that he was ready to be out of his bed, and then she'd proceeded to take out his stitches, all while lecturing him on how he still needed to mind his wound and wasn't strong enough to work for a mine just yet.

But Kate had said he could help with the trading post if he was careful.

And he had. Mr. Darrow had eaten dinner with the family in the kitchen, then spent yesterday evening folding blankets and straightening supplies in the store.

Today he'd risen early and eaten breakfast with them, then gone across the street to the warehouse and helped Inessa inventory beaver pelts.

"Well," he asked, that faint grin tipping up the sides of his mouth once again. "Where is it?"

"What?"

He gave his head a small shake. "Please tell me you don't plan to get this distracted while you're teaching today."

She wouldn't. But only because Mr. Darrow wouldn't be in the room with her.

"The jailhouse," he asked again. "I need to know where it is."

Right. That's what he'd been asking. "It's down the road, two blocks, then turn— Wait. Why do you want to know where the jailhouse is?"

"Someone stole two hundred dollars from Simon Volker, didn't they?"

"Yes."

"Has the thief been found?"

"No."

"Then I'm off to see what I can learn about the thief. Unless you think I'll benefit from lying in the exam room listening to you assign letters to the various sounds in the Tlingit language."

She plunged the bowl into the wash water, her shoulders stiff. "That's hardly a foolish endeavor."

"I didn't say it was." He held up his hands in a gesture of innocence. "But I'm also not sure I need to listen to your lecture, pretty as your voice sounds through the wall."

Did he really think her voice was pretty? Her face heated yet again. Oh, what was it about this man that invoked the incessant need for her to blush?

"Lina." Kate rushed into the room. "The laundress is downstairs asking for you."

Evelina frowned. "Why? You usually pay her for the laundry."

"It's not about the laundry. Her landlord is trying to evict her from the house she's been renting, but she's late getting paid for some of her work. She says she'll have the money if he'll just wait a few more days."

"And what does she expect me to do about it?" *Please, God, don't let it be what I think.*

Kate rolled her eyes. "Don't pretend like you don't know."

The knot in her stomach twisted into a sickening sensation. "I can't, Kate. You know that."

"Tell me you're not serious. She's about to be thrown out of her home. She needs help, and you have the ability to help her."

"I'll only make the mess bigger."

"Lina, please. I understand you might not feel like you can help, especially after what happened last time, but God is 'able to do exceeding abundantly above all that we ask or think.'"

Of course Kate would quote that verse of Scripture at her.

It was Kate's favorite, and she'd spent her entire life armed with it, using it like a shield when they'd gone to Boston, then again when they returned to Alaska and Kate started taking patients.

The problem was, she wasn't Kate, and she wasn't strong enough to go out every day and do a man's job and face all the criticism that came with it. "There's a lawyer on Third Street. Timothy Miller. He's young, but he has a decent reputation for helping people. Tell the woman downstairs to go there, that there's nothing more I can do."

Kate narrowed her eyes. "That's a lie, and you know it."

She shook her head. It wasn't a lie. It was the absolute truth. "I'm sorry."

"Lina!" Kate threw up her hands. "Just because last time didn't go as you hoped doesn't mean—"

"But it does." Tears smarted her eyes. "I'm not you, Kate. I can't just go and go and go while the rest of society looks on, mocking me. You and I might look the same, but we both know that two people could never be more different. I don't like taking on a man's job in a man's world. I don't get some sort of energy from proving a man wrong or exceeding other people's expectations. I don't—"

"You used to get energy from helping people, just the same as I do when I save a man's life." Kate glanced at Jonas. "Even if he's balking the whole time about being tended by a female doctor."

"Don't you understand? I can't help people. At least not anymore." Even now the memories were coming back, the way every eye in the packed room had been pinned to her, waiting for her next statement. The way her words had deserted her, her mind had gone blank, and her tongue had felt as if it were wrapped in cotton. The laughter that had trickled through the crowd, quickly turning into taunts and jeers.

She drew in a breath, then looked around. The stuffy room

filled with people faded away until she found herself standing in the kitchen above the trading post. Only two pairs of eyes were looking at her. The first pair was an identical reflection of her own, and they did not look happy. But the second pair looked horribly confused.

She must seem heartless, standing there arguing with her sister and refusing to help someone in need.

But it wasn't something she felt like explaining, not to Mr. Darrow, not to the woman downstairs, and not to anyone else she might come across—not ever again.

"Please see to it that the woman downstairs is gone by the time I need to teach my class." And with that, she swept from the room.

13

Sitka, Four Days Later

Alexei studied the supply list Yuri had created for the ship, then moved his eyes back to the detailed diagram he'd drawn on his own. "Yes, that will be enough wood, but maybe we should consider having a Douglas fir shipped up for the mast rather than using Sitka spruce."

The Amos Family Shipbuilders had certainly built ships more difficult than this in the past. But it had been four years since they'd been commissioned for such a large project, and he wanted to make sure every last detail was right.

"Looks good to me." Bjorn Thagaard, their master shipbuilder, cocked his head to the side, his blue eyes scanning Alexei's diagram yet again before he straightened. "But I don't need a fancy picture to build a sealing clipper. You know how many clippers I've built over the years?"

It didn't matter if they were clippers, schooners, cutters, yawls, or sloops. The man had built too many to bother counting. The Danish shipbuilder had been working for their family for more than thirty years, a trade he'd learned from his father back in Denmark, and from his grandfather before that.

There was something to be said for a man with three lifetimes' worth of shipbuilding experience behind him.

"How much longer will it take to finish fixing the hull on the cutter in dry dock?" Yuri jabbed a thumb over his shoulder.

Alexei looked to his left, where the ship was clearly displayed through one of several windows on the west side of the office that overlooked the shipyard.

Much like the series of windows on the western wall, there was also a series of windows on the southern wall, allowing anyone inside to overlook both the work being done in the shipyard and the ships entering the mouth of the sound.

It was a rather uncommon setup with exceptionally beautiful views for an office that had been stashed on the second floor of a warehouse. But it seemed to work, because no matter how many hours Alexei found himself spending in this office, he could always assess the state of the shipyard, the progress of a ship being unloaded, or the arrival of a new ship headed toward either the trading company dock or the larger wharf to the east that supplied most of the town.

"We should be finished with the cutter in drydock sometime next week." Bjorn rubbed a meaty hand along the back of his neck. "But we might need to wait another week or two until the first of our supplies come in for the clipper before we start."

"If Sacha returns soon, maybe we can send Tavish and the *Aurora* on a quick trip down to Bellingham to get supplies before he leaves for Japan." Yuri took a sip of coffee, eyes narrowed at the diagram with an unusual amount of concentration.

"*If* he returns by then." Alexei had been in Sitka for a week and a half, and Sacha had yet to return.

It was all he could do not to worry.

He pushed himself up from the desk, leaving Bjorn and Yuri to review the list of supplies he'd put together, though moving around didn't exactly calm him.

He stopped at the series of western-facing windows, leaning an arm against one of the log beams separating two of the windows as he looked down into the shipyard. The men were busy working, but with Bjorn up here, that left only five down below.

He scanned the spot where they'd stored lumber for decades upon decades. There had been a time, back in the early days of his childhood, when it was filled with oak and pine, mahogany and cedar. They'd even brought teak in from Southeast Asia on occasion, if the ship that had been commissioned required it.

Now the series of lean-tos that shielded the lumber from the rain at the back of the property sat nearly empty, with just enough oak, pine, and cedar to repair damaged vessels.

He wanted to say it was his fault for letting work at the shipyard slow, but if anyone was to be blamed, it was his father.

Unlike his grandfather, and his great-grandfather before that, Rurik Amos hadn't been enchanted with shipbuilding, with the notion of taking nothing but wood and air and creating a grand vessel that could travel the world, withstanding storms and barging through ice and bringing the entirety of the planet closer together through trade.

No. Exploring had excited Rurik, much like it did Mikhail and Ilya. Their father had spent his days charting maps to places unknown and finding the deepest, darkest forest and seeing what resources the land was willing to offer.

And it had paid off. Rurik Amos had built the Sitka Trading Company to a grand size.

It wasn't that he'd ignored the shipyard in the process, but instead of working with his hands to learn the same skills their ancestors had learned clear back in England in the 1500's, their father had traveled to Denmark, hired Bjorn, and left the ship-yard to the Dane.

And then Rurik had taught his children the ins and outs of running a trading company, of keeping inventory and negoti-ating trades with the native tribes and establishing trading posts in remote sections of the interior.

As Alexei and his brother Ivan had grown older, they'd been called into his father's office numerous times to discuss the best trade routes for their ships and which trading posts in the interior were proving most lucrative.

But his father had never taught any of them how to build ships—right at a time when naval architecture was changing. The ships that had once seemed large now looked tiny compared to the barges and freighters that could carry three times the cargo in a single journey as one of their clippers or schooners.

Alexei dragged a hand through his hair. He'd been deter-mined to change all of that once. To build the Amos Family Shipyard into what it had once been and then expand it into a company that could compete with the giant shipyards in Cali-fornia and Maine.

As a youth, he'd apprenticed with Bjorn, choosing to stay in Sitka and build ships rather than accompany their father on voyages the way his brothers had.

But Bjorn only knew how to build wooden ships, so when he turned eighteen, Alexei had up and gone to college in San Francisco to study naval architecture. It had seemed like a wise decision at the time.

And it probably would still look like a wise decision, had his father and stepmother not been lost at sea during a storm.

Had Ivan not died in a terrible accident on the same night.

Had he not needed to return to Sitka a year shy of finishing his studies.

The trading company had been making more money than the shipyard at that point, and it's what he'd had to focus on, especially after the loss of the brother he'd been closest to, both in age and in spirit.

Oh the dreams the two of them had once had. Ivan had a business brain about him, more so than anyone else Alexei had ever known. He'd put together a business plan to restore the shipyard to its previous level of production.

Ivan had said it would take five years, and then they could expand to a second shipyard in Seattle, where iron and steel were easier to come by and could be shipped via rail.

But nine years later, those dreams were nothing more than faded memories, shriveled and fallen to dust. As a thirty-year-old man, Alexei was farther away from achieving them now than he'd been as a boy of Ilya's age, one with his entire future ahead of him.

Alexei clenched his hand into a fist against the wall as he looked down at the workers. It hardly seemed fair. All he'd done since he'd gotten that fateful telegram nine years ago was try. Try his hardest to be the father his younger siblings had all lacked. Try his hardest to maintain the trade routes his father had worked so hard to establish. Try his hardest to bring in the money needed to keep their family businesses afloat.

But other than building the *Aurora*, which Sacha now captained, he'd left Bjorn to manage the shipyard.

"So do you want to try to find a mast from Washington, or do you want me to have one cut of Sitka spruce?" Yuri asked from behind him. "You never did say."

Alexei blinked. "What was that?" He headed back to the desk where Yuri and Bjorn still stood.

Yuri smirked.

"You're distracted thinking about the dance the day after tomorrow, aren't you? Just admit it, you're going to have fun. Might even find a lady you'd care to dance with a second time, or a third."

"Is that true, Alexei?" Bjorn slapped him on the back, the force of the stocky shipbuilder's meaty hand almost enough to cause Alexei to cough. "There finally a lady in town that's caught your eye?"

He scowled. "Not hardly."

"He's determined to go to his grave single." Yuri's body shook with a mock shudder. "Have no fear, Bjorn. I fully intend to carry on the Amos family name in Alexei's stead. My problem is quite different, though. Rather than not being able to find a single woman to wed, there are so many lovely ones here in Sitka that I don't know how I'll ever . . ."

Yuri's eyes narrowed on a point beyond Alexei's shoulder. "Sacha's back."

Alexei turned toward the windows facing the harbor and followed his brother's gaze. "Where?"

Yuri gestured toward the entrance to the sound, where two rocks marked the place where the open waters of the Pacific met the calm, mountain-shielded waters of the sound. "That has to be the *Aurora* there."

He was right. The cutter glided elegantly across the water, its sails full and its three masts standing out like guards against the backdrop of the hazy mountains behind it. He could tell it was the *Aurora* even from this distance. Not too many ships were built for the sole purpose of cutting through ice, but the *Aurora* was one of them. Built not just of six-inch-thick oak boards and an iron frame, the entire hull was lined with Australian ironwood, the tough, durable wood that gave the ship the strength needed to break up ice in the Arctic.

It was one of the things he was most proud of in his life.

He'd built it the year after his parents died, when he'd returned to Sitka, a twenty-one-year-old in charge of seven younger siblings, six of whom were under the age of eighteen.

His mind had dreamed up that ship while he'd been in naval architecture school. His classes might have been about iron hulls and bigger barges, but he'd wanted something that could plow through arctic ice, and so he'd built the *Aurora*— back when he'd had a head full of dreams and a heart full of hope.

"Let's hope all is well, and Sacha's delay was for a good reason," Bjorn said, his mouth set in a grim line as he watched the ship glide toward the wharf in front of their dry dock.

Alexei slanted Bjorn a glance, then looked over at Yuri, who wasn't smiling any longer either. They all felt the heaviness in the room. Oh sure, there was excitement about the ship's arrival, as there always was whenever a ship arrived in port, but just beneath it was a swell of worry.

They headed down the stairs as a group, their boots creating a thunderous cacophony of clomping against the worn wood, before they pushed their way outside.

The men from the shipyard had already stopped their repairs and gone to the warehouse where the handcarts were stored. Rather than employ stevedores to unload their ships, the Amos family had always paid their shipbuilders to pause their work and help unload the vessels.

Alexei lengthened his gait, beating Yuri and Bjorn to the far edge of the wharf, and trying to ignore the hard knot in his stomach. What if, after the gangway was lowered, the first mate appeared with a grim look on his face, bearing news that—?

"Ahoy, mate," a familiar voice called from the ship.

Alexei looked up to find Sacha standing at the rail, his shoulders and chest so broad they took up the same amount of space as the two sailors standing beside him.

"You're home." He didn't speak loudly enough for his words to carry up to Sacha, but a sense of peace settled inside him.

The bottom of the gangway landed on the wharf, and Alexei was the first man up it.

Sacha laughed when he saw him coming, a deep belly laugh that sounded almost identical to their father's from years gone by. Then he opened his arms, and Alexei crashed into them.

"You're back." He didn't care if he looked as weak as a woman, hugging his brother on the deck of a ship for all to see.

"And you were worried." Sacha gave him a slap on the back. "Don't tell me you weren't."

"Of course I was worried. I'm your older brother, and you're two weeks late. It's my job to worry."

"Step aside, brother," Yuri said from behind him. "You're not the only one who wants to greet him."

Alexei moved aside so that Sacha could fold Yuri in a hug, followed by Bjorn.

"What kept you?" Bjorn asked as he pulled away from Sacha.

Sacha scratched the side of his beard, his form so large that he looked like a giant next to Yuri and Bjorn, and neither of them were small. "In the Arctic? Ice. Last winter was harsh, even now there's more than usual. It was hard to break through."

Alexei raised his brows. "Even for the *Aurora*?"

"Even for the *Aurora*, but before I reached Barrow the first time, I happened upon a wreck near the Kotzebue Sound. The sailors were stranded, but the ship was salvageable, so I towed it back to Unalaska."

"You towed a ship from Kotzebue Sound clear back to Unalaska?" Alexei rubbed the back of his neck. It was a miracle his brother was only two weeks late after something like that. Unalaska was just under a thousand nautical miles north of Sitka on the Aleutian Island Chain, where Inessa and Ilya's mother had been from. But Kotzebue was much farther north than Unalaska. He'd have to look at a map to be certain, but he'd guess maybe six hundred nautical miles separated Kotzebue from Unalaska.

Sacha shrugged as though taking a two-week detour was as common as sneezing. "She was a new vessel, and a beauty. If I'd left her, I'm not sure how long she would have lasted with the waves, but we got her hull patched enough that the sailors limped her to the closest dry dock."

"And you followed?"

Again, Sacha's wide shoulders moved in a careless shrug. "You'd have wanted another ship to do the same had the *Aurora* been the one that wrecked."

He would have, yes. But the delay in Sacha's return was sure to cost them money they didn't have.

"What happened that caused her to wreck?" Bjorn asked. "Was there a storm?"

Sacha's sun-weathered face darkened into a scowl. "More like the sailors they hired on in San Francisco or Bellingham— or maybe even Virginia—had never seen a lick of ice before. They think they're going to come up here and get rich sealing and whaling, but they don't have a clue what to do once they're here." Sacha crossed his arms, causing his chest to look even more imposing. "I swear there's been more wrecks this year than there were in the last two decades when Russia owned Alaska."

"Trouble is, these kinds of tales never reach California," Bjorn muttered. "Only the stories of captains and their crews getting fat—"

"Sacha!" a nasally voice called from the gangway. "Did you get it? Tell me you got it!"

Alexei turned to see none other than Alaska's one and only minister of education, Rev. Sheldon Jackson—who also happened to be Sitka's resident Presbyterian minister—appear at the top of the gangway.

The reverend scanned the deck, excitement lighting his eyes the moment he spotted them. He started toward them, practically tripping over his own feet in his haste to reach Sacha. "Well? Were you able to find one? Don't keep me in suspense!"

"Find one what?" Yuri muttered.

Alexei resisted the urge to roll his eyes, but barely. One never knew what to expect when it came to Sheldon Jackson.

"Not only did I get her, but I put her in my cabin." Sacha jabbed his thumb over his shoulder. "Told the boys she wasn't to go in the hold with everything else."

Bjorn raised his bushy eyebrows at the reverend. "What, exactly, was Sacha supposed to get for you?"

A wide smile swept across the reverend's face. "A whaling suit, of course."

"A whaling suit?" Alexei repeated. "Why do you . . .?"

But Rev. Jackson was already running toward the captain's quarters.

Alexei looked at Sacha. "Tell me this isn't what I think."

Sacha chuckled. "Oh, it's exactly what you think. And I better follow him before he tears apart my cabin in search of it."

Sacha headed toward the bow of the ship.

"I guess the rest of us should get busy. There's still a ship to unload." Yuri turned and started toward one of the empty handcarts that had been left on the deck.

Bjorn grabbed another, and the two of them wheeled their

carts to where cargo from the hold was being piled onto the deck.

Rather than grab a handcart for himself, Alexei followed Sacha and the reverend up the stairs to the upper deck. Just what had his brother gotten himself into? And with Rev. Jackson, no less.

"Isn't it wonderful?" The reverend's nasally voice floated around the side of the wheelhouse. "Oh, who would have thought I'd be able to acquire one!"

Alexei rounded the wheelhouse, then stopped in the narrow doorway to his brother's cabin.

Things were exactly as Sacha had said. There was a bonafide whaling suit lying over one of the chairs in Sacha's quarters. Made out of seal intestines, the waterproof suit was a nearly translucent shade of white.

The native tribes of Alaska wore whaling suits when hunting seals and whales in the frigid waters of the Bering Sea, and even though they would look odd to someone living in California or Washington Territory, they really were expertly designed. All the stitching was done on the inside of the suit, with reeds that would expand when they got wet, sealing up any holes so that water couldn't penetrate.

Commercial whalers and sealers wore oilskin hats and slickers, much the same as those the crew aboard the *Aurora* or the *Alliance* wore. But they were heavy and cumbersome, whereas the natives' lightweight suits allowed greater freedom of movement.

"It's magnificent. Simply magnificent." Rev. Jackson picked up the suit by its shoulders, holding it up to the light of the window with a look of wonder on his face. "I am in your deepest debt, Sacha."

"Are you now?" Sacha sent Alexei a smirk.

Alexei leaned a shoulder against the doorway. "So when do you leave on your whale hunt, Reverend?"

"I'm not going whaling!" the older man sputtered, pressing a hand to his chest. "Good heavens, I am but a humble minister of the gospel."

And the minister of education for all of Alaska. Which didn't seem like such a humble position, in Alexei's opinion. "Then why do you need a whaling suit?"

The man blinked through his thick glasses, as though a bit baffled by the question. "For the museum, of course. Indigenous cultures must be preserved. Why else do you think I've been collecting artifacts? You should come by and see my collection of totem poles. It is quite extensive. We recently acquired a seal-blubber lamp."

He should have guessed. If the reverend wasn't yammering on about the immorality of the natives living in a single longhouse or the need to assimilate the native youth into American culture, he was waxing eloquent about the museum he was building to preserve their culture.

"Tell me, Reverend Jackson, does your interest in preserving the different native cultures of Alaska mean you've decided to let the students at your school speak in their own languages?" It wasn't the first time they'd had this conversation, but he couldn't stand there and watch the man pretend that preserving a seal-blubber lamp was the same thing as letting Ilya and Inessa's cousins speak the language they'd grown up with while at boarding school. "I'm sure you'd hate to see their languages grow obsolete given all you've invested in the education of the native children."

Jackson stiffened, bringing himself up to his full height, never mind that the man was impossibly short. "English is the language of the future. Not these small dialects that only a few thousand people know. You, of all people, should understand the only way forward for the native populations of Alaska is assimilation. If the youth don't learn to adapt to our ways, they will be left behind, relegated to sewing beads onto leather and carving totem poles while the world moves on. And none of us would want that, would we?"

Alexei pushed himself off the doorway and stepped closer. "Maybe you should ask the students in your school just how grateful they are for your endeavors."

The reverend shoved his glasses higher onto his nose. "And perhaps, if you're so concerned about the future of the Alaskan Indians, you should consider making a contribution to our aboriginal benevolence fund. It's quite clear you can afford to be generous, yet I don't recall ever seeing a banknote from your family. Such a contribution would help native populations far more disadvantaged than yourself."

Rev. Jackson leaned forward, his eyes aflame with an indignation that he would probably describe as righteous. "In fact, I didn't even see you in church this past Sunday, where we prayed specifically for the Aleut people, who are having a harder and harder time finding food due to the extensive whaling and sealing operations in the Bering Sea."

"That's because I went to St. Michael's," Alexei gritted. "With Father Andrew. I'm a member there."

It wasn't the first time he'd told the reverend he was a member at St. Michael's, but the man still blinked, as though he hadn't considered a person might attend any church other than his own. Never mind that St. Michael's was Russian Orthodox, and the obvious place for any Russians remaining in Sitka to attend church.

Rev. Jackson sniffed, his hands tightening around the whaling suit. "I best get this back to the museum where it can be properly displayed. But should you wish to pray for the aboriginal peoples of Alaska, we would certainly welcome your presence next Sunday. In the meantime, I look forward to receiving that benevolence check from your family."

Alexei moved to the wall, allowing the reverend a clear path to the door. "I would hate to keep you from your duties."

But before leaving, Rev. Jackson turned back to Sacha. "Captain Amos, have you any idea when your sister might return?"

"My sister isn't here?" Sacha raised his eyebrows. "Which one? Evelina?"

The man sent Sacha a baffled look, as though not quite able to comprehend that Sacha had been gone for three months and thus wouldn't know about Evelina, Kate, and Inessa moving to Juneau. "Yes, Evelina has been in Juneau for the past sixty-eight days, and I'm wondering if you have any idea when she might return. I have a rather important question to ask her."

"I'm sure you could write her a letter."

The man's brow furrowed. "This is the type of thing best asked in person."

Alexei stifled a groan. There was only one question a man like Sheldon Jackson would want to ask in person rather than in a letter.

"Juneau is only a couple days away." Sacha gave the man a simple shrug. "If it's that important, you could pay a visit."

"Yes, yes, perhaps I could, but the needs of the schools are so great this time of year that it's not easy for a man such as myself to get away."

The corner of Sacha's mouth twitched beneath his beard, but other than that, he managed to keep a straight face. "I'm sure. You are a very busy man indeed."

Alexei met his brother's gaze above the reverend's short head. "Scott Paddington took a job as a guide in the interior while I was in California, so the women are in Juneau to tend the trading post until I can find someone to replace Scott."

"You mean Evelina is there unchaperoned?" Rev. Jackson stiffened, his eyes growing wide. "In a place as rugged as Juneau? Why, that town's little more than a mining camp, and certainly no place for a woman of her refinement."

Alexei's hand curled into a fist at his side. Did the man purposely try to anger him each time they spoke, or was he truly that much of a dunce? "I'm afraid that's my problem to worry about, not yours."

"Yes, well, if I ever get a chance to speak with Evelina, then perhaps she won't be your problem to worry about anymore."

"That is not what I meant. I don't consider any of my sisters to be a problem." Especially not Evelina. "The problem is finding a manager for the trading post. And Evelina isn't there by herself. Both of her sisters and Ilya are with her."

"That hardly seems proper given the rapscallions that Juneau tends to attract." The reverend turned back to Sacha, a bit too quick to show Alexei his back. "I best be off now, but thank you again for my whaling suit. I am most grateful for the trouble you went through to procure it."

"Anytime." Sacha reached out and patted the man on the back, the size of his hand large enough to cover the reverend's entire shoulder. "Just make sure you stop by the office and pay for it on your way out."

"Of course." The reverend gave a dutiful nod. "How much did you say it was?"

"Fifty dollars."

Fifty dollars? Alexei nearly choked. Had Sacha lost his mind?

But the reverend seemed to be taking him seriously. In fact, the short little man gave Sacha another dutiful nod. "I will go to the office and pay directly. Before you leave again, I'll decide which item I'd like you to procure for me next."

Sacha flashed the man a disarming smile. "Excellent."

The reverend smiled in return, then trotted out the door, holding the suit out in front of him as he muttered something about the intricate stitching.

Alexei waited for him to round the corner before speaking. "Fifty dollars for a whaling suit? Since when do we engage in extortion?"

The side of Sacha's mouth tilted up beneath his beard. "I figure if the man is fool enough to pay me several months' wages for a whaling suit, then I may as well let him."

"Charging a price like that should be illegal, no matter how ridiculous the man purchasing it is." Alexei scrubbed a hand over his face. "Where do you even suppose he gets the money to pay such high prices?"

Sacha grinned. "I daresay it's the benevolence fund, dear brother."

"No." Alexei's gaze shot to his brother's. "He said that money went to help the different tribes."

"It does, by preserving their culture in a little square building where Americans can come and gawk at the curiosities."

"I am not giving that man a single dollar."

Sacha tilted his head back and loosed a full, hearty laugh.

Alexei only shook his head. "Did you pay anything for that suit?"

"I traded a few blankets and a sack of grain for it. I got it from Inessa and Ilya's grandfather when I visited Unalaska, and he refused to take anything more. But honestly, I don't know why you waste time fighting with Reverend Jackson. Neither of you is ever going to persuade the other."

Alexei stared at the door where the man had disappeared. How did he explain that he couldn't help looking at Inessa and Ilya and wondering if, in another fifty years, the only place whaling suits would exist anymore was in museums.

And if their language would be completely forgotten.

And if the Aleut and Tlingit, Yupik and Inupiat peoples would be so thoroughly "assimilated"—as the reverend liked to say—that their customs and beliefs and ways of doing things that had existed for centuries would disappear altogether.

Even now, few people called the Inupiat and Yupik by their tribal names. Most simply referred to them as Eskimos. Would even the Inupiat Yupik names disappear?

"Sacha, there you are." Yuri barreled into the cabin. "Tavish is looking for you. He has a question about whether the whale blubber needs to be unloaded here, or if it's going to one of the . . ."

Yuri's words trailed off as he looked between the two of them. "Don't tell me Alexei's got you talking about something serious already. You've only just arrived."

"Serious indeed." Sacha winked. "I'm afraid that's all Alexei knows how to be."

"You need to convince him to come to the dance in two days' time. If we find him the right wife, he might remember how to smile."

"Is that what you need?" Sacha ran his gaze down Alexei, another smirk tipping the side of his mouth up beneath his beard. "A wife to help you be less serious?"

"Not in the least," he gritted. "I smile plenty."

"You hear that, Yuri?" Sacha elbowed Yuri in the ribs. "He thinks he smiles."

"He probably considers any time he's not glowering to be a smile." Yuri swung an arm around Sacha's shoulders. "But you're not too busy for a little fun and dancing, are you?"

"After being at sea for the past three months? Never." Sacha looked at Alexei, his eyebrow raised. "So how about it? Want to come to the dance?"

Alexei sighed. Why was it so important he attend some

frivolous dance? "I don't have time. I still haven't finished going over the shipping routes, and I need to make sure all our supplies are ordered before I leave for Juneau next week."

"See," Yuri quipped. "What did I tell you? He's always serious these days. Not sure he even remembers what a real smile feels like."

"There really is no hope for him, is there?" Sacha shook his head.

Alexei frowned at his brothers. "I'm not going to apologize for . . ." But his brothers were already walking away from him, likely to finish unloading the ship. ". . . Being responsible," he muttered under his breath. That's what he was going to say.

Neither of them understood what it was like to run two companies and a family at once. Something always needed doing—like finding a manager for the trading post at Juneau and having supplies for the new clipper delivered to Sitka. And even though he had a slew of siblings, it seemed there were never enough hands for all the work.

And speaking of work, the cargo being unloaded wasn't going to come to life and check itself against the shipping manifest. So he followed his brothers out of the room.

14

Juneau, One Day Later

The smell of coffee and some sort of baked confection reached Jonas halfway up the stairs. He yawned, then rolled his shoulders, loosening up the knots that had formed in the night as he stepped into the kitchen.

"Good morning," Evelina greeted him.

He couldn't help the way his lips turned up into a small smile. She stood at the stove frying up some eggs, the very picture of loveliness and femininity. Kate and Inessa were there too. One twin stood at the stove leisurely cooking eggs with a smile on her face, while the other tromped around the kitchen, firm lines wreathing her face as she set plates and silverware on the table with her typical brisk efficiency.

"Have a seat." Evelina used the spatula in her hand to gesture to the chair at the head of the table. "The eggs are nearly done, and I already poured you a cup of coffee."

"Thank you." He stifled a yawn, then blinked the heaviness away from his eyelids. Evidently Evelina had noticed his morning habit of not being able to string more than a handful of words together until he'd had his coffee.

He sank into the chair that had unofficially become his and reached for the coffee. The aroma alone made him know he'd be asking for a second cup about five minutes into breakfast.

Evelina carried the plate of eggs to the table and set it in the center beside some sort of white cake that looked to be dotted with raisins, then slid into the chair on his left. "Do you have plans this morning?"

"I want to head back to the jail. Ask Volker a few more questions."

"Haven't you questioned him before?" Inessa took a sip of her water.

"More than once, if I recall." Kate quirked an eyebrow at him.

He'd questioned Volker four times—Volker's friends too—trying to figure out who had stolen his money. While the men could all remember Orville, the long-haired man in the red shirt who'd been with them on the ship, no one seemed to know where he'd gone.

Not even the prospectors who wandered into town every so often and had themselves a drink at one of the bars. Which he knew because he'd made a habit of heading down to the bar a few times, seating himself at one of the tables at the back, and listening to the locals.

Could the man have left the area entirely? It seemed likely, given that he'd yet to find a single clue as to where this Orville fellow might have gone.

"Jonas, would you care to pray for our meal?" Kate plopped down into the chair on his right, directly across from Evelina.

"Aren't we going to wait for Ilya?" Evelina glanced at the door. "I thought you sent him to the bakery for bread."

Kate huffed. "I sent him to China Joe's nearly half an hour

ago. Who knows when he'll return. We can use the *zapekanka* to sop up the eggs."

"Zapen-what?" Jonas jutted his chin toward the cake in the center. "Is that what this is called?"

"*Zapekanka*," Inessa answered. "And yes, it's a Russian breakfast cake made with semolina and cheese and raisins."

"Cheese?" Jonas raised an eyebrow. "In a breakfast sweet?"

"It's not very sweet. More hearty than anything." Kate began slicing the cake. "The cheese makes it moist."

Jonas eyed the confection, which seemed more suspicious by the second. Just when would Ilya be back with the bread?

"Here, try some." Evelina slid a piece onto his plate. "You'll like it, I promise."

"The way I liked the blood soup last night?"

Evelina and Inessa giggled, but Kate grew stiff. "There wasn't any blood in last night's soup. How many times do I have to tell you? Borscht is made with beets. That's what turns it red."

"I'll have to take your word for it." He'd had a few bites, but that was about all he could manage. It wasn't that the soup had tasted bad, but there was something about spooning bright red broth into his mouth that he simply couldn't tolerate.

"You'll like the *zapekanka*." Evelina nodded at the piece sitting on his plate. "If you go ahead and pray, we can start."

"You don't want to wait for Ilya either?"

Evelina glanced around the table. "Kate's right. The eggs will get cold if we wait much longer, and who knows when he'll return."

"Very well." Jonas bowed his head. "Dear Heavenly Father—"

"There's a murder!" Ilya raced into the kitchen. "Mr. Darrow, you have to come. We need to figure out who did it."

Jonas stilled, the opening words from his prayer still

hanging from his lips. "I . . . A murder? What makes you think I can figure out who did it?"

Ilya rounded the table and gripped his arm, trying to tug him from the chair. "All the men in town are helping. It's not like the Marshal's here to run the investigation."

He looked around the table. "Is that what happens when there's been a murder? The men help until the Marshal arrives?"

"It is, yes," Evelina answered before swinging her gaze back to Ilya. "Do you know who it was?"

"The laundress, the one who wanted you to stop her from getting evicted."

Evelina's face paled. "You don't think her landlord . . ."

Ilya shrugged. "That's what we got to figure out, but she wasn't killed at the boarding house. She was killed down at the laundry."

"That poor woman." Evelina twisted her hands together in her skirt. "Maybe if I'd helped, she—"

"You're not doing yourself any favors with thoughts like that." Kate rose and grabbed a piece of cake. "I doubt this had anything to do with a dispute about rent."

Pounding sounded on the door downstairs.

"That's probably Mr. Hemming from the Committee of Public Safety." Kate wrapped the cake in a napkin. "He'll want me to examine the body and declare a cause of death. I'll eat my breakfast on the way. Jonas, are you coming?"

"I . . . uh . . ." His hands slicked with sweat. There was a part of him that wanted to say no, that he'd seen too many dead bodies already in his lifetime.

But what if there was something he could do? Some insight he might have, given his former line of work? After all, a murderer on the loose was a threat to every man, woman, and child in Juneau—including the Amoses.

He rose from the table, never mind that his legs trembled slightly beneath his weight. "Yes, I'll go with you."

No ONE in Juneau knew how to handle a crime scene. That much had been clear from the moment Jonas entered the wash-house to discover men tromping all over the dirt floor—a dirt floor that should have yielded some clue as to which door the murderer had used and whether the laundress had known her attacker.

Instead, the floor was a mess of footprints, and the blood had already been scrubbed off the table. The only thing that hadn't been moved was the woman's body. Her eyes stared vacantly at the ceiling, and even though Kate was in the middle of her examination, the bruising around the victim's neck told him she'd been strangled to death.

But he couldn't tell if there had been a struggle. Or if the attacker had come up from behind and surprised her or gotten angry in the middle of an argument and strangled her out of frustration. Any evidence of such a struggle—spilled laundry soap, toppled crates, and clothes strewn on the floor—had probably been cleaned up by the well-meaning townsfolk crammed into the small laundry building.

Jonas blew out a breath. It was one thing to ask him to help with a murder investigation. It was another thing entirely to expect him to help when the crime scene had been ruined. The murderer would likely never be found now, the motive never determined unless there was a letter of some sort back at the woman's apartment that might give clues.

Either that or a witness who came forward.

Jonas turned to one of the men on the Committee of Public

Safety, Grover Hanover, the grocer who had questioned him after he'd been stabbed. "Where did Miss Clement live?"

"She just moved to Mrs. Mills's boarding house over on Second Street."

"Second Street," he repeated. "Has anyone searched her things?"

The man blinked at him, as though the thought of looking through a murder victim's personal items hadn't occurred to him. "We usually just collect the victim's things and leave them for the Marshal to sort out."

The Marshal, who still hadn't arrived in Juneau even though he'd been summoned after the stabbing almost three weeks ago. The Marshal who hadn't so much as lifted a finger to find Orville Jacobs, the man who had likely stolen Simon Volker's two hundred dollars.

"And when do you think the Marshal will find the time to investigate this murder?"

Hanover shrugged. "Hopefully by the end of the week. He tends to prioritize murder investigations—once he gets word that a murder has been committed."

Jonas wasn't going to ask how long that might take. "So it's no problem if I head to the boarding house and collect Miss Clement's things? Or do you want me to stay here?"

Hanover waved him off. "Go on and collect Miss Clement's things and bring them to the jailhouse. That will be fine."

"Thanks." He turned and made his way to the closest exit, which happened to be the back door. A faint drizzle was falling outside, and the air held the coming chill of winter. Fortunately he'd taken a fur coat with him when he left the trading post, rather than a slicker like Kate had worn. Everyone in town might think him odd for wearing a fur coat in October, but his

Texas blood still wasn't used to the constant chill in the Juneau air.

Jonas paused for a moment and surveyed the yard, which looked to be untouched—unlike inside the building. The laundry vats in the yard sat empty, almost as though waiting for the proprietress to come and fill them with boiling water and clothes. There were multiple sets of footprints. Most of them were the same size, running from the back door to the giant washtubs, then back inside the building. But there was a larger pair of footprints. A large, fresh pair.

It looked as though they led into the woods that lined the yard and climbed the mountain behind the town. The person had been in a hurry. Jonas could see that from the way the tracks dug deeply into the earth.

But there was a third set of prints. These ones small and light and . . . leading behind the barrels?

Jonas approached the barrels nestled against the back of the building. "Hello? Is anyone there?"

"Mr. Darrow?"

A small voice came from where two barrels touched, leaving a little crevice against the wall.

"It's me."

A girl stood from behind the barrels—a small, thin girl that he now saw every afternoon when he went to the bakery. It was none other than Sally Shephard.

"What are you doing behind there?"

She looked down, causing a wave of dirty blond hair to cascade over her face.

He crouched down to her level, even though she still stood behind the barrels.

Did you see something that made you frightened? Why are you at the laundry? These questions and more rushed through his mind, but the tremble in her jaw made him bite his tongue. "Are you stuck? Do you need help getting out?"

She shook her head, then vaulted her little body on top of one of the barrels and climbed down the other side. She looked around, carefully surveying the woods before turning back to him. "It was the man you've been looking for."

"The man I've been looking for?"

"The one who stole two hundred dollars from Mr. Volker. The one you keep asking everyone in town if they've seen. That's who killed Miss Clement. He has a long gray ponytail. Remember?"

Jonas felt his blood turn cold. "I remember, but how do you know he killed Miss Clement?"

Sally shifted, her hands twisting together in front of her. "Miss Clement . . . she pays me to deliver laundry. Two cents per trip. Ma was sick yesterday, and I had to stay home to care for Jim, which meant I had extra laundry to deliver today, so I came early. Miss Clement leaves the laundry for me bundled by the back door, so it's no trouble to come early before she starts working. But when I got here, there were two voices inside the building."

Sally looked around, scanning the woods as though she expected the murderer to suddenly appear. "One voice belonged to a man, and he wasn't happy. He told Miss Clement she needed to do better. She said she needed more money. That she'd been kicked out of her house because he hadn't paid her, and that if he didn't pay up, she'd go to the Marshal. Then there were a lot of noises, banging and slamming. Some things must have been knocked over for that much noise. Then Miss Clement screamed, and it scared me. So I . . ."

Sally looked back toward where she'd been hiding.

"What happened after that?" He was almost afraid to ask, almost afraid to extrapolate events based on the testimony of such a young child. But as far as he knew, there weren't any other witnesses, and he needed as much information as he could get.

Especially if the man who had murdered Betty Clement was the same man who had stolen from Simon Volker. The same man with the gray ponytail that Volker had identified as Orville Jacobs when he questioned Volker at the jail.

"There were more sounds," she whispered. "More banging and crashing."

"Did you look through the window?"

She shook her head, strands of long blond hair cascading about her shoulders. "I was too scared."

"Reckon I would have been too scared too." He reached out and patted her hand. "So when did you see him, the man with the gray ponytail?"

"He ran out the back door and into the woods."

"Did he see you? Was there any chance that he might have . . .?" His words stopped in his throat, because if the man with the gray ponytail—Orville Jacobs—had seen her, then Sally just might be his next victim.

But Sally just shook her head. "I was hiding when he came out."

Jonas crouched down, looking directly into her eyes. "What I'm about to tell you is very important, and I need you to listen, to do exactly what I say. Do you understand?"

She nodded, her blue eyes wide and somber.

"You can't tell anyone what you just told me. No one can know that you saw a man leaving the laundry. Not Mr. Hanover or Mr. Hemming or even the Marshal. It has to be our secret."

Her eyes filled with tears. "But Miss Clement is dead, and if I don't tell anyone, the man with the ponytail might get away."

"He won't get away." Jonas patted her shoulder. "I'm going to catch him, and after he's caught, we can tell people."

"But what if you don't catch him."

"I will. I promise." Jonas straightened and held out his hand. "Now I'm going to walk you home. No laundry deliveries today."

Sally slipped her little fingers into his hand. "Can we stop by the bakery and get some bread first, before the Finch boys figure out where I am?"

"Sure." He gave her hand a squeeze and slowed his pace to match hers, all the time surveying the woods and hoping that a man with a long silver ponytail wasn't watching.

Dear God—he tilted his head to the sky—*why can't there be a sheriff? Or at the very least, why can't you send the Marshal? I shouldn't be the one to go into the woods after Orville Jacobs. My lawman days are done.*

But that didn't change the fact that a murderer needed to be caught, and he was the only person in town who knew how to catch him.

SHE'D MISSED A STITCH, again. Evelina sighed as she set her crotchet needles down and began pulling out her most recent stitch. And the one before that, and the one before that, and the one before that.

She really had no business crocheting, not when she was paying far more attention to the door of the trading post than the scarf in her hands.

But it didn't matter how many times she looked up from her work, how black the sky grew outside, or how hard the wind howled, the door stayed firmly shut. And that door was the sole reason she was sitting downstairs in the trading post and not up in her room dressed in her nightgown and rocking by the window.

Because Jonas had yet to return. He'd been gone for over twelve hours. All she knew was that he came back to the trading post for a few minutes and went into the exam room. When he reemerged, a pistol had been strapped to his hip beneath his coat. He said he needed to do a bit more investigating and had left.

The men from the Committee of Public Safety had spent the day questioning the people who lived and owned shops up and down the street before concluding the murderer had skipped town on the ship that had left just after dawn.

But no one had seen Jonas. He hadn't decided to leave town too, had he?

Surely not. His carpetbag was still stuffed under his bed, and no ships had docked after the murder had been discovered.

But where could—?

The door opened, and Evelina stood, the breath rushing out of her as Jonas's tall, familiar form stepped inside and shut the door behind him.

"Are you all right? What took so long? Did you find the murderer?" The words tumbled out in a giant rush.

Jonas met her gaze, his eyes serious. "No."

That was the only word he said. Nothing about where he'd been, though the twigs tangled on his arm and back told her he'd been in the woods. Clearly he'd been in the woods.

She came closer, reaching for his coat to hang it on the peg by the door. "I'm glad you took one of the furs with you today. It was cold."

Jonas shrugged. "For the first time since I moved here, I don't think I noticed."

"I saved dinner for you. And lunch too, if you want that reheated."

"I'm not hungry."

"Oh, but . . ." She ran her eyes down him, ready to argue that he must need nourishment after spending a day in the mountains, but his shoulders were hunched, dark shadows hugged the skin beneath his eyes, and his eyes held a haunted look.

"Why did you spend the day in the woods?" she whispered. "Don't you think the murderer left on the ship first thing this morning?"

"That's what everyone is saying."

"But you don't believe it?"

"No."

It felt like he was keeping something from her. But before she could come up with another question, he brushed past her and headed toward his room.

"Are you sure you don't need anything?" she called after him. "Maybe a cup of hot tea and a biscuit?"

"My bed." He didn't even turn to look at her when he spoke. "That's the only thing I need."

And then he shut the door, leaving her to do nothing but stare blankly at the plain slab of wood . . .

And wonder just what had transpired in the forest.

15

Sitka, One Day Later

Alexei gritted his teeth. Why did everyone at the dance look so blasted happy?

Especially when these dances were nothing but work? The volunteer committee had spent the entire week emptying the large warehouse on the wharf of supplies, stringing decorations from the rafters, and organizing who was bringing what food for the dinner.

It seemed every last person in town had been roped into helping in some form or other—at least everyone but him—and now he stood in a cavernous room filled with too many bodies and laden with warring scents of food, while the three fiddlers and single bass player strummed an endless series of tunes.

What was it about dancing that made people want to smile and laugh? Why did Yuri and Sacha want him to be here so badly when he could be home in his study, poring over trade maps or business ledgers or the list of supplies needed to build the clipper?

Even the Widow Benford—who never smiled at anyone—had a grin plastered on her face as one of the old fishermen in town twirled her around the dance floor.

A chorus of feminine laughter filled the air, and Alexei looked over to find Yuri had stopped dancing and was standing a few feet away with a gaggle of women about him.

Of course, the men closest to Yuri were all glaring.

And why wouldn't they be? There were maybe four dozen women in all of Sitka—most of whom were married—and well over two hundred men. Yet there Yuri was, entertaining five single women at once.

He'd be glaring too, if he was of a mind to dance. Instead, he scanned the group of women. There was Freya and Jane and Millicent . . . and Rosalind Caldwell?

Alexei straightened. What was she doing with Yuri?

A quick glance around the room told him that her father, Preston Caldwell, hadn't noticed where she was. He practically kept his daughter shackled to his side. Why, Alexei didn't know. Most men of Caldwell's standing with daughters of marriageable age sent them to Boston or New York to live with relatives and find some city slicker of a husband. But not Caldwell.

He'd warned Yuri not to dance with Rosalind tonight, but would his younger brother remember? Because there was something about the way Yuri angled his body toward Rosalind when he spoke, something about how he tilted his head just a little lower to hear her—

"You're supposed to be smiling."

Alexei looked over to find Sacha at his side.

"At least you need to smile if you're going to convince any of the women to dance with you."

"I'm not planning to dance."

Sacha gave his head a somber-looking shake. "Then why come?"

"Because if I hadn't, you and Yuri would have spent the next eight decades harassing me about it."

That, and because the rest of the town expected him to make some sort of appearance. He could hardly afford not to, considering how the governor was here along with two captains in the Revenue Cutter Service. There were a slew of other government bureaucrats in attendance as well. He didn't know what all of them did or why they needed to be in Alaska, but they had no trouble dancing.

Even little Ingrid Eriksson was being twirled around the dance floor by the governor's sixteen-year-old son.

"There. Look. The dance is ending." Sacha gave him a little nudge. "You should ask Freya Eriksson for the next dance."

Alexei leveled a glare at his brother. "Do you know how many rumors that would start?"

Besides, if he was going to move from where he'd been standing against the wall for the last fifteen minutes, it would be for the sole purpose of wrenching Yuri away from Rosalind Caldwell.

Now all he had to do was figure out how to accomplish that without causing a scene.

"Dancing with Freya won't start any rumors," Sacha said. "Everyone is dancing with someone tonight. Surely you can't mean to come here and be a complete curmudgeon."

"I can and I will. Now if you'll excuse me, I need to go manufacture some way to get Yuri—"

"Mr. Amos. Mr. Amos!"

Alexei winced. He didn't need to turn to know who was calling his name. The nasally voice could belong to only one man.

"See?" Sacha thumped him on the shoulder. "Told ya you

should have danced with Freya. Now you'll be stuck talking to the reverend."

"At least I won't be the only one."

Sacha grinned. "But you will. I'm dancing this next set with Millicent." And then his brother was off, weaving his way across the warehouse toward her.

"Mr. Amos." Rev. Jackson came to a halt beside him, the older man's eyes blinking owlishly behind his thick spectacles. "I'm glad I found you."

"Yes, hard to imagine attending a dance without the two of us talking," Alexei muttered.

The reverend pushed his spectacles higher onto his nose. "After we spoke yesterday, I expected to receive a banknote for my benevolence fund."

Alexei coughed. He couldn't help it. That's why the reverend was tracking him down? Because he still wanted money? "I'm afraid I'm going to need a bit more information about what projects the benevolence fund supports and the process for appropriating funds once a . . ."

Alexei narrowed his eyes at the opposite wall of the warehouse, where Preston Caldwell and the governor had fallen into a conversation that looked rather serious.

"I'll have you know I run my benevolence fund with complete transparency."

"I'm sure you do," Alexei said, not taking his gaze away from the men on the other side of the room. He didn't like this. Not one bit. What were the two of them talking about? The only type of plans Caldwell ever hatched were ones sure to line his own pockets—often at the expense of others in Alaska.

He needed to get closer. Maybe if he got himself a cup of punch, he could stand close enough to the men to overhear—

"Are you even listening to me?"

Alexei tore his gaze away from Caldwell long enough to

glance at Rev. Jackson. "If you'll excuse me. There's a matter I must attend to."

The reverend sputtered, gaping at him like a fish trying to spit a hook out of its mouth. "What is this matter? We were in the middle of a highly important . . ."

But Alexei didn't hear anything else the man said, because he was off, weaving his way around the outskirts of the dance floor, trying to look as though he was nothing other than thirsty as he sidled his way around the perimeter of the room.

The trouble was, the reverend was following him, calling after him and making something of a commotion. And while the music was loud enough to drown out most of the ruckus, those in the reverend's path couldn't help but notice the man was trying to run him down.

This would never do. He could hardly look innocuous standing at the punch table with the reverend shouting his name.

Why hadn't he thought this through better? He should have realized the reverend wouldn't let him slip away. Perhaps if he made it look as though he was going home . . .

Yes, that's what he'd do. He was almost to the back door of the warehouse, and he seemed to be putting distance between himself and the reverend. If he slipped out the door, maybe the reverend would assume the urgent business he was attending to was at home, and the other man would choose to stay at the dance.

It was the best plan he had.

The moment he reached the door, he glanced briefly over his shoulder, then turned the knob and stepped into the night. He waited there for a moment, his chest heaving as he pressed his back to the wall of the warehouse.

Would the door swing open in another moment? Would the reverend follow him outside?

He wouldn't put it past the man. But the door stayed closed as one song ended and the fiddlers struck up a different tune. It was long enough for his breathing to return to normal and his face to grow cold with the faint droplets of mist brushing his skin.

Maybe he should just do as he'd led the reverend to believe and head home. He'd only been at the ball for half an hour, but that was long enough for others to take note that he'd attended. Though part of him was sorely tempted to head back inside if for no other reason than to remind Yuri to stay away from—

"Mr. Amos. Oh, good, you're still here." A slender woman with blond hair piled atop her head slid through the back doorway. "I've been wanting to speak to you."

Alexei stiffened, his body instantly on alert as he stared at the silhouette of none other than Rosalind Caldwell.

She gave a quick peek over her shoulder before closing the door behind her.

"I'm sorry. Did you say you've been wanting to speak with me?" He looked around, just to make sure someone else wasn't also loitering outside the back door.

"My father knows about the study." Miss Caldwell's voice sounded rushed and breathy, almost as though she'd run through a field to talk to him rather than taking a few steps outside.

He blinked at her.

This had better not be some type of ploy, something her father was putting her up to.

But what could the man intend by having the two of them alone out here in the dark? The only ploy he could think of was to have someone catch them together, insinuate something inappropriate had happened, and insist on marriage.

The idea was laughable. Preston Caldwell didn't want their families joined together any more than Alexei did.

"My father knows about the study," Rosalind whispered again into the darkness, her crystal-blue eyes deadly serious.

"I'm afraid I don't know what study you're talking about. Or why it would affect me."

Rosalind gave a petulant little huff, the type of sound he might imagine a wealthy child making when she didn't get her way. "Don't play the fool, Mr. Amos. It won't help matters. I'm not sure how my father found out, but the study is all he's been talking about for the past month. I figured you should know."

Alexei scratched the back of his head. Was she talking about Mikhail's expedition into the interior? What could Caldwell possibly know about the expedition that the rest of Sitka didn't already know—including himself?

"That's why he's taking your contracts. That's why he's starting the Bering Shipping Company."

The Bering Shipping Company. He'd seen that name on the letter from the most recent cannery to cancel their shipping contract.

Could Preston Caldwell be starting his own trading company for no other reason than to run the Sitka Trading Company out of business?

But why? What had he ever done to Caldwell to provoke such a ruthless string of actions? It was true that the two of them had never liked each other, but scathing looks and clipped, forced conversations were as far as their differences had gone.

"My father says it's only fair." Miss Caldwell glanced over her shoulder as though expecting the door to open any second to reveal her father. "That if you're going to take his revenue, then he's going to take yours. He's giving the canneries money to pay the early termination fee on your contracts. That's why they're all switching."

"I don't understand. What does Mikhail's expedition have to do with—?"

The back door swung open.

Alexei took a few steps away from the door and pressed himself against the shadowed wall of the building.

"Rosalind, there you are." Freya Eriksson peeked her head out. "Your father is looking for you, and he's not happy you appear to be missing. You'd better hurry."

"Yes, of course. I was just catching a breath of fresh air. The warehouse is feeling a bit cramped with all the people, wouldn't you say?"

Miss Caldwell disappeared inside with Freya, as though he and Miss Caldwell hadn't just been in the middle of a conversation.

As though the part of the conversation they'd had was somehow helpful rather than confusing.

Because she has no choice, you dolt. Because if she's trying to help you, she can't have her father find out.

But why would Rosalind Caldwell be trying to help him?

And why was her father starting a shipping company in direct competition and paying the early termination fees for the companies that left?

16

Juneau, Seven Days Later

Jonas looked at the ledger, then at the panning supplies sitting atop the largest cabinet in the trading post. According to what had been recorded, he should have twenty-two pans with screens, but he counted only twenty-one.

Could someone have slipped a pan and screen into their pack while whoever had been attending the store was busy with another customer?

He didn't know which Amos woman had last inventoried the supplies that had been brought over from the warehouse, but the writing in the ledger was both feminine and neat. It wasn't as though he was accidentally mistaking a one for a two.

But it was possible that she had miscounted. He'd nearly miscounted the beaver pelts earlier when Ilya had come up and started talking to him.

He made a mark beside the entry so that he'd remember to ask Evelina about it later, then closed the book. The trading post was empty at that moment, but a ship had arrived two days ago, bringing passengers up from San Francisco, and the trading company had been inundated with men who'd caught gold fever. Some of them had arrived well supplied for their prospecting ventures, but others had needed to purchase every last one of their supplies, and he and the Amos sisters had been busy.

The store might be experiencing a brief lull this afternoon, but the *Alliance* was due to arrive tomorrow, and according to Evelina and Kate, the store would once again be filled with customers for a day or two after its arrival.

But Jonas wasn't going to complain. Truth be told, there was something calming about working in the store. He never would have guessed he'd enjoy stocking rucksacks and pickaxes or chatting with the men who came in, each one determined he would be the next person to discover a vein of gold worth millions of dollars. After so many years of moving around, of sleeping in his own bed for only about a week before he was off on another mission, staying in one place felt rather nice.

Even if his knife wound still pained him.

In fact, the only thing he would change about the past week or so was his inability to track down Orville Jacobs.

He'd searched for the man every day, no matter how busy the store was. Some days that meant getting up early, missing breakfast or skipping dinner, and heading into the mountains for the last few hours of daylight. Or even stepping away in the middle of the day if Kate could tend the store.

But his searches had yielded nothing. In a creek, he'd lost the original trail he'd followed the day of the murder, and nothing he followed, no one he asked, had seen hide nor hair of a man matching the description of Orville Jacobs.

Prospectors up in the mountains weren't too keen on a stranger walking into their camp and asking questions, but Jonas wasn't going to apologize for trying to find the man who had murdered Betty Clement—and who would probably turn around and murder Sally Shephard if he learned what she knew.

Of course, there was always the possibility the man really had skipped town on the *Dockett*, the ship that had left the morning of the murder.

Everyone had thought the thief skipped town with Volker's money, but Jonas never quite believed it. And then he'd conveniently reappeared to murder the laundress, who had been expecting some type of payment from him.

That wasn't the pattern of a man who had skipped town but of a man who was hiding somewhere close.

Now if he could just figure out where.

A chorus of laughter filtered through the wall on the other side of the store, followed by the sound of Evelina's voice.

Jonas blinked away any thoughts of Orville Jacobs and turned to look at the door to the classroom.

As Evelina had feared, only a handful of students had shown up the day after Miss Thompson had barged into her classroom. But that had been two weeks ago, and the missing students had gradually filtered back into the classroom a day at a time until Evelina had all but two of her original students back.

More laughter echoed from the room, followed by the sound of Evelina calling the children to order again.

He couldn't help but smile—at the thought of her standing in front of the chalkboard teaching her students. At the sound of her voice. At the taste of her cooking. At the sight of her.

It seemed everything about Evelina Amos made him want to smile.

And why wouldn't it? She was gentle and kind and always volunteering to help. Plus, she loved her students something fierce.

And that said nothing about the way she looked when she tugged her scarf off her head and let her reddish-brown hair tumble in waves about her shoulders, or the way her eyes were the shade of a rich, deep emerald.

Jonas swallowed. It was almost enough to make a man want to get stabbed in the chest all over again if it meant he could stay with the Amos family a little longer.

But maybe he could stay anyway. Alexei was looking for a store manager, and even though the oldest Amos sibling had been gone for a couple of weeks, he hadn't sent anyone over from Sitka to take on the role.

He could always ask Alexei about hiring on as the trading-post manager the next time Alexei returned from Sitka.

But was that what he wanted?

Because for a man who'd come to Alaska to disappear, settling himself into the middle of a family business was only a step removed from putting down roots.

"Ship approaching!" a voice filtered in from outside the trading post.

More voices filled the air, and Jonas headed toward the window behind the counter to find a three-masted ship making its way toward the wharf. If he wasn't mistaken, it was the *Alliance* arriving a day ahead of schedule.

He stuffed the ledger they used to keep track of store inventory beneath the counter, then looked for the book that contained the orders expected to come in on the *Alliance*.

Where was it?

Kate had gone over it with him yesterday, showing him what had been ordered and then explaining that after the goods were unloaded, they would be taken to the trading post and checked against the ship's manifest before being handed over to the customers who'd ordered them.

Certain orders were standard and due to arrive every three

weeks. Like vegetables for the grocer, beef for the butcher, and flour and sugar for China Joe's bakery. But other items varied based on need.

Jonas had volunteered to check the goods they received against the orders and see to it that everything was stored in its proper place.

Now if only he could find the ledger.

"Mr. Darrow?"

At the sound of Inessa's voice, Jonas peeked his head over the counter. Both Inessa and Ilya had left the schoolroom.

"Lina said we could leave school to help!" Ilya bounced up onto the balls of his feet, his smile wide at the prospect of skipping out on a few hours of learning.

"That's what we usually do whenever one of our ships arrives." Inessa shoved a lock of long black hair behind her shoulder. "Keeping track of everything that's delivered is a bit much for one person. And I'm sure Kate is already on her way here. She would have seen the *Alliance* docking across the channel while she was at the Tlingit village."

"Good," he muttered, moving a stack of ledgers from the shelf to search behind it.

"What are you doing?" Inessa peered around the counter.

"I'm looking for the proposed shipping manifest. I went over it with Kate just yesterday, but now I can't seem to—"

"You mean this?" Ilya grabbed the ledger that had been lying on the far side of the counter against the wall.

Jonas sighed. "Yes, that." Why had he not thought to look on top of the counter? "I must not have put it away."

Ilya handed the ledger to him, then darted toward the door. "Let's go."

Jonas Darrow was a natural.

When Evelina had dismissed school a half hour early and headed over to the warehouse to help inventory the delivery, she'd expected to find a man overwhelmed by the activity and the sheer amount of goods being dropped off.

Instead, she found a man who was easily controlling the situation. He'd pulled a couple of the stevedores away from unloading the ship and had them using their handcarts to take supplies deeper into the warehouse. He'd drawn a map of the warehouse that he'd tacked to the wall, indicating which section of the warehouse stored which supplies, and he had Inessa, Ilya, and Kate checking goods off the list of orders as they got dropped off at the door.

Jonas stood in the middle of it all, a towering rock anchored in the ebb and flow of people around him.

She would offer to help, but she wasn't quite sure what she should do. He had every last bit of the unloading and storage process down to a science.

"Seems like he knows what he's doing, doesn't he?"

Evelina jumped at the sound of the voice, then turned to find Alexei standing behind her.

"You're back!" She threw her arms around her older brother.

"I am, though I'm not sure I'm needed." Alexei gave her a tight squeeze, lifting her off her toes for a moment before setting her back on the ground. "It seems Mr. Darrow has things under control."

"As soon as he was able to get out of bed, he started finding things to do around the store. You wouldn't think it by looking at him, but I swear he can sell three gold pans to a man who only needs one. And after the man buys all three, he leaves with a smile on his face. I try to sell one gold pan, and I get told I'm charging too much."

Alexei chuckled, his gaze drifting toward Jonas. "I'm happy to hear it. And of course I'm happy to see he's recovering. Do you know how much longer he plans to stay?"

She shook her head. "He hasn't mentioned leaving, which is probably for the best. I can't imagine him being a miner, can you?"

Her brother studied Jonas for a minute, his face growing serious as he gave a slow shake of his head. "He's large enough to haul rock. But as for actually enjoying the mining? No, I can't envision it."

Evelina let her own gaze slip back to Jonas, who was in discussion with one of the stevedores.

Then Jonas hefted an unusually large sack off the handcart onto his shoulder and strode toward the back of the warehouse. Her throat went dry. He was wearing a shirt today, so she couldn't see how the muscles played across his back. But after seeing him shirtless for over a week, she could well imagine how those muscles bunched and pulled beneath the weight of the heavy sack.

"Did you find anyone in Sitka to manage the store?" she asked, her eyes still pinned to the spot where Jonas would reappear in another moment or two.

"I didn't." Alexei heaved a sigh. "It's the same problem there as it is here. Everyone with any knowledge of mining or the area is being hired by wealthy prospecting teams."

"Maybe . . ." She shifted her weight and cleared her throat, then turned back to her brother. "Maybe you already have a manager. Maybe all you need to do is ask Jonas."

"Jonas, is it? He's not Mr. Darrow to you anymore?"

Her cheeks heated as memories rose of her and Jonas sitting by the fire one night last week, her knitting and him reading.

Mr. Darrow, do you think my students would enjoy hearing about living in a place where it's always sunny and warm, like where you're from? Would you mind coming into my class later this week and telling them about it?

They might enjoy that, yes, but do you know what I would enjoy?

She shook her head, the light from the fire casting orange shadows over his ruddy face.

Hearing you use my first name. Two people comfortable enough with each other to share an evening by a fire shouldn't be using surnames, don't you think?

She'd been calling him Jonas ever since.

"Is that a blush on your cheeks?"

She looked back up at her brother, then dropped her eyes to where her ankle boots peeked out from beneath the hem of her skirt. "I don't know what you're talking about."

"He'd make a fine husband."

Her gaze shot straight back to Alexei. "What would possess you to say that?" And how could her brother read her thoughts so easily?

Oh, she had to find a way to stop her heart from running away on her whenever Jonas was near. The man had never shown any type of romantic interest in her. And even more, she couldn't say why she was so attracted to him.

He was pleasing to look at, yes, and they might be using first names, but that didn't explain why she remembered every last detail of his muscled chest, especially now that he'd been wearing a shirt for two weeks.

Or why she still remembered the way his hand had felt clasped over hers, his thumb gently brushing her knuckle as he murmured kind words after Miss Thompson had barged into her classroom.

Oh, goodness. What had gotten into her? She needed to find a way to stop herself from being ridiculous whenever Jonas was around. He was a worker at the store, much the same as

Scott Paddington had been or Stephan Miller before him. Both of them had been bachelors, and she'd never had this kind of reaction to either of them.

"Reverend Jackson is curious to know when you'll return to Sitka. He says he has a question to ask you, and it's not the type of thing one asks in a letter."

She closed her eyes and groaned. "Did you know he's been sending me letters three times a week?"

Alexei smirked. "Gotta credit the man for being tenacious, especially considering how you wrote him and said you weren't interested in his attentions."

She shifted her weight from one foot to the other. "I . . . ah . . . didn't ever send that letter."

"Seriously, Lina?" Alexei raised an eyebrow, the action somehow filled with censure.

"I still don't know how to say what needs to be said."

"Figure it out—unless you want to marry the dunderhead?"

She slanted a sidelong glance at her brother. "Can't you tell him that I'm not interested in his attentions?"

"You think he'll listen to me?"

She sighed. That was the problem. As well-intentioned as the man was, he didn't have a lick of common sense—and wasn't willing to listen to anyone who did. "I don't suppose telling him that another man is courting me would deter him at all."

"I'd wager it would only make him hop on a boat here and propose."

She rubbed a brow, where a small headache was beginning to form above her eyes. "Does he know about my school yet?"

"He doesn't appear to, no, or I'm sure he would have said something. But it's only a matter of time."

She blew out a breath, her shoulders slumping as the air

deflated from her lungs. "I'll write to him and try to explain that I'm not interested in any sort of a future together."

"I doubt it will be enough to deter his feelings, but it's certainly a place to start." Alexei cocked his head to the side, watching Jonas as he hefted yet another heavy sack onto his shoulders and started down the aisle. "Do you know, when I arrived a few minutes ago, Grover Hanover saw me and came right over. He had an interesting story about how Janice Thompson barged into your schoolroom one day, spewing all kinds of uncharitable things about you and our family and your school. And then he said Jonas Darrow stepped in to defend you."

Her brother was going to switch from talking about Sheldon Jackson to talking about Jonas in a matter of seconds? It didn't seem like those two should belong in the same conversation. "He did, yes. I was quite flustered and wasn't sure what to say. He had a way of calming down the situation."

"First he saves Ilya." Alexei held up a hand with a single finger raised before raising a second finger. "Then he steps in to defend you when I'm gone, and now I arrive to find him running the *Alliance* delivery with more efficiency than an army sergeant." Alexei raised a third finger, then dropped his hand altogether. "And earlier you asked me why I think he'd make you a good husband?"

Alexei didn't even know that Jonas had spent the past two weeks keeping bullies away from little Sally Shephard, or that when someone stole a quarter from one of her students on the way home from school, Jonas had tracked down the thief and carted him to the jail, or how determined he'd been to figure out who had stolen two hundred dollars from Simon Volker. And that was before Betty Clement had been murdered. Now he spent every minute of his spare time searching the mountains for her killer, and with such intensity that she was starting to think Jonas might actually find him.

And somehow, in spite of all of that, he'd found time to take Ilya and his new friend Gushklin out prospecting twice.

"There's no question that Juneau is better for having Jonas here, but that doesn't mean he's interested in courting me. Maybe he has eyes for Kate."

"Kate doesn't look at him the way you do."

She clamped her mouth shut. Was she looking at Jonas Darrow with her heart in her eyes?

And if so, was there a problem with it?

Alexei leaned closer. "Have you told him that you're a lawyer yet?"

Evelina couldn't stop her entire body from tensing, never mind that her brother's voice was unusually soft, or that compassion filled the deep brown of his eyes. "Why would I do that? I'm not a lawyer anymore."

"You're still a lawyer."

"I am no such thing."

He sighed. "You passed the bar, Lina, and you write all the shipping contracts for the trading company."

"The contracts we keep losing? I don't see how that's very helpful of me."

Alexei clamped his jaw shut. "That doesn't change the fact that if you think Jonas might make you a good husband, then there are some things he should know about you—like that you graduated at the top of your class from Harvard Law School, one of only three women in a sea of men."

"But then I'd have to tell him about the Haliburtons." She nearly choked on the name. "And why I stopped practicing law."

Her brother looked at her as though she were daft. "Of course you'd have to tell him about the Haliburtons. One doesn't decide to up and marry a man while keeping this kind of thing secret—especially when everyone in Sitka knows what happened. And trust me, if Jonas stays here for any length of time, he'll make it to Sitka. Do you want him finding out about the Haliburtons from a bunch of gossips?"

She didn't want him finding out at all.

Or at least, she hadn't thought she did, but as she watched him help a Tlingit woman sort through a chest of tiny beads that had just been delivered to the warehouse, then offer one of her children a lollipop, she could almost see herself telling him. Almost see him understanding her story. Not just the horrors of what had happened during her last case six months ago—when she'd thought she'd been helping an abused woman—but what had propelled her to seek out a law degree in the first place.

And why she couldn't have helped Betty Clement with her lease before she'd been murdered.

Or why she didn't feel as though she could ever practice law again.

She looked back at Jonas, who patted the head of the small Tlingit girl happily sucking on her bright-red lollipop.

Could he be the one to understand all these things about her?

And did that mean the two of them just might have a future together?

17

He didn't remember the last time he'd felt so full. Jonas leaned back on his bed, his hand splayed over his distended stomach. After they'd finished unloading the *Alliance* and had inventoried all the items from the ship, Alexei had taken the entire family out to dinner at one of the hotels. They'd feasted like kings. Halibut and roasted potatoes, green beans and garlic sauce, and on the list went.

The dinner was a goodbye of sorts, because Alexei would be leaving on the *Alliance* when it set sail in the morning. He'd said something about needing to procure supplies to build a clipper, and he had been determined to make the most of his time with his siblings.

The man had been full of stories, half of them relayed from Sacha and his latest adventures in the Arctic, and half of them involving Yuri, who was evidently the youngest of his full siblings and who kept himself quite busy charming the women of Sitka.

Of course, Ilya had responded with his own stories, including giving his own account of when Jonas had stepped in to defend Evelina to Miss Thompson, and when he'd tracked down the boy who had robbed Gushklin, his Tlingit friend, on his way home from school.

All in all, it was a good time. And the Amos family was almost starting to feel just like that—a family.

Maybe even *his* family.

For some reason, that didn't make him want to run the other direction. If anything, it made him want to settle in.

A knock sounded on his door.

Jonas sat up straighter on the bed. "Come in."

Alexei had said he wanted to talk, and at the end of their conversation, Jonas expected to be a little more settled in Juneau—as the official manager of the Sitka Trading Company.

In some ways, it seemed too simple, especially after everything he'd gone through in Texas. But if his past work stayed exactly there—in the past—then why wait to create a new life for himself in Alaska?

Yet it was Evelina, not Alexei, who stepped into the room, her rich chestnut hair cascading in waves around her face.

"Is something wrong?" He stood from the bed. "Where's Alexei?"

"No, no. Nothing's wrong." She offered him a tentative smile. "I was just going through the mail that arrived on the *Alliance*, and you have a letter."

A letter? His shoulders tensed. He shouldn't have a letter. No one knew where he was, save his sister, and he'd given her explicit instructions not to contact him for four years, long enough to ensure he could safely start a new life under his new name and that no one from his past was searching for him. "Are you sure it's for me?"

Evelina raised an eyebrow, her eyes scanning his face as she stepped forward with the envelope. "Quite certain. It says your name, right here on the front. See? Jonas Darrow."

196 Written on the Mist

That was impossible. Everyone from Texas, from his years as a lawman, knew him by his real name—Jonas Redding.

He snatched the letter from her, only to find his false name really was written on the front—in his sister's dainty handwriting.

He sucked in a breath, the letter trembling in his hand. Why was she writing him so soon? Had her husband died? Or one of her children?

Could his sister and her family even now be dead because of him?

"I . . . um . . . I'll leave you to read it privately."

He heard Evelina's words, but they sounded far away as he stared at the letter.

The second the door closed behind her, he tore open the envelope, then scanned the feminine handwriting.

I pray you won't be upset when you receive this, seeing as how you told me not to write you. But after what happened today, I wanted you to know. There was a man who came to our house. He claimed to be a reporter named Luke, and he wanted to know where you were. I didn't tell him, of course, but I did promise I'd write to you and pass along his information.

She told him that she would write? Jonas's heart pounded against his chest. Was she daft?

What part of him telling her *no contact for four years* had been unclear?

He hadn't the faintest idea who this Luke was. Perhaps he was a reporter, or perhaps the reporter job was a disguise, and the man was really someone else . . .

Like Lucas Crowe?

Jonas suddenly felt sick. The seasoned criminal had escaped from prison in Texas shortly before he'd left for Alaska. He and his gang had been responsible for over a dozen bank and stage-coach robberies before Jonas had finally tracked him down outside of Amarillo. What if the man was bent on seeking revenge against the person who'd put him behind bars?

All this Luke fellow had to do was pay the worker at the general store to write down the addressee on Olivia's letter, and he would have his location.

Jonas pressed his eyes shut. All his hard work, all his efforts to leave what had happened behind him and start again some-where safe, and a single letter had ruined it.

Why hadn't Olivia listened to him? Why hadn't she cut off all communication?

Why had she even admitted to knowing him rather than claiming the man had the wrong house?

Did she want to end up like their mother? Like Harriet?

Could she even now be dead, murdered in cold blood after Luke obtained his address?

His stomach lurched, and nausea swelled in his belly. *Dear God, please protect her. Please don't let anything I did lead to her death.*

He sucked in a breath through his nose, though it did little to calm him as he forced his eyes back to the letter.

Please come home, Jonas. I'm as devastated as you about what happened to Ma and Harriet, but I don't feel as though that means I should lose my brother too. You're all I have left of our family, and waiting four years for you to visit is simply too long. If something happens to you in Alaska, will I even be informed? Or will you disappear into the wilderness, never to be heard from again?

Jonas's hands curled around the edges of the paper. Had his sister listened to nothing he'd said during their visit? Did she not understand how much jeopardy she'd just put the both of them in?

Think. He needed to think.

He drew in another breath, raising his gaze to the wooden beams of the ceiling above.

The letter had already been written and sent. There was nothing he could do to change that.

But what about this Luke character? He didn't remember any reporters back in Austin with that name—and more than a dozen of them had interviewed him after he'd helped bring down a Mexican crime lord.

Did that mean Luke the reporter was really Lucas Crowe?

No. No. No. He gave his head a small shake. He needed to calm himself, to think rationally.

Maybe this Luke fellow was harmless. Someone who really had interviewed him and needed some clarification on his notes, and he was letting himself get worked up for nothing.

But he had no way of knowing if his sister's visitor had been dangerous or well-intentioned. No way of knowing if Olivia and her family were even still alive, or if this Luke fellow had returned to her house after dark with deadly intentions.

Jonas pulled the envelope out from beneath the letter and looked down at it.

Olivia hadn't put a specific address on it. She'd just written "Jonas Darrow, Juneau, Alaska."

Seeing as how half the town already knew him as Jonas Darrow, the man Simon Volker had stabbed, he couldn't exactly change his last name without drawing even more suspicion to himself.

A quick glance back at the envelope told him the letter was postmarked nearly four weeks ago, plenty of time for "Luke" to travel to Juneau. In fact, he might have arrived on the *Alliance*, right along with the mail.

And Luke would track him straight here, to the trading post where Evelina and Ilya, Inessa and Kate all lived.

Jonas tossed the letter onto the bed, then crouched down,

reached beneath the frame, and pulled out his carpetbag and satchel. He didn't have much to pack, just an extra pair of trousers and a shirt. He'd need to buy panning supplies from the store, but he'd simply leave a note with some money for the supplies under his pillow.

"Jonas. I was wondering if you might . . ."

At the sound of the voice, Jonas turned to find Alexei standing in the doorway to his room. Had Alexei even knocked?

"What are you doing?" Alexei frowned at him. "Don't tell me you're leaving."

"I can't stay. I'm sorry."

Alexei pulled the door shut and came to the bed, his brow furrowed. "Why?"

"I just received news from home—urgent news."

The man rocked back onto his heels. "Did you tell the others you're leaving?"

"No. But I'll . . ." A sudden lump rose in his throat. Could he leave that easily? Ilya would be devastated, and Evelina . . .

Oh, how had things come to this? How had he let himself get so attached to the Amos family when he'd never planned to stay?

". . . I'll leave a note atop my pillow explaining that I needed to leave." His hand involuntarily gripped the spare shirt he'd just laid in his carpetbag. "Either Ilya or Evelina will find it."

"It'll be Evelina." Alexei spoke the words casually, but there was nothing casual about them. The trading-company owner was watching him with dark eyes, taking in everything he could about the situation.

An image of Evelina at dinner floated through his mind. Her long chestnut hair covered with a beautiful scarf that allowed locks to slip out and frame her heart-shaped face and deep-green eyes. Her lips curving into a smile as Alexei told them of Yuri's antics, and the gentle way she leaned over and squeezed Ilya's hand when the boy started relaying a story of his own.

There was part of him that could imagine himself staying here, running the trading post and seeing Evelina's smiling face at breakfast every morning, hearing her voice filter through the wall that separated the main part of the store from her schoolroom, listening to her tell stories of her students' endeavors each night at dinner.

Would she miss him? Be sad that he'd left?

"Were you even planning to say good-bye?" Alexei's words were sharp, cutting through the room with the authority of a man used to controlling everything and everyone around him.

And why wouldn't he speak that way? Alexei was in charge of five ships, countless trading posts scattered throughout Alaska's interior, and a shipbuilding company.

"I . . . No. None of this was planned, but it's best if I just go."

Alexei narrowed his eyes, and the air between them turned as chilling as the rain splattering the window outside. "I assume there's more to this situation than you suddenly deciding to leave for no reason."

Jonas closed and latched the bag and satchel with brisk movements that reminded him of Kate examining his wound. "I'm sorry. I wasn't planning to leave like this, but I got a letter this evening, and I . . . it . . . it changes things."

"I see." Alexei's shoulders slumped, and he blew out a breath, raking his hand through his hair. "It's just . . . Evelina has a delicate heart. She won't understand you leaving like this."

Jonas dropped his head. "Please tell her I never meant to hurt her."

"You'll hurt her anyway."

Would he? Did Evelina have feelings for him?

It didn't matter. He had no choice about leaving, at least not if he wanted to ensure her safety. "I knew another woman like your sister once. She was kind and gentle with a delicate heart."

Alexei cocked an eyebrow at him. "And you didn't bring her with you to Juneau?"

"She died earlier this year." The words filled the room, dark and heavy, and taking up so much space that it seemed there was hardly any air left to breathe.

Jonas waited for the pain to pass, for the hot, searing sensation that had lanced his heart to fade into a dull ache before he spoke again. "That's why I have to leave. So what happened to Harriet doesn't happen to your family. I hope you understand."

Alexei had grown stiff beside him, every last trace of understanding evaporating from his eyes. "Did you put my family in danger by staying with us, Darrow?"

Jonas looked at the letter still lying on the bed. "I . . . I didn't think I was. But now . . . I don't know."

"Get out." Alexei shoved his hand toward the door. "And I don't just mean go up into the mountains and then return to Juneau with the rest of the prospectors in a few more weeks when the snow comes. I mean you need to leave Alaska entirely. Do I make myself clear?"

Jonas's body turned as stiff as Alexei's. They could have been two statues placed in the room, staring at each other with bodies of stone rather than flesh.

"There's another ship due in port tomorrow. I'll look at booking passage on that one rather than the *Alliance.*"

It was a lie. He wasn't going to leave, not with Orville Jacobs hiding in the mountains, but Alexei didn't need to know that.

"It looks like you're finished packing." Alexei jutted his chin toward the carpetbag. "I'll escort you out and explain that you left in the morning. No need for the letter."

"I'd like to write one anyway."

"Not if it's as you say. Not if each minute you're here puts my family in danger."

Jonas swallowed. He didn't know for certain that his presence would bring danger, but at the same time, he couldn't guarantee the Amoses' safety. Pretending otherwise was nothing more than a lie.

And yet, he couldn't leave without attempting to explain himself. "Just a few sentences. I'll be quick."

Alexei crossed his arms over his chest. "There's pen and paper behind the counter at the front of the store. You can write your letter there. And then I expect you to disappear. Do you understand?"

"Completely."

The man turned and stalked from the room, leaving Jonas alone but for the sound of the cold rain hitting the window.

How had things turned into such a mess?

He'd come to Alaska to be alone, to rid his heart of the painful memories and dark emptiness that had been plaguing it.

So why did leaving the Amos family and heading off into the mountains suddenly make him feel more desolate and lonely than he'd been when he'd first started his journey?

18

Evelina stared at the note in front of her, her chest filling with heaviness. Never mind that she sat on a fallen log on the edge of a sandy stretch of beach. Never mind that the clouds above were light and wispy, covering the sun with a faint mist that might evaporate sometime later in the afternoon.

Never mind that she had a clear view of the mountains on the northern tip of Douglas Island or that the water in the channel was still as glass.

It was almost as though the beautiful scenery was mocking her.

And maybe it was, mocking both her and Jonas. How many times had Ilya bragged to him about Southeast Alaska being the most beautiful place on earth when it was sunny?

Now here was the first sunny day they'd had in all the weeks Jonas had been in Juneau, and he'd up and left.

In the middle of the night.

Without even trying to say good-bye.

She glanced down at the letter in her hand, the edges crinkled from holding it too tightly.

Dear Amos Family,

Her hand tightened even more around the paper. Jonas hadn't left a letter for her. He'd addressed it to everyone in the entire family.

And why wouldn't it be for the entire family? It wasn't as though they'd been courting. Wasn't as though he'd ever said or done anything that made her think he felt any differently about her than he did about Kate or Inessa or Ilya.

So why did her eyes insist on burning each time she read the greeting in the letter?

Why did her heart feel too heavy for her chest at the news that he'd left Juneau? Or her lungs struggle to draw breath?

She forced her gaze back to the half-memorized letter.

I'm afraid the things that first drove me to Alaska might well be following me here, which means I can't stay any longer. I thought about waiting to say good-bye in the morning, but time is of the essence, and it's best that I depart. Thank you for nursing me back to health and giving me a place to sleep for a few weeks. I will remember my time with your family with great fondness, and I wish everyone well in your future endeavors.

Sincerely,

Jonas Darrow

Evelina huffed.

Thank you for nursing me back to health? Was that all his time with her family had meant to him? Sure, he said he'd think of them with fondness, but the words felt so final, like he was never planning to come back.

Had he already left? Was he even now on his way back to California or wherever he'd come from?

Her eyes burned anew.

"Evelina?"

Alexei's voice carried on the air, and footsteps sounded on the sand behind her. She didn't turn around to look at her brother. Instead, she stared straight ahead, her gaze blindly focused on the mountain peak across the water.

"You should have told someone before coming out here." Alexei stepped over the log, then settled beside her on the dried piece of wood. "No one knew where you'd gone."

"If I'd told you, then you would have found me sooner."

Alexei was silent beside her, letting the sounds of the water and wind and birds fill the space between them.

It was almost worse than him talking. Her brother wasn't the type to traipse to the northern edge of town and pick his way down to the beach only to sit in silence.

"I know you had something to do with this." She shoved the letter at him.

He sighed. "It was Darrow's decision to leave."

"But you knew about it last night. Didn't you? Knew about it and didn't come get me. Didn't let me say good-bye. You just . . . what? Let him leave?" She shifted so she could look straight at her brother. "Did you even tell him I would miss him? Did you say anything about me to him at all?"

Dark shadows filled the space beneath his eyes, and faint lines creased the skin on the sides and around his mouth. "Jonas didn't want to hurt you. He wanted to protect you, even more than he wanted to protect Ilya, and that's saying something considering the bond between the two of them."

"And you just let him go in the middle of the night."

Again, her brother was silent. Too silent. It wasn't like him to say nothing, not when asked a direct question.

"Or are you the one responsible for him leaving entirely?" Tears filled her eyes, and her lungs burned.

"Not entirely, no." Alexei's jaw stiffened as he stared out over the channel. "But he won't be coming back."

She sniffled. "I don't understand. Why would you send him away?"

"I need you to trust me."

I don't. The words were on the tip of her tongue, ready to be flung out into the air between them. But her mouth refused to open.

Because the truth was, she did trust her brother. Ever since their parents and Ivan had died, Alexei had done nothing but take care of them and protect them.

But sending Jonas away? It caused a place deep inside her to ache. A place she hadn't even known existed.

"I was going to leave for Seattle today on the *Alliance.*" Alexei drew in a breath. "But I've decided to stay until Yuri gets here."

Those words alone were more revealing than Alexei probably realized. She might not know precisely what had happened between Jonas and Alexei, but her brother was clearly worried about leaving her and her siblings alone, when he hadn't given it a single thought yesterday.

"After Yuri arrives," Alexei continued, "I'll take the next ship south to Seattle. You should come with me."

"Come with you?" She reared back. "To Seattle?"

"We can find some kind of position for you down there. Perhaps as a nanny or a nurse. Heaven knows you have enough experience helping Kate that any hospital will hire you. But if you really want, you could go back to school and get your teaching certificate."

"And what would happen with the school I've started here? Am I just supposed to send my students to Miss Thompson's class? Even Inessa and Ilya?"

Alexei's dark eyes held her own with an intensity that made her suddenly want to shift on the log. "You don't want to be a teacher. Not really. I'm not saying you don't care for your students, but it's something to fill the time, not something you want to do forever."

Her skin suddenly felt too tight for her body. "So what's the real purpose of me going to Seattle?"

He extended his legs in front of him in the sand, stretching out as though relaxing. "To find you a husband, one from somewhere other than here. Alaska doesn't exactly attract the type of men I see you happy marrying."

She couldn't argue, at least not about that. "I don't need a husband to be happy."

"Oh, really? And just how happy are you here in Juneau? Or how happy were you before that in Sitka? If you were to work at a hospital, that would put you in contact with doctors. If you worked as a nanny for a widower, he might also be looking for a wife. I could see you happy raising a family with a husband like that."

She drew in a breath, long and full, letting the calming scent of the sea fill her lungs. Yesterday she would have said she was plenty happy in Juneau between teaching and seeing Jonas every day.

But now?

Everything felt so empty, and she'd not even realized that Jonas had meant so much to her.

Alexei picked up a small stick, then used the tip to draw a swirly pattern in the sand. "I look at Kate, and she could be perfectly happy doctoring for the rest of her days, whether or not she has a family. But you, Lina? You might look the same as your sister, but you're not drawn of the same cloth."

"Maybe you should have thought of that before you went and scared off Jonas Darrow."

Alexei jabbed the stick straight down into the sand. "I didn't scare him off, and you need to put any notion of a future with him from your head. He's got secrets, lots of them."

Memories of Jonas's bare chest rose in her mind. Not the strong, sculpted muscles but the scars that had marred them.

Yes, Jonas had secrets, and yet . . . "He's not some kind of criminal."

"How do you know?" Alexei's eyes darkened, his face growing so serious that a chill traveled up her spine.

Dear heavens, what had her brother and Jonas talked about last night? "You insisted on him leaving, didn't you? Even if he hadn't wanted to leave, you still would have forced him to go, and probably in the dead of night without letting him say good-bye."

"Alaska is a wild place. I won't apologize for wanting to keep you safe."

"Where did he go?"

"Even if I knew, I wouldn't tell you."

"You're the most high-handed, frustrating person I have ever met!" Her fingers dug into the smooth side of the log that the elements had long ago stripped of bark.

"If you don't want to get a job in Seattle, then let me write to a few acquaintances I have there. I'm sure you could stay with the family of one of our business associates for a few months, go to some parties and balls, meet some men your age. We've money enough to pay for a new wardrobe and some of the other fripperies. Maybe you'll meet someone who can make you happy."

"Will the man in your imagination be happy with me when he learns I'm a lawyer?" she gritted. "Or that, just six months ago, I made a public embarrassment of myself and my family?"

Maybe that's why Jonas's leaving bothered her so much. He was the first man she'd met that she could envision telling her story and not seeing disdain creep into his eyes. In fact, if she told him, he just might open his arms and draw her into his chest.

And then she'd know what it felt like to be pressed against

him, to have his big, strong arms surrounding her while the steadiness of his heartbeat thumped beneath her ear.

Alexei sighed beside her, the softening of his eyes saying he had about as much faith in the men of Seattle as she did, once they learned about her degree.

It didn't really matter that she and Kate came from a prominent business family in Sitka. Their chosen professions and Creole half half siblings were the types of things whispered about at parties and discussed in hushed voices in fancy churches filled with city folk.

Evelina dug her toes into the cool sand at her feet. "If your goal is to marry me off, then perhaps I should return to Sitka and pay more mind to Reverend Jackson's attentions."

The reverend knew everything about her, and he was still willing to marry her.

Maybe she was being too quick to discount him.

Alexei dragged in a breath, then reached out and settled his hand over hers atop the bare log. "My goal is to see you happy, remember? Don't try telling me that Reverend Jackson will make you happy."

Her brother was right. Again. And that only made her eyes burn anew, for what had to be the hundredth time.

"Evelina?" A voice called from farther down the beach. "Evelina? There you are."

She turned to find Kate crossing the beach with long, quick strides that seemed at odds with the peaceful beauty surrounding them.

"I've been looking all over for you."

Evelina stood, hope springing in her chest. "What is it? Has Jonas returned?"

Alexei let out a low growl, but Kate was already shaking her head. "There's a woman at the trading post. She wants to leave her husband and go back to Saint Louis, and she's asking for help."

"Oh." Evelina drew in a breath, but the air seemed to freeze in her lungs, turning into a thousand jagged pieces of ice. "You know my answer, Kate. I don't practice law anymore."

"Please, Lina." Her sister reached out and gripped her hand. "It's Myra Dressner. I know she's not our closest acquaintance, but you've heard the stories about her husband. Myra showed up half an hour ago with a black eye and bruises around her wrist, and I'm worried that if she doesn't get away from him . . ."

Evelina pressed her eyes shut for a moment, memories flashing of another woman with a black eye and bruises—and how she devised the wrong sort of plan to help the woman get away from her husband. "What did you tell her?"

Kate extended her hands to encompass her surroundings. "She read about the Haliburton case in the paper back when it happened. She already knows you can help. We *all* know you can help. The question is, will you?"

Evelina pressed a hand to her throat. There was a part of her that wanted to say no, that wanted nothing to do with the mess this kind of situation could lead to.

Because the only thing her involvement ever seemed to do was make these things messier.

But the last time she'd said no had been to Betty Clement, and one of the reasons she'd done so was because an argument with a landlord typically didn't put a woman in danger.

Even in Betty's case, her former landlord had been cleared of any murder charges.

Myra Dressner . . .

Evelina had seen her around town a time or two, always pale and gaunt, as though she never got enough food or fresh air. Always too skittish to make eye contact with another woman, let alone talk to her.

From what she knew, Myra's husband had been up in the mountains working a claim since the snow had melted last spring, but he must have returned.

If she'd come to the trading post for help, then the situation might be dire indeed.

And it was the entire reason she'd decided to study law.

She drew a shaky breath into her lungs, then met her sister's eyes. "All right, I'll meet with her."

Surprise flashed in Kate's eyes.

"But just this once. And only because the woman's in danger."

"Thank you." Kate closed the distance between them and wrapped her in a fierce hug. "Think of the difference you'll be able to make."

It was just the type of thing Kate would say. How one person could be so eternally optimistic about the impact a single woman could have on the world, she didn't know. But Kate had been that way for as long as she could remember.

"Just pray that things end better this time than they did last time," she whispered into her sister's ear.

And then she set off down the beach. Because no matter what had happened with the Haliburtons, she couldn't stand by and watch innocent blood be shed at the hands of a violent man.

19

Near Juneau, Fourteen Days Later

Another camp. Another dead end. Jonas tromped away from the campsite he'd spent the morning spying on. Everyone had risen from their tents after dawn and shared breakfast around the fire, all while he'd been crouched in the brush, looking for Orville Jacobs.

But there was no man with a silvery ponytail working this claim, just like there'd been no blue-eyed man with a silvery ponytail working the claim before that, or the one before that.

He'd been in the mountains two weeks, searching for Simon Volker's thief and Miss Clement's murderer, but no matter how many claims he visited or conversations he struck up on the trails, he hadn't found a single clue as to where Orville Jacobs had gone.

Maybe the rumors flying around town were true. Maybe Jacobs had left Juneau the morning of the murder. Maybe he'd planned it that way.

But Jonas still couldn't bring himself to believe it. Not

considering how the man had similarly vanished after stealing from Volker, only to return to town for the murder.

That was a pattern of movement from a man who was hiding somewhere in the area. If Jacobs hadn't left town after stealing, he would bet everything he had that Jacobs hadn't left town after committing a murder. And he needed to find Jacobs before someone else got hurt.

Like little Sally Shephard.

Or the Amoses.

Jonas sucked in a breath. Where had that thought come from? There was nothing to indicate Orville Jacobs had turned his attention on the Amos family.

But then there'd been nothing to indicate that Jacobs had set his sights on Miss Clement either. In fact, there'd been nothing to indicate the two of them had even known each other.

At least not in Miss Clement's things. Which he'd gone through four different times in the week after the murder.

A gust of wind blew down from the top of the mountain, and Jonas snuggled deeper into his coat, thankful for the thick fur that kept him warm as the days turned progressively colder.

Most of the men he met on the mountain were still wearing slickers and thought him strange for wearing a winter coat when winter had yet to arrive. But it would arrive soon enough, and the prospectors would head out of the mountains.

What about Orville Jacobs? Would he skip town then? Find a ship to take him to warmer weather in Washington or California?

Would he winter in the mountains?

Or would he come to town and pay another early morning visit on a defenseless woman?

Jonas didn't know. So he ducked his head against the bitter wind and trudged down the faint path toward the next claim.

SITKA, **Nine Days Later**

"Yes, Mrs. Traverton. I believe you've mentioned your niece before." Alexei attempted to smile at the woman in front of him, but the muscles around his mouth felt tight. "More than once, actually."

The gray-haired widow blinked. "I have? Did I tell you she's coming to visit next summer?"

"You did," Alexei gritted, looking past the woman toward the large building behind her that housed the government offices in Sitka.

"Perhaps I can have you over for dinner. I think you might really enjoy her company."

"Perhaps." He rubbed the back of his neck. "But she might enjoy the company of another gentleman too, of which Sitka has plenty."

The woman stepped forward and patted his arm, a kindly smile on her face. "That may be, but none are in need of a wife quite so much as you."

I'm not in need of a wife. But rather than growl the words at the sweet old widow, he pressed his lips shut.

Why did everyone think he needed a wife? Because he was the oldest of his siblings? Because his family owned two long-standing Alaska businesses?

Or was there another reason?

He shook his head, then stepped away from the good-hearted woman whose husband had spent more than twenty years working at their family's shipyard before suffering a heart episode and dying. "It's very kind of you to be concerned about my marital status. Now if you'll excuse me, I need to speak with the Marshal."

If he could find the man.

After being gone from Sitka for a few weeks, Alexei had arrived back in town last night to learn that the Marshal was finally back in Sitka. Apparently the man had returned a day or two after Alexei had left.

"The Marshal?" Widow Traverton's gray eyes rounded in concern. "Whatever for? Has someone committed a crime?"

"Not that I'm aware of." And he wasn't about to elaborate, no matter how large the widow's eyes grew; otherwise, Winifred Traverton would have news of his visit with the Marshal spread around town before lunch. "I heard there might be a change to the tariffs on goods imported from Japan, and I want to make sure I understand them."

The widow gave him a blank look, then patted his arm again—for what had to be the tenth time in a matter of five minutes. "Oh, well, I best let you get to it."

"Thank you, ma'am." He gave her a nod, which he tried to make look polite rather than hurried, then slid past her before she figured out that if he had a question about tariffs, he needed to visit the office for the Revenue Cutter Service, not the Marshal's office.

Alexei tugged the collar of his slicker closer to his neck to ward off the wind coming from the ocean as he trudged the rest of the way up the hill. A fine rain was falling, which the widow hadn't seemed to notice when she'd spied him heading up the path to the government offices that sat atop Castle Hill.

Alexei pushed open the large wooden door with its series of ornate carvings, then let it fall closed behind him, trying to ignore how the Americans had reduced the once stately governor's mansion, with its elaborate foyer and intricate woodwork, into nothing more than a series of offices.

It should be a crime, really, to take such a lovely display of Russian architecture and reduce it to something so boringly practical. But muttering about it each time he entered the building was hardly going to change things, so he headed up the grand, curving stairs to what had once been the mansion's bedrooms.

The Marshal's office had been stuffed into a room that was probably a bathroom or small dressing chamber before renovations had given the room a door that opened directly into the hallway.

Alexei knocked once, then cracked open the door to find Norman Hibbs seated behind his desk, a cookie in his hand as he studied a stack of papers on his desk.

"Good morning, Marshal."

"Alexei." The Marshal stood, his chair screeching as it scooted backward against the wood floor. "I heard you were out of town. It's good to see you back."

"I arrived last night." Alexei stepped into the office and closed the door behind him.

"Here. Sit, sit." The man gestured to one of the empty chairs across from his desk, then held out a plate of cookies. "Want one?"

"I . . ." Alexei blinked at the plate, which looked to already have a couple cookies gone, never mind that it wasn't yet time for lunch. "No, thank you." He seated himself on the chair.

Marshal Hibbs took a seat as well, sweat beading along his balding head despite the cold rain outside. The man's stomach was so large, he couldn't pull himself fully up to his desk, and Alexei couldn't imagine the Marshal ever catching a criminal in a footrace.

And yet, this was the only Marshal Alaska had and it wasn't as though there was a younger, healthier assistant who could be called on to chase a particularly lithe outlaw.

The Marshal swiped another cookie from the plate, then stuffed a bite into his mouth before speaking around the food. "How are you this morning?"

"I'm . . ." He wanted to say good. That was the acceptable thing to say. But was he good? He didn't know how to tell such a thing anymore. And more importantly, it had nothing to do with why he'd come.

"I'm busy." He nodded toward the desk covered in papers. "I can see you're the same, so I'll keep this quick."

The man took another bite of cookie, then handed him two separate sets of papers. "Did you come here for the results of the murder investigation over in Juneau, or the official ruling on the Simon Volker case? Those are both the reports."

"The murder investigation?"

"Into Betty Clement's murder? Your sisters used her for their laundry. Kate determined the cause of death, and Evelina gave testimony as to her upstanding character. Both their names are in the report."

Alexei flipped through the handful of papers until he found Kate's name and a copy of the death certificate with her signature, followed by Evelina's name, with a glowing statement about how diligent Betty Clement was at picking up and returning their laundry in a timely manner.

Juneau had been abuzz with news of the laundress's death when he'd stopped there on his way to Seattle, but he'd been too preoccupied with family matters to pay much attention. "Did you find who killed her?"

The Marshal shook his head. "No, and I don't expect we ever will. The murderer skipped town on the ship that left at dawn."

"Do you know why she was murdered?"

Again, the Marshal shook his head. "All I know is that she was late paying rent. She told the landlord one of her customers hadn't paid her, but no one seems to know who, and it must have been a large amount of laundry if a single customer refusing to pay meant the difference between having rent money or not."

"Perhaps it was the hotel or one of the boarding houses."

"No. I checked. The hotel maids do their own wash, and all four of the boarding houses I checked had receipts for their most recent payments to Miss Clement."

Alexei studied the paper for a few more seconds. Something about the case seemed odd. Why would a washerwoman not have enough money for rent if all her large clients seemed to have paid?

But solving a cold murder case wasn't why he'd come. He set the report back on the Marshal's desk and scanned the official court report for the Volker case. He paused when he reached the words printed in bold at the very bottom of the paper. *Sentence: Five years.*

"As for Simon Volker, you'll be happy to know that the man who attacked your friend was sentenced to five years in prison." The Marshal shoved a particularly crumbly bite of cookie into his mouth, causing crumbs to scatter across his desk. "The Revenue Cutter Service will be transferring him to the penitentiary down in Washington by the end of the week."

A sense of calm should have come over him. It was excellent news, the kind of thing he would normally be happy to hear. But the sight of Jonas Darrow's name in the report only made his stomach twist. "He's not my friend."

The Marshal blinked. "What was that?"

"The man who was stabbed . . . Jonas Darrow. He's not my friend. In fact, he's why I came to see you."

The Marshal frowned. "He was the person Simon Volker stabbed, correct? No one in Juneau argued that point."

"Yes, he was stabbed trying to defend Ilya, and Simon Volker certainly deserves a prison sentence for his actions. But I'm concerned about why Jonas Darrow came to Alaska in the first place. At first I thought he was honorable. I mean, I left him alone at the trading post with my sisters so Kate could tend him while he recovered. But the longer he was there, the more something about him seemed off. He came to Alaska because he's running from something, and I'm wondering if what he's running from . . ." Alexei cleared his throat, resisting the sudden urge to start squirming in his chair. "If maybe he's running from the law."

The Marshal sat back, his half-eaten cookie falling to the desk. "You think Jonas Darrow is a wanted man?"

"I doubt his real name is Darrow, but yes. Or at least, I think it's worth checking into. Was he there for the trial?"

"No. He left town a couple weeks before I arrived."

Good. If the man hadn't returned for the trial, then hopefully he'd left Alaska entirely rather than heading up into the mountains.

"What does the report say he looked like again?" Marshal Hibbs reached for it, and Alexei handed it over. "He's tall. Probably six foot or better, with curly red hair that he keeps cut fairly short."

"And his eyes? What color are those?" The Marshal stood and headed toward a shelf filled with papers. "We can always check the wanted posters and see if his description matches."

"Brown." A deep, sincere brown that seemed at odds with the man being a criminal. But the fear in Jonas's eyes on the night he'd left Juneau had been a real thing. He was running from something, and he was scared.

What could a man like that be running from other than the law?

The whole situation made him want to shake his fist at the sky. How could he have let such a dangerous man so near his siblings? What kind of brother was he to not see the threats a stranger like Darrow might pose?

He was the kind of brother who'd been thankful Ilya hadn't been injured.

But why would a criminal on the run—someone who clearly had no trouble shunning the laws and mores of society—step in and voluntarily protect a Creole boy he barely knew?

Alexei sat back in his chair, a long breath shuddering from his lungs. That was the part he still couldn't make sense of, no matter how many times he went over it in his head. That, and Darrow's concern over the possibility he might put others at the trading post in danger.

Because there was no question he'd been worried on the night he left, but a law-abiding man arriving at the trading post wouldn't pose a danger to his family, and Jonas had definitely seemed worried for them.

Alexei didn't know how to get to the bottom of it, at least not without asking the Marshal. So here he was, sitting in a hard wooden chair while the Marshal riffled through a thick stack of wanted posters.

"This one has red curly hair and brown eyes." The Marshal pulled a thick, crinkled paper from the stack and handed it over. "What do you think?"

Alexei studied the drawing staring back at him. The likeness wasn't perfect, but if the artist had never seen the man before, maybe this was the best sketch a person could draw. All of the other details seemed to match. According to the poster, the wanted man—Jedidiah Cuthbertson—was over six feet tall with curly red hair and brown eyes.

"It says here that he's wanted for counterfeiting?" That didn't seem terribly dangerous.

"Yes." There was a team of four counterfeiters in Montana. They got into a gunfight with the Marshal and sheriff who found them." Marshal Hibbs's face turned grave, and he dabbed at his sweaty hairline with his handkerchief. "The sheriff didn't make it, I'm afraid. Two of the criminals were caught at the scene, but Cuthbertson and another man, Milo Simmons, escaped. Simmons was caught a month later in California, but there's been no sign of Cuthbertson, and the rumor is he escaped with most of the counterfeit money."

"Montana's not terribly far from Seattle," Alexei muttered. And if Cuthbertson didn't know that Simmons had been arrested, he might assume the other man was still searching for him—right along with every lawman on the West Coast. That would give Darrow reason to believe Evelina and Ilya might be in danger if the other criminal came looking for him.

"No. Seattle ain't far from Montana." Marshal Hibbs slid his damp handkerchief back into his breast pocket. "And from there, it's just a few days' ship ride up the coast."

"It is, indeed."

"Does the man on the poster look like Jonas Darrow? If so, I'll send word to the other Marshal offices and have his alias put on the next printing of the poster."

Alexei sighed. He didn't know. Could the same person who saved his brother also have killed a sheriff? He didn't want to falsely accuse a man of a crime he didn't commit.

But what other reason would Jonas have for running to Alaska, and then turning around and needing to flee after getting a letter?

If only the likeness on the poster looked a little more like Darrow, maybe he could give Marshal Hibbs a more definitive answer.

A brisk knock sounded on the door, and it flung open behind him.

Alexei turned to see none other than Rev. Sheldon Jackson rush inside.

"Alexei. There you are. You're a rather hard man to track down."

"Reverend." Alexei pushed to his feet. "You're looking for me? Not the Marshal?"

"Yes, yes. The post just came, and I got the most disturbing letter from Miss Thompson. Do you know who Miss Thompson is?" The man came closer, not stopping until the tips of his shoes were only a few inches away from Alexei's boots.

"Ah . . . one of your teachers?"

"The teacher at the day school in Juneau."

"All right."

"It says the most outrageous thing! I would hate to cast any aspersions on Miss Thompson's character." The reverend flapped the letter around, not bothering to hold it still long enough for anyone else to confirm anything other than the obvious fact that the paper was, indeed, a letter. "And I'd certainly never accuse Miss Thompson of lying, but she must be lying. Truly she must. Because it says here that Evelina opened her own school in Juneau, in direct competition with the new one where Miss Thompson is teaching!"

Oh. *That*. Now the wild gesticulations and high pitch of the reverend's voice made a bit more sense.

"I don't believe it," the Marshal blustered. "Evelina Amos would never do such a thing. Why, she values the education of the natives nearly as much as you do, Reverend. Surely this must be some kind of misunderstanding."

Alexei winced. "I . . . um . . . wouldn't call it a misunderstanding, per se."

The reverend blinked at him, two wide, owl-like eyes staring through the thick lenses of his spectacles. "Then what would you call it?"

"You should think of Evelina's efforts in Juneau more as tutoring than a formal school. Not all of the students are able to attend school for a full day, so my sister is trying to give them a semblance of an education. I'm sure it's not nearly as good as the education the students would be receiving from Miss Thompson." Alexei ignored the churning in his stomach as he forced the bitter words from his tongue. It was all he could do to keep a straight face, but he needed Jackson to believe him, or it would only mean trouble for Evelina. "You're aware my sister doesn't have her teaching certificate."

"Yes, I am aware Evelina doesn't have her teaching certificate—yet. But she has such a heart for the indigenous population. If the two of us were to marry, and she were to do an apprenticeship at the industrial school—under my direction, of course—I'm sure I could get one of the colleges back home to grant her a teaching certificate. Then think of all the good we could do together for the aboriginal peoples of Alaska!" The reverend's voice pitched even higher, his eyes bright.

"Your sister wants to marry the reverend?" The Marshal brushed some crumbs from his cookie onto his vest.

Alexei cleared his throat. "I think it's more that the reverend wants to marry her."

The Marshal leaned back against his chair and smiled. "Well, that's an excellent idea. I can't think of a more well-suited match. She needs a bit of . . . stability in her life, wouldn't you say, Alexei?"

Alexei slanted a glance at the Marshal. "You're referring to the Haliburton debacle, I assume?"

"Yes." The Marshal tugged his handkerchief back out of his pocket and mopped at the sweat beading anew on his brow. "We certainly don't need a repeat of that."

To his way of thinking, the only part that didn't need to be repeated was everyone laughing at his sister and her fleeing the courtroom in tears—but that wouldn't be the part the Marshal was referring to.

"Of course." Rev. Jackson straightened, drawing himself up

to his full height—which was probably a good three inches shorter than Evelina's. "There will be no more scenes like what happened with the Haliburton case once Evelina is married to me."

Alexei's shoulders tensed. "Has it occurred to you that my sister might not want to marry?"

"But why ever not?" The reverend blinked at him from behind his ridiculously thick glasses. "She's twenty-one. Or is it twenty-two?"

She was twenty-four—not that he was going to explain that to the reverend.

"And she's clearly in need of a husband. And here I am in need of a wife. It's a match made in heaven."

"Right."

"When you go to Juneau next, I simply must accompany you. Then I shall ask her to marry me and bring her back to Sitka. I was going to wait until she returned on her own, but now I must investigate this tutoring business and see for myself why Miss Thompson is so upset. Plus, the longer your sister is gone, the more keenly I feel her absence. And she's not very good at returning letters—something I'll be sure to work with her to rectify once we're married. So as you can see, I simply must go to Juneau with you. When is your next trip planned?"

In two days. "I'm not sure."

"I can pay you handsomely for the passage. And you can help me procure a spruce-root basket for my museum while we're gone."

Because that's what he wanted to do. Help the reverend get more frivolous things for his museum on his way to propose to Evelina. Alexei clamped his lips together, careful not to agree to anything.

Though if the reverend was truly set on accompanying him

to Juneau, he wasn't sure he'd be able to wriggle out of bringing the man along.

When he left Evelina, she'd still been upset with him and pining after Darrow. Now when he returned to Juneau, he'd be bringing a man who'd be furious when he saw her school but would probably still propose, convinced he'd be able to change Evelina's ways once they wed.

At this rate, he'd be lucky if his sister ever spoke to him again.

20

Near Juneau, Two Days Later

K ate had been right. He wasn't nearly strong enough to be hauling rock out of the earth.

Jonas slumped against the side of the crude bunkhouse that had been slapped together with poorly-fitted logs. After more than two weeks of wandering around attempting to find Orville Jacobs, he'd made his way over to Silver Bow Basin, thinking that perhaps the man might be blending in with other miners at one of the operations along Gold Creek, and he could find Jacobs best by blending in.

Even though it was late in the season, the Perseverance Mine had three times as much work as they did men. Getting hired on had been simple enough, but after five days of pushing carts laden with rock out of the tunnel and up to the surface of the mountain, he could tell his knife wound was on the brink of tearing itself open again.

Jace, the foreman who lived in the cabin next to the bunkhouse, had given him the day off to recover, and with tomorrow being Sunday, he'd have that off as well. But two days wasn't going to be long enough to regain strength in his chest.

Jonas drew in a breath, staring out at the peak of Mount Juneau rising out of the north side of the basin. Not that he was complaining. The view above ground was beautiful—and certainly less foggy than the bottom of the valley where Juneau sat. But it didn't make up for the dark tunnel where he'd spent the past five days or the cold, dank air that surrounded him underground. Nor would he miss living in a bunkhouse with men who went by names just as false as Darrow and looked just as shady as the criminals he used to track for a living.

But what would he do with himself once he left?

With winter coming on fast, the Perseverance Mine would pack up for the season as soon as the creek froze.

He'd give that about another week. Maybe two.

He could search for Jacobs until the snow came, but then what? He'd need to either head back to Juneau or learn how to winter in the mountains.

The trouble was, if he got snowed in, he wouldn't be able to look for Jacobs or keep an eye on things in Juneau.

As it was, he'd made time to slip into town at least once a week—and not just to see if Jacobs had been spotted.

It had been almost a month since he'd received that letter from Olivia, and two since she had written it. Yet to the best of his knowledge, no one had arrived looking for a man by the name of Jonas Darrow.

If whoever was looking for him had paid off the clerk at the post office, then he should have arrived in Juneau long before this.

Did that mean he'd been worried about nothing? Had the "Luke" his sister had written of truly been a reporter? Or was Lucas Crowe out there searching for him, determined to seek revenge on the man who had put him and his gang behind bars?

He didn't know. But it seemed the immediate danger—if there had ever been any—had passed.

Which meant he'd left the Amos family for nothing.

His heart hurt when he thought about it. Yet another regret to plague him each night when he lay down and attempted to sleep.

But why did leaving the Amos family bother him so much?

He'd said good-bye to his sister's family with nary a thought, yet here he'd stayed with the Amoses for a handful of weeks, and he found himself wondering what Ilya would talk about if the boy were with him, traipsing through the forest looking for gold.

He also found himself thinking of Evelina's smile, or recalling the way her hair reflected in the . . .

Singing. Someone was singing. No, not someone. A woman. All the way up in the mountains.

Jonas turned his head in the direction of the voice, just as a figure in a dress appeared through the trees on the forested path that led to town.

What reason did a woman have to come up to Silver Bow Basin?

And was it just him, or was there something familiar about the voice that was singing?

The woman stepped into the clearing, and he had no doubt it was one of the twin Amos sisters.

Maybe it was Kate? Coming for some kind of medical emergency?

He looked toward the entrance of the mine, but there was no indication anyone had been injured. And if someone had needed to go to town for the doc, Jace probably would have sent him, seeing as how he was too weak to lift anything.

Did Kate come up to the basin for routine medical checks?

Except the woman crossing the clearing wasn't Kate. First,

because she was singing, and Kate Amos wouldn't dare waste time doing something so frivolous. And second, because Kate always pulled her hair into a bun and walked with a brisk sort of efficiency.

The woman on the opposite side of the clearing had a brightly-patterned scarf covering her long hair, and gently picked her way around a rock and over a fallen branch.

What was Evelina doing here? And by herself? He watched the path through the woods for any other sign of movement. Maybe she was taking Ilya and Inessa for a walk in the mountains? Or maybe she was accompanying Alexei or one of her other brothers up here?

But it seemed as though she was alone.

Completely, entirely alone.

While there was a murderer on the loose in the mountains.

Though to be fair, Evelina didn't know that last bit—no one did except for him.

She carried a basket on one arm, and her voice rose and fell with the melody of a song as she walked, a beautiful, rich contrast to the pulsing thrum of the stamp mill.

She didn't pause to glance around the basin but headed straight toward the foreman's house.

That was even stranger. Why would she be visiting the foreman? He was probably in his office at the moment, or perhaps in the mine.

She stopped singing as she approached the door, then knocked. A moment later the door opened and she slipped inside.

Jonas shoved himself off the side of the bunkhouse and started across the mossy ground. He had to be imagining what he'd just seen. Surely Evelina hadn't just entered a man's house by herself.

But the door to the little house stayed firmly closed.

"THIS IS EXCELLENT WORK, Job. See how much your handwriting has improved since we started lessons?" Evelina pulled one of the papers she'd collected on her first trip to Silver Bow Basin from the folder inside her hamper and slid it across the table to the boy.

"Yes! See how far you've come?" Job's older sister, Agnes, sent the small boy a smile.

Job picked up the old paper, a lock of dark hair falling over his forehead.

There was hardly enough light to see the words. The foreman's hastily-built cabin had only one window, and it was barely big enough to provide light for cooking, let alone reading. When she'd first started coming up to the basin, the weather had been warm enough that they could open the door, allowing enough light to do their lessons, but the air today was too chilly for such a thing.

Job's eyes moved between the old paper and the most recent round of copy work he'd done, then a smile crept across his face. "You think I'll be able to write as good as Pa one day?"

"Don't see why it matters." George, the middle of the three Lidding siblings, muttered. "No one but foremen and mine owners need ta be able to read and write. And there's only so many of those types of jobs to go around."

Agnes stiffened. "I, for one, am thankful for Miss Amos coming all the way up here to—"

The door to the cabin burst open, bringing a chilly gust of wind with it.

"Evelina? Is everything all right?"

She straightened at the sound of the voice, then turned to find none other than Jonas Darrow standing in the doorway.

She could only stare. At the tall form filling the doorway.

At the broad expanse of his muscled chest. At the strong set to his jaw and the dark look in his eyes.

"What . . . ? What are you doing here?" she rasped.

He'd been gone from the trading post for nearly a month, but during that time, she assumed he'd gone back to California or Oregon or wherever he was from. That he'd settled in somewhere, found a job, and moved on with his life.

But he clearly hadn't left Alaska, and now he was towering in the doorway with a glowering look on his face.

She wasn't sure whether she should glare at him and demand to know why he'd left in the dead of night, or run to him, throw her arms around him, and say she was glad to see him.

Because she *was* glad to see him. And because she still thought of him too many times throughout the day. When she sat down to breakfast with the rest of her family. When Miss Thompson came back to the school, and Evelina defended herself rather than allowing someone else to do it. When a ship docked and she and Kate found themselves scrambling to inventory the goods being unloaded without Jonas's help.

When she lay down at night and dreamed of one day finding a man who wouldn't be ashamed of her.

Her cheeks burned. Oh, goodness, here she'd been in Jonas Darrow's presence for a matter of seconds, and her thoughts were already running away on her.

"Do ya need somethin'?" George asked, his gaze leveled at Mr. Darrow. "'Cuz I'm pretty sure they're still workin' in the mine. Ain't that where you're supposed to be?"

Jonas stepped farther into the cabin, barely sparing the boy a glance. "I was checking on Miss Amos. I saw her come up the trail and thought it strange she'd be headed to the cabin of an unmarried miner."

That's why he'd come to check on her? Because he thought she and Mr. Lidding were . . . were . . . ?

"I'm teaching school," she bit out, shoving her hand toward where the children were seated around the table.

"On a Saturday?" He crossed his arms in a manner that made his chest seem impossibly broad.

"I can't very well teach during the week, at least not without letting my other students down."

"Miss Amos comes every three weeks to teach us," Agnes said, her voice soft in the cabin. "We don't got no ma to do it. We'll be headed to Treadwell as soon as the creek freezes and go to school there, but Miss Amos didn't want us to get behind."

Jonas surveyed the room. Hopefully he was taking note of the papers and books scattered across the table, and the large hamper with school supplies.

She wanted to ask how he was, if he'd been in the basin ever since he'd left town, if mining suited him. But all she seemed to be able to do was stare. His hair had grown long enough to curl around the edges of his ears. But his shoulders seemed even broader than she remembered, his eyes an even deeper shade of brown.

Why did you leave us like that? The words almost burst from her tongue, but she held them in. He didn't owe her an explanation.

Except it felt like he did. Like there had been something growing between them—even if the two of them had never spoken of it. Even if he'd never asked to court her.

Then she'd woken up one morning to find nothing but cold air in the place Jonas Darrow had once occupied in her life.

"Where's your brother?" Mr. Darrow scanned the cabin.

That's what he decided to ask? She was probably a fool for letting it bother her. But really, of all the words that could have come out of his mouth, he was asking about Ilya? "He went

with Kate to hold a clinic in the Tlingit village across the channel. He's become friends with one of the boys from school
and—"

"I'm not talking about Ilya," he snapped. "I'm talking
about Alexei or Yuri or either of your other brothers old
enough to act as your escort while you traipse about the
mountains."

"Oh." She winced. Alexei would not be happy if he learned
she was up here by herself, though Yuri would be more rational
about it. "My brothers are all in Sitka at the moment. Yuri's
been in Juneau for most of the month though, and he should
return sometime next week. He just had to make a quick trip to
Sitka."

"But he's not here now." Mr. Darrow stalked to the wooden
chair beside the cabin's single bed and plopped himself down.

She frowned. "Whatever are you doing?"

"Ensuring your safety. Now carry on." He gestured toward
the table, where the three Lidding siblings were watching them,
as though their odd conversation was the most interesting thing
that had happened all month.

And it probably was. Not much beyond mining took place
in these mountains.

But surely Mr. Darrow didn't mean to sit there the entire
time she taught? She'd be here for at least another two hours.

"Shouldn't you be working in the mine?" George glared at
Mr. Darrow.

"Got the day off." Jonas's hand slid to his chest, resting over
his injury.

Was it paining him?

"I hope your day proves restful," she muttered, because for
some reason, the thought of him being in any pain, even a pinch
of it, made her own chest ache.

Which was utterly foolish. The man had already walked

out of her life once. He'd have no trouble doing it again in twenty minutes when he grew bored of her teaching.

So she turned back to her students, bracing herself for Mr. Darrow's inevitable departure and promising herself she wasn't going to let herself care when it happened.

Except he didn't leave. He sat there the entire time, watching her with a look she couldn't quite explain but also wouldn't be able to forget.

When she finally packed up her books two hours later, confident the Lidding children had enough schoolwork to get them through when the creek froze and the mine closed, he stood and picked up her hamper.

"I'll carry this."

She shook her head. "Thank you for the offer, but I'm headed back to town now."

"Town . . . another mining camp with children who need to be taught . . ." He waved his hands absently. "You can go wherever you want, but you're not going by yourself."

Part of her wanted to tell him she didn't need his assistance. It's certainly what Kate would have done.

But Alexei truly would hate the idea of her coming up to Silver Bow Basin by herself. And while she'd never had any trouble with men in Juneau treating her poorly, the trip here had been awful lonely.

"Thank you, Mr. Darrow. I won't insist upon having your escort, but I won't claim not to be grateful for it either. The choice is yours."

"I choose to escort you," he said. "And I choose to carry this basket."

21

"I really can carry the basket. It's no trouble."

Why was Evelina offering to carry the basket again? Jonas looked at her on the trail ahead of him, her brightly-patterned scarf pulled up to hide her hair. It had to be the fifth time she'd offered, and it seemed as though they had just left the mining camp.

Jonas grunted in response, then shifted his balance to maneuver around a rock in the trail. That meant bearing most of the weight from the basket on his left arm, which caused pain to flash through his wound.

Another grunt erupted from his mouth, and this one had nothing to do with the ridiculous notion of letting Evelina carry a hamper full of books down the mountain.

"Please, Mr. Darrow. I can tell that your chest is paining you, and I'm perfectly capable of carrying it."

Mr. Darrow. She'd been calling him that ever since he'd shown up at the foreman's cabin. As though this was the first time they'd met, and they were little more than strangers.

He probably deserved it. After all, he'd been the one to up and leave her family with only a simple letter of explanation.

But he still missed the sound of his name on her tongue. She had such a soft way of speaking it, as if she were using her words to give him a hug.

"I have two arms. I'm just as capable of carrying the basket as you." And he'd be hanged if he let a woman cart such a heavy load down the mountain while he carried nothing.

She sighed. "When we get back to the trading post, you should wait for Kate to return from the Tlingit village. She'll want to inspect your injury."

"I need to get back up the mountain before dark." It wasn't true. He was perfectly comfortable navigating the mountain path at night. After he saw Evelina to the trading post, he'd head down to the bar and listen to the chatter, see if anyone had arrived in Juneau looking for a man with red hair and brown eyes.

Or if anyone had seen a man with a long ponytail.

A rather steep section of trail stretched before them, and Jonas shifted the basket so he could hold it with both hands. He groaned again, the weight of the books tugging at his knife wound.

Evelina sighed, but she didn't say anything more about carrying the basket. She also hadn't said anything about his abrupt disappearance, leaving her and her family without so much as a good-bye.

They'd been walking about a quarter hour, and he'd expected it to be the first thing out of her mouth once they were alone. Instead, she'd been mostly silent, and he didn't have the first clue what she was thinking.

Had she been surprised to find him at the Perseverance Mine?

Had she been disappointed when she'd woken one morning a month ago and found him gone?

Had she missed him?

Jonas swallowed, his palms turning slick against the handle of the basket. Should he ask?

Or maybe he should tell her that he'd missed her.

Which was ridiculous. Because he hadn't missed her.

He'd just thought of her. A lot.

Like how she left her hair long and free, falling about her shoulders in thick chestnut waves. How she was so quick to smile at her students when they arrived for class each day, and so gentle when she spoke to Ilya, telling the boy things like no, he really couldn't take three days off school to prospect down by Sheep Creek himself.

He also couldn't help thinking about how he'd enjoyed sitting at the table with her family and taking part in their playful banter. Or witnessing the way they all cared so genuinely for one another.

Jonas pressed his free hand to his chest.

"Your wound is paining you again."

This time it wasn't. But just how was he supposed to explain the real reason for the ache beneath his breastbone?

"My wound is healing a bit more every day."

Her eyes flashed. "Mr. Darrow, you can stand there and insist that you have to carry the hamper because I'm a woman and you're a man and you're too stubborn to use common sense. But don't lie to me. It's beneath you."

He blew out a breath. "Fine, perhaps my wound has become aggravated lately, but I have no doubt it will heal in time."

She huffed and lengthened her stride, eking ahead of him as she rounded a bend in the trail.

"Evelina." He quickened his own pace. "It does me no good

to escort you down the mountain if you refuse to walk beside me."

"I told you I didn't need an escort."

It was a simple task. Escort a single woman home. He'd done it more times than he could count over the years.

And yet he was mucking it up today.

He sighed, then tipped his head back to stare at the sky. Except he couldn't see the sky. Swirling gray mist greeted him instead. No vast blue or wide expanses, no landscape that allowed him to see for miles. The sky was clearer in the mountains than it ever was down in Juneau, and there were even a few days where the sun had broken through the misty wisps of clouds. But even then the views weren't as clear as back home.

"I miss Texas," he muttered.

Evelina stopped, her head cocking to the side. "Is that where you're from? Texas?"

He hadn't meant to give that away, but he didn't want to feed her any more stories either. "Yes, I lived there my entire life."

He expected the questions to come—a slew of them about why he'd left and what had really brought him to Juneau.

But instead, Evelina's brows pinched together, and she waited for him to catch up to her. "What do you miss most?"

He barked out a laugh. "The sun."

"Yes, I daresay I'd miss the sun too, if I were from Texas." She gave her head a small shake, surveying the gray mist that grew thicker with each step they descended into the valley. "And here I thought you were going to say you missed your family the most."

"My family's dead."

The words were out before he could stop them, almost as though his brain couldn't quite manage to work with Evelina walking so close to him. Because he certainly hadn't meant to tell her that—or anyone else in Alaska.

Her throat worked. "I'm so sorry. I had no idea."

"No need to apologize. It's not your fault."

It was his.

She reached out and gripped his free hand, her palm warm and comforting as she skimmed her thumb over his knuckles. "I'm not apologizing because I had some kind of part in it. I'm apologizing because losing family hurts."

Jonas blew out a breath. "Thank you."

"Was it recent?" Her brows pinched together, concern creasing into lines around her eyes and mouth.

"We best keep going." He pulled his hand away from her and started down the trail at a pace so brisk, Evelina had to rush to keep up.

She didn't complain, just hiked up her skirt a few inches and hurried over the uneven terrain. "What was it like, growing up in Texas? Did you grow up in the city or the country? Did you have a horse? A ranch where you raised cattle? Don't people do that in Texas?"

He didn't quite smile, but there was something about her statement, about how very little she understood regarding cattle, that made him *want* to smile, even after talking about his family.

"Yes, people ranch in Texas, but my pa was the blacksmith in a small town a couple days' ride from Austin, the capital. He died when I was a boy, and my ma moved us to Austin. Easier for a woman to find work in the city."

She had more questions. He could tell it by the way her brows had pinched together again and she poked her tongue into the side of her cheek.

"What about you?" He blurted before she could ask anything else. "Where did you grow up?"

She gave him an odd look. "You already know that. Sitka."

Right. So maybe that wasn't the best question to distract her with.

"What was it like?" He cast a glance at the dark fog that was beading into watery drops atop the thick fur of his coat, even if he couldn't see any rain. "And please tell me it's not as rainy as Juneau."

She laughed, a bright, sparkly sound that contrasted with the gloom around them. "You and the sunshine. It's almost as if you're obsessed with it. But no, Sitka is on the open ocean, and while the mountains still hold air from the ocean overtop of them, it's not quite as dreary and enclosed as Juneau. There the rain comes and goes. In Juneau, the dense clouds just sit on top of you, trapped between the mountains on Douglas Island and the mountains behind us. But honestly, more than missing the weather in Sitka, I miss the culture."

"Culture?" What type of culture could possibly exist in the wet, muddy mess that was Southeast Alaska?

"When Alaska was owned by the Russians, they called Sitka the jewel of the Pacific, and they sent the very best of the best to Sitka. Did you know that our last Russian governor was married to a princess?"

Our last governor. She spoke as though she considered herself more Russian than American, even though she couldn't have been more than a few years old when America purchased Alaska.

"There were plays and operas and ballets, things of beauty that everyone on the island could enjoy." She waved her hand haphazardly down the trail toward Juneau. "The Americans, on the other hand, think of Alaska as something to be exploited. There are no plays anymore, no traveling orchestras. The American government keeps putting men who don't understand a thing about Alaska here and expecting them to govern it. It is quite sad."

He rubbed the back of his neck. He'd never stopped to consider just how haphazard the American way of doing things might look to a family that was familiar with Russian rule. "So why don't you return to Russia like everyone else?"

"Because there's nothing for our family in Russia, no city or town with aunts and uncles. Everything we have is here. My great-grandfather was a shipbuilder from Maine. He came to Russian America in 1790 and started the Amos Shipbuilding Company. Back then, the Russian-American Company was responsible for all the trade in Russian America. But there was nowhere for the ships that the company owned to be repaired, and most of those ships were sailed from the capital of Russia, Saint Petersburg, which is near Finland on the Baltic Sea. That meant the ships had to cross the Atlantic and sail clear around the cape of South America before coming north up the Pacific Ocean."

That would be quite a trip. Any man with half a head for business would be able to see the need for a shipyard. "I'm sure the Russian-American Company greatly appreciated your English ancestor choosing Sitka as the place he wanted to start his shipyard."

"I'm sure you're right, but not as much as my great-grandfather appreciated the daughter of the governor who was stationed in Sitka at that time." She sent him a wink.

An actual wink.

It was all Jonas could do not to choke on his tongue.

"They married, and he used his skill with wood to build a house on Sitka, one that our family still owns to this day."

Jonas cleared his throat. "Just like you still own the shipyard."

"Exactly."

He cocked his head to the side, studying how a lock of hair had worked its way out from beneath the side of her scarf, creating a rich contrast between the reddish-brown color and the deep pink-and-blue hues of her head covering.

And there he was letting himself get distracted again. He needed to focus on Evelina's story, not on how she looked walking through the woods.

It wasn't as though he'd asked her permission to take her for a walk or had invited her on a picnic or anything of the like. "Coming from Maine to Sitka would have been quite the trip to make, especially back in those days."

Evelina made a small humming sound in the back of her throat. "I don't think my great-grandfather had much choice, at least not after he was charged with murder."

"Murder?" He stopped on the trail, his eyebrows shooting up.

Evelina trotted past.

"Was he guilty?" He stumbled forward before she made it to the next bend in the trail.

She shrugged. "It's hard to tell, though I read the legal filings when I was in Boston."

"You were in Boston because of Kate, right? Isn't that where she went to medical school?"

"Yes."

He tried to imagine her sitting there, poring over a century-old stack of files in the cramped basement of a courthouse. "What did the filings tell you?"

"That he was wanted for the murder of a woman he'd been courting. But as I said, it was quite unclear whether he'd done it. She was from a family far wealthier than his, you see."

"Wealthier than a family of shipbuilders?" Jonas rubbed the back of his neck. That was a bit hard to imagine, considering how Alexei seemed to own the world.

"Much wealthier than that, unfortunately. My great-grand-father, Ezra was his name, had no contact with Elisabeth the day she was murdered and had spent all day and part of the evening at the shipyard. Apparently the shipyard was on a deadline to complete a ship by the end of the week, and employees were working long into the night. But when Elisabeth was discovered strangled to death in her room the next day, a warrant was issued for his arrest, and he fled. It was quite the scandal. Every newspaper in New England ran articles on it."

They continued down the trail in lockstep, drawing nearer and nearer to town. "Let me guess. They all said Ezra was guilty, and that was why he fled."

"That's where it gets interesting." She tucked the wayward lock of hair back beneath her scarf. "Many of the articles I read surmised that Elisabeth's father was guilty, either him or her eldest brother, both of whom were known for their tempers. But accusing the owner of a prominent fur trading company—who also happened to be friends with a member of America's newly formed Senate—of murdering his daughter . . ." She shrugged. "Well, why do that when it's much easier to blame a shipbuilder's son?"

His mind was spinning, trying to connect the clues she'd given him. He'd spent too many years as a lawman to turn that part of his brain off, even for a hundred-year-old case. "Seems like Elisabeth's father had a good reason to want attention pointed toward your great-grandfather. But it also seems rather suspicious that Ezra didn't stay to defend himself. Why not proclaim his innocence in court?"

"Maybe because he was facing such a powerful adversary that he knew he'd end up convicted, regardless of the truth."

Jonas's breath froze in his chest. *It's not the same. Not what I went through with Ma and Harriet.*

244 Written on the Mist

After all, he hadn't been framed for a murder he didn't commit.

No, that had been another man, barely eighteen years of age, who'd gotten tangled up in his last case. The true killers had been found before the framed man went to court, but the adversary they'd faced had almost been powerful enough to see an innocent man hanged for a crime he didn't commit.

Just like their adversary had been powerful enough to kill the family of anyone trying to stand in his way.

Jonas tried to suck in a breath, but his lungs still seemed frozen, the world going dark around him.

"Mr. Darrow? Are you all right?"

Evelina's voice sounded far away.

"It's the basket, isn't it?" She sunk her teeth into the side of her lip. "Oh, I knew it was too heavy for you. Here. Let me take it. We're almost to town."

She tried to tug the hamper away from him, but his hands clamped down on it.

"It's not the basket," he rasped.

"Then what?"

He gave his head a small shake. "Something you said. It just . . . brought back memories."

Wrinkles creased her forehead, and concern filled her eyes. "Not very good ones, it seems."

He grunted, then straightened and took a small step forward. "This story about your great-grandfather being framed for murder, has it been passed down through the years, from one generation to the next?"

"It has." Evelina didn't say anything about him ignoring her statement and moving back to her story. Perhaps somehow she understood that he needed a distraction. "Ezra Amos lived to be an old man. At some point, long after the fur trader had died, he told the story to his wife and children, and on the story lives."

"And that explains how the Amos family came to be. A Russian family with a British surname living in America."

"Yes, or perhaps we are just an Alaskan family."

Yes, the Amos family had deeper roots in Sitka than many ranchers did in Texas. "Did your grandfather and father marry Russian women or American ones?" Just how American were the Amoses?

The last of the trees gave way, revealing the rough and tumble collection of log buildings that was Juneau. It was raining in earnest now, making the town even drearier than the last time he'd traveled down the mountain.

Evelina pulled her scarf tighter about her head and surged ahead of him as the trail widened into a road. "Officers sent to Russian America had to be married and bring their wives with them. It was the tsar's decree. So there were always women in Sitka. Both my father and grandfather before him found wives without issue. In fact, my mother was the governor's daughter."

"Didn't you say your great-grandfather also married the governor's daughter?" Now he was the one rushing to keep up with Evelina as she turned down one road, then another, weaving her way through the streets of Juneau toward the trading post.

"It seems to run in our family." She slid him a glance, a faint blush tingeing her cheeks. "Just ask Alexei, if you don't believe me."

"Don't say your brother is in love with the current governor's daughter?" He scrubbed a hand over his face. "I didn't think Alexei thought highly of how Alaska is being run."

"Oh, not this governor, no. That was several governors ago." A frown creased Evelina's brow. "And it didn't turn out as happily as the story of my great-grandfather's or my father's. In fact, now that I think of it, you best not mention it to him. I have no idea how he would respond."

He hadn't planned to. It wasn't as though he'd be staying in Juneau for more than a few minutes, and the two of them weren't exactly friends, especially considering how adamant Alexei had been that he leave and never return.

But the idea was intriguing. Alexei Amos looked and acted as though he controlled the world. Could a woman have caused him so much misery that he was unwilling to speak of the subject?

Bang! Bang! Bang! A pounding sound echoed through the town.

He and Evelina turned the corner onto the main road that ran between the wharf and trading post.

Bang! Bang! Bang!

Through the rain, Jonas could just make out a large man banging on the door of the trading post. He lifted his hand to pound again, but Evelina was already rushing forward.

"Mr. Dressner. Can I help you?"

The man turned, and something about the way he moved had Jonas quickening his pace too.

"You," he bellowed, narrowing red, bloodshot eyes at Evelina. "I want my wife."

Evelina stopped in front of him, plastering a smile on her face that even a babe could tell was fake. "I'm afraid I don't know what you're . . ."

The brute raised his hand as though to strike her, but Jonas was faster, dropping the hamper into the mud and stepping between the drunken man and Evelina. "Is there a problem? Because I'm sure you weren't about to strike a woman. Just like I'm sure you're aware an action like that will land you in jail for the night, sheriff or not."

"She stole my wife," the large man wheezed. "I know she's

got Myra locked up in there. Fred said he saw her standing by the curtain before lunch, and I'm here to take her back home."

"She's a person, Mr. Dressner," Evelina snapped from behind him. "Not a piece of property."

"Oh, I'll own her, all right. As soon as I get my hands on her, I'll—"

"Treat her with the utmost respect, as you would any woman." Jonas straightened to his full height. He had no idea how Evelina had ended up hiding this man's wife, but the last thing he was going to do was release her to a drunkard with violence glittering in his eyes.

Dressner's jaw clenched. "If you don't give Myra to me, I'll report you to the Marshal. Have you brought up on kidnapping charges."

"On what grounds?" Evelina planted her hands on her hips, her eyes blazing green fire. "Your wife has filed for legal separation, which will be granted on Monday, and which will be followed by a divorce once she returns home to her family. She is not yours in any way, and if you wanted her to stay living as your wife, then you shouldn't have been so cruel to her."

The large man lunged toward Evelina, but once again Jonas was faster, moving in front of the drunk before he could take so much as a step in Evelina's direction. "You hit Miss Amos, and you'll be in jail for more than just one night. I guarantee it."

Dressner didn't so much as look at him. Instead, he kept his gaze latched on Evelina, his eyes seething with rage. "You're wrong, you know. The judge isn't going to grant you that separation. He's going to take one look at you on Monday, and he's gonna laugh you out of that courtroom, just like last time."

Jonas felt more than saw Evelina go stiff behind him, felt more than saw the fear swirling through her.

It shouldn't be possible to feel things that another person felt, especially without looking at her. But there was no other way to explain the sudden coldness he felt swirling through his own body.

"Spousal abuse is not a laughing matter." Jonas met the man's gaze. "Now you've got five seconds to get out of my sight, and if you're not gone by the time I'm done counting, I'm going to haul you to the jailhouse. Threatening another person is just as much of a crime as disorderly conduct. I don't care if I need to call for a meeting of the Committee of Public Safety. I'll see to it that you spend tonight in jail, and maybe tomorrow, and the night after that."

"I'm going, I'm going." The man took a step back. "But I'll be back, and I'll see to it the lot of you pay."

Jonas watched for a moment as the man stumbled his way down the road, then he turned to Evelina. The backbone she'd used to face the drunk seemed to have completely disappeared, leaving her looking vulnerable and frightened.

Jonas settled a hand on her shoulder. "What is he talking about with court on Monday? And how did you end up tangled up in the middle of this?"

"The hearing for Myra's separation is on Monday, when the traveling judge will be in town. If she wants the judge to grant it, she needs to testify against her husband."

"But how does this involve you?"

She swallowed, then looked down, the rain plastering her scarf to her head and causing a wet tendril of hair to cling to her cheek. "Remember earlier how I said that I went to Boston with Kate?"

"Yes."

"And remember before, when I told you that I went to teaching school in Boston, but it was miserable and I dropped out?"

"Yes."

"Well, after I dropped out of teaching school, I went to law school."

Law school. He could only stare. Since when did they let women into law school?

But Evelina didn't seem to expect him to have any questions about how a woman might obtain a law degree, because she was prattling on about making a terrible lawyer and dropping out of teaching school and not practicing law anymore. About how everyone in Juneau knew Bruce Dressner beat his wife when he was drunk, and no one would be surprised to find her dead one morning. So when Myra came to her for help, she hadn't been able to say no.

And then Evelina was silent, looking up at him with her large green eyes and nervously twisting her fingers together in front of her.

"A lawyer," he whispered.

The gentle woman in front of him. The woman who tried to help every last person she met. She'd gone to law school and embarked on a profession reserved for men.

He couldn't understand the courage that must have taken, the complete and utter resilience.

It was all he could do to leave his hands at his sides, when he wanted nothing more than to pull her against him and tell her she was the bravest woman he knew.

22

"What do you mean you said he could stay downstairs?" Evelina stilled, her knife poised above the onion she was about to mince. "Mr. Darrow already left us once. I see little reason to invite him back."

"Says the person who told Myra Dressner she could stay with us." Kate didn't look up from where she stood on the other side of the kitchen table, rolling out the dough for the pelmeni —traditional Russian dumplings—that they would soon be having for dinner.

"That doesn't mean Mr. Darrow is welcome." It was one thing to see Jonas up in Silver Bow Basin after not knowing where he was or what he'd been doing for the past four weeks. It was another thing entirely to invite him back into their home —into their lives.

Mr. Darrow had been completely irrational after Mr. Dressner left. The man had refused to leave the trading post, claiming it wasn't safe to leave her or Myra or the rest of the family unprotected and proclaiming he was staying until Yuri returned from Sitka.

Then after Kate returned and looked at his injury, the two of them had emerged from the examination room both convinced that Mr. Darrow should stay at the trading post.

It was most infuriating.

Evelina drove the knife down into the onion. "Alexei wasn't pleased with Mr. Darrow when he left last time."

Kate snorted. "You were the one who was most upset. You and Ilya. I don't think Alexei ever expected him to stay."

He didn't? But she'd thought . . .

Oh, it didn't matter.

All that mattered was Mr. Darrow had left once, and while she might be able to smile at him if they passed each other on the street, she didn't intend to let him back into her life as fully as she had before—not when he could up and leave again at any time.

"If this would have happened last week when Yuri was here, then we could send Jonas on his way. But Yuri won't be back for a few more days." Kate picked up the glass cup on the table, turned it upside down, and used it to cut the dough into circles with brisk, methodical movements. "So if having Jonas stay here until Yuri returns will deter Bruce Dressner, then he is more than welcome."

"We're perfectly capable of taking care of ourselves." Evelina sliced through the remainder of the onion, dicing the pieces as small as possible to mix with the ground venison and spices that would soon fill the dumplings.

"You're being ridiculous." Kate cut the last circle, then set the glass down with a thump. "I don't fancy myself strong enough to take on the likes of Bruce Dressner if he decides to barge in here in the middle of the night. And I don't know why you would think that you could either."

Kate used the bottom of her apron to wipe a bit of flour from her cheek. "Truly, Lina, what were you thinking? Myra

252 Written on the Mist

might need help, but why did you say she could stay here while Alexei was gone? Bruce Dressner is cruel and violent when he drinks—the entire town knows it—and it's not too much to think that he might try to attack one of us for hiding his wife."

Evelina stirred the dumpling filling with her hands, blending the onion and spices and venison together before plopping the first bit of filling into the center of a doughy circle. "What was I supposed to do when she showed up this morning with a broken arm and a black eye? Send her away?"

Kate's shoulders slumped. "No, I wouldn't have wanted that. I probably would have done the same thing, but I certainly wouldn't be upset that Mr. Darrow appeared and wants to stay here. That seems like a blessing from God. What do you have against the man?" Kate pinched the dough on the edge of the filled dumplings together, sealing them for cooking. "He deserves our thanks for what he's doing."

"He left us in the dead of night," she whispered. The pain of waking up the next morning and reading the curt letter he'd left opened anew in her chest. She might have been civil with him on the walk down the mountain. Might have even enjoyed telling him about her family history and learning that he was from Texas. He'd always been a kind, considerate man. But that didn't mean she was willing to trust him again, especially not as easily as she had last time.

"He saved Ilya and has shown other kindnesses to our family. That should count for something." Kate sealed another dumpling. "Besides, this is just for a few days. When did you say Myra went to court? How long will she be here?"

Evelina drew in a breath. Perhaps she was being dramatic, making this whole situation into something bigger than it was. "Three nights, assuming her petition for separation goes through on Monday, that is."

"Then that's all the longer Jonas needs to stay. After that, we'll ask him to leave, even if Yuri still hasn't returned."

"But what if Myra doesn't win the petition?" This would be the first time she'd be in court since the Haliburton case, and just the thought of Judge Lincham glaring down at her from the bench caused her tongue to turn dry.

What if she messed up again? What if she ruined everything because—?

"Judge Lincham will have no choice but to grant the separation." Kate tucked a wayward strand of hair that had escaped her bun behind her ear. "The entire town knows Myra's husband beats her."

It was true. Usually Dressner was up in the mountains until the snow came, but this year he'd returned to town twice. The first time had been a month ago, after which they'd filed the petition for separation. The bank attendant who also worked as the clerk when court was in session had tried to deliver the court papers to Dressner but hadn't been able to find him in the mountains.

But Dressner must have gotten word of the coming court date somehow, because he'd returned.

"So what happens after court?"

Evelina blinked at her sister. "Hmm?"

"You said Myra only needed a place to stay for three nights, that's tonight, tomorrow, and Monday night." Kate scooped the dumplings into her apron and carried them to the stove, where she dumped them into the pot of already-boiling water. "Then what happens?"

"The *Alliance* is due back in town on Tuesday, and Myra wants to return to Saint Louis, where her brother lives, until the divorce can be finalized."

"Does she have money to pay for the trip?"

"I told her Alexei would grant her free passage to San Francisco." Evelina grabbed the rag from the sink and turned back to the flour-covered table.

"And after that?" Kate covered the pot with a lid. "I'm assuming her abusive husband isn't going to give her money for passage from San Francisco to Saint Louis so she can divorce him."

Evelina pinned her gaze to one of the worn grooves in the table as she washed it. "I may have given her a bit of my spending money."

"Of course you did."

"Don't act like I'm doing something wrong."

"You're not. You're just . . ."—Kate dusted her hands on her apron—"being you. Which means you're trying to help others at any cost. Or without first stopping to consider what that cost might be. It's not bad, but it can certainly make things difficult on us. Now keep an eye on the dumplings while I gather the others for dinner."

"I'm not trying to . . ." *Make things difficult.* But Kate had already left the room.

It was probably just as well. She was twenty-four years old, and she still hadn't figured out how to defend herself to her sister.

Kate was so sure about everything she did, never questioning herself or wondering whether she might be wrong, even when that meant she went toe-to-toe with a male doctor who'd been practicing medicine for fifty years.

And then there was her. Evelina rounded the table and trotted toward the sink. She couldn't stop wondering whether she was wrong, no matter what she did or how much she tried to help others.

She pumped water into the sink and rinsed out the rag, then waited a few minutes for the dumplings to finish cooking.

She took a plate to Myra first. The poor woman was

nursing both a broken arm and a black eye and didn't feel up to eating in the kitchen.

When Evelina returned, she found Ilya, Inessa, Kate, and Mr. Darrow all seated at the table. She took the empty chair at the far corner, as far as possible from where Mr. Darrow sat at the head.

Ilya's smile was ten shades brighter than it had been at breakfast that morning. As soon as they finished praying, he regaled Mr. Darrow with tales of how he'd gone prospecting down by Sheep Creek and explored the woods with Gushklin, one of the Tlingit boys from her class who had gold fever almost as bad as Ilya.

Evelina pushed dumplings around on her plate as Mr. Darrow turned the conversation from Ilya to Kate, asking how her medical clinic went at the Tlingit village that day. After that, he asked about other goings-on in town. If the Finch boys had been leaving little Sally Shephard alone, how China Joe's bakery was doing, and if anyone in town had spotted the man with the ponytail who had stolen Simon Volker's money.

It all seemed so normal, like a dinnertime conversation they might have had weeks ago, before Mr. Darrow left.

Was she the only one who cared that he'd walked out on them one night, disappearing into the mist?

"Are you okay, Lina?" Inessa leaned close, keeping her voice down while Ilya informed Mr. Darrow that Simon Volker had gone to trial and gotten himself locked up for five years, then had been shipped to Washington for prison.

"I'm fine." Evelina speared a dumpling with her fork, but rather than put it in her mouth, she pushed it around the side of her plate.

"Is it court on Monday? Is that what you're worried about?"

"You're worried about court?" Ilya piped up from his spot

across the table. "You got nothin' to be afraid of. You'll show them this time. Just wait. It won't be like last time."

"I'm glad you're doing this." Kate sent her a smile. "It will be nice to see you back where you belong."

Except she didn't belong there. That was the problem.

And everyone was far too excited about Monday, because helping a woman like Myra was a far cry from practicing law in full.

"I'm not going back. I just want to see Myra's petition granted." She took a sip of water. "Actually, Kate, I was wondering if you might go to court in my stead. The case is simple. I can tell you what to say, and if you wear a scarf and keep your hair down rather than pull it back into a bun, everyone will assume you're me."

Kate narrowed her eyes. "Until I open my mouth."

"That's why you should be the one to go. You're better at thinking on your feet, and after last time with Judge Lincham . . ." Her throat grew tight, every last bit of moisture leeching from her mouth.

And there she sat, completely tongue-tied, just like she'd been in court that day last spring, while everyone at the table stared at her as though she'd grown a third ear on her forehead or an antler from her chin.

At least her family wasn't laughing at her the way all the men had. That was something.

"What happened last time?" A deep voice filled the kitchen, and her head swung toward Mr. Darrow.

For a few minutes, she'd forgotten he was there. "Nothing."

"Her defendant lied," Ilya pronounced, his voice happy and carefree. "Mrs. Haliburton told Lina that she didn't kill her husband on purpose, that it was self-defense when he was trying to beat her silly, but she planned it all along. Got herself some arsenal and put it in his coffee one morning after he beat on her."

"Arsenic," Inessa corrected. "Arsenal is a pile of guns. Arsenic is a poison."

Mr. Darrow glanced at Inessa, then Ilya, before raising his eyes to meet Evelina's, their gazes tangling across the table. "So you lost the case?"

Lost the case.

He made it sound so simple, as though it was a mundane thing every lawyer went through, when the ordeal had been so much more than that. "I feel a headache coming on. I best retire for the night."

"Lina." Kate sighed. "Don't forget. God is able to do—"

"Exceeding abundantly above all that I ask or think. Yes, yes. I know." But if that was true, why had God allowed the Haliburton case to turn into a spectacle in front of the entirety of Sitka?

"Excuse me." She stood, then set her bowl of untouched dumplings by the sink. Silence filled the kitchen behind her, but she didn't say so much as a word as she strode out of the kitchen.

The moment she entered the hallway, chatter exploded behind her, just as she'd known it would.

But at least she wouldn't need to see the expression of horror come over Mr. Darrow's face when he learned just how much embarrassment she'd brought her family.

23

E velina's eyes shot open, her heart pounding against her chest as she frantically searched the darkness.

There'd been a sound. She'd heard it in her sleep, though she couldn't say what had woken her.

Had Mr. Dressner returned to the trading post? Was he trying to enter the building?

She stood, wrapping the cover from her bed around her, then padding to the window on bare feet. Inky blackness greeted her, the dark and dreary day having turned into an even darker and drearier night.

She saw nothing below, but the window faced the back of the trading post, not the front that would reveal the road and wharf on the other side of the street.

Thwack!

Another sound, this one in the distance, followed by laughter and the low rumble of masculine voices.

The sounds were too far away and the window too thick to make out what the men were saying. They were probably outside one of the bars. Or maybe the bar owner had even tossed them onto the street for being too rowdy.

But was that another sound coming from somewhere below? The sloshing of boots through mud, perhaps?

Or maybe it was nothing more than the sound of the wind in the trees, but she was awake, and there was no harm in checking to see if anyone was on the street.

She padded through the room, weaving her way around where Inessa lay on the floor so that Myra could take her bed; then she crept by Kate, who slept soundly on her bed by the door.

Cracking the door open, she made her way along the hallway and down the stairs, careful to avoid the step with the creaking board.

From the bottom of the stairs, the windows facing the harbor looked just as black as the one in the bedroom.

She crept closer. If she went to the window, hopefully she'd be able to make enough sense of the shadows to see if someone was in the street. And she might even be able to tell just where the voices earlier—

Oof!

She was only a couple feet from the window when her foot hit something soft and thick. She stumbled forward and would have fallen into the wall, but large hands reached out to catch her.

"Evelina?"

She suddenly found herself hauled against a warm, broad chest. "Mr. Darrow?"

"You really can call me Jonas." His voice rumbled out of his chest, deep and thick.

"Whatever are you doing here?" She could just make out the shadow of his face in the darkness.

"Preventing you from tripping over my bedroll, it appears."

She looked down, where she could barely make out the form of the bedroll at her feet. "But why are you out here and not in the examination room?"

"Thought it best to sleep in front of the door. I think the better question is, what are you doing down here?" Again, his voice emerged low and rough, and she could feel it rumble deep inside his chest.

His chest. Oh dear, what was she doing still pressed against his chest? And with his arms wrapped around her, no less?

She scrambled back, but that only caused her feet to tangle in his bedroll once more. She would have fallen a second time, but Mr. Darrow was there again, his hands clasping onto her upper arms and helping her straighten.

"Are you all right?"

"I'm sorry. It appears my feet keep getting tangled."

He released her, his hands dropping back to his sides. "That doesn't answer why you're down here in the first place."

"I thought I heard a noise outside. And voices, though they were farther down the street."

"And you came to check? Alone?"

Now there was nothing soothing about his voice. It was still deep, but it made her want to straighten her spine and clench her teeth. So what if she'd wanted to come downstairs and make sure no one was near the trading post? This was her family's building, not his. She had just as much of a right—if not more of a right—to protect it than he did.

"What if there was someone down here?" His voice turned even sharper. "And I'd already been knocked out?"

"Something woke me, and I wanted to check on things. This is hardly the first time I've done such a thing since moving to Juneau, and I'm not going to apologize for that."

He disapproved, she could feel it in the air between them, but far-off voices sounded again.

Evelina stepped closer to the window. One look was all she wanted. Then she'd head back upstairs.

Jonas let her pass, but just like before, she saw nothing but blackness. The shadows from both the trading post and the warehouses on the opposite side of the street cast the road in so much darkness she could barely make it out, let alone a person who might happen to be walking down it.

"Satisfied now?" Mr. Darrow asked. "You can go back to bed."

She should be satisfied. She'd done what she came to do. But what if there was someone hiding around the corner of the building? Or even beneath the window where she stood?

"Has there been any indication someone is outside the trading post?"

"No." His voice was still sharp and tight, as though he truly didn't like her being down here.

Or maybe he wasn't short because she was down here but because he didn't enjoy needing to spend the night on the floor.

She let out a long sigh, her shoulders deflating along with her lungs. "I truly am sorry for all of this. When I said Myra could stay with us, I never thought—"

"Don't apologize for helping a woman flee an abusive husband. I don't mind guarding the building."

Then what had set him so on edge? She ran her eyes down him again, not that she could see much. But there was something about how he was handling all of this. If Yuri was here, he might have thought to sleep downstairs, but he never would have slept in front of the door. Neither would Alexei.

"Just what did you do for work back in Texas?" she whispered.

His body stiffened. "Why did you stop practicing law?"

"You know why. My siblings were only too happy to convey that story over dinner."

"They told me that your defendant lied to you and ended up confessing the truth on the stand. But they couldn't tell me why you stopped practicing afterward."

"Because I was a failure." The answer slipped out of her mouth unbidden, a natural response to a natural question. Never mind that she hadn't intended on sharing such a thing.

"A failure?" Though he only spoke two words, they somehow seemed gentle and concerned, a complete turnabout from how he'd been snapping at her thirty seconds earlier.

But really, she might as well tell him. What was the harm in it? He'd be gone again in a few more days. "When I was a girl, there was this woman in Sitka. Her husband beat her and the children, and the whole town knew it. My mother tried to be kind to her. We brought her soup and bread and sat by her in church."

She pressed her eyes shut, the memories vivid, even though she'd been only seven at the time. "Then we went a week or so without seeing anyone from the family. Not the children in school or the wife or even the wastrel of a man. So some men from town went out to check on the family . . ."

She shuddered, still remembering the conversation her parents had had in the office that night, not realizing she was standing just outside the door. "He'd killed his wife and disappeared with his two daughters."

"I'm so sorry."

"I remember thinking that we should have cared more. Done something to help get her away from her husband. Everyone knew he was violent, but most of the town looked the other way. A few women like my mother tried to be compassionate, but that wasn't enough to save her life. Mrs. Smirnov needed to get away from her husband, and no one knew how to help her."

Evelina drew in a breath. "So when I found myself stuck

in Boston and not wanting to finish teaching school, I decided to go to law school. Partly because I knew my knowledge of the law could help Alexei with shipping contracts and maritime law but also because I never forgot Mrs. Smirnov. I've always wondered what happened to her two daughters. Did they end up like their mother? Victims of their father's violence? There are so many women like Mrs. Smirnov and Myra. Women with terrible husbands who hurt them. Once I had my law degree, I thought I'd be able to—" She clamped her mouth shut, letting silence fill the darkness between them.

"It turned out differently than you expected, I'm sure."

She sighed. "I'm not strong enough to wake up every day and fight for the chance to do my job, at least not in the way Kate does. I don't get a sense of satisfaction from proving people wrong. And all I ended up doing was tiptoeing around the men who thought I had no business being a lawyer. That and embarrassing my family."

Jonas was quiet for a moment, and she suddenly wished it wasn't so dark, that one of them had lit a lamp so she could see what, if any, emotions played across his face.

"Did your family say they were embarrassed?"

Had they? She thought back, trying to remember. "The entire courtroom laughed at me. They said a woman had no business being a lawyer. That a man would have figured out Sophie was lying long before I put her on that stand."

"Is that true?"

She blinked. "What?"

"Would a man have been able to figure out Sophie was lying?"

"Probably. Or at the very least, they wouldn't have been so quick to believe her story. I took one look at her broken nose and sprained arm, and it never occurred to me that her husband's death had been anything other than self-defense like she claimed."

"And you don't think a male lawyer would have done the same thing?"

"No."

"I disagree."

Her head snapped up. "How could you possibly know such a thing? You weren't there."

"No, and I'm not a lawyer either, but I happen to know a few back in Texas, ones who defended women with abusive husbands. Most lawyers would take one look at a case like Sophie's and step up to defend the woman, not the man."

She tugged on a strand of hair that had fallen beside her face, absently twirling it about her finger. Was Mr. Darrow right? Would most lawyers have done what she did and believed the woman?

"That still doesn't change what happened." Nor did it change the fact that she'd have to walk into court in two more days and face the same judge who had laughed at her the last time she'd made an appearance.

A hand settled on her shoulder, warm and large. "I have no doubt you'll succeed with Myra."

She sunk her teeth into her lip. "I'm afraid you have too much confidence in me."

"You can call on me to testify if you'd like. I'm happy to repeat the threats I heard Dressner make against both you and Myra."

She looked up, trying to find his eyes in the darkness. The notion of court scared most men silly. They didn't want to swear an oath and testify to anything, even if they were expected to say something as simple as the sky was blue. Yet Jonas didn't seem to have any qualms about making claims against another man.

But there was something about how he said the words, about how he stood there discussing court while exuding a calm sort of confidence. This wouldn't be his first appearance in court. Just like this wasn't the first time he'd stayed awake into the wee hours of the night to protect a building.

A memory of his first morning in Juneau sprang into her mind. She could still smell the rain from the downpour outside, feel the dampness of the air as she unwound the bandage covering his stab wound. Still remember how, before she'd replaced the bandage, her eyes had been drawn to the small bullet scar just below his collarbone, to the vicious knife wounds farther down his abdomen and on his back.

"What did you say you did for work back in Texas?" she whispered again, more to herself than anything.

But he heard.

Once again his body went stiff beside her, and he took a step away. "I already told you. It's none of your concern."

"That's where you're wrong. It's very much my concern, because you're standing here in my family's building, watching the street as though you know what you're looking for, acting as though you're confident in your ability to handle Bruce Dressner, should he appear."

"That's because I am confident."

"You were a sheriff, weren't you?"

"My past isn't something I wish to discuss."

"Then at least tell me what drove you to Juneau. Surely you can discuss that."

He took a step away from her. "Has your brother found a manager for the trading post yet?"

She blinked. "What?"

"A manager. You know, the job he was going to offer me before I had to leave last time?"

"He hasn't, no."

"Good. Then I accept the position."

"Wait . . . what? You can't." Her shoulders tightened, and she drew herself up to her full height. "You left us, remember?"

"And now I'm back."

"Alexei wasn't happy when you left."

"I can convince him to hire me, if I've a mind to."

Every muscle in her body turned suddenly hard. "Oh, so you could have convinced him to hire you last time, but you decided to leave instead?"

"Something like that."

"That doesn't make things better, not when we've got no guarantee you won't up and leave again. Alexei needs someone dependable to manage this post."

"I'm perfectly dependable," he gritted. "So dependable, in fact, that if I think my presence will bring others danger, the first thing I'll do is leave. You can depend on me for that before you depend on me for anything else. Because the last thing I ever want to do is stand in front of . . ." His voice cracked and his words stopped.

She could ask him to finish his sentence, but he wouldn't tell her. She could tell that from the way the air between them seemed to snap and crackle despite the lingering dampness from the rain that afternoon.

"You claim you were in some type of danger when you were staying with us before? That's why you say you left?"

He raked a hand through his hair. "I told you I'm not willing to speak of this."

"And I'm not willing to be made a fool!" She took a step toward him. "You might say you were in danger, I but know the truth. I know what I brought you before you left. A letter from a woman. Then the next day you were gone, without even bothering to give us a proper good-bye. You just disappeared one morning, as though we . . . our family . . . as though we meant nothing to you."

Oh, goodness, why were her eyes hot? Why was her throat turning thick and her hand trembling?

Jonas Darrow didn't owe her an explanation. He'd been right about that all along, and she just wanted him to leave. Leave the trading post, leave Juneau, leave Alaska altogether.

Now. While she expected it.

Because the last thing she wanted to do was get close to him a second time, only to have him up and disappear again.

JONAS STARED down at Evelina's shadowed form, her head bent and her thick hair falling in waves about her shoulders.

Her words still hung in the air between them.

You left after you got a letter from a woman. You left as though we meant nothing to you . . .

Did she have feelings for him? Feelings that went deeper than the soft smile she sent his direction or the kind way she always asked about his day?

No. She couldn't. The last thing he'd ever do was put another woman in danger, not after what had happened to Harriet.

But what if there wasn't any danger? What if this Luke fellow who'd sought out his sister had been a harmless reporter and nothing more? What if he was completely safe here in Juneau?

Did that mean he was free to . . . ?

What?

Pursue a relationship with Evelina? Did he want to open up his heart that way?

What if he came to love her, and she caught ill? Or there was an accident at sea and the ship she was on went down?

What if he lost Evelina, just like he'd lost Harriet?

He shook his head. His mind was getting ahead of him. He needed to deal with the facts, not conjecture or worries or hope. Just like working a case.

And the one thing he knew for certain was that he'd hurt Evelina when he left last time. And he hadn't meant to.

"The letter was from my sister," he whispered.

She raised her head to look at him. "What?"

"You're right about me being a lawman in Texas." Though he hadn't been a sheriff like she'd assumed. He'd been a step above that. He scrubbed his hand over his face, though it did little to erase the memories. "There was a case, and it went bad. People died, and I . . . I decided to hang up my guns and take off my badge. To start over again, someplace where no one knew me. That's how I ended up in Juneau."

Hopefully that would be enough to satisfy her, because while he didn't want to hurt her, he wasn't prepared to tell her more either.

"The letter from your sister . . ." Evelina's voice was soft against the darkness. "It spoke of danger?"

"It spoke of a man seeking her out and asking after me. I didn't know why. Didn't know if he might have been a criminal and traced the letter Olivia sent up here to Juneau. So I thought it best I head into the mountains and keep an eye on things from a distance." His training demanded nothing less.

Evelina cocked her head to the side, and even though he couldn't see her face, he could feel the concern rolling off her. "No one has come to the trading post looking for you."

"I'm aware."

"But how would you . . . Oh." She straightened. "You said you were keeping an eye on things from a distance. Does that mean you've been snooping about Juneau even though you haven't been staying in town?"

"I wanted to make sure I hadn't brought any danger to your doorstep."

"What about bringing danger to you?"

His own safety had been the least of his concerns. "Like I said. I thought it best to watch from a distance."

"For nearly a month?"

"Yes. Though after this much time, the risk of danger has passed."

"And that means you can stay and manage the trading post and warehouse?"

"And look out for you." He wasn't sure what possessed him to say that last bit, but he couldn't deny the truth of it. If Evelina had a mind to go about rescuing women, then someone needed to ensure her safety, and without any of her brothers here, there weren't a lot of people volunteering for that duty.

The strange part was, he didn't seem to mind.

"Jonas," she whispered softly, then took a step closer to him.

Jonas. For the first time since he'd left, she said his name. It sounded soft and gentle on her lips, and he couldn't stop himself from leaning closer to her.

She laid a hand on his forearm. "I might not know everything that happened in Texas, or precisely what sent you here, but I want you to know that I'm sorry for it."

"I . . ." He reached out, fingering a strand of her silky hair in the darkness. "Thank you."

All of a sudden, her arms were around him, her body pressing close in an embrace that felt so natural he couldn't help but wrap his arms around her in return. The faint scent of vanilla and cinnamon wound around him, while the heat from her body radiated into his.

"I'm not sorry you came to Juneau." Her breath fanned against his chin. "And I'm not sorry you're here now."

He wasn't sorry either.

Maybe there was some truth to the verse Kate had reminded everyone of at dinner, about God being able to do exceeding abundantly above all that he asked or thought. Because when he first arrived aboard the *Alliance*, he never would have guessed that he'd find a home with a sprawling family like the Amoses, or that holding any woman besides Harriet could feel right.

But standing here, with Evelina in his arms, her face so close he could feel her breath on his chin, it was almost enough to make a man lean forward and . . .

Crash!

The window to his left shattered, spraying both him and Evelina with glass. A flaming torch flew through the air and landed on the floor near one of the stands holding fur coats.

Evelina gasped, then opened her mouth, likely to scream, but Jonas clamped his hand over it. "Quiet. Give me a chance to catch him before you go making a commotion. Use my bedroll to smother the fire, then grab the pail of water from Kate's examination room and keep it handy, just in case."

Jonas released her, gave his shirt a small shake to dislodge the glass bits that had showered him, then slipped out the door into the darkness.

A shadowy form stood near the wall by the undamaged window that faced the street. Jonas moved swiftly forward, but he wasn't quite fast enough to prevent another match from being struck.

He had to give the man credit. He wasn't trying to burn the building from the outside, not with how wet the logs were from the rain earlier in the day. But aiming for the dry interior of the store? Targeting a stand of fur coats that would go up in flames in under a minute? That was rather smart work for a drunkard.

Jonas crept along the storefront, using the darkness to his benefit. That, and the man was obviously having trouble lighting the second torch in the dampness. The first match flickered out, but it took only a couple of seconds to light another and hold it to the torch.

The moment the pitch on the torch lit, Jonas cocked his gun. "Drop it right there in the mud, or I'll put a bullet in your head."

"Fire!" A cry echoed from somewhere down the street.

Someone else must have seen what was happening, but Jonas didn't look up to figure out who. Voices sounded from inside the trading post too, where he expected Evelina had put out the fire and roused the others.

But Jonas kept his eyes pinned on the man with the torch. It wasn't Bruce Dressner. The man was too short and thin. "I said, drop the torch."

The man did as commanded, and the flames died a quick death in the soggy mud.

"Good." Jonas raised his gun a bit higher. "Now stick your hands up."

Again, the man obeyed.

"Let's head to the jail."

The arsonist didn't try to fight it, just turned and started trudging through the mud. Jonas followed behind, his gun pointed at the man's back while he tried to figure out why someone other than Bruce Dressner was trying to burn down the Amoses' trading post.

24

"I'm going to give you one more chance." Jonas narrowed his eyes at the small man tied to the chair in the office at the front of the jail.

Despite the late hour, three men from the Committee of Public Safety had been roused, and all had stood watching him for the past half hour as he tried to pry information out of the arsonist.

It wasn't going well.

Jonas moved closer, hovering over him in a way that should seem intimidating. "Who hired you to burn down the building?"

The man didn't look the least bit intimidated. Instead, he tried to shrug, but the way his hands were tied behind his chair prevented him from moving his shoulders more than an inch. "I already told ya. It were my idea. Weren't no one else's."

Jonas didn't believe it, but no matter how many different times he asked the question or how many ways he managed to phrase it, the arsonist was being consistent with his answers.

That made it impossible for Jonas to poke holes in his story, regardless of how unbelievable it was.

"Were you aware that a threat had been made against the owners of the trading post earlier in the day?"

"I weren't aware of nothin'. Just bored is all. Seemed like somethin' ta do."

There wasn't so much as a whiff of liquor on the man, not on his breath, not on his coat, not on anything. The arson attempt couldn't have been the result of a drunken dare. But so far that was all he'd been able to figure out.

The man hadn't said a word about Bruce Dressner either.

"You came to town with four torches soaked in pitch. That's the kind of thing a man plans, not something that happens because he's bored."

The man gave another half shrug.

"Jonas, I say we wait until the Marshal gets here." One of the men said from behind him. "Let a trained professional question him."

A trained professional? He *was* a trained professional.

Not that any of the men in the room knew that. Of the three men on the Committee of Public Safety who'd been roused from their beds, he had a grocer, a banker, and a blacksmith.

And he'd be hanged if he was going to sit around and wait for the Marshal. It had taken more than four weeks for the Marshal to arrive last time, and the Marshal hadn't even bothered trying to track down Betty Clement's murderer.

Now a man was trying to burn down the Amoses' trading post, and not the same man who had issued threats earlier that day.

It made him think Dressner had men working with him, and if the drunkard had been able to find one man willing to commit arson, chances were he'd be able to find a second.

"What's the Marshal going to do that we can't?" Jonas turned to face the men. All three of them were standing on the opposite side of the room, almost as though afraid to come any closer, never mind the arsonist was tied up. "He still hasn't found Betty Clement's murderer or whoever stole that two hundred dollars from Simon Volker."

Grover Hanover flinched. "Not sure how much effort he put into either of those things, to tell ya the truth. Especially since the murderer skipped town."

"Exactly." Jonas crossed his arms over his chest. "So if he can't ferret out a thief or be bothered to send out a memorandum about the murderer to other Marshals, what makes you think he's going to figure out who's behind an arson attempt?"

"Ya already know who's behind the arson attempt," the man said from behind him. "It was me. I ain't trying to deny it."

Which was yet another thing Jonas didn't like. He'd spent six years as a lawman, and never before had he encountered a criminal so willing to admit to his crime.

It was almost as though Dressner had offered to pay the lout more if he claimed sole responsibility for the crime.

Almost as though Dressner was trying to keep the lot of them stuffed in this tiny office and distracted while . . .

The breath clogged in his chest. "Is anyone watching the trading post?"

The three men looked between each other, then Dwain Hemming, the town banker, cleared his throat. "We already caught the arsonist. Why would anyone need to watch it?"

"In case the first attempt was a distraction," he said as he barreled toward the door.

"Get him locked up," he called over his shoulder as he raced into the night.

He ran down the street, mud sucking at his boots and slowing his stride. The main road was only a block away, but it took half a minute too long to reach it. He slid around the corner and looked ahead to the trading post. It was several blocks away, nearly at the end of town. Faint, hazy light spilled from a couple of the windows into the mist. But no flames licked the walls or lapped at the roof.

That was a good sign, but it didn't mean the danger had passed. What if Dressner had snuck in the back door while everyone had been dealing with the fire at the front of the building?

What if he arrived to find Evelina lying in a pool of her own blood, with a gaping bullet hole in her chest?

Or Ilya suffocated with a pillow?

What if someone had thrown a stick of dynamite through the broken window, and it was about to explode, killing everyone inside?

What if . . . ?

The possibilities grew in his mind, each one worse than the last as he ran. His wound hurt slightly, but more from the dampness and rain than because he'd strained it during the night. Unlike his work in the mine, nothing he'd done that night had involved pushing and carrying heavy things.

Jonas didn't pause when he finally reached the door, just burst inside. "Evelina? Kate? Ilya? Inessa?"

All was quiet, but that only caused his heart to beat harder inside his chest. Often the houses where the most heinous crimes had been committed looked peaceful and quiet from the outside.

His hand automatically went to his side, searching for the pistol he'd kept strapped to his side ever since Betty Clement's murder.

His hand slid over the familiar butt of the gun and drew it from the holster, then crept forward.

He shouldn't have shouted, not when he didn't know who

might be in the building. If Dressner was inside, all he'd done was give warning that he was coming.

Footsteps thundered down the stairs. Ilya. If he'd heard the boy barrel down the stairs once, he'd heard it a hundred times.

But was the boy running because he was excited or because something was dreadfully wrong?

Jonas slid his gun back into his holster but kept his hand nearby, ready to draw and shoot.

"Mr. Darrow!" Ilya bounded onto the trading-post floor, then ran straight toward him. "Did you get him locked up? What did he say? Did Mr. Dressner pay him to try burning down the building?"

Jonas caught the boy in his arms, then hefted him into the air. "Are you all right? Is everyone here all right? Dressner didn't try to come into the building, did he? Has someone searched the street? The ally? Do you know if . . . ?"

"Jonas?"

He shifted Ilya, looking over the boy's shoulder in the direction of the soft voice that had said his name.

Evelina stood at the bottom of the stairs, concern etched across her brow. "Are you all right? Did something happen with the arsonist?"

"I . . . no. Nothing happened with him. He wouldn't even tell me his name."

Ilya settled his head onto his shoulder, then reached out and gave him an awkward pat on the back. "Mr. Darrow was worried about us. Like something might have happened while he was at the jail."

"Did it? Did anyone try to . . . ?" His voice gave out, as images of the charred rubble that had once been his mother's house rose in his mind.

"We're all fine." She came toward him, her steps small and

graceful, as though she floated over the wooden planks of the floor. "Myra is upset, and Kate and I have been trying to calm her. That's all that's happened here. Was Dressner the one behind the fire?"

"I don't know." He relaxed his grip on Ilya, letting him slide to the floor.

"Are you sure you're all right?" Evelina asked. "You seem upset."

"I'm fine. I just . . ." He turned, sweeping the room in a single gaze. "Light more lamps. I need to search the building and board up the window."

Evelina hugged Ilya to her side, worry creasing her brow. "Do you think we might still be in danger?"

"I don't know."

All he knew was that something about the arsonist's behavior didn't sit right—that and he wasn't going to let anything happen to the Amos family.

———

HE SPENT two hours searching the building. Every crack and crevice, every closet and cupboard.

Inessa and Ilya had confirmed that there weren't any knives missing from the collections inside the trading post or the kitchen while he triple-checked the locks and made sure no one was hiding in a closet.

And the entire time, his gun had been strapped to his side. The weight of it didn't feel heavy like it had after Betty Clement's murder. If anything, the feel of his pistol against his hip gave him comfort. If Bruce Dressner had snuck into the building and hidden while everyone was trying to put out the fire, then Jonas was going to be ready when he found the man.

But Dressner wasn't hiding in the building. Or outside it. Or in the warehouse across the street.

No. It seemed like the man had gone back to wherever he'd been holed up in the mountains for most of the summer and fall. And it seemed like Jonas was the only one worried. Everyone else had gone to bed, hoping to get at least a couple hours of sleep before dawn.

He was about to go downstairs and find his bedroll—which he was still keeping in front of the door—when the door to the women's bedroom opened and Evelina emerged. "You're still awake?"

"I could ask you the same question."

"Myra had a nightmare. She's worried about her husband returning. I was going to get her a glass of water."

"I'd have nightmares too, in her situation." He moved away from the kitchen doorway, making room for Evelina to enter.

She came forward, her steps light, but when she reached the doorway, she stood there and looked at him, eyes wide and luminous.

Only then did he notice she was in her nightgown. She'd probably been in her nightgown since she'd first come downstairs to look out the windows, but it had been too dark for him to see her, and then he'd been dealing with the arsonist and searching the building.

But now she stood before him in some gauzy, lace-trimmed gown that stopped just above her toes. It was the kind of thing that he could imagine her wearing to bed, feminine and delicate and beautiful.

She reached out and rested a hand on his arm, her fingers warm against his skin. "I'm so sorry."

He frowned, then looked past her toward the bedroom door. "For what? Is something wrong? What did you say happened with Myra?"

"I'm sorry for you, Jonas, not Myra. For whatever happened to you back in Texas. Whatever made you so worried tonight when you came back from the jail."

A breath shuddered out of him, and he pressed his eyes shut. "It occurred to me that Dressner might have paid the other man to create a distraction, all while intending to sneak into the trading post and do you harm, and I couldn't stop imagining the trading post exploding with all of you in it."

"Is that what happened back in Texas? A building exploded, and it killed your family?"

He opened his eyes and met her gaze. "My mother's house."

Her mouth opened, but no sound came out. Instead, she stood there looking at him, her eyes round with a stunned sort of horror.

Then her arms were around him, pulling him close while the scents of cinnamon and vanilla wafted from her hair. "Was your mother . . . ? Was she . . . inside?"

"Yes. As was my fiancée, Harriet. They were both killed instantly."

She pressed her head into the crook of his shoulder, burying her face in the rough fabric of his shirt. "How terrible."

He wrapped an arm around her back, then used his free hand to stroke a strand of hair behind her ear.

"That's why I was so worried earlier. Because if anything were to happen to you or Ilya, to anyone in your family . . ." The words clogged in his throat, and he shook his head. "This was never supposed to happen."

"What?" she whispered, her eyes two green, watery pools.

"I wasn't supposed to care. I was going to come to Alaska and disappear. So that if anyone ever came looking for me, if anyone wanted to do me harm, no one else would be hurt too."

"So you were supposed to die in the explosion? Not your mother or your fiancée?"

"Yes." The word rasped out from a place deep inside him, grating against his vocal cords until his throat felt raw.

He had been the target of that attack, and if not for him, both his mother and Harriet would still be alive.

Silence hung between them, heavy and somber. Then Evelina pulled far enough back to meet his gaze. "Maybe, just maybe, God led you here for a reason. Maybe it's as Kate always says, that God is 'able to do exceeding abundantly above all that we ask or think.' And so God brought you to us."

Could God really have brought him to the Amos family? Have led him here for a purpose, even though he'd thought he was coming to escape?

He gave his head a small shake. "Why would God want me here?"

"So you could save us tonight. No one else would have been able to watch the building the way you did. No one else would have been awake when that torch came through the window."

He swallowed. Was Evelina right? Had God worked something good out of his coming to Juneau? He hadn't asked God once about coming here. Hadn't stopped to pray or consider what God wanted. He'd just run.

"And maybe God led you here so that we could help you heal," she whispered, the heat of her breath brushing his neck.

Is that what was happening to him? Was he healing?

He stared at Evelina in the dimly-lit hallway, her delicate frame illuminated by the soft lamplight spilling from the kitchen. He could feel the warmth of her body through her nightgown, could smell the sweet aromas of vanilla and spice on her skin. And the longer he stood there, wrapping her in his arms in the stillness of night, feeling the gentle rise and fall of her side beneath his hand, the more he wasn't sure what to do with himself . . .

Other than lean down and kiss her.

So he did.

It was a mistake. The moment their lips touched, he felt himself slipping. As if all the things he had been certain of, all the things he thought he'd known in coming to Alaska had vanished into the thick Juneau mist.

Her lips moved gently beneath his, almost as though she'd been waiting for him to lean down and kiss her. A soft sigh shuddered up from her, and she pressed onto her tiptoes, then wrapped her arms around his neck, bringing their bodies closer.

He tightened his grip on her back, then used his free hand to tilt her head to the side, deepening the angle of the kiss.

She'd said God might have brought him to Alaska to heal, but could a kiss heal as well? Because the longer he stood there, holding her in his arms with their mouths fused together, the more the memories from Austin faded, until there was no explosion, no new tombstones in the cemetery, no pain or sorrow or death.

There was only Evelina, and she was bright and warm, alive and vibrant—and filled with a shiny hope that drew him closer and closer.

Then she broke away, right in the middle of the kiss, pulling the hope and light and warmth with her as she took a step back.

She pressed the back of her hand to her mouth. "I'm so sorry. I didn't mean to . . . How horrible of me! Please forgive me."

Forgive her for what? Kissing him back? Making him feel whole again? Showing him that maybe, just maybe, his life didn't need to be as dark as he'd imagined?

"There's nothing to forgive. I kissed you, remember?" And

heaven help him, he wanted to wrap her in his arms and do it again.

Never mind that she stood there looking utterly mortified, with her cheeks an unnatural shade of pink and her chest rising and falling briskly beneath the fabric of her nightgown.

"How long ago was the explosion? How long ago did you lose your fiancée?"

He groaned. Why was she bringing up Harriet? And now of all times? "July."

Her eyes filled with tears. "Then you're not ready for this. You're not ready to love again."

"Evelina, I . . ."

But she turned and fled, rushing back to her room as though a fire licked at her heels.

I didn't love Harriet in that way. The words were on the tip of his tongue, ready to spill out.

It wasn't that he hadn't loved Harriet, of course he had, but they were more like friends than anything else. They'd grown up next door to each other, and Harriet had been something of a sister to him—a sister who had understood how his work as a lawman took him away from home for weeks or even months at a time. A sister who had never complained about his devotion to his job.

But with each turn of the calendar, he came one step closer to thirty—and so had Harriet. At twenty-six, she had passed the age that most women married, and he had still needed a wife. So he'd proposed, and they'd settled into a comfortable relationship, the kind where she came over for dinner when he was home and they set a wedding date far off in the future. The kind where they made good companions.

But she didn't fill his thoughts whenever he left Austin, and he'd never had such a strong hankering to reach out and feel the softness of her hair or lean forward and kiss her.

He stared at the door behind which Evelina had disappeared. He needed to explain his relationship with Harriet to her. He didn't want her to assume it had been different than what it actually was.

But what was the point of explaining it when he still didn't know if he could let himself love Evelina?

25

He'd failed. Again. Jonas hunkered deeper down into his fur coat as he trudged down the streets of Juneau. A slight mist was falling, causing water to pool on the thick hide he was burrowed beneath as shadows crept into the street.

How was it he could track numerous bands of criminals across the desert for miles, but he couldn't seem to find a man who disappeared into the mountains?

Was it because the frequent rains washed away tracks so quickly, or the fact that the forest was so dense, one couldn't see for miles like in Texas?

He couldn't say for certain. All he knew was that spending an entire day trying to track Bruce Dressner had proved just as futile as spending four weeks trying to track Orville Jacobs. The mountains and woods of Southeast Alaska had a way of hiding men that the Texan desert didn't.

Either that or he'd lost all skill as a lawman the day he'd watched his mother's house burn.

At least the pain in his ribs was subsiding now that he was

done hauling things. He'd barely noticed it while he'd been searching for Dressner.

"Mr. Darrow. Mr. Darrow."

At the sound of the young voice calling his name, he turned, searching the shadows of the buildings that lined the road.

A head of dirty blond hair appeared around the side of the building, then a small form came toward him. Little Sally Shephard.

"The Finch boys are leaving me alone now." She came up and gripped his hands, her small fingers wrapping tightly around his larger ones.

"I don't know what you said to scare them off, but it worked. They let me get bread every day."

She smiled up at him, her grin bright.

"I'm glad."

"Did you find him yet?" The smile dropped from her face. "The man with the gray ponytail? Or do I still need to keep my secret?"

He sighed. "I'm afraid it still needs to stay secret."

"Everyone says the man who killed Miss Clement left town on a ship."

"I know."

"Do you think that's what he did, left town? Could he have made it look like he was going into the woods, then come back to the wharf, just to trick us?"

"It's possible." In fact, he was starting to think that might be the only realistic scenario. Because if Orville Jacobs were up in the mountains surrounding Juneau, surely someone would have seen him at some point in the past month.

Though something about that scenario just didn't settle right.

"The Marshal came to town and did his investigation," Sally said.

"I know."

"He didn't arrest anyone."

"That's what I heard." Because there'd been no one to arrest.

She looked around the darkening buildings. "So maybe the man with the ponytail really did leave, and I don't need to worry anymore."

"Yes, maybe he left." He wasn't sure he agreed with the words, but he couldn't stomach the thought of this precious child living in fear that Jacobs might come for her one day.

"But until we catch him, I still want you to keep our secret."

Her grip on his hand tightened, but she nodded. "It's all right if you don't catch him. No one else is even looking for who killed Miss Clement."

Maybe not, but he'd still like to see justice served. If only he hadn't lost the trail on the day of the murder. This was supposed to be a simple case, with the criminal caught by the end of the day and a clear motive for the murder emerging.

But a month later, he still had nothing.

Where had the killer gotten off to? And why had Orville Jacobs killed the town laundress?

It was yet another set of questions he didn't have answers to, just like he didn't know where Bruce Dressner had disappeared to.

———

"THAT'S all you need to say. That you fear for your safety." Evelina reached across the kitchen table for Myra's hand.

They were due in court in less than an hour, and Evelina

had wanted to go over what Myra needed to say to the judge one final time. Or at least that's what she'd told Myra.

More than anything, she'd wanted to calm the nerves writhing in her own stomach, but the closer the clock ticked to the top of the hour, the more fretful Myra became.

Once on the stand, would she remember the things they'd rehearsed? Or would the woman take one look at the people filling the room and forget everything they'd discussed?

Evelina shifted. She couldn't blame Myra if she became tongue-tied. After all, it's what had happened to her the last time she'd made an appearance in court, and she'd been the lawyer.

"I fear for my safety," Myra whispered softly, then looked up, strands of dark blond hair hanging beside hollow cheeks that spoke of too many missed meals.

She and Kate had made a point of plying Myra with as much food as possible during the two days she'd been at the trading post, but their bountiful meals and endless offering of snacks hadn't gone on long enough for the woman to fill out. Hopefully once she reached her brother in Saint Louis, she'd be able to regain some of her weight.

"What if the judge doesn't grant the separation?" Myra whispered into the stillness.

"He will." Evelina patted her hand. "Judge Lincham won't send you back to a monster like your husband."

"How do you know?"

"Because there is a recorded history of your husband injuring you." A deep voice filled the kitchen, and Evelina looked over to find Jonas entering the room.

She dropped her gaze, memories from Sunday's early morning kiss spiraling through her head. She'd spent all of yesterday and a good part of the morning avoiding Jonas.

He'd tried talking to her several times, but she wasn't of a mind to get swept into a conversation.

After all, what was she supposed to say?

That she wanted to kiss him again?

That she just might be falling in love with him, even though he was still in love with his late fiancée?

That she thought of him even when he wasn't in the room or when she drifted off to sleep each night?

That her life was richer and fuller with him in it, and she really hoped Alexei hired him as the store manager . . . even if he wasn't ready to open his heart to love again?

Because she'd rather have him close than far away. Because she wanted to see him every morning at breakfast, and again at lunch and dinner.

Even if she spent most of their meals avoiding his gaze.

But honestly, how could she not have feelings for him? First he'd saved Ilya, then he'd defended her to Miss Thompson, and protected her from Bruce Dressner, and that was all before he'd prevented the trading post from burning to the ground.

She'd even told him she was a lawyer, and he hadn't balked, hadn't acted embarrassed or told her a courtroom was no place for a woman.

Because Jonas Darrow was a truly good man. Honorable and hardworking and upright. And though he might be grieving his fiancée now, at some point, his heart would heal.

And she was willing to wait for that day to come.

She just didn't want anyone in her large, nosy, boisterous family to know that she was waiting for him.

"Even if the judge doesn't grant the separation . . ."

Evelina blinked, Jonas's words drawing her mind away from visions of her future and back to the sparse kitchen.

". . . We know your husband's not in Juneau, so if you go

home, he won't be there to hurt you. But any judge with half a brain will grant the separation in thirty seconds."

It was true. Jonas had spent all of yesterday searching Juneau and the surrounding mountains for Bruce Dressner.

And with a black eye and a broken arm, Myra was all but guaranteed a win in court.

Dressner was supposed to show up at court today, but if he didn't, that was yet another mark in Myra's favor, because there would be no one to contradict her story.

"Are you two ready?" Jonas pumped a glass of water for himself from the sink, then turned to face them.

"Don't want to be late to court."

"You're coming?" Myra squeaked.

She'd looked small and lonely sitting at the table before, but since Jonas had entered, she'd shrunk into herself even more, refusing to look at the man who had saved their building.

Jonas took a step back from the table, as though he somehow sensed Myra's fear. It was a nice gesture, even if he was too large and broad of chest to ever be unassuming.

"Figured I'd escort you there," Jonas answered. "The others are downstairs waiting, and I hung the Closed sign in the window."

Evelina had to fight the urge to twist her hands together. Of course her family would be there to watch her. It was the supportive thing to do. The type of thing one expected from family. And she needed Kate to testify about Myra's injuries.

But why did courtrooms have to be open to the public? Didn't anyone understand this would be so much easier if it was just her and the judge, Myra and Mr. Dressner—and maybe Dressner's lawyer, if the brute bothered to show up and bring one.

The witnesses could come in only for their testimonies and

then leave immediately after. It seemed like such an easier way of going about things. Far less nerve-wracking, to be sure.

A hand landed on her shoulder, and her gaze traveled up until it met Jonas's soft brown eyes. "You're going to do great. And remember, I'm more than willing to testify on Myra's behalf if needed."

The warmth in his eyes traveled straight down to her heart, giving her the courage she needed to stand from the table. "Thank you."

26

"Where is everyone?" Yuri asked. "This place looks deserted."

Alexei glanced over at Yuri as they tied their little sloop to the wharf in front of the warehouse.

His younger brother was right. For the middle of a Monday afternoon, Juneau seemed completely deserted.

"Dear heavens." Reverend Jackson wrung his hands together. "Do you think some type of tragedy has befallen the town? What if typhus has struck?"

Alexei tried not to cringe as he hopped up onto the wharf. "Typhus seems a bit extreme."

But that was probably the best way to describe the past two days of sailing from Sitka to Juneau. Extreme.

It wasn't that the weather had been extreme. Or that their boat had struck a rock and needed to be repaired. No. The extreme part was Rev. Jackson and his endless questions about the ways of the native tribes, or monologues on the importance of assimilating native children to American culture, or his fanciful dreams about just how wonderful his life would be once he married Evelina.

Alexei had tried to explain that Evelina wasn't going to marry him. At least once an hour. So had Yuri. But the man couldn't seem to fathom the idea that someone might not want to become his wife.

"I was here last week, and there wasn't any sign of typhus—or any other illness." Yuri used the ladder to climb up to the wharf two rungs at a time.

"Yes, but typhus can sweep through a town in a day or two. Anything might have happened while you were gone."

"If it's typhus, Kate will have converted the trading post into a hospital. We'll head there first." Alexei extended his hand to the reverend. "Do you need help up?"

The man blinked at him, then at the three feet from the bottom of the boat to the edge of the wharf. "I'll use the ladder, thank you. But what should I do with my bags?"

"We can either stow them in the hull or bring them along with us to the trading post."

The reverend's eyes widened. "And have my bags exposed to typhus?"

Yuri choked back a laugh, but Alexei had an undeniable urge to grind his teeth together. They would probably already know why the town was deserted if Rev. Jackson hadn't taken so long getting out of the boat. And he was willing to bet all five of the ships his family owned that it wasn't due to typhus.

The reverend made a show of stowing all three of his bags inside the small cabin at the front of the boat. Why the man needed three bags when he was only going to be gone a week, Alexei didn't know, but he wasn't about to ask.

When the reverend returned, he climbed the ladder about as slowly as a small child who was on a ladder for the first time.

"If you're really that worried about typhus, you can wait

here." Alexei turned on his heel and stalked across the wharf and the large, open space between the pier and the street, that allowed the stevedores to move between the ships in port and the various warehouses lining the water. Yuri hurried to keep pace beside him, while Rev. Jackson hung back, trailing slowly and clutching the button at the front of his fur coat as though doing so might ward off any lurking danger.

They didn't need to walk far to see a window had been boarded up on the front of the trading post. A Closed sign hung in the opposite window, and the door was locked.

"That's odd. How do you think the window got broken?" Yuri asked.

Alexei shrugged. "I don't know, but this is hardly the first time we've needed to replace a window at a trading post." Any number of accidents might have broken it.

"But do you think something happened to our family?" Yuri looked around the deserted street.

"No, I think something of importance is going on, and that's where everyone is." Alexei waved at the reverend, who had stopped on the opposite side of the road. "There's no typhus— or any other kind of epidemic."

"Are you certain?" The reverend hesitantly stepped into the road.

"I am. Now let's head into town and see what's going on." They started off down the main street, only to find that the closer they drew to the heart of town, the more businesses were shuttered. China Joe's bakery had a Closed sign hanging in the window, as did the Hanover's grocery store beside it.

"You have to admit this is a little strange." Yuri's long strides ate up the muddy ground. "We should have found someone by now."

"Do you think something happened to make everyone disappear?" The reverend glanced around the town through the thick lenses of his glasses. "Maybe there was an earthquake, and the entire town disappeared into the mountains for safety."

Alexei rolled his eyes. How had this man been tasked with overseeing education for the entirety of Alaska? For all the book learning he claimed to have, he didn't seem to have a lick of common sense. "All the buildings are still standing. Does that look like evidence of an earth . . ." Voices floated on the air, hushed chatter mixed with deeper undertones.

"The church." Why hadn't he thought to check there first? If anything of importance was happening, it was likely to be there.

Alexei lengthened his gait, striding ahead of the others as he rounded the corner of Seventh Street to find people spilling out of the little white Presbyterian church in the center of town.

Was someone getting married? No, the serious faces of the men crowded on the steps and peeking into the windows told him nothing worth celebrating was happening.

Was it a funeral then? Had someone of significance died?

He quickened his pace even more. Yuri did the same, leaving the reverend even farther behind as they approached the steps crowded with people.

"What's happening?" Alexei whispered to a man with leathery skin and a grizzled beard standing at the edge of the crowd.

The man turned and ran his eyes down him once, then looked back toward the open door of the building. "Your sister's trying to get Dressner's wife away from her husband and make it all legal-like."

"My sister?"

The prospector scratched the back of his head. "There's something about . . . a motion? And a separation too. Whatever that means."

Alexei pressed himself up onto his tiptoes, but he couldn't begin to see what was happening inside, not given how the church building itself sat a good four steps up from the road.

"Are you sure Evelina's arguing a case?" He must have misunderstood. Evelina wanted nothing to do with a court-room. "Do you know—?"

"The judge said he won't be hearing nothin' about the fire today. Reckon that's what brought most of the folks out. But that there judge says the Marshal's gotta come to town and file charges all official-like before he can hear what yer sister has ta say about it."

"There was a fire?" Rev. Jackson asked, his face turning pale.

"Yes," Yuri shifted closer to the grizzled man. "What fire are you talking about?"

"The one the stranger tried to start at the trading post Saturday night." The man gave them all an odd look, then released a gust of stale breath that wheezed out from between yellowed teeth. "Don't you know nothin'?"

Evidently not. Because he was starting to feel very, very lost.

"Who did you say tried to start a fire?" Yuri flashed the man a disarming smile—not unlike the smile he used to draw every single woman in Sitka to his side. "Forgive me, but I've been gone for a few days. Do you mind starting from the beginning?"

The smile worked its usual charm, even on the grizzled miner, because the man shoved a leathery hand toward the open door of the church and started talking again. "Bruce Dressner's been up in the mountains working some kind of secret claim he don't want ta say nothin' about. He came back to town a month ago and beat his wife somethin' fierce. After he left for his claim, yer sister got this separation thing started for his wife. Then Dressner came back an' found out about the separation, and he beat his wife again 'cuz don't no man cotton to the idea of his wife up and leavin' him. Miss Amos found out about it and done said his wife could stay at the trading post until court. Reckon yer sister was worried what Dressner would do ta his wife if she stayed with him."

Alexei rubbed the back of his neck. He didn't recall anyone by the last name of Dressner, but he also didn't spend enough time in Juneau to know every last person—especially the prospectors who spent more time in the mountains than in town during the summer.

"I call Mr. Jonas Darrow to the stand." Evelina's voice rose above the hushed chatter on the steps, and Alexei's heart stilled.

Darrow. The man whom he'd ordered to leave Alaska? The man who might well be wanted for counterfeiting money and killing a sheriff back in Montana? The man who, the last time they'd talked, had said that staying in Juneau would put the Amos family in danger?

What was he doing back in town?

And why was his sister calling him as a witness?

Had he somehow been involved in the fire Saturday night, bringing danger to his family after he swore he was leaving town? Alexei shoved his way forward.

He didn't recognize half of the people on the steps, but they all seemed to know him, because every last person stepped aside, creating a path for him and Yuri and Rev. Jackson.

When they reached the back of the church, three of the men on the back pew hopped up and offered their seats.

Alexei waved one of the men back down. His muscles were too tense to sit. Besides, standing gave him a better view of the goings-on at the front of the church, where the pulpit had been turned into a makeshift judge's bench and the side of the platform was being used as a witness stand. Kate, Ilya, and Inessa all sat in the second pew, as close to the proceedings as possible.

But Evelina had positioned herself in front of the stand, behind which Jonas Darrow was seated. And though she'd been loud earlier, he had to strain his ears to hear the soft timbre of her voice as she questioned Darrow.

"What did Mr. Dressner say to you then?"

"That he would see to it the whole lot of us paid," Darrow responded, his voice loud and clear.

"And Mr. Dressner said this directly after you said you would get the Committee of Public Safety involved if he didn't leave the premises?"

"He did. Yes."

"How did Mr. Dressner respond to your statement?"

"He left, but someone returned later that night, after dark, with several torches covered in pitch, one of which he tossed through a window in an attempt to set the trading post on fire. We were able to put the fire out before it spread, but the relationship between Mr. Dressner and the arsonist is still under investigation."

Alexei had to give Darrow credit. It wasn't just that his voice was twice as loud as Evelina's. There was something about how he held himself on the stand, about the certainty with which he answered questions that drew the attention of every person in the room.

It wasn't the type of behavior one would expect of a man running from the law.

"Who are you?" he whispered quietly. "And why are you so comfortable in a courtroom?"

"What was that?" Yuri quirked an eyebrow from where he sat at the end of the nearest pew.

Alexei gave a small shake of his head. It wasn't something he was about to discuss with his brother now.

"How did you know of the arsonist's plans?" Evelina's voice grew louder inside the room, almost as though hearing Darrow's answers filled her with a new sense of determination.

"After he threw the first torch through the window, I ran outside to see if I could find who had thrown it. That's where I found the arsonist, on the street outside another window trying to light a second torch."

"I didn't pay no arsonist to do nothin'," Dressner shouted from where he sat behind a table at the front of the church.

"Order in the court!" Judge Lincham banged his gavel on the pulpit. "Order in the court!"

Dressner quieted, and Evelina went on to ask more questions. Judging by the nods and the whispers that trickled through the room, each time Jonas gave an answer, he seemed to convince more and more people to see his side of things.

Even Judge Lincham listened carefully, never mind that the judge could barely look at Evelina without a bored expression crossing his face.

Alexei swallowed. Was Darrow the counterfeiter from Montana, or someone else?

Marshal Hibbs would need to figure that out—and he'd be sending for the Marshal as soon as court was dismissed, seeing as how Darrow hadn't left Alaska after all.

But it would still take several days for the Marshal to get here. In the meantime, what did he know of Jonas Darrow?

If Darrow wasn't running from the law but was in some true kind of danger, could he have been the real target of the arsonist?

Alexei rubbed his jaw. He didn't know much about the fire —something he'd rectify the second the judge made his ruling and he could speak with a member or two of the Committee of Public Safety—but he knew Dressner denied hiring the person who had set it.

And he knew when Yuri had left Juneau a few days ago, his sisters had been safe.

Now they'd returned to find their family in danger again.

And the only thing that was different between then and now was Darrow's presence.

27

E velina looked around the deserted room, the empty desks where her students usually sat, the window that was letting in light from the unusual bit of misty sunshine, the chalkboard she'd forgotten to erase after class on Friday.

It was a nice room, and she enjoyed teaching. But standing in the courtroom earlier, seeing the look on Myra's face when the judge granted her order of separation, and hearing the cheers from the townsfolk at the ruling, had filled a place deep inside her. A place she hadn't realized had been empty.

Judge Lincham still didn't think she belonged in a courtroom. That much was obvious by the way he'd glowered and frowned at her through half of the hearing. But the man had still ruled in Myra's favor.

She sat back in her chair, a feeling of satisfaction welling in her chest. Whether she was in the courtroom or not, her law degree was useful to her family. She wrote all of the shipping contracts Alexei needed and stayed abreast of any changes to maritime and trade law. But writing contracts and reading legal documents wasn't the same as helping someone who genuinely needed the protection of the law.

Would she take more cases in the future? She enjoyed seeing her students make progress every day in class. Truly she did. But maybe if the case was right, if it was a cause she believed in—

"There you are."

The door to the schoolroom opened, and she looked up to find Jonas standing in the doorway.

"I've been looking everywhere for you."

She smiled, his words causing a burst of warmth to release inside her. Hopefully he hadn't gone through too much effort to find her. She gladly would have told him where she was. "I thought you were going to take Dressner to the jail and question him about the arson attempt. Have you finished already?"

Court hadn't even been out for an hour. But the church building had been packed with so many people, she'd slipped out a side door, leaving Myra to walk back to the trading post with Kate and Inessa.

She might be able to see herself back in a courtroom, but she'd never been one who liked a crowd or too much attention, and practicing law wasn't going to change that.

Jonas walked down the aisle toward her, his lips twisting into a scowl. "I tried to question Dressner, but the Committee of Public Safety said they didn't need my help."

She frowned. "Whyever not? You're a sheriff."

"I'm not, Evelina. Not anymore." He paused for a moment, almost as though choosing his next words carefully, or maybe debating whether he wanted to say something at all. "Besides nobody here knows what I used to do back in Texas."

She rose from her chair. "You should tell them. I'm sure you'd do a better job questioning Dressner than any of them."

"After how little information I got out of the arsonist?" He cocked an eyebrow at her. "I'm not sure anyone would believe me."

"Maybe you'll get another chance to question him then."

His jaw turned hard. "I doubt it. If he and the arsonist are connected, their stories will be well-rehearsed. I suspect Dressner will disappear back into the mountains the second the committee is done questioning him."

"Will you try following him?"

"Me? No. Not after I just testified against him in court." The corner of his mouth twitched up into a smile. "But I might have paid the Finch boys to trail him for a bit, see if they can figure out where his claim is."

Her eyes widened. "You paid the Finch boys to follow him?"

He shrugged. "Figure if they're trailing Dressner, they'll be too busy to steal bread from Sally when she comes to the bakery later."

She smiled. It was a brilliant idea, really, because the Finch boys were just insolent enough for Dressner to believe they were randomly trotting through the woods looking for gold—if Dressner encountered the boys and they didn't stay hidden, that was. "I hope they figure out where the claim is."

"Me too, but even if they only trail him for an hour or so, I'll know the direction of the claim."

She sighed. "That makes sense, but I still don't understand why the committee wouldn't let you question Dressner."

His gaze darkened. "That was your brother's doing."

She straightened. What? She'd seen Alexei and Yuri after court. They'd both come up and offered her hugs, explaining that they'd arrived in the middle of the hearing. But then Alexei had muttered something about needing to conduct business and meeting her back at the trading post.

She hadn't taken that to mean he was talking to the Committee of Public Safety.

But of course he was, because he would have heard about the arson attempt, and he'd want to learn everything he could.

The trouble was, Jonas was the person Alexei should be talking to. But how would Alexei know that? "What did my brother say to you?"

"Not a word. It was more what he got others to say. I was in the office with Hemmings and Stubbins and had asked Dressner a few questions when Alexei came in with Hanover, and Hanover asked me to leave. Seeing as how I'd just testified against Dressner in court, he didn't think I was the best person to question him."

"Is he right? Is it poor form to question a man after you just testified against him?"

A muscle ticked at the side of Jonas's jaw. "Lawmen interrogate criminals and testify against them in court all the time. The one hardly excludes the other."

She rested a hand on his arm. "Which only proves that you need to tell the committee you're a lawman."

"No." The muscles of his upper arm tensed beneath her hand. "Those days are done. I'm not going back."

"But you saved the trading post from burning, and that was after you prevented Ilya from getting stabbed. Maybe your lawman days aren't as done as you think." She spoke the words softly, letting them linger between them in the quietness of the room.

Jonas drew in a breath, his shoulders heaving with the movement, then looked down at where her hand still rested on his upper arm. "This isn't what I came here to talk to you about."

"What then? Is something else wrong?"

A smile curved the edges of his lips, and his other hand

came up to cover hers. "Not in the least. I came to compliment you on how you did in court today."

"Oh." She stepped away. "It wasn't me. It was you. Your testimony swayed the minds of every person in that room, including the judge."

"I daresay that was Myra's testimony, and Kate's, especially when she gave an account of all the injuries she's treated Myra for over the last few months."

"But everyone listened to you. You have quite a way of commanding a courtroom."

He shrugged. "It used to be part of my job. If I wanted to make sure criminals were put away for life, then I needed to be impressive on the witness stand, so I learned to do just that. But I can't take credit for the judge's ruling." He took a step closer to her, erasing the distance she'd just put between them, then reached out and clasped her hand in his.

"That was you. Myra was brave going up to the stand and listing all her grievances against her husband. But she never would have filed that motion if not for you. Never would have been able to get away from her husband."

She looked down, staring absently at where the toes of her boots peeked out from beneath the hem of her skirt. "I figured if I didn't help her, one of them would end up dead. Either Bruce would come back one night and beat Myra until he killed her, or Myra would follow in Sophie Haliburton's steps and become so oppressed she'd kill her husband."

"You're probably right, but at the moment, I'm most concerned about you. Was it really so terrifying being in a courtroom again?"

She pressed her eyes shut and drew in a breath. She'd been so terrified she would fail. So scared she would bring more embarrassment and shame to her family.

But Bruce Dressner was the only person who had walked

out of the courtroom in shame. "Everyone in my family seemed happy or proud about how I handled the case. Alexei even smiled when he came up and gave me a hug—and he smiles about as often as the sun shines in Juneau."

"Of course they did. It was impossible not to be proud of you. But I'm not asking about how your family felt. I'm asking about you. How did you feel being up there in front of so many people?"

His eyes bored into hers, and she almost looked away, but instead she answered his question, drawing on the same confidence she'd tried to use in court. "I felt afraid. I can't lie about that. But there was a part of being there that felt good too. Myra needed help, and if I hadn't stepped in, I don't know that she would have gotten it."

"Then I'd say you have good reason to feel proud, not just for winning, but for being willing to do something you found so terrifying, and all so you could help another person." He opened his arms, and she couldn't stop herself from stepping into his embrace any more than she could stop the tide from rising.

She drew in the scent of him, rain and earth and man, and felt her heartbeat slow, her spirit calm. Had she been too quick to step away from practicing law last time? Jonas had said many male lawyers would have made the same mistake she did and believed Sophie's testimony about her husband.

And the townsfolk hadn't dismissed her or the merits of her case merely because she was a woman. Not considering how everyone knew the way Bruce Dressner treated his wife. The arson attempt had only helped to put people on her side—even if Dressner's exact connection to the arson had yet to be proven.

She pulled back far enough to look into his eyes. "Though

for a few seconds, I wondered if the judge would refuse the motion for separation just to spite me."

Jonas's chuckle rumbled low and deep in his chest. "He didn't seem to be much of a fan."

"Not of me. But he's certainly a fan of you."

"Then he's a fool." Jonas ran a hand over her hair. "He should be a fan of you. I am."

Her heart almost melted. Perhaps at his words, or maybe at his touch; she didn't know which. All she knew was that when she looked up to meet his gaze, their lips were only a few inches apart.

"Jonas . . ." she whispered.

And then his lips were on hers. Again.

And oh, was he strong. His chest was firm against her, his arms wrapping around her like a warm blanket, making her want to snuggle up against him and never let him go. And his mouth moved with a delicate precision that made her heart feel light and her cheeks warm.

How many times had she replayed their first kiss in her head? It had plagued both her dreams and her waking thoughts. But her memories hadn't done the kiss justice, because they hadn't quite recalled how the heat from Jonas's body radiated into her own, or how large and strong his hand felt as it splayed against her back, pressing her even closer.

Did Jonas feel the same things she did when they kissed? Did he feel—

"Step away from my sister!"

Jonas's arms stiffened around her for a fraction of a second, and then he dropped them and took a step back.

She was tempted to follow his retreat, to step back into his arms, or even just lay a hand on his chest, which was rising and falling rather quickly.

"What is the meaning of this?"

She blinked, then turned toward the doorway, even though she didn't need to look to know who was barking at them like a feral dog. "I . . . we were just . . ."

But Alexei wasn't the only one standing in the doorway. Her entire family had crowded into the room, everyone from Kate to Inessa to Ilya and Ilya's friend Gushklin.

But Yuri was the worst, because while Alexei might have a cold glower on his face, Yuri was grinning from ear to ear.

"Look at that, brother." Yuri slapped Alexei on the back. "I think Evelina here might just break the curse for you."

"Curse?" Jonas asked softly. "What curse?"

"Lina and Jonas were kissing. You saw that, right Gushklin?" Ilya shoved his friend in the shoulder.

"I saw it." Gushklin smiled right back at Ilya.

Evelina groaned. The two boys were going to tell the entire world. Then everyone in Juneau would be expecting marriage, and if she wanted to keep teaching, she and Jonas would need to—

"Come on." Ilya grabbed Gushklin by the sleeve. "We gotta go tell the others."

The two boys turned to leave, but Alexei reached out and gripped Ilya by the back of the neck. "Not so fast. I don't want either of you to breathe a word of this to anyone. Do you understand?"

"But Lina was kissing Mr. Darrow. That means they've got to get married, and we're going to have a great big wedding." Ilya twisted in Alexei's grip and looked over at her. "Can there be cake? Lots and lots of cake?"

"I want chocolate," Gushklin said.

"There's not going to be any cake, or any wedding, or any speaking of what you saw here. Am I clear?" Alexei leveled his gaze at Jonas. "All this means is that Mr. Darrow will be leaving us. Immediately."

A chill swept through her. Why was her brother so angry? There'd been a time when Alexei had thought Jonas would make her a good husband. It wasn't as though Jonas had forced himself on her. She'd been kissing him back. Surely her brother had seen that.

But before she could say something to defend either herself or Jonas, Ilya broke free of Alexei's hold and raced up the aisle toward Jonas.

"You're leaving again?" Ilya wrapped his spindly arms around Jonas's waist, his eyes filled with worry. "But you said you'd stay. That you'd run the trading post. You promised to take Gushklin and me down to Sheep Creek tomorrow. Remember? You said we could go prospecting."

Jonas patted Ilya's back, then crouched down, looking him directly in the eyes. "I need to talk to your brother first. There's been a bit of a misunderstanding."

"Misunderstanding?" Alexei stalked forward. "Were you or were you not kissing my sister?"

Jonas straightened, somehow seeming even taller and larger than before as he met Alexei's hard gaze. "I was. And I'm not going to apologize for it."

"Everyone out," Alexei snapped. "I need to talk to Mr. Darrow. And no, Ilya, leaving does *not* mean you can tell others what you saw. At least, not unless you've got a mind to ruin your sister's reputation and have me marry her off to the first man I can find."

Ilya's eyes lit with hope. "Does that mean you'll marry her off to Mr. Darrow? Then he could be my brother!"

"No!"

Ilya huffed. "If kissing means a lady has to get married, then I vote she marries Mr. Darrow."

"Me too," Inessa said from behind Alexei. "He'd make a nice brother-in-law."

"I agree." Yuri slung an arm around Kate's shoulders and grinned. "Did you see him up there behind the witness stand? He'll do right by our Lina."

Alexei glared at Jonas. "If he was interested in doing right by her, he wouldn't have kissed her in the first place."

Jonas crossed his arms over his chest. "You realize we can both hear you, right? And we're people, not a ship that can be owned and managed and moved around at—"

"Evelina! Evelina!" A nasally voice filled the store, and then a man rushed through the doorway, barreling through the mass of bodies standing in front of him.

"There you are, my sweet." Sheldon Jackson raced across the rough floorboards toward her.

Evelina could only stare. What was he doing here? Had her brothers brought him from Sitka? She hadn't seen him in the courthouse.

"Evelina, darling." He hurried forward, moving so quickly that she was half afraid he might plow into her. But he stopped just shy of colliding, then reached out and took her hand. "Here you are. I've been looking all over for you. There's something we simply must discuss, and it can't . . ."

He blinked, the thickness of his glasses only seeming to magnify his already large eyes as he studied his surroundings.

The chalkboard behind her, the teacher's desk at the front of the room, and fourteen student desks arranged into straight lines.

"What is the meaning of this? It looks like . . . like you really have started a school?"

"I . . . um . . ." She tugged her hand away from the reverend and shifted awkwardly from one foot to another.

"I told you, it's more of a tutoring arrangement." Alexei held out a hand to encompass the desks. "The students are here for only a few hours each day."

"But . . ." the reverend sputtered, pushing his glasses higher onto his nose. "But surely you know that the Ministry of Education established a school here just last year. That Miss Janice Thompson is teaching, and she's doing a rather fine job of it."

"She's not doing that fine of a job, actually." The words were out before she had time to think about them.

The reverend blinked at her with owlish eyes. "My dearest Evelina, whatever do you mean?"

"Go on." Jonas reached out and squeezed her hand, then tilted his head toward the reverend. "Tell him."

She wasn't sure whether it was the feel of Jonas's strong fingers wrapped around her own, or the way he was looking at her with faith in his eyes. Or maybe it was the stories the Tlingit children shared around town, or her own frustration with Janice Thompson. But for some reason, she opened her mouth, and her mind didn't freeze, nor did her tongue feel thick and woolen.

"Miss Thompson might be teaching, but she beats the children's hands bloody with her yardstick and won't let them speak a lick of their own language and—"

"But that makes her a good teacher!" The reverend sputtered again. "And these are the very latest, most improved education methods—which you would be aware of if you had a teaching certificate."

Oh, she was done with all the nonsense about not having a teaching certificate. What did that prove? She'd decided she didn't want a certificate on her second week of schooling in Boston, and that still hadn't changed. She didn't expect it ever would, not if having one meant hurting her students or forbidding them from speaking in the tongue they'd known from birth.

"You're right, reverend. I don't have a teaching certificate. I have a law degree, which I just used to get a woman free of a man who beat her with a board the last time they were alone together. I wonder if that board started out as a ruler, and his teacher struck him when he was in school."

The reverend blinked at her, almost as though she was speaking in Tlingit rather than English, and he couldn't comprehend what she'd said. Or more likely, that he couldn't comprehend someone having an opinion so very different from his own.

"Evelina, dearest, I came all this way to ask you to be my wife, but I cannot be married to a woman who insists on practicing law. It's unheard of. Now if I were to work with you and you get your teaching license, then the two of us could . . ."

"I have no intention of getting my teaching license—or becoming your wife."

"But how could you . . ." The reverend's jaw fell open. "That is . . . I'm offering you a chance to redeem your name. To detach yourself from the scandal that unfolded the last time you practiced law and—"

"Trying to save a woman from an abusive husband isn't a scandal." She stepped closer, squaring her shoulders and dragging a breath into her lungs. "The scandal is that people like you know what Sophie Haliburton was enduring at her husband's hands and did nothing."

The reverend's eyes grew even wider, which shouldn't have been possible considering they already looked like two moons taking up half his face.

And then they filled with . . . tears?

That was ridiculous. Certainly the man wasn't about to cry because she thought more people should have tried to help Sophie Haliburton, or that children should learn to read without having their hands rapped bloody.

"And here I thought you cared about those less fortunate than yourself." The reverend's voice pitched high, then cracked. "About the Indians. That you shared my burden for educating and assimilating them into society. But you only care about what? What is this? Why would you do this to a good woman like Miss Thompson? Why would you steal her students away?"

"While Miss Thompson might have a sincere heart, I already told you, there's nothing good about her teaching methods—or yours. All they do is hurt the children you're trying to help."

"No. This is not an issue you've studied, not something you can know. You're the last person who can offer an objective opinion on the best way to assimilate the various tribes of Alaska into American life—not considering your half siblings, who you're not even educating in a decent manner."

"I'm their legal guardian." Alexei stepped forward. "If you have questions about their education, you come to me. And mark my words, the last place you will ever find Inessa or Ilya is in one of your schools."

The reverend didn't even look at Alexei, never mind that her brother's eyes were so hot, they just might singe the reverend's coat. "Should you wish to actually help the Indians —rather than damage their chances at ever belonging in society —come visit me in Sitka."

And then the short little man turned on his heel and left, his fancy shoes clacking overly loud against the wood floor.

The moment he slammed the door behind him, everyone in the room sighed.

"He is the most condescending, horrendous little man." Kate's hands balled into fists at her side.

"Thank you for not making us go to one of his schools." Inessa looked across the room at Alexei.

"My cousin goes to Miss Thompson's school," Gushklin said. "He comes home with bloody knuckles once a week."

"You should have heard yourself, Lina." Yuri plowed forward and wrapped her in a giant hug. "For a moment, you almost sounded like Kate. I'm so proud."

He dropped her back on her feet, then gave her a slap on the back that probably stung a bit more than he intended.

She smiled at him anyway. "Thank you. It felt . . . nice."

"Don't tell me you were truly considering marrying him," Jonas said from behind her.

There might have been a time when she'd felt compelled to marry Rev. Jackson. Like after the Haliburton case, when it seemed as though she couldn't show her face around Sitka without people whispering.

But after meeting Jonas and starting her own school? "No, absolutely not."

"Good." He swept her hand into his, then held it down at his side, as though he couldn't stand to be so close but not touch.

She knew exactly how he felt.

But Alexei was glaring at their clasped hands. "Everybody out. Darrow and I need to talk."

"Come on. You heard Alexei." Yuri headed back across the room, herding everyone out. "Show's over."

Evelina sighed. She didn't even want to think about the stories that Gushklin would take back to his clan later that night.

"You too, Lina." Alexei jutted his chin toward the door.

She narrowed her eyes at her brother. "You expect me to leave?"

"I do."

She dropped Jonas's hand and crossed her arms over her chest. "If the two of you are going to talk about me, I fully intend to be present for it."

Alexei didn't argue. Instead, he fastened his gaze to Jonas,

314   Written on the Mist

the look in his eyes so sharp she half expected Jonas to start bleeding. "Darrow here told me he was leaving. Told me he needed to leave to keep you safe. Imagine my surprise when I returned today not just to find him back in Juneau but living here, no less, and that someone tried to burn down the trading post after he returned."

Alexei thought Jonas was the reason the trading post had almost burned? Her mouth fell open, but once again, her brain refused to form thoughts, and her words deserted her.

"You think the arsonist tried to burn down the building because of me?" Jonas's body tensed, something cold churning in his blood. He'd gone searching for Evelina partly to congratulate her on a job well done, but also because he'd wanted to explain the truth of his relationship with Harriet. How had it turned into this?

"When I left Juneau last, my siblings were perfectly safe." Alexei took a step closer, his eyes blazing. "And when I returned, I found someone tried to burn down this building while they slept. The only thing that changed in all of that was you. I don't care what kind of feelings you have for my sister. You're not staying at this trading post, and you're not to have any contact with her or anyone else in my family."

"Alexei, no," Evelina gasped, covering her mouth with her hand.

Jonas slanted her a glance. She'd taken a few steps away from them and was leaning against her desk, her arms wrapped around herself in a loose hug.

"You're mixing things up." She glanced between the two of them. "That's not what happened. Jonas saved us. Again. For a second time. He didn't bring any danger."

"Then how do you explain the attempt to burn down our building?" Alexei snapped.

"Clearly you don't have the whole story." She pushed herself off her desk and came toward her brother. "Because he stopped it from burning down, not the other way around."

"We can't rule out that he might have been the target of the fire." Alexei looked at him, his eyes narrowed into thin slits. "Or didn't he tell you why he left the last time?"

"He told me, and the arsonist had nothing to do with him."

"How do you know?"

She tossed her hands into the air. "Because I know! Because Jonas is good-hearted and gentle and kind. Because he'd never do anything to hurt another person, and here you are accusing him of that very thing."

"I find it awful suspicious he showed up while I was gone."

Evelina jabbed a finger into Alexei's shoulder. "You've been gone two other times, and he didn't come back."

"Yes, Amos," Jonas drawled. "Why don't you ask your sister why I returned?"

"He was helping me," Evelina explained. "He escorted me back from the mine and—"

"Back from what mine?" Alexei asked.

Evelina sighed. "The Perseverance, if you must know. I've been going up there to teach the foreman's children."

"I know you've been doing that, but why did you need an escort on the way home?" A muscle pulsed on the side of Alexei's jaw. "Don't tell me you went up there by yourself."

Evelina shifted, then sent him a quick glance before drawing her gaze back to her brother. "Well, Kate was running a medical clinic for the Tlingits, and Ilya and Inessa were helping her, so I—"

"Went up there alone anyway." All the tension slumped out of Alexei, causing his shoulders to go limp and his head to bow. "Why, Lina? Why would you go and do something like that?"

The stiffness drained from Evelina's body too. "Because the Lidding children needed to be taught. I visit only every three weeks, and they were expecting me. I would have needed to walk up there just to send word that I wasn't coming, so it seemed easiest to teach. When Jonas saw me up there by myself, he insisted on escorting me home. He was planning on turning around and going straight back up to the Perseverance, but Dressner was waiting for me at the door."

"I didn't feel it was safe to leave her—or anyone else in your family—after the threats Dressner made," Jonas said.

Alexei pinched between his eyebrows and drew in a breath. "It appears I am in debt to you yet again, Darrow."

"I tried to send Jonas away after he scared off Mr. Dressner," Evelina said softly. "But he and Kate both insisted that a man needed to be here so long as Myra was with us, just in case Dressner tried something."

"Which he did," Jonas added. "He just didn't do it himself."

Alexei moved his gaze between the two of them. "And somehow him staying led to the two of you kissing in the schoolroom."

Evelina's face turned bright red, but Jonas simply met Alexei's gaze. "I already told you, I'm not going to apologize for kissing your sister."

Alexei rubbed his hand over his firm jaw. "You can't stay. I don't care what kind of feelings you and Lina might have for each other. I can't risk anything happening to my family."

"Nothing will happen to them. The threat from a month ago is gone."

"Is that a promise or a hope?" Alexei took a step closer. "Just how do you know for certain that the threat is gone?"

Jonas opened his mouth, ready to launch into the same explanation he'd given Evelina two nights ago, about how whoever was looking for him had plenty of time to trace him to Alaska, about how no one had come to Juneau looking for a man by his name. About how he'd missed the Amoses—the whole messy lot of them—and was ready to come down from the mountains and start living again.

But none of the words would come.

Because Alexei was right. He didn't know for a fact that all possibility of danger had passed. He hoped it was gone. It seemed likely it was gone, but that didn't mean the danger was gone entirely.

And just how long would it take him to be certain of that? One year? Two? Five?

Part of him wanted to say that he could stay, that he wanted to fight for Evelina and the future they might one day have.

But the other part of him, the part that had watched flames ravage his mother's house, that had returned to Austin and stood over the shadows of two new tombstones in the cemetery, didn't want to protest.

It wanted to keep the woman beside him as safe as possible, and that meant being nowhere near a man whom criminals might be hunting this very moment.

"I'll pack my bags." The words were quiet, but they landed in the room with the force of a landslide, shaking the air around them before settling into a deathly quiet.

"Wait." Evelina stepped to him, her eyes wide and watery. "Please don't go. Please stay. Please . . ."

He wrapped his arms around her, drawing her against his chest.

She came willingly, letting him rest his cheek atop her silky hair.

"I'll give you two a moment to say good-bye." Alexei

headed toward the door. "But then I expect you to be gone, Darrow, and never to come back. Am I clear?"

Jonas swallowed, his grip involuntarily tightening around Evelina's back. "Perfectly."

The second the door closed behind Alexei, Evelina leaned back to look at him. "Please, Jonas. Don't let him do this."

He stroked a hand down her hair, the tresses long and smooth. "Your brother is right. I can't promise I won't bring you harm, and the thought of that, after what happened to my mother and Harriet—" His throat closed off. "I need to leave. Please try to understand."

"But if you just tell Alexei what happened in Texas, why you came here—"

"It won't change the truth. We both know that arsonist had nothing to do with me, but someone might come looking for me one day. And I can't bear the thought of putting you—or anyone else here—in danger."

She buried her face in his shoulder. "Ilya will be devastated."

Ilya wasn't the only one. Even now, standing there with Evelina in his arms, with the scent of cinnamon and vanilla twining around him, and her hair falling in soft waves over his shirt, he felt a hole open inside him.

Not unlike the one he'd felt the night he stood on the street watching as his mother's home burned to ash.

He'd not realized that hole had begun to fill again. But now it had emptied itself once more, leaving nothing but a gaping hollowness inside him.

28

The sun was already tracking westward in the sky by the time Jonas trudged up the side of the mountain, its rays painting the forest in a vibrant brush of gold.

It reminded him of his first day in Alaska, when Ilya had told him that Juneau was the most beautiful place in the world when the sun was shining. He hadn't believed the boy then, but standing on the mountain with the blue waters of the Gastineau Channel sparkling below him and tree-covered mountains rising on all sides, it was hard to argue.

But the sunny day seemed wrong somehow. All the good things that had happened to him since coming to Alaska had been encased in the endless mist and rain that shrouded the valley. But now, on the day when he'd lost every last bit of the new life he'd been trying to build, the sun decided to shine on the town.

It was almost as though the sun was mocking him. As though it had looked down from its place in the sky, seen his misery, and decided to cast a bright, happy glow on the world.

Jonas hunched his shoulders and continued up the path.

Hopefully he'd be able to convince Jace to hire him back on at the Perseverance, at least for another week or so until the creek froze.

And after that, maybe he really would learn to winter in the mountains. Or he'd go to Treadwell and work there like everyone else. Maybe he'd get used to the smell of the chlorination plant, to the constant pounding of the stamp mill.

Jonas dragged a hand down his face.

Was this to be his lot? Was he to be a vagabond for the rest of his life?

He'd thought that was what he wanted when he decided to leave Texas, but now?

He didn't want to leave another place, especially not one that was starting to feel like home.

He wanted to stay with the Amoses, with Evelina and her sweet kisses and soft hair and kind heart, with Ilya and his love for life and excitement for everything he came across. He'd even miss Kate and her determined ways and endless practicality, and Inessa with her quiet observations.

But at what cost?

What's next, God? He raised his head to the heavens, allowed himself to feel the weak warmth from the sun on his face. *I don't understand. I thought I was doing the right thing by coming here, that I was protecting both myself and my sister. Then I arrived and met the Amoses, and I know you didn't want me to walk away from Ilya on the wharf. I know you wanted me to step in. But then . . .*

What?

He raked in a jagged breath, though the air that entered his lungs felt sharp as glass. He'd thought he was healing, that maybe there had been something to what Evelina had said the other night, that God had brought him to Alaska—to the Amoses—to heal.

But there was nothing healing in all of this. It was sheer misery, like losing his mother and Harriet all over again.

Or maybe even worse, because he had little hope that he'd ever be anything more than a vagabond.

God is able to do exceeding abundantly above all that we ask or think.

Though Kate was the one who always quoted that verse, it was the sound of the words on Evelina's tongue the night of the arson attempt that floated back to him.

"Am I missing something, God?" He looked back up at the sky. "When are you going to do exceeding abundantly above all that I ask? Because it doesn't seem like I'm asking for a whole lot. Just a chance to stay with the Amoses. Just a chance to have a normal family. Just a chance to . . ."

Be whole again.

But no answer floated down from the sunlight or whispered through the trees, no sense of peace or belonging filled his soul.

If anything, his soul felt even blacker and darker than before.

So he continued his trudge up the mountainside.

Because what better place was there for a man filled with blackness to work than in the deep, dark bowels of the earth?

"THERE YOU ARE."

At the sound of her sister's voice, Evelina looked over her shoulder to find Kate coming up behind her.

"Everyone's been looking for you." Kate plopped down on the piece of driftwood beside her, the same piece of driftwood they'd sat on a month ago, when Jonas had left the first time. Across the channel, the mountain on the tip of Douglas Island rose into the sky, its slopes blanketed with the dark green of Sitka spruce and moss-covered earth.

"Tell everyone I'm not interested in being found," she muttered.

Kate scooted a bit closer on the log, then reached out and gripped her hand. "You did well in court today. I think even Judge Lincham was impressed—for about two seconds until he remembered you're a woman."

She smiled faintly. "There was a part of me that liked being back in a courtroom."

"I could tell." Kate gave her foot a little nudge. "Beyond liking it, you're also a good lawyer."

Evelina sighed. "Maybe, but we both know that's not why I'm out here."

"Are your feelings for Darrow really that strong?"

"I think so. Maybe." She shoved a hand through her hair. "Oh, how does a woman tell if she's in love?"

"She can't stop thinking about the man she's in love with, I suppose. And she wants to be with him all the time, and . . . I don't know. I can't call what I had with Peter back in Boston love, at least not now that I look back on it. Alexei would be the one to ask."

Her shoulders stiffened. "I'm never speaking to Alexei again."

"Maybe he'll come back."

"Alexei? I hope he leaves in the morning and doesn't ever return." Evelina reached down and scooped a rock off the beach. "I hope he goes back to Sitka and stays there until he's old and gray."

"You don't mean that."

She did. This was the second time he'd scared off the man she was coming to love, and it hurt.

"I wasn't even talking about Alexei. Maybe Jonas will return."

Evelina's hand tightened around the rock. "Even if he does, Alexei won't let him anywhere near us. He's that upset."

"It doesn't sound like he's upset. It sounds like he's lost his ever-loving mind."

Evelina drew in a breath, her shoulders slumping. "Maybe he has. He's convinced Jonas's presence puts us in danger, and he's convinced the arson attempt was meant for Jonas."

"Sometimes our oldest brother has more stubbornness than he has sense."

Evelina snorted. "I think that's an Amos family trait."

Silence stretched between them, leaving nothing more than the sound of a raven cawing and the rising tide lapping at the beach.

"Isn't this about the time where you tell me that life isn't so bleak?" Evelina looked out at the calm water glinting in the sunlight.

"It isn't. There's always a reason to have hope. Sometimes we just have to look a little harder for it than other times."

"What about when it feels like all hope has deserted you?"

Rather than try to convince her she was wrong or that she needed more hope or faith or joyful spirits, Kate merely reached up and stroked her back, up and down, up and down. The movement was familiar, something Kate used to do during their childhood, whenever she was upset.

Evelina drew in a breath, then leaned her head on her sister's shoulder. Kate tilted her head too, letting them rest against each other as they both stared out at the beach.

"Do you ever look at our lives now and think they look nothing like we imagined as girls?" Evelina whispered.

"I'm a doctor." Kate's hand kept moving against her back in long, smooth motions. "And for the first time since I got my medical license, I have patients. Real patients with real problems, not just a list of rich women wanting me to make house calls for female complaints and fits of nerves. This is exactly what I imagined when I was little."

"But you're not married."

"I was never the one who wanted to get married." Kate shrugged, even though the weight of both their heads still rested on her shoulder. "I figured it would happen because I'm a woman and that's what we do, get married and have babies, but I'd much rather be single than married to a man who thinks I should raise children instead of practice medicine."

"I want to be a mother. I like teaching well enough. I mean, I certainly like seeing the students progressing a bit more each day. And I loved how I was able to help Myra. But more than anything, I want a family."

"Maybe you need to leave Alaska, then. Go somewhere that the men are a little more . . . reputable. Unless you're of a mind to marry a miner with unkempt hair and only half his teeth."

She pulled away from Kate. "Jonas isn't missing half his teeth, and I like it when his curls are a little unruly."

"Are you set on marrying him?"

She dug her toe into the damp, cool sand. "When I told him I was a lawyer, he didn't balk. He didn't look at me as though I'd lost my mind or tell me I belonged in the schoolroom or needed a husband and family to occupy my time. If anything, he looked proud of me. Even when I explained the Haliburton case. He didn't think I was crazy for believing Sophie or trying to defend her. He said the lawyers he knew back in Texas would have taken Sophie's side in the case, that it was an honest mistake."

Kate grew still beside her. "Then maybe he really is the right man for you."

"I think he might be. But what am I to do when Alexei keeps sending him away? Run off in the dead of night and marry in secret?" The thought brought tears to her eyes. So much would change if she did that. Her relationship with Alexei would never be the same, and it probably wouldn't be the same with anyone else in her family. And that didn't even take into account that Jonas had just lost his fiancée and wasn't ready to love again.

"Maybe Alexei will have a change of heart about Jonas," Kate said.

Evelina blinked away the burning sensation in her eyes. She hoped her sister was right.

Because she suddenly couldn't imagine any kind of future for herself—unless Jonas Darrow was in it.

29

K nock. Knock. Knock.
    "Lina?"
Evelina looked up from her desk inside the schoolroom to find none other than Alexei poking his head through the doorway. "I'm still not talking to you, so you can turn right back around."

Alexei sighed, but rather than listen, he stepped into the room. "It's been two days. You can't expect to keep this up much longer."

She narrowed her eyes. "Try me."

He looked back out the door, said something she couldn't quite make out, then stepped back inside and closed the door. "I didn't realize Darrow meant that much to you. I thought that if I—"

"Then maybe you should have asked before you went around accusing him of being the reason someone tried to burn the building down."

Alexei raked a hand through his hair. "That's just it. We still don't know that Darrow isn't the reason."

She held up a hand. "I'm not doing this. Just leave. Please." She said the words as an order, not a request.

"Gushklin's mother wants to talk to you."

"Is that who's on the other side of the door?"

"Yes."

She straightened the papers she'd been grading, then drew in a long breath, pushing all thoughts of her brother and Jonas and her lack of future aside. "Send her in."

A woman stepped through the doorway a moment later, her dark hair pulled back into a long, thick braid. "Thank you for meeting. I am Kaaguneteen."

She spoke with a thick accent, but her English was passable enough to converse.

"It's my pleasure." Evelina stood and grabbed one of the students' chairs, then positioned it next to the desk. "I'm happy with how Gushklin is progressing in school. He's both reading and writing in English, and his math has—"

"I didn't come here about Gushklin." The woman moved silently down the aisle, then slid into the open chair.

Evelina sank down into her own chair behind her desk. "Then what is it?"

"You helped the woman with the cruel husband . . . Mrs. Dressner, yes?"

"Yes."

"And you're a lawyer? You can . . . You can go to court? You can help me?"

She shifted uncomfortably in her chair. "That depends on what you need help with." Was Kaaguneteen in some kind of trouble? Gushklin had never mentioned such a thing.

The woman straightened. "I need Gushklin's brother back."

Evelina blinked. "Gushklin's brother? Is he gone for some reason?"

"Their father—my husband—he died earlier this year."

"I'm so sorry." She'd already known about Gushklin's father, but having his widow in front of her, the woman's dark eyes filled with sorrow, made the loss seem new.

"It is hard now that we are in white men's houses." Kaaguneteen kept her hands on her lap as she spoke, her shoulders back and her chin straight. The only sign of her distress was the way the fingers on her right hand toyed with the edge of the sleeve on her left. "Before, in the longhouses, our family was all together. There were others to care for those in the clan when a husband died. But now it is just us, and I need Xetsuwu to come home, to go back to work digging the ditch."

"Xetsuwu? Is that your oldest son's name?" She tried to pronounce the word as Gushklin's mother did, but just as with most Tlingit words, it seemed to stick on her tongue.

Kaaguneteen nodded. "Yes. That is him."

"And where is he?"

"At Mr. Jackson's industrial school in Sitka."

Evelina frowned. "So do you need help asking the school to send Xetsuwu home?"

"I already have." The woman slipped a letter out from her pocket and handed it over. "They refused to send him."

Evelina took the letter and scanned the words, her stomach growing more and more sour with each line she read. This couldn't be true. She had to be misconstruing something.

But the words were clear as day. Rev. Jackson said he couldn't allow Xetsuwu to be released from the school because the school had legal custody over him, not his mother, and that custody had been given up when she agreed to enroll him in the school for five years.

"Can you help?" Kaaguneteen leaned forward, her eyes shining with a hope that Evelina didn't want to think about.

"I don't know. Did you sign something when you agreed to

have Xetsuwu attend Reverend Jackson's school? A piece of paper or some sort of contract?"

"Yes. He made all parents sign it. He said we needed to in order to make sure our children would have proper training."

"I need a copy of what you signed." Evelina drew in a shaky breath.

Kaaguneteen slid a single-page contract across the desk.

Even though the contract was short, she'd need to go over it in detail later. But surely the reverend wasn't asking native parents to give up their rights to their children just so they could go to the school. She and the reverend might have differences of opinion regarding the best way to educate the native populations of Alaska, but this went too far.

Except what if he was truly asking such a thing? And even if Kaaguneteen hadn't signed something giving up her parental rights, Rev. Jackson was still claiming the school had custody of Xetsuwu. And there was only one place for a dispute like this to be settled. In court.

But filing such a lawsuit would attract instant attention. People didn't take schools to court, especially not Alaskan natives, and especially not a school like Sheldon Jackson's Industrial and Trading School. She might think Rev. Jackson a nincompoop, but the newspapers in California loved him, and Presbyterians across the entirety of America sent money to fund his schools.

It would be like the Haliburton case all over again, except with more attention on it right from the beginning. She could already see the headlines from San Francisco in her mind: "Indian Woman Claims Prestigious School Kidnapped Son." Or "Tlingit Mother Takes School to Court for Teaching Valuable Skills." Or even worse, "Female Attorney and Tlingit Mother Bring Laughable Case against Education for Natives in Alaska."

It was sure to spell disaster.

But none of that changed the fact that Xetsuwu's family needed him, and Sheldon Jackson was refusing to let him go home.

Evelina slid both the letter and the contract into the top drawer of her desk. "Give me some time to think about how I might help. Perhaps there's another way, other than going to court, that might convince the school to release Xetsuwu."

At the very least, she could write the reverend a letter. Not that she expected it to get very far with the stubborn man. But at least she'd be doing something, and a lawsuit seemed like the last method they should try to have Xetsuwu returned.

"Thank you for your time. I appreciate anything you can do to help." Kaaguneteen sent her a weak smile and looked around the room. "Now where is Gushklin? I'd like to speak with him before school starts."

"What do you mean? Isn't he at the Tlingit village with Ilya?" Evelina glanced at the wall clock. "But I imagine the boys will arrive soon. School starts in only twenty minutes."

"No." Kaaguneteen gave a firm shake of her head. "The boys are not at the village. Gushklin said he was coming here after breakfast."

"Something must have gotten mixed up, because Ilya said he was going to your village. That the two of them were going to help repair a leaking roof."

"They are not at the village. Gushklin took our canoe first thing this morning. He said he was coming here to speak to Ilya. I borrowed my brother's canoe to row across the channel and see you."

"Your canoe is gone? Do you think the boys may have taken it down the channel by themselves?" The words nearly clogged in her throat. The islands and inlets near Juneau were familiar, yes, but also dangerous. And if the boys had ventured off in the canoe, they could be nearly anywhere. What would possess the boys to go off on their own and . . .

But she knew the answer. Jonas had promised Ilya they'd go prospecting somewhere near Sheep Creek.

Then Alexei had sent Jonas away, and Ilya was every bit as upset with Alexei as she was.

Which meant he was probably mad enough to go off prospecting on his own.

She turned to Kaaguneteen. "Let's give the boys another hour or so to return, but if they're not back by two, we might need to organize a search party."

The boys weren't back by two, and as a search party was organized, Evelina couldn't say precisely how she knew something was wrong—only that she did.

———

ALEXEI YANKED open the door to the trading post and trudged in from the cold rain. He shivered, trying to ward off the chill of the wintery air. He wouldn't be surprised if the rain turned to snow overnight. Water and mud from his boots tracked inside the store, creating a mess.

He couldn't bring himself to care, not when his brother was gone and no one had been able to find him. The sickening sensation that had been twisting in his stomach all afternoon while they'd organized a search party and looked for the boys writhed yet again.

Though Ilya didn't love the water, he was still good with a canoe, and Gushklin would be better. Even if the boys had planned to go prospecting on their own in the morning, they should have returned in time for school—or maybe a few minutes late if they had lost track of time.

332 Written on the Mist

Ilya would never intentionally return late, especially considering both his father and mother had been lost at sea.

A shiver traveled up his spine as he entered the school-room, which had been turned into a makeshift headquarters for the search. Sandwiches were laid out on a table along the wall, and the sweet aroma of China Joe's cookies filled the air.

He didn't need to ask if anyone had found Ilya. The somber faces of the men inside the room told him everything he needed to know.

"Still no sign of them?" Evelina approached, her eyes filled with a hope he didn't want to think about.

"Nothing." He took off his dripping slicker and hung it on one of the coat trees by the door.

"Not even their canoe?"

"No." And he didn't know what to do about it. Men from Gushklin's clan had spent the afternoon and evening searching alongside residents of Juneau, and Sheep Creek was scoured a dozen times over, never mind that it lay about ten miles south of town.

Someone should have discovered something.

Now night was descending, and they'd need to wait until morning to resume the search. Was it too much to hope the rain would stop and no snow would come? Any tracks Ilya and Gushklin left needed to be preserved.

Evelina bit into her bottom lip. "I wish we knew where their canoe was. Then we would at least know we were looking in the right spot."

"Do you suppose they went north of town, not south?" Yuri asked, studying the map of the area that someone had pinned to the cork strip at the top of the chalkboard at the front of the room.

"Hadn't thought of that," Grover Hanover said from where he stood at the back of the room, eating one of the sandwiches.

He was there along with the other members of the Committee of Public Safety, Hemming and Stubbins.

A group of Tlingit men entered, their faces just as grim as they explained there were too many trails and footprints around Sheep Creek to determine which ones, if any, belonged to the boys.

"Should we start searching north of town in the morning, then?" Mr. Hemming asked, still dressed in his three-piece suit from the bank.

"He has a point." Yuri scratched the side of his head. "We haven't found any evidence that the boys actually went clear down to Sheep Creek. Maybe they went somewhere closer."

"Where?" Alexei huffed. "Ilya wanted to go to Sheep Creek. It's all he's talked about for the past month. I can't imagine he'd go anywhere other than that, can you?"

Yuri shrugged, and the conversation continued, the Tlingit men agreeing they should switch search areas and look north of town in the morning, while Alexei thought Sheep Creek still hadn't been scoured thoroughly.

For once in his life, he wished for Marshal Hibbs. The man might not be able to outrun a criminal, but he'd led the search when their parents' ship had been lost at sea.

The Marshal was supposed to arrive tomorrow or the next day to question the arsonist, but Alexei didn't plan on waiting that long to find Ilya.

"I'm going out." Evelina picked up her cloak from where it was lying across one of the desks and slipped it on.

Alexei glanced outside. Frigid rain pounded against the window. "Why? Don't tell me you plan to search Sheep Creek by yourself after dark."

"Not hardly. I'm going to the Perseverance." She raised the hood of her cloak over her head, then nabbed a sandwich off the table and slid it into her pocket.

"Why?" Alexei came toward her. He knew she was worried about Ilya—they all were—but that didn't explain why his sister would lose all sense.

"Why do you think?" She rolled her eyes. "To get Jonas Darrow."

Darrow? What could he possibly do?

"I hadn't thought of Darrow." Hemming snapped his fingers. "He might know where we should search."

"That's why I intend to get him." Evelina started toward the door, but Alexei reached out and grabbed her arm.

"What am I missing here? Why will he be more helpful than anyone else? Unless . . . Do you think he might have taken Ilya?"

"What is wrong with you?" She jerked her arm away, her eyes shooting green fire. "Why do you keep assuming the worst about Jonas? He used to be a sheriff. That's why I'm going to get him. Because he'll know a heap more than you about how to conduct this search."

"He used to be a sheriff?" Hemming stuffed a bite of sandwich into his mouth. Heaven forbid the search for Ilya interrupt the fancy banker's dinner. "Why didn't he say so?"

Grover Hanover scratched his head. "That explains why he was so good at questioning Volker and the arsonist."

"He couldn't even get the arsonist to give us his name," Alexei gritted.

"He got more out of the man than the rest of us did, you included," Hanover responded. "And he got Volker to tell him all about the man with long hair that Darrow's convinced stole the two hundred dollars."

"Like I said, I'm going to get Jonas." Evelina turned back toward the door.

"Not by yourself, you're not." Alexei stomped over to where he'd hung his slicker. One lost sibling was enough.

The trek up the mountain was arduous. Alexei hunkered down beneath the thick fur of his coat, which he'd grabbed in place of his slicker before heading out into the night. The rain descended in sheets from the heavens, stealing the small beams of light emanating from their lamps. He let Evelina lead the way, and she charged up the mountain, never mind the mud soiling the bottom of her skirt and the water dripping from her wide-brimmed hat.

At least the rain hadn't yet turned to snow.

When they reached a particularly steep stretch of trail and their feet started sliding on the soft earth, Alexei sidled in front of her and picked his way over the steep terrain, then turned back and extended his hand.

Their eyes met through the slashing rain. "How do you know Darrow's a sheriff?" He couldn't stop himself from asking.

She stiffened at the question, a look of indignation crossing her face. "He told me so."

"What if he lied?"

Her glare turned harder as she scrambled up the slope, then stopped beside him. "Lied? You think he lied? You should have seen him watching our building on Saturday night. He wasn't just sitting on a chair next to the window eating snacks. He had every light off. He knew exactly where to stand in the shadows so that no one on the outside of the building could see him. He spread out his bedroll in front of the door. Our trading post certainly isn't the first building he's guarded into the wee hours of the morning.

"And you watched him save Ilya from Volker." She jabbed her finger into his chest. "Tell me, did he seem like he knew what he was doing when a group of angry drunkards was surrounding him? Did he know how to conduct himself? How to get Ilya away from the men and focus their attention on him?"

"He did, yes." Alexei sighed. "And I didn't realize that was how he guarded the building."

"Well it was. And if you had questions about it, you could have asked. Instead, you marched into the schoolroom and accused him of being the reason the torch was thrown through the window."

"I wasn't trying to—"

"Clearly, you haven't seen his chest, or you'd know there is no way he's lying about being a sheriff."

"Have *you* seen his chest?" Alexei growled, taking a step closer.

"He was shirtless in our sickroom for over a week. Who do you think changed his bandage every day? Who do you think gave him sponge baths? Who do you think—?"

"This is why most doctors are men. So there's never any question of propriety."

"I'm not a doctor." Evelina swept past him and continued up the trail. "And I certainly wasn't acting as a doctor when I changed his bandage. That's a nurse's job, and nurses see men with bare chests and bare legs and bare groins all the time!"

"Then maybe I don't want you to be a nurse anymore."

Alexei rushed to keep up with her, but she just lengthened her stride. "Not only are you being ridiculous, but you're missing my point, which is that Jonas was injured before by a bullet, plus he suffered multiple stabbings that looked as though they should have killed him. What kind of person has that many knife and bullet scars if he's not a lawman?"

"A seasoned criminal."

She halted on the trail and jerked around, her mouth flying open. "You think . . . you think Jonas is a criminal?"

"I spoke to the Marshal after Jonas left the last time. He left so suddenly, and he was so sure danger was coming, that it felt odd." Alexei tilted his head, causing the rain that had pooled on the brim of his hat to pour onto the ground. "It got me wondering why he was here in the first place. Where he'd come from, and what he'd left behind."

"Well, I'm not sure what took you so long." She turned back around and started walking again. "I was wondering that on his first day in Juneau. He's from Texas, and he left because—"

"There's a criminal from Montana on the run." Alexei used his long strides to catch up with her, but the rain was so hard, his neck and face were getting wet despite his hat and coat. "A counterfeit money operation was raided by the US Marshals, and one of the men is still on the loose. A man with red hair and brown eyes. I'm sorry, Evelina, but I think Jonas Darrow might really be—"

"From Texas." She whirled on him. "Jonas is from Texas. Or are you going to tell me he's been faking that southern drawl this whole time?"

"Men can learn to speak with new accents."

"When they're delirious from pain after being stabbed?"

Alexei's mouth clamped shut. "I hadn't thought of that."

"Tell me, how many men who live in America have brown eyes?"

"I don't know."

"Neither do I, but we both know it's more than one, seeing as it's the color not just of your eyes but also of Ilya's and Inessa's and Mikhail's. Oh, and Jonas. He has brown eyes too. As does this criminal from Montana who's missing."

Alexei sighed.

"Now let's play the game again with red hair. How many men in this country do you think have red hair?"

"I understand your point."

"Do you?"

He used his gloved hand to wipe the rain from his face. "I should have asked more questions, given Darrow a chance to explain."

"I understand having questions about the fire, but considering all he's done for us, you should have at least trusted him enough to ask him a few more questions. To have a conversation."

"If he was such a good sheriff back in Texas, what brought him to Alaska?"

Evelina rubbed her arms, as though suddenly cold, even though there hadn't been a particularly strong gust of wind to chill her. "A case went bad, and a criminal killed his family."

"Oh." He couldn't imagine what it would feel like to have a criminal kill his family, especially if he'd just been doing his job. "I suppose that would cause a man to want to start over again."

"It would."

"Did he . . ." Alexei glanced over at his sister. "Did he have a wife?"

"No. A fiancée and a mother. The criminal threw a stick of dynamite into his mother's house. He was supposed to be there."

The twisting sensation returned to his stomach. How terrible. After Ivan and his parents had died, his heart had felt so heavy that he struggled to get out of bed some mornings, struggled to eat. He couldn't imagine how much worse the pain would have been had he inadvertently been the cause of their deaths. "I assume his mother and fiancée were there instead?"

Evelina nodded, her eyes shining with a moisture that probably had nothing to do with the rain streaming around them.

"I'm sorry," he whispered.

"I'm not the one you need to apologize to."

"I wasn't saying I was sorry because I assumed he was a criminal. I'm sorry because you're falling in love with him, but if he just lost his fiancée . . ."

"He's not ready to move on. I know." Evelina turned her head and stared up the mountain, her breath puffing white against the frigid air. "That's why I was so mad when you sent him away. He wanted to stay in Juneau, to manage the trading post. I wanted him to have time to heal but still be close. Perhaps it's selfish to want such a thing, but I can't bear the thought of him up here in the mountains all alone. I think the thing he needs most is people, even though that scares him."

"You're probably right." Alexei put his head down and trudged forward passing his sister as the first pellet of sleet landed on his arm. Lovely. Now the rain was changing to snow. "But if he's really a lawman, and if he lost his mother and fiancée, why couldn't he promise not to bring danger to the trading post? Why couldn't he promise that the arson attack hadn't been intended for him?"

Evelina sighed, her shoulders deflating. "When he left the first time, it was because someone had come to his sister's house looking for him, and his sister sent a letter telling him of it. Jonas was worried it might be a criminal, but after a month passed and no one seemed to have followed him to Juneau, he assumed everything was safe. So I'm guessing that when you asked him about danger on Monday, he left because he can't promise no one will come looking for him ever, that one of the criminals he put away won't escape from prison and try to track him down."

Alexei swallowed. "That wasn't what I meant."

"But that's how he probably took it."

"I see." He stared straight ahead at the trail, quickening his pace. "Can you go any faster? I owe someone an apology."

Now it was Evelina's turn to rush to match his gait. "Will

that apology come before or after you beg him to help you find Ilya?"

———

HIS CHEST WAS ALREADY BACK to aching. He'd been back to work for only two days, and already his wound felt like it was ready to split open again. The second he stopped pushing and hauling things, it improved.

But it wasn't as though there were a whole lot of jobs for him to work that didn't involve moving rock.

Jonas leaned back in one of the wooden chairs beside the fireplace, keeping an eye on the table in the middle of the bunkhouse, where a half dozen other miners were playing a game of poker.

Last night one of the men had tried cheating, and the game had ended with a fight. But now that the cheater had been barred from playing again, the game seemed to be progressing as expected.

Jonas rubbed a hand over the back of his neck. The air outside was downright frigid tonight, and the rain that had hammered the mountain earlier in the afternoon had turned to a wet, slushy snow. The creek probably wouldn't be frozen in the morning, but it would freeze soon enough, and then what would he do?

He'd head to Treadwell. He had no choice. He didn't want to try finding a job in Juneau on the off chance someone would arrive on a ship looking for him one day. The farther away he was from Evelina and Ilya, the better he could ensure their safety.

Yet as he sat there beside the crackling fire with snow and sleet battering the ground outside, all he wanted was to sit beside a different fire, with Ilya squeezing himself into the same overstuffed chair, opening one of his prospecting books, and Evelina softly humming something on the other side of the fire as she knitted a mitten or scarf.

Jonas blew out a breath, slamming his eyes shut against the image in his mind. That type of scene wasn't in his future, not with Evelina, not with Ilya, and probably not with anyone.

A sharp knock sounded at the door, and his eyes sprang open.

The miner with the bunk closest to the door rolled off his bed and pulled the door open.

"I'm looking for Jonas Darrow." A firm voice filled the bunkhouse.

Jonas was instantly on his feet, shoving his way past the poker table as he strode forward. "Alexei?"

The shipyard owner stepped inside, followed by a smaller form shrouded in a fur cloak and hood. Dainty hands reached up and pushed the hood back from her head, revealing a torrent of rich chestnut hair and somber green eyes.

He wanted to smile, to pull Evelina into his arms and not let her go for a solid week—until he glimpsed the worried look on her face.

"What is it?" He looked between them, his heart thundering against his chest. "What brought the two of you up here?"

After dark. In the snow and sleet.

The answer couldn't be good.

"It's Ilya." Evelina's eyes filled with tears. "He and Gushklin went out prospecting this morning, and they haven't come back."

"Ilya?" he repeated. "He's lost?"

It couldn't be. Not Ilya, the boy he'd promised to take prospecting. Not the boy who could pull a smile from his mouth and fill his heart with warmth. Not the boy who'd sat on his bed and dreamed of growing bigger and exploring unnamed mountains and valleys, of discovering gold for himself.

Dear God, please not Ilya. Anyone but him.

Alexei scanned him, his mannerisms nothing like that of the tense, angry man who'd sent him away on Monday. "Evelina says that you were a sheriff in Texas."

He hadn't been a sheriff, but he'd been awful close to one, and the details were hardly worth hashing out if Ilya was lost outside somewhere in the snow and sleet.

"We've been searching for Ilya and Gushklin for half the day," Alexei continued, his voice growing scratchy. "But we haven't found any clues as to where they might be. Can you return to Juneau and run the search?"

Of course. He had to help. There was no way he could refuse.

But he'd run searches many times before, and these were the worst search conditions a lawman could imagine. Water, mountains, and thick forests already surrounded Juneau, making the terrain nearly impossible to search. And that wasn't taking into account the rain-turned-snow they'd had for most of the day that would either wash away or cover tracks, or the fact that there were already numerous tracks in the woods left by hundreds of men scouring the mountains in search of gold.

It would be a miracle if they found either of the boys alive.

30

"We're going to lay out the search area like this." Jonas raised his voice loudly enough to be heard throughout the packed schoolroom. The sky was just beginning to lighten from black into a misty gray, and it seemed as though every last person from Juneau and the Tlingit village had come to help search for Ilya and Gushklin.

"I want people in teams of at least three. I've numbered each grid on the map. When you finish searching one grid, report back here and you'll be assigned another. We're starting with the grids closest to Sheep Creek." Jonas used the yardstick leaning against the wall to tap Sheep Creek on the map hanging from the cork strip above the chalkboard. It was one of the southernmost features on the map, a good ten miles or so outside of town. "After each of those have been searched, we'll expand to the grids farther away. If you're familiar with a particular area on the grid, let Evelina know, and she'll assign you to it."

He gestured to where Evelina sat at the back of the room.

They'd cleared space on one of the food tables for her to assign grid numbers to the teams as they left.

"I'd rather have people familiar with the terrain searching than people who have never seen it before. And that goes for the water too. If you fish a lot and are familiar with the shoreline, you can search for the canoe. Finding that will give us our biggest clue as to where the boys might have gone. Are there any questions?"

He scanned the room. A few men looked around, but no one asked anything. Word that he was a former lawman must have spread quickly through the town, because no one seemed to have any questions. If anything, they looked at him with a new level of respect, especially the men from the Committee of Public Safety. "Very well. Break off into groups of three or four and head out. Remember to report back and grab a bite to eat once you've finished searching your grid. You're all going to search better on a full stomach."

Chatter filled the room once again, the men deciding whom they wanted to search with and then approaching Evelina and Kate to get their assignments.

The two women had stayed up into the wee hours of the night helping him lay out the grids over the map and number them, all so that the teams could start the search at dawn.

"Mr. Darrow! Mr. Darrow!" The Finch boys shoved their way through the crowd of men surrounding the back table and headed straight toward him.

"We followed Mr. Dressner for you." The shorter of the two boys reached him first. Robbie, if he recalled.

"Did you now?" He'd looked for the boys before he left Juneau on Monday evening, but when he hadn't been able to find them, he'd assumed they were still tracking Dressner. "What did you find?"

Harry, the taller of the two boys, puffed out his chest. "You said Mr. Dressner's claim was down by Sheep Creek, but that's not the direction he went."

"No? What way did he go?"

"North of town," Harry said, the words practically bursting from his lips.

Jonas scratched the back of his head. That was odd. All the prospectors around Juneau said Dressner had a claim south of town, near the area that Ilya and Gushklin had gone prospecting, in fact. So why would he have headed north? "Did you find his claim?"

The boys shook their heads.

Robbie shoved a thatch of dark brown hair away from his face. "He lost us."

Harry nodded. "He tried being sneaky at first, because he started off in the direction of Sheep Creek, but then after a half hour or so, he swung back around and crossed Gold Creek."

"That's where we lost him. He walked in the creek for a ways, and we couldn't find where he climbed out."

"Thank you." Jonas reached for his billfold and pulled out two quarters. "Appreciate it."

"Do you need us to help find Ilya next?" Robbie asked.

"You don't have to pay us this time. We wanna help." Harry took a step closer to him. "If Robbie and I were the ones who got lost, Ilya would want to help find us."

Jonas patted Harry on the shoulder. "I'd sure appreciate it. Why don't the two of you split up and see if you can each find a team of men?"

"Sure." Harry spun around and disappeared into the crowd, probably heading toward the table where he'd join the next group that left.

But Robbie stayed beside him. "Can I join your team, Mr. Darrow? I'd really like to go with you."

Jonas shrugged. "I suppose." He didn't exactly know which

346   Written on the Mist

men he was searching with yet, but bringing one of the Finch boys along shouldn't pose a problem. If the boy learned enough about tracking, then maybe the next time he needed someone tracked, the Finch boys wouldn't lose the person in a creek bed.

"Mr. Darrel . . . Did I say that correctly?" Jonas looked up to find a native woman with heavy eyes approaching. Gushklin's mother. He'd met her briefly that morning, but he hadn't had much time to speak with her before others started arriving at the trading post.

"It's Darrow, but that's close enough."

"Thank you again for all you are doing." The woman's dark eyes went to the map. "My people, they are good in the woods and on the sea, but they wouldn't know how to do what you did with that map. How to let everyone help without people stumbling on top of each other."

"It's an honor to lead the search."

"Will you take my brother, Gushklin's uncle, with you? He knows these woods better than anyone in our clan."

Jonas straightened and met the eyes of the man standing behind her. They were dark but not unkind. If anything, they looked filled with worry—just like the eyes of every other person in the room. "Do you know English?"

"I do." The man stood tall and strong, clearly not a stranger to hard work.

"Then I'd be honored to go with you."

"I assume you're taking the grid that covers the bottom portion of Sheep Creek?"

He was actually taking all four of the grids that covered Sheep Creek, because unlike everyone else, he wasn't planning to return until nightfall—unless he found Ilya and Gushklin.

Evelina and Kate knew of his plans and would send a messenger for him if the boys were found. But with each hour they remained gone, the chances of finding them alive and healthy dwindled. He'd intended to find a prospector familiar with Sheep Creek to search with him, but searching with a Tlingit man might prove even better.

"Yes, we'll start at the mouth of the creek and work our way up. Robbie here will be going with us too. My name is Jonas. Jonas Darrow." Jonas extended his hand for the other man to shake.

"And I'm Kajun-sad."

"Kajun-sad," Jonas repeated, the sounds unfamiliar on his tongue. "Please let Evelina know that you and Robbie will be joining my team."

"Thank you."

"And thank you." Gushklin's mother stepped closer. "For doing what you can to find my son."

"I'll do everything in my power to find him." *But that doesn't guarantee I'll find him alive.*

The words were there, on the tip of his tongue, but he didn't have the heart to say them. Most search missions resulted in bodies being found, not living people. But Ilya and Gushklin were smart in the woods. Even if their canoe had sprung a leak and they'd been stuck in the woods overnight, the boys were savvy enough to find a cave to hole up in.

Hopefully they'd also be able to find some dry sticks or moss to use in a fire.

He had to let himself think that, because he couldn't bear the thought of any other kind of outcome.

"Darrow, who's on your search team?" Alexei approached, crossing the nearly empty room with long, powerful strides. "Would you like to join Yuri and me?"

"I'm actually taking the grids that run along Sheep Creek. I want to try tracking where the boys might have gone myself."

"Then Yuri and I will go with you."

"No. I told Evelina to assign you and some of the Tlingit

groups to grids along the water. You know what the shoreline looks like, and I need you searching for that canoe, seeing if the boys hid it in some thick brush."

He didn't like that no one had found it yesterday. It was the one thing in all of this that didn't seem to fit. Ilya and Gushklin going prospecting on their own? He could see that. Something waylaying them, or one of the boys getting injured and them being stuck in the woods overnight? He could see that too.

But no canoe? That made him wonder if the boys went somewhere other than Sheep Creek. Either that, or maybe someone had stolen their canoe.

But why would someone steal it? And if it was stolen, wouldn't it show up on the beach somewhere else around Juneau?

Jonas rubbed the back of his neck, trying to chase away the feeling of foreboding that settled in his chest.

"Well, if you're sure you don't want to come with us, then we're going to head out," Alexei said.

"I would say I'd search with you tomorrow, but . . ."

"There better not be a search again tomorrow." Worry flashed in Alexei's eyes.

"Exactly." Jonas clapped him on the shoulder. "Now if you'll excuse me, I need to go see if Evelina found anyone else to add to my search team."

"Take care, and when I see you next, I sure hope one of us has my brother with him." Alexei turned and headed back to where Yuri stood by the door.

Me too. Jonas drew in a breath, then headed to the table, where a middle-aged man with long, matted hair and a gold tooth stood beside Kajun-sad.

To others in the room, the lot of them probably looked like the most mismatched search party to ever exist. But Jonas was hoping their combined knowledge would give them the tools they needed to find the lost boys quickly.

JONAS PUSHED his hat down farther on his head as he studied the print on the ground. It looked smaller than most. Could it be from Ilya or Gushklin?

Or was it from one of the people who'd spent yesterday searching for the boys?

He crouched closer and bent his head to further study the footprint, but that only caused a stream of water from his hat brim to pour into the track.

He pressed his lips together, his jaw clenching. Between the downpour that had started an hour after they arrived at the creek and the hundreds of tracks that had been left yesterday, he hadn't found a single, helpful clue. It seemed that the entirety of Juneau had canoed down to Sheep Creek to search for the boys.

In fact, he couldn't even say with certainty whether the boys had stepped foot anywhere near Sheep Creek.

Even now, as they inched deeper into the forest and up the side of the mountain, it was hard to find any tracks at all in the soft moss-covered earth, let alone any small enough to belong to a pair of ten-year-old boys.

Two moccasined feet stopped in front of Jonas, and he looked up to find Kajun-sad standing in front of him, his face grim. "We aren't going to find anything in this weather. We should head back to the trading post and see if anyone else found something."

Kajun-sad was probably right. Jonas had planned on searching until dark, but any hope he'd had of the creek yielding helpful information had been washed away hours ago.

Around lunchtime, Evelina had sent a messenger telling them that no one had discovered the canoe in the first round of searching. But it was now nearing time for dinner.

Jonas pushed to his feet. "You're right. We may as well—"

"I think I found something!" Robbie shouted from higher up in the creek bed.

Jonas didn't bother to hurry as he moved toward the boy. The first time Robbie had hollered, he'd been hopeful. And the second and third, but this was probably the twentieth time Robbie Finch had thought he'd discovered something.

"That's my footprint from earlier," the prospector, Charley Moulder, appeared at the top of a small moss-covered rock wall and stared at the place where Robbie was crouched. "And no, I didn't find anything down this trail, at least not anything that looks like it could have belonged to the boys. Someone spent a few weeks digging farther down the trail, probably in hopes of finding a vein, but it looks like they abandoned the claim months ago."

"All right. It's time to call it a day."

Robbie blinked up at him. "But we haven't found them, Mr. Darrow."

"I know." As he spoke, that hollow place in his chest opened once more. "But there's nothing for us to track here."

"And no sign they were ever here in the first place," Kajun-sad said from behind him.

It seemed their thoughts were both headed in the same direction.

"We'll head back to town and see what the other parties have found." Even if the canoe hadn't been found, maybe someone had spotted a lost hat or a scrap of fabric caught on a bush. Then they'd at least have an idea of where to search.

The four of them were silent as they trudged down to the channel, climbed into Kajun-sad's canoe, and paddled clear back to the trading post. Jonas's wound throbbed lightly in his chest, but the pain was mild compared to how it would have felt after a day in the mine—and nothing like the pain in his chest when he walked into the trading post to discover none of the other search parties had found anything of use either.

Not a hat, not a scrap of fabric, and certainly not a canoe.

Evelina went instantly to him, her somber eyes searching his. He wanted nothing more than to pull her to him, bury his head in her hair. But he couldn't do any of that, at least not with so many people from the community milling about.

"Maybe the weather will be better tomorrow," someone said from behind him.

"Should we try searching Douglas Island next?"

"Has anyone gone over to Treadwell, just to make sure the boys didn't end up there?"

Jonas tried to answer the questions as best he could before shooing everyone out the door, telling them that if they wanted to be helpful tomorrow, they needed a good night's rest.

It was an excuse more than anything. He wasn't of a mood to be around people, not after the day's search had gone so poorly.

When only a few people remained, Jonas pulled a chair in front of the map, slid into it, and tilted his head back to study each section of stream and shoreline and mountain marked on the thick paper.

Dear God, what am I missing?

"Seems to me you're not taking your own advice."

Jonas looked over to find Alexei standing beside his chair with a bowl of halibut chowder in his hand.

"It's better to search on a full belly than a hungry one, remember?" Alexei handed him the soup.

Jonas stared down at the creamy liquid as Alexei walked

off. He didn't feel like eating much of anything, but he plunged the spoon into the bowl and managed a couple of bites.

Alexei returned with a chair that he settled right beside Jonas's, then handed him a biscuit. "Figured you might want this too."

He didn't want any of it. Not the food or the company. He just wanted Ilya.

"What are we looking for?" Alexei studied the map in front of them.

Jonas shrugged. "Anything. Any clue to where they might be, any idea we might have."

"Do you still think they're around Sheep Creek?"

Jonas dunked his biscuit into the soup and took a bite. "No. I mean, they might have gone there briefly yesterday, but they're certainly not near there now."

"What if we don't—"

"Don't say it." His heart wasn't ready to admit Ilya might be lost, not yet. "Both boys know their way around the woods."

"I really wish you'd told me you were a lawman." Alexei hung his head. "Then maybe I wouldn't have . . ."

Jonas slanted a glance at Alexei. There was something about the way his shoulders slumped, about the regret etched across his face. "Wouldn't have what?"

"After you left so suddenly the first time, I went back to Sitka and had a word with the Marshal about you." He scrubbed a hand over his face.

"Did you?" Had the Marshal figured out who he was? He wasn't as bothered by that now as he would have been after he first arrived.

"Turns out there's a criminal from Montana on the loose, one with red hair and brown eyes."

"The counterfeiter? Jedidiah Cuthbertson? They still

haven't caught him?" Jonas took another bite of soup. The poor Marshal in charge of that case. He didn't envy the man.

Alexei shrugged. "I thought you might be him."

Jonas choked, a chunk of halibut sticking in his throat. "You what?"

"I thought you were hiding from the law. I didn't realize you were really hiding from criminals."

Jonas stared at the map. It was easier than looking at Alexei. "I'm here to make sure criminals don't come after your sister the way they did my mother and fiancée."

"Evelina told me what happened."

"I assumed as much, seeing as how you trekked clear up to Silver Bow Basin to ask me for help."

"I'm sorry for sending you away."

Jonas swallowed, even though there was no food stuck in his throat. He didn't know how to respond. Maybe if he had been honest from the beginning, if he had told Alexei everything...

Would that have changed things? He didn't know. He couldn't quite claim his wounds from Texas had healed, though holding Evelina in his arms sure seemed to help him forget everything that had happened before meeting her.

"After this is done—whether Ilya is found or not—I'd like you to stay on at the store." Alexei clamped a hand on his shoulder. "I'd be honored to hire you as a manager. I can't think of a better person to watch over my siblings."

"Do you mean that?" He sucked in a breath. "Because I can't promise . . ."

"That no criminal will come looking for you? No, I'm sure you can't, and I don't expect you to either. If someone does search you out, I know you'll do everything in your power to keep my family safe, and likely a much better job of protecting them than Yuri, Sacha, Mikhail, or I could ever do."

"Thank you." He couldn't say why the words meant so much to him. Perhaps because this now meant there was a place he could stay. Three days ago, he'd been asking God if he was meant to be a vagabond for the rest of his life, and now he had a place he could belong.

Alexei cleared his throat. "And when you're done grieving your fiancée, I just might know of a lovely woman with chestnut hair and green eyes who's more than a little attracted to you."

Jonas's lips curved. "I'm still grieving my fiancée, yes, but not in the way you mean. Harriet and I were friends. We'd grown up together, and it was time for me to settle down and get married, so I proposed. I miss her, yes. I wish she was still here, but mainly because I feel guilt over her death."

"You're not still grieving her?" said a soft voice from the back of the room.

Jonas turned in his chair to find Evelina standing beside the door, her eyes wide. He'd thought she and Kate had gone upstairs to start assigning various teams to different sections of the grid for tomorrow. But she must have come back to gather some of the papers from the table.

Jonas set his bowl on the floor and stood, then crossed the floor to her. "As I said, we were friends. I loved her as a sister more than anything. She was tolerant of the long hours I worked, of how my job sometimes led me to be away from home. She never gave me any trouble about it, and we were both nearing thirty, so I proposed. She would have made a nice companion. We were both very comfortable with each other."

He dropped his hands to Evelina's shoulders, holding her in front of him, letting the heat from her body radiate through her dress and into his palms. "I wanted to tell you after court the other day. That's why I was looking for you. Because I knew you assumed my feelings for Harriet were different than they actually were."

"And then I interrupted your conversation on Monday and told you to leave Juneau." Alexei stood from his chair. "But this time I won't."

He headed toward the door, then clicked it shut behind him, leaving Jonas to stare down at the beautiful woman who'd been filling his dreams since his first night in Alaska.

"I LOVE YOU," Evelina blurted the second the door closed behind her brother.

She wasn't sure if there was a moment when most people knew they'd fallen in love. She'd realized it when she arrived at the Perseverance Mine yesterday and told Jonas what had happened to Ilya.

Let me get my coat and bags. That was all he'd said. Just those few words. And that was the moment her heart had gone into a freefall for the man standing before her.

He hadn't complained about how Alexei had sent him away just four days earlier or mentioned how much he'd already lost in his own life.

Instead, he'd returned to Juneau and stayed up until the wee hours of the morning preparing for the search. He hadn't even cared that she'd told half the town he'd once been a lawman.

Or that she'd told Alexei what had happened to his fiancée and mother back in Texas.

And all of that made her realize she loved the man standing before her, with his dark eyes and curling hair and broad chest. And she couldn't keep the words inside a second longer.

"I love you," she said again, a bit louder this time. "I know you'll probably say it's too soon, or that I can't be so certain of my feelings when we've known each other only a couple of months. But I'm telling you, Jonas Darrow, I love you, and there's nothing you can do to make me take it back."

His lips tilted up into a smile, but it stopped short of his eyes. Stopped short of transforming his face into something that resembled the joy welling up in her own heart. "Evelina, I . . . My feelings for you . . ."

He reached out and smoothed a strand of hair behind her ear, his fingers lingering in the tender place where her ear met her jaw.

Then he sighed and stepped away. "I'm worried I might love you too."

There was something wrong. She could feel it in the way he pulled back and tensed his shoulders.

But why? This was the man who had pulled her into his arms and kissed her, not just once, but twice. If he wasn't still grieving his late fiancée the way she'd assumed, wasn't still heartbroken over her loss, then why was he pulling away from her?

She reached out, her hand hovering in the space between them, unsure of whether to bridge the gap or let it widen further. "You should be hugging me right now, or kissing me. Not moving away."

And certainly not looking at her with a frown on his face.

His eyes locked onto hers, and she could see the struggle within him, the conflict playing out in his furrowed brow and the way his fingers twitched by his side.

"Maybe if Ilya wasn't missing," he rasped. "Maybe if someone in Oklahoma wasn't looking for me or I hadn't served so long as a lawman before . . . Maybe then I'd . . ."

His voice trailed off, leaving only silence to fill the wide expanse of the room.

"You're not ready to love again," she whispered. "You're still not ready to open up your heart."

Jonas raked a hand through his hair, then shook his head. "It's not that. In fact, there's someone I already love very much. But I'm not willing to put you at risk. Because loving you, caring what happens to you and your family, means the last thing I can do is be near you."

Tears pricked the backs of her eyes. "But you said yourself that any danger from Oklahoma or Texas had passed. I just heard you tell Alexei."

"And then Ilya went and disappeared." Jonas pressed his eyes shut, his face a mask of raw, unfiltered anguish. Then he opened his eyes, and his gaze sought hers. "Don't you understand? If something happens to him, I'm not sure how I'll go on."

She wanted to say nothing would happen, that Ilya would be found safe tomorrow morning. But her brother had been missing for more than thirty hours already, and it would be another eight hours before search parties left to look for him again.

"You'll go on with God's grace," she whispered.

"What grace, Evelina? Does it really exist? Or is that just a word people use to create a false sense of comfort when something goes terribly wrong? Let's say we were searching in the wrong spot today. Let's say tomorrow we find Ilya, and all is well. Then what happens? Do we court for a few months? Maybe marry in the spring? What if someone arrives a month later looking for me? One of the men I put behind bars—Lucas Crowe—escaped from prison this summer. Did you know that? What if he comes to Juneau? What if he wants revenge?

"If I'm managing the store for your brother and nothing more, I can leave on a moment's notice. But if we marry, that's forever. Whoever is searching for me could ask anyone in town where I live, and that would lead them straight to you, my wife. I couldn't live with myself if something happened to you because of me. Going through that once was hard enough, but you're so full of life. You're so happy and kind. You take pleasure in helping everyone you meet. The world would be a darker place without you in it, and I just can't put you at risk, no matter how much I . . ." His throat worked, and he looked away.

"How much you what?" She stepped closer. "Finish the sentence."

He hung his head, but she took another step closer, then another and another until they were standing toe-to-toe, and he had no choice but to look down into her face. "What were you going to say? *Love me?* Is that it? No matter how much you love me? Because you do love me, don't you? All these feelings I have for you, you have them for me too. I know you do. You're just too scared to admit it."

He drew in a breath and took a step away from her, putting the space she'd just crossed back between them, then he stalked to the window. In reality, only a few feet separated them. But it might as well have been a few thousand miles given the way he withdrew into himself, an impenetrable wall of a man.

"What I was going to say doesn't matter." Shadows haunted his eyes as he stared out the rain-streaked window. "Because I can't act on it. Because at the end of the day, I'm still not going to do anything that puts you and your family at risk."

"Then why did you kiss me? Why did you tell Alexei you'd take the job here? Why do you look at me as though you want nothing more than to haul me into your arms and carry me down to the preacher?"

"I'm sorry. I'll do better." His hand reached out, gripping the molding on the window until his knuckles turned white. "No more kissing, no more touching. I promise I'll . . ."

"So you're still going to work here? You just, what? Expect that the two of us will never be alone together? You expect me to be fine with you coming to dinner and sitting at our family table now that you've rejected me?" Tears scalded her eyes, but she refused to let them come. "No. Leave. Go back into the mountains."

He whirled on her, his eyes ablaze with fury. "So someone can burn down the trading post the next time you try to help a woman with a violent husband? I'm not leaving you, Evelina. Someone needs to watch over your family, and who better than a trained lawman?"

"What if I don't want you to stay?"

He raised his chin and crossed his arms over his chest. "I'm going to stay. This is where I belong, where God led me. I just don't belong with you—at least not in the way either of us want."

She wanted to cry. No. She wanted to scream. Or even better, she wanted to close her eyes and never see the man in front of her again. The man who loved her but refused to say it. The man who insisted he needed to work at the trading post to protect her but also insisted they couldn't marry to protect her.

Dear God, what do I do? What do I say? She didn't know. She felt hollow inside, as though a great gaping crevice had carved itself into where her heart had once been.

And then a verse came back to her, one that their priest had shared after her parents died, when she'd been fearful of ever getting on a boat again and had sworn she'd stay in Sitka the rest of her life so that she didn't have to sail.

"'God has not given us a spirit of fear, but of power and love and a sound mind.'" She straightened as she said the words. "And do you know what that verse makes me think? That you're afraid."

She wiped a tear from her cheek. "That you're not walking

away from what's between us because it's best for me or best for you. You're doing it because you're fearful. Because you don't want to lose me the way you lost Harriet. Because you're afraid Ilya might be lost—and please understand, I'm afraid of that very thing—but at the end of the day, whether we find my brother or not, I know that God loves me, and he doesn't want me to live my life in fear. I learned that after my parents died, but even though you've lost two people you loved, I don't think that's a lesson you've learned."

She wasn't sure what she'd been hoping for when she quoted the verse, but it certainly wasn't that Jonas's shoulders would tense and his jaw would go hard. And it certainly wasn't that he'd look at her with shuttered eyes void of any emotion. "We should both get to bed. It's been a long day, and tomorrow will be just as long."

He started for the door, but a different verse came back to her, another one from the days after her parents died, even though she hadn't thought of it much recently. "'God works all things together for good. Don't forget that either.'"

Jonas's hand paused on the door handle, though he didn't turn around.

"Do you understand that? It's from Romans eight. 'And we know that all things work together for good to them that love God, to them who are the called according to his purpose.'"

"You almost sound like your sister," he muttered, turning around to face her. "I suppose next you'll be telling me that God is going to do exceeding abundantly above all I ask or think, even though your brother's missing."

"Because he will." She came nearer, searching Jonas's face, the rough, familiar plains and shadows, the firm line of his jaw, the hard veil over his normally warm eyes. "Because God is ultimately in control, and he has the power to bring good out of the worst situations."

A muscle ticked at the side of his jaw. "Nothing good has come of Ilya missing."

"That's how I feel right now too." She reached up and rested a hand on his upper arm, his muscles strong and hard beneath her fingers. "But then I think of how your mother and fiancée died, and how that must have been a terrible, painful thing, and yet God brought good out of it."

"There's nothing good that came out of their deaths."

"But if not for their deaths, God never would have brought you here, to us. Ilya very well may have died on the wharf. My sisters and I could have died in the fire that arsonist tried to set. And even if we'd survived that, there'd be no one to lead the search for Ilya now. We'd all be waiting on the Marshal."

"Maybe," he said, then he flung open the door and stalked from the room.

The moment she was alone, the room suddenly felt too big, too haunting, with the map of the area on the wall and the students' desks scooted to the side of the room to make room for the tables with food.

She wasn't sure what she'd do if they didn't find Ilya tomorrow.

But for some reason, Jonas turning his back and walking away was almost as difficult to watch as the expression on his face when he'd returned to learn that no one had found Ilya an hour earlier.

31

J onas turned on his bed, the quilt tangling around his legs as he settled onto his back, then rolled onto his side, then turned to his other side. But no matter the position, he couldn't sleep.

If not for their deaths, God never would have brought you here, to us.

He should be exhausted considering how little he'd slept last night when he'd been plotting the search grid with Evelina and Kate. Then he'd spent the entire day in the cold, rainy woods, studying every last indentation and marking in the soft ground.

The second his head hit the pillow, he should have been slumbering like Rip Van Winkle. Yet here he was, hours later, staring up at the ceiling while Evelina's words swirled through his mind.

Was she right?

Nothing about his mother's and Harriet's deaths felt just or right or fair. And yet he couldn't deny that their deaths had led him here, to a place he was growing to love—and a certain brown-haired, smiling boy.

And a woman with rich chestnut hair and a gentle smile.

And even that woman's older brother, with his stiff shoulders and constant scowls and sharp eyes. And that woman's twin sister, even though she wielded her tongue the way most backwoodsmen did a knife blade. And then there was Inessa, who was not quite a woman but no longer a girl. She was probably the quietest of all the Amoses, but that didn't mean she was to be underestimated. Intelligence lurked in her gaze, and he had a feeling she might one day outshine everyone else in her family.

And oh, hang it all. Because somehow, somewhere, he'd up and fallen in love with the entire Amos family.

But he'd fallen even more in love with Evelina.

I love you. He could still see the look in her eyes as she'd said those words, still smell the hints of vanilla and cinnamon curling up from her hair and hear the excitement in her voice.

She was so certain of her feelings for him, even standing there, in a room filled with reminders of her missing brother, she'd been able to look beyond that, to see the future.

But as for him?

Jonas rolled onto his back again. *God has not given us the spirit of fear.* Again, her words came back to him.

Was he letting his fear control him? Did the reason he'd held himself stiff and stepped away from her have more to do with fear than love and protection?

She would know. She'd lost her parents to the sea and an older brother in some kind of accident, yet she wasn't afraid to trek up the mountainside by herself. Wasn't afraid to step onto a boat and move from Sitka to Juneau. She didn't even seem afraid for Alexei each time he left to go to Seattle or Sitka or wherever else the man's business ventures took him.

Evelina had found a way to move past the tragedy that life had brought her, but not him.

He'd thought his actions, everything from leaving Texas to refusing to pursue Evelina, had been driven by love.

But what if they were really being driven by fear, and that was the reason he wasn't allowing himself to love her?

THE NEXT MORNING they started the search north of town. Half the men were sent to Douglas Island and the other half stayed on the mainland. Jonas continued searching with his team from the day before. The morning was bright and sunny, unusual for so late into the fall, but even with the beautiful weather, they found no clues as to where Ilya or Gushklin might be, not even their canoe.

The sun was sliding behind the mountains to the west when Jonas, Kajun-sad, Charley, and Robbie all trudged back to the trading post.

"Still nothing?" Evelina came up to him the second he walked through the doorway.

Others watched him as well. In fact, it seemed every eye in the busy room turned to him.

"No. Nothing," he gritted out, his chest aching with the words.

"Should we try again tomorrow?" one of the men asked.

"Is there any hope of finding them after so much time?" This from a woman who was helping with the food.

"Could they have been killed by a bear?"

"Maybe there's no sense in searching any longer."

"A bear might have got one of them, but both? Surely one would have got away while the other was being chased."

"That doesn't explain why we haven't found their canoe."

The comments swirled around him, each person trying to make sense of a situation that was completely senseless. Because in all his years as a lawman, never once had he taken part in a search that had yielded nothing. Not a footprint. Not a scrap of cloth or a lost horse or a witness who'd seen the missing person at some point.

He didn't have a single clue.

"Go home." He raised his voice to be heard above the commotion, never mind the ache in his heart as he spoke. "Get a good night's sleep. We'll start again tomorrow."

"And if we don't find the boys then?" This from Kajun-sad, who looked at him with dark, somber eyes.

Jonas shook his head. "Then we'll have to assume them lost."

The words nearly broke him, but he held his head high and kept his back straight as he turned and stalked out of the room. He went next door to the examination room, where he'd slept the past few nights, ignoring the smell of antiseptic stinging his nose as he climbed onto the bed.

He pressed his eyes shut against the burning sensation threatening to overwhelm him. *Dear God, what am I missing? What am I doing wrong?*

No answer came.

Please not Ilya, Father. You can't mean to take him home, not a boy with his whole life spread in front of him, not when he's so young . . .

A knock sounded at his door.

"Come in," he mumbled, not bothering to get up.

It opened a crack, and there stood Kate, with the same beautiful features as the woman he loved, but she held her shoulders a bit too straight and had pulled her hair back into a severe bun that left nothing soft about her.

"Do you need to use the room?" He pushed himself off the bed. "I can go elsewhere."

"It's not that. A few of us have gathered next door to pray. Would you like to join?"

He wanted to say no, which was a bit ridiculous, seeing as how he'd just been praying. He didn't want to look into yet another hope-filled face and explain he had no idea where Ilya might be.

But people would expect him to be there, so he stood on shaky legs and lumbered next door. The entire Amos family was in the room, along with the Committee of Public Safety members and a few others. The moment Kate stepped inside the room behind him, Evelina went straight to her, wrapping her twin in a hug.

The embrace made his own arms feel empty, but he couldn't blame anyone other than himself.

Alexei cleared his throat. "We probably should have done this days ago, when Ilya first went missing. Instead, we were all so busy searching that . . ." His words tapered off, and his throat muscles worked for a moment. "We might not know where Ilya is or what happened, but we need to remember that God does. So let's go to him."

Alexei crossed himself, as did Yuri, Kate, Inessa, and Evelina. Then Alexei reached out and took Yuri's hand, who then took Grover's hand, and on the chain went until Jonas found himself standing between Alexei and Inessa, holding each of their hands.

Alexei bowed his head, and they prayed.

And prayed.

And prayed.

And prayed.

They went around the room in a circle, everyone praying

once, and once they'd finished that, some felt led to pray a second time.

When everyone had finished, Jonas raised his head and drew in a breath. Ilya was still missing, but at least there was a semblance of peace in his heart, something other than the sorrow threatening to consume him.

Then the door to the schoolroom opened, and large man with a short beard and broad chest stepped inside.

"There they are." He looked around, the smile dropping from his face as his brows drew down into a frown. "What on earth is going on?"

"Sacha!" Inessa ran to him and wrapped her arms around his waist.

Sacha. So this man was one of the Amos siblings. The explorer?

No, the explorer was named Mikhail. Sacha must be the ship captain.

Jonas could see the family resemblance now, the strong jaw —even if it was buried under a scruff of beard—the straight nose, the sharp eyes. Sacha's chest was probably twice as broad as Alexei's, and thick muscles corded his forearms where his sleeves had been rolled up.

Sacha hugged Inessa, then Kate and Evelina, whom he probably hadn't seen since the spring. When he pulled back from Evelina, he looked around. "What happened to the storeroom?"

"Is this Jedidiah Cuthbertson?" A man with a balding head and round midsection stepped out from behind Sacha and started straight for Jonas.

Jonas frowned. "I'm not Cuthbertson, no."

"That won't work on me." The man unhooked a pair of handcuffs from his belt as he approached. A faint wheeze puffed from his mouth with each breath he took, almost as though the exertion of walking halfway across the room exhausted him. "Put your hands behind your back, Mr. Cuthbertson. You are under arrest for counterfeiting US currency and murder."

Jonas raised an eyebrow. Who was this man? Certainly not the Marshal for all of Alaska. His health was far too poor for him to bear such a heavy responsibility.

The man cleared his throat. "I said put your hands behind your back. I'll draw my gun if I need to."

"I'd raise my hands," Jonas drawled, "if I were actually Jedidiah Cuthbertson."

The man settled his palm on his gun, which remained holstered. It gave Jonas an almost irresistible urge to grind his teeth together. If he really were Jedidiah Cuthbertson, the counterfeiter from Montana who had been on the run for six months or better, he would have the Marshal's gun in his own hand by this point.

"Your name change won't work on me. I've already had discussions with Mr. Amos about your person. Now put your hands behind your back, unless you want to be staring down the business end of my pistol."

Jonas almost wished he was staring down the business end of the pistol. At least that would mean the Marshal was somewhat competent. Instead, it seemed as though the Marshals Service had sent the worst Marshal in their employ to Alaska.

At least now he didn't need to wonder why it had taken over a month to get Simon Volker convicted. In fact, getting any kind of conviction at all was probably a small miracle.

"I was mistaken, Marshal Hibbs." Alexei approached them, his boots clacking overly loud against the wooden planks of the floor. "This isn't Jedidiah Cuthbertson. Jonas here was a sheriff back in Texas before coming to Juneau."

A sheriff. That's what everyone thought. And he'd been

happy to let them think it, because it meant no one might recognize him or realize who he truly was, that his name had been plastered across newspapers from New York to Los Angeles.

But here he was, running a search for Ilya that he certainly wasn't going to turn over to the bumbling bundle of incompetence in front of him.

Maybe it was time to tell the rest of his story.

"He's lying." Marshal Hibbs pulled his pistol from his holster and pointed it straight at Jonas's chest. "I recognize him from that wanted poster I showed you."

Jonas tried to feel fear, truly he did. It seemed like the thing to do with a pistol pointed at his chest. But he just couldn't manage it, because he had no confidence the Marshal had the courage to fire a shot.

"I don't think the likenesses match." Alexei rubbed his jaw, his head cocked slightly to the side as he studied him.

"Then why do I recognize him?" The Marshal moved his thumb to the pistol's hammer, though he stopped shy of cocking it.

And Jonas still didn't feel so much as a twinge of fear. "Probably because you've seen my face in a newspaper a time or twenty. My name is Jonas Redding, and I was a US Marshal, just like yourself, right up until the beginning of August."

The man stepped back, wheezing in a heavy breath as he blinked at him. "You're . . . you're Jonas Redding? The Marshal from Texas?" He turned toward the door. "You there, girl, bring me my case."

Marshal Hibbs had probably been telling Inessa to bring him his case, but Evelina was the one who retrieved it and carried it over.

"You were a Marshal?" Her eyes latched onto his. "But I thought . . ."

"That I was a sheriff. I know." He dragged a breath into his lungs. "And I'm sorry for letting you think it for so long. When you first said something about me being a sheriff, it wasn't really a correction I felt like making, though I see little point in hiding it now."

"Just a minute here. There's something I want to check." The Marshal opened his satchel and pulled out a thick stack of papers, which he began riffling through.

"As I was saying, this man was clearly a lawman back in Texas." Alexei stepped closer to the Marshal, viewing the papers that looked to be a mixture of both newspaper clippings and wanted posters. "I was mistaken before."

"Jonas Redding?" Sacha came up and joined their group. "Is that what you said your name is?"

"I did, yes." Jonas couldn't quite explain it, but at the sound of his true name on another man's lips, his chest filled with pride.

"Why does that name sound familiar?"

"Yes, it does sound familiar, now that you mention it." Alexei glanced up from the papers, his eyes narrowed.

"I was thinking the same thing." Yuri edged his way up to the group, with Inessa and Kate following behind him.

"That's because he's been in the papers, or at least, the real Jonas Redding has been in the papers. Now if I could just find an article . . ." The Marshal held up one of the clippings, his eyes moving between Jonas and the ragged newspaper cutting. "Well, I'll be . . . You're Jonas Redding."

A quick glance at the headline told Jonas it was from the *Austin City Gazette*. And there he was, one of three men in the picture right below the headline, right alongside his friend Cain and Cain's father. "Trio of Lawmen Kill Powerful Mexican Criminal."

"You brought down the most-wanted criminal in the Southwest." Marshal Hibbs's voice filled with a reverent sort of wonder.

"Ah, that was Cain Whitelaw." Jonas shifted from one foot to the other. "I was just . . ."

"The one who killed Eduardo Velez." The Marshal had clearly read every last detail about the case.

Jonas shouldn't have been surprised. The Marshals Service had sent out two dozen memos or better about the case and were incorporating it into their training materials for new Marshals.

A warm sensation started in his chest and worked its way up the back of his neck to the tips of his ears, which were sure to be a bright shade of red. He and Cain hadn't brought down Javier Velez and his criminal empire for acclaim. They'd done it because the man was wreaking havoc on the people of Northern Mexico and Southwest Texas, and he needed to be stopped.

"Javier Velez was based in Mexico." The Marshal handed the clipping to Alexei, who started reading. "But he had operations in Texas too, from El Paso clear over to Laredo, and as far north as Austin. We're standing in the presence of a hero."

Jonas pressed his eyes shut. Could he disappear into the floor now? Or maybe the earth would open up and swallow him? That had to be better than standing in the center of the room with every eye pinned to him as though he was deserving of some special type of honor.

"That was very brave of you." It was Evelina who spoke up, who stepped forward and took his hand in hers, meeting his gaze. "Thank you for bringing such a dangerous man to justice. I'm sure Texas is a much safer place because of your actions."

Her hand tightened around his, soft and warm and comforting, and he sucked in a breath. "I'm not a hero."

"That's not how these articles make it sound," someone said, but Jonas didn't look up to figure out who was speaking.

He couldn't, not for all the money in the Amos family bank account. All he could do was stare down into the soft, warm eyes of the only other person in the world who seemed to understand how he felt, how hard this was, how he wished more than anything he could go back in time and prevent his mother and Harriet from dying. How, even though he'd done his job and made Texas safer and brought down a dangerous criminal, he couldn't proclaim himself a hero, because a hero didn't get people killed while solving a case.

"It says here that Javier Velez was paying off men inside both the Marshals' and Rangers' offices. Does that mean he was paying off your boss?" Yuri asked.

"It does," Jonas gritted, still not able to look away from Evelina.

"Whatever are you doing up here? Why not stay in Texas? Surely you were offered some kind of promotion."

"Read this article, you dolt." Inessa's voice cut through the chatter. "One of Velez's men burned down his mother's house. His mother and fiancée were inside."

Hearing the words aloud made Jonas feel suddenly sick, but then Evelina squeezed his hand again.

"It will be all right," she whispered. "You were strong and brave. You did what you had to so this Velez character couldn't hurt anyone else. You saved lives."

He drew in a breath. Yes. He'd saved lives, and he had no idea that his boss was on Velez's payroll at the time of the explosion, no idea the man he'd been reporting to had reason to want him dead for pursuing criminal charges against Velez.

Maybe it was time to stop letting guilt consume him whenever he thought of his mother and Harriet.

"Ah, this is good to know. Really, it is. I like the idea of my sister falling in love with a man who can keep her safe." Sacha's voice cut through the room. "But can someone here tell me why there's a map tacked over the chalkboard and a bunch of food in the back of the room? And where's Ilya? I would have expected him to be the first one to greet me—then ask me if I brought him back a keepsake or twenty."

"Ilya's missing." Evelina dropped his hand, the comforting grip of her fingers leaving his as she turned to face her brother. "He went prospecting with one of his friends from my school, but they never came back."

"Missing?" Sacha's face drained of color. "How long?"

"Two and a half days," Alexei handed the stack of clippings pertaining to the Velez case back to the Marshal. "Darrow—or is it Redding?—has been leading the search party, and he's done a good job of it. But we haven't found anything."

"We just finished praying," Kate said. "We're hoping that maybe tomorrow . . ." Her voice trailed off.

"Tell me everything." Sacha crossed his arms over his chest, making him look even larger and more imposing than before.

Jonas let the others fill Sacha in on the details, the other man's expression growing more worried with each word.

Jonas couldn't stop his own mind from spinning. Sacha said he'd spotted a clearing on the northern tip of Douglas Island.

"I don't suppose you noticed an abandoned canoe along the coast on your way here." Jonas walked to the map, trying to study it with fresh eyes, but he'd spent so many hours staring at it that the lines and markings all seemed to blur together.

"Not a canoe, no, but there was a small yawl dropping a few men off on the opposite side of Douglas Island." Sacha shrugged. "I wouldn't have thought anything of it, except the ship pulled away from the coast and made a beeline around the north side of the island as soon as the lookout spotted me. Not too many ships head north along there. It was almost as though the captain wanted to get out of sight."

"Where did it drop the men?" Jonas narrowed his gaze on the northern tip of the island. "And how many men were there?"

"Looked like maybe two, plus whoever was in the boat. The boat seemed a bit familiar, like maybe I've seen it around Sitka before." Sacha stepped to the map and pointed to a little cove on the west side, near the north end.

The Tlingit had searched the east side of the island, where everyone assumed the boys were because it was the side that faced the channel. But what if the boys had gone to the west side of the island? The island had to be about twenty miles long and two, maybe three miles wide. Two days didn't make for enough time to search every inch of it.

"I assumed there was a mine going in," Sacha said. "The men each had a load of supplies. And like I said, it looked like there might be a small clearing farther up the mountain."

"I haven't heard of any mine over there." Alexei strode over to them.

"Me either," Grover said, also sauntering over to look at the map.

In fact, the entire group that had congregated in the center of the room now ambled over to the map, including Kate, Evelina, and the Marshal.

"Where's the clearing?" Jonas turned to Sacha.

"Well, I can't say for certain it's a clearing." Sacha scratched the side of his beard. "There was just a change in the trees. I wouldn't have spotted it on a cloudy day, truth be told. It's too high up the mountain. But with the sun out, and seeing as how the men had just been dropped off, I was studying the mountain a little closer than normal. There's some kind of gap in the trees. I assumed it was a mine, but maybe there was a small landslide. "That could cause the gap.

Jonas shifted. Why did the idea of something being north of town seem unsettling? Almost as though someone had mentioned something about heading north of Juneau recently, but he couldn't quite recall where he'd heard it.

"So it was somewhere around here?" Jonas tapped the slope of the mountain near where Sacha had spotted the boat.

"More like here." Sacha patted a spot even higher on the mountain. As I said, the clouds would have covered it on a normal day.

"I want to search it. We didn't send any teams to the west side of the island. Until now, we had no indication anything was even going on over there." Perhaps it was nothing, but they'd had so few clues about where Ilya and Gushklin had gone that he had little choice but to check it out.

"You want to search it now?" Evelina asked. "It's nearly dark."

"We'll take lanterns." That was better than leaving Ilya and Gushklin alone in the woods for a third straight night—if the other men and the clearing had something to do with their disappearance.

And there was certainly no guarantee of that.

"I'll go with you," Alexei said.

"Me too," Yuri piped up.

"Just how many men do you need, Darrow—er, Redding?" Grover asked. "Reckon everyone here is willing to go with you, and we could call back more men from the town if needed."

Jonas glanced around the group, made up mostly of the Amos family and men from the Committee of Public Safety. "I'll take the Amos men. I need Sacha to show us what he spotted, and if I take Alexei and Yuri, that gives us four people. Then we'll stop by the Tlingit village across the channel and get Kajun-sad. He knows these woods better than anyone, and we'll need a guide if we're going to trek up the side of a mountain after dark."

"Wait for me." The Marshal, still standing in the middle of the room, fumbled to stuff his papers back into his satchel. "I'm the lawman, and I should be running the search. Redding here resigned from the Marshals Service."

Jonas grimaced. The "lawman" was still more concerned with his old newspaper clippings than studying the map of the search area.

"Actually, I was hoping you would go to the jailhouse and interview the arsonist. I haven't been able to get a lick of information out of him, but something in my gut tells me Dressner hired him to burn down this building." Jonas headed back to the Marshal and slung an arm around his shoulders. "You seem like the type of man who's good at conducting an interrogation."

At least he hoped the man was good at interrogations. Surely the Marshal had some redeeming qualities, even if he wasn't in the best of health.

"Oh yes, and if you finish there early, we could certainly use your help figuring out where to conduct the search tomorrow." Evelina swept toward Marshal Hibbs, a charming smile on her face. "I'd be happy to show you a map of the places we've already covered. You have so much experience, and we could certainly use a pair of fresh eyes."

"Yes, yes, we need to get this arson business cleared up." Grover came toward them, a serious expression on his face. "Anyone can search a mountain, but no one has been able to crack the arsonist."

"I'd like to observe Marshal Hibbs as he questions the arsonist. The man won't even tell us his name." This from Mr.

Hemming, who was already moving to where his coat hung near the door.

Jonas waited until Marshal Hibbs and all three men on the Committee of Public Safety left for the jail before slipping out the door with the Amos brothers.

He tried not to get his hopes up too much as they all grabbed lanterns and headed across the street to the wharf. The men who'd been dropped off on the west side of the island could have just been prospectors, and the gap in the trees could have been the result of a small landslide. That was the most likely way for the topography of a mountain to change, especially considering all the rain Douglas Island got.

But he wasn't going to apologize for wanting to investigate it before news had time to spread.

32

Jonas clamped the side of the boat, his knuckles whitening on the smooth wood as Sacha navigated around the west side of the island and steered the boat toward a patch of dense forest. The final streaks of twilight painted the sky purple and orange, giving them just enough light to see.

"This looks like a good place to hide a canoe. Much brush." Kajun-sad said as he surveyed the coast.

Sacha loosened the sails, letting them sag in the wind before he lowered them. The boat glided to a stop in the shallow waters just off the forested shoreline.

"See how the land is flat for a bit?" Kajun-sad nodded toward the moss-covered rocks and shrubs. "It's a good place for a larger boat to drop men off or even seek harbor."

Jonas surveyed the area. He didn't have the eye of either a native or a sailor, but Kajun-sad's reasoning made sense. "Let's search the beach."

"Don't you want to head to the clearing?" Yuri moved to the back of the boat and let down the anchor. "Isn't that where you expect to find the boys?"

"I'd rather find something that tells us we're looking in the right spot first. And as Kajun-sad said, there're many places to hide a canoe along here." Jonas grabbed one of the lanterns, then hopped out of the boat into calf-deep water.

Alexei jumped out behind him, followed by the others.

"Let's spread out. We'll cover more ground faster." Jonas headed to the left of the boat, thinking to take the far edge of the search. The Amos brothers and Kajun-sad had no trouble fanning out after him, but the dim light and thick undergrowth of the forest made it impossible to see more than a few feet of shore at a time, even with the soft glow of the lanterns.

They searched in silence, each of them looking for something that might be amiss. Even in the growing darkness, Kajun-sad seemed to cover twice as much ground as the rest of them, his skill traversing the rocks and brush and water on full display.

But Jonas couldn't help glancing up the side of the mountain every few minutes. Was someone watching them? The light from the lanterns seemed dim, but what if it was bright enough to attract the attention of someone higher up the mountain—someone who didn't want to be found?

"I found a trail!" Yuri called. "Looks like it heads up the mountain!"

A trail. That meant the clearing Sacha had spotted could well have been made by humans. Jonas trudged toward where Yuri stood atop a moss-covered rock on the edge of the water.

"It's right here. See?" Yuri pointed to a thin path that led between two bushes and up into the forest.

"Indeed." A chill traveled down Jonas's spine. The trail was too defined to belong to two men who had beaten a path through the woods once on nothing more than a whim. This trail certainly belonged to someone—or maybe even a group of people.

Jonas took a few steps backward and let his gaze travel up the mountain again, though it was barely light enough to make out its hulking shadow anymore.

Who are you, and what are you doing up there? Working a claim was the most obvious answer. But that didn't mean the men working the claim knew anything about Ilya or Gushklin.

It was still best not to get his hopes up.

"What does this canoe we're searching for look like?" Sacha called softly from farther down the shore. He was the only person who hadn't come to investigate the trail, and he was crouching down, studying a stretch of ground and a thick stand of shrubs. "Something with a smooth bottom was dragged through here within the past few days."

Kajun-sad leaped into the water, racing through the shallows toward Sacha, while barely making a sound.

Yuri jumped off the rock where he'd been standing and landed in the water, creating a loud splash.

"Move slow and quiet." Jonas scanned the mountainside again. "I don't want to do anything that might call attention to us."

There was certainly a part of him that wanted to run forward, to trample the brush and see if there was, in fact, a canoe hiding in the shrubs. But he wanted to be cautious. He didn't know where the yawl came from earlier, and should it appear, he didn't know whether he'd face friend or foe. Just like he didn't know where the men from a couple hours earlier had gone or how friendly they would be.

By the time they reached where Sacha had been standing, the ship captain and Kajun-sad had moved onto the bank and were standing in a patch of shrubs that came to their chests. Their surroundings had grown so dark that if not for the narrow light of his lantern, Jonas wouldn't have been able to find them.

"We found it," Kajun-sad whispered.

"Show me," Yuri panted, his chest heaving with the effort of running.

Jonas followed Alexei out of the water, examining the mossy ground to find it just as Sacha had claimed—something large and smooth had been dragged across the earth here a few days earlier.

Alexei forged his way into the shrubs, then stopped beside Sacha. "Yes, that's the canoe."

"It might not be the one Ilya used, though." Yuri rubbed the back of his neck. "It could belong to whoever has been using that trail up the mountain. Maybe they have two boats."

"It is Gushklin's canoe." Kajun-sad bent down and retrieved a small leather pouch that had been tied shut. He loosened the fastenings, then pulled out a piece of paper, soggy from the days of rain. "It looks like there was some kind of map on here before the rain faded it."

"And this is Ilya's hat." Sacha picked up a smaller version of the wide-brimmed hat every man in Juneau wore when it rained.

"Of course he would leave his hat." Alexei's voice emerged raw and hoarse. "He's always leaving it behind, even in a downpour. It's like the boy doesn't feel rain."

"Does this mean we can head up the mountain?" Yuri raised his head and looked around, scanning the water. "I'd rather find Ilya than his hat, and I'd rather disappear into the woods before that boat comes back and spots us."

"I agree." Something about this didn't settle right. They knew Ilya and Gushklin had been here, and they also knew the boys weren't alone. Why hadn't whoever found them returned them to Juneau?

He'd likely have his answer when they reached the clearing.

They silently made their way over to the trail and started

up the mountain. Jonas's wound pained him slightly on the trek up, but after spending the past two days searching the woods, the pain was small compared to what he'd feel after two days of working in the mine.

Silvery light trickled into the forest from the moon above. Between that and the lanterns, Jonas was able to just make out the narrow path that led them around rocks and over tree roots, the ground soft beneath their feet.

But Kajun-sad seemed to possess the ability to see in the dark. He led the way, traveling twice as quickly as the rest of them, often forging ahead, only to come back down the trail and report on what lay ahead.

They followed the trail for fifteen minutes or better, and the longer they climbed, the harder Jonas's chest worked to suck in air and the quicker his heartbeat raced.

Because the trail was growing ever steeper. Surely that was it. Not because he was worried about what he might find when he reached the clearing.

Had Ilya and Gushklin walked this very path three days earlier? If so, what had befallen them at the top?

Could they have happened upon a claim, and the miners working it were none too happy to be found? What might angry miners do to a pair of—?

"Stop walking," Kajun-sad said from the darkness.

Jonas suddenly found himself standing at the edge of a shallow pit, the chasm so wide that the thin beam of his lantern barely reached across it.

"Someone's got a full-fledged mine up here after all," Alexei said from behind him. "And somehow no one knew about it."

"Is that what this is?" Jonas blinked at it. The chasm wasn't very deep, but it was large in diameter. Someone had obviously been digging.

"That's the rock they've dug out of the pit over there." Sacha pointed to the opposite side of the hole, where a large pile of rock sat in the shadows. "Bet they're stashing the gold in their camp, wherever that is."

"The trail goes farther up the mountain." Alexei slid past him and would have started up the path, but Jonas reached out and grabbed his arm.

"Let Kajun-sad and me go first."

Alexei turned back to him, his eyes flashing in the lantern light. "My brother is somewhere up here, and I—"

"Maybe he is, and maybe he isn't. But if he is somewhere ahead, I can guarantee you he isn't alone. That means whoever found him—if he's still alive—has a reason for keeping him hidden. Tell me, how many boys have you rescued from kidnappers?"

"You've done this before?" Yuri asked from behind him.

"It was part of my job."

"Do cases like this . . . ?" Sacha shifted his lumbering form from one foot to the other. "Do they ever end well?"

"I recovered all but one of my abductees alive."

"Forgive me." Alexei stepped aside, leaving room for him to pass on the trail. "I got ahead of myself for a moment."

"Put your lanterns out. We'll use the moonlight to guide us." Hopefully the moon would provide enough light they could make out the basic path of the trail without lanterns. "Set them here by this tree. We can't risk whoever might be ahead seeing their light or them getting in the way if we carry them. Do all of you have guns?"

"This is Alaska." Alexei slid his hand to a holster at his side. "What do you think?"

"Good. Keep your pistols at the ready and watch for my signal. I don't know how many men we'll find, or whether Ilya and Gushklin . . ." He shook his head, not quite able to bring himself to say the words he feared most. "Hopefully they're alive."

"Maybe whoever found them is using them to work in the mine." Yuri set his lantern down at the base of the tree.

"Maybe." That was the best outcome he could hope for, because then the boys would not only be alive but would also have been given food and water over the past three days. "If that's the case, they're still being held against their will, and we don't know by how many men."

Please, God, let them still be alive. Let us find them. Jonas's heart stuttered over the prayer as he and Kajun-sad crept farther up the trail. Kajun-sad moved ahead of him, his feet not making so much as a sound, but Jonas moved slower, carefully picking his way slowly over the damp earth so that he didn't reveal himself.

Or at least he hoped he wasn't revealing himself. But his heartbeat thrummed so loudly in his ears that he wondered if Alexei, Yuri, and Sacha could hear it behind him.

This was why the Marshals Service never assigned cases to a Marshal who knew a victim's family. It got too personal. It was too easy for the Marshal to let feelings get in the way.

And Jonas had feelings aplenty for Ilya.

It didn't help that the last time he'd been in a situation like this had been down in Mexico, when he'd killed Eduardo Velez.

His mother's and fiancée's deaths had been barely two weeks old, and his gun had shaken in his hand as he'd held it.

All he'd wanted to do that day was escape, to flee someplace where no one knew him and start over again, a place where he could forget what happened. A place where he'd never need to hold a gun again.

But this time his hand didn't shake as he slid it over the butt of his pistol and pulled the gun from his holster.

And he didn't regret the Amoses knowing he'd once been a lawman. Didn't regret leading the search, even if they'd been looking in the wrong area for the past two days.

His only regret was not finding this trail sooner.

A sound floated on the air, and Jonas stilled, holding up his hand for the others behind him to do the same. He could just make out the deep timbre of a voice ahead, though the exact words were muffled.

Another voice joined in, and Jonas gave the signal to move closer.

He was even quieter than before, creeping over the unfamiliar ground at the pace of a slug. A large shaft of moonlight filtered through the trees ahead, indicating he was approaching another clearing. Kajun-sad crouched near the base of one of the trees still shrouded in shadows.

"They're talking about searching again tomorrow," a man said from ahead, his voice growing clearer with each step Jonas took. "Last I looked, they don't have this side of the island marked for searching, but if that changes . . ."

"We need to get rid of them." Another voice, its timbre darker and deeper.

"We needed to get rid of them from the start. I told you this was a stupid idea, that nothing but trouble would come from keeping them alive." A third voice, this one brisk and filled with venom.

"No, you told us we'd get paid handsomely to make trouble for the Amoses." The first voice said.

"The boys are good workers, the both of them."

Jonas froze, recognition jolting through him at the sound of a fourth voice. The last time he'd heard it had been on Monday, when the church had been converted into a courtroom and he'd testified against the churlish brute of a man.

It looked like he'd found where Bruce Dressner had gone

after court that day. North, as the Finch boys had said. But not just north. North and across the channel.

"I'd rather them haul the rock out of that stupid pit than me," Dressner continued.

"It's not stupid. That pit is going to make us filthy rich," one of the other men snapped.

Jonas stopped moving and looked back at the Amos brothers. They all watched him, their faces grim.

He held up his hand again, indicating he wanted them to stay put once more, then he removed his hat and set it against a tree before creeping the last few feet to the large tree where Kajun-sad crouched. Holding his breath, he poked his head around it.

There was a clearing all right, a place where the mountain evened out for maybe thirty yards before a wall of rock extended up toward the sky. A crude, windowless cabin had been built of rough logs on flat ground, and a gaping tunnel had been dug into the rock face behind it. He saw no piles of gold ore, but that could be in the cabin or hidden somewhere in the woods.

A small fire flickered in the space between the cabin and the tunnel, and four men gathered around it.

Jonas studied the men in the moonlight. Just as he suspected, Bruce Dressner was among them, his broad shoulders and large form towering over the other men even while they sat.

Had Dressner intentionally kidnapped Ilya in an attempt to get back at the Amoses? Or had Ilya and Gushklin accidentally stumbled upon the claim, and Dressner kidnapped them merely because the opportunity had presented itself?

Jonas let his gaze linger on Dressner for another moment, then he shifted it to the next man in the group—and stilled.

The man's face held familiar lines and angles, though Jonas

had seen it only once before. A long, silvery-blond ponytail cascaded over the man's shoulders and down his back.

His heart pounded against his chest and sweat slicked his hands. Betty Clement's killer was with Bruce Dressner? And here he'd been blaming himself for not being able to track the man, when he'd never even thought to search Douglas Island, let alone the far side of it.

Jonas forced a breath out of his lungs, trying to calm himself. He needed to keep his wits about him if he was going to apprehend Orville Jacobs—and he didn't want to do anything that might give away how dangerous the man was until after he was locked in a jail cell. He couldn't risk anything happening to little Sally Shephard.

Jonas recognized the third man—the one who was talking about keeping the boys around to work the mine—from the search party, though he didn't recall his name. He'd probably been sent to town to keep an eye on things after Ilya and Gushklin had been kidnapped.

The fourth man Jonas had never seen before.

The man sailing the yawl would make a fifth person, though they had little hope of apprehending him unless Sacha happened to find the boat hidden in a cove or inlet in the morning.

And Jonas would wager there had been a sixth man a week ago—but now he was sitting in the jailhouse after attempting to burn down the trading post at Dressner's behest.

Something tapped his shoulder, and Jonas jerked around, raising his gun only to find Alexei staring at him, impatience smoldering in his gaze.

"What are you waiting for," he whispered, his voice barely audible in the darkness. "We outnumber them."

"Information," Jonas whispered back. "Once we reveal

ourselves, I can't promise these men will answer any of our questions." The arsonist certainly hadn't.

"One of us should go to Sitka and tell Caldwell we got the Amos boy," said the man who'd been helping with the search. "See what he wants to do."

Jacobs lifted his cigar to his lips and drew on it. "He'll be happy, and he'll pay us extra. You'll see."

Jonas raised a brow at Alexei. "Who is Caldwell?"

"It doesn't matter." Alexei's jaw hardened. "What matters is that we get my brother back."

He had a feeling it mattered very much. If the missing money from the ship and the arson attempt and Ilya's disappearance could all be tied to this Caldwell fellow, then maybe his work as a voluntary lawman wouldn't be finished after they rescued Ilya and Gushklin.

"Having the boys here is a danger. They need to go. Now." This from the slender man that Jonas hadn't seen a single time since coming to Juneau. He had light hair and a smaller build than the others.

"You haven't seen the search map back at the trading post. It'll take them two weeks to work their way around to searching this part of the island, and they'll declare it a lost cause long before then. Most of the townsfolk are ready to stop searching as it is."

"How much is Caldwell going to pay us for kidnapping the boys?" Dressner asked, his voice dark.

"Probably nothing." The small man tilted a flask to his lips and took a sip, then shuddered and wiped his mouth on his sleeve. "Who says Caldwell isn't angry about it?"

"I already told ya he won't be angry. He said he'd pay us extra if we cause trouble for the Amoses, and that's exactly what kidnapping the half breed is doing. Causing them trouble." Orville sounded rather certain of himself. In fact, he spoke with enough authority that Jonas was starting to think of him as the leader. "Bet I can take the yawl up the coast and steal a couple more shipping contracts from the canneries while Alexei's distracted looking for his brother. That'll make Caldwell happy for sure."

Jonas sent Alexei a questioning gaze, but all three Amos men had turned stiff as trees. Was something going on with this Caldwell fellow and Alexei's shipping contracts? If so, no one had breathed so much as a word about it to him.

"When is he going to pay us?" Dressner asked, reaching for the jug of moonshine sitting between him and Orville. "My wife's gone, and I'd just as soon take my earnings and leave, but I want to get paid first."

"You don't want to keep mining the claim?" Jacobs swiped the jug from Dressner's hand and took a swig. "We get enough gold from this, and you could be a millionaire by this time next year."

"I'd rather sell my part to Caldwell outright—for about five times what it's worth—then take my money and go somewhere comfortable."

"You have enough information," Alexei whispered to Jonas. "Let's get Ilya back."

"Yes," Kajun-sad said from where he still crouched near the ground. "We know enough. It is time to get Gushklin."

Jonas drew in a breath, his eyes narrowing on Orville Jacobs. The men were right; he had plenty of information to wedge between the men during questioning. It should be easy to get them to turn on each other, which would lead to even more information being revealed.

Jonas took a few steps away from the tree, then motioned for Alexei and Kajun-sad to follow. He wasn't going to discuss their plan where they might be overheard. They silently moved back down the trail until they reached the mining pit.

"Caldwell's behind everything," Alexei whispered, tension radiating off every fiber of his body. "I think he's a partner in the claim, and he's paying the men working it extra if they can make trouble for us."

"Caldwell." Though he said only one word, ice filled Sacha's voice. "Of course it would be him."

"At least now I know for certain he's the one who's been trying to take my shipping contracts."

Sacha's lips twisted into a scowl. "Why? He doesn't own a shipping company."

"But he knows how much we'll be hurting if we lose our contracts," Yuri muttered.

"I'm trying to figure out why." Alexei's glower was as dark as Sacha's. "But I haven't been able to make any sense of the little information I've gotten so far."

Jonas looked among the men. "Who is Caldwell?"

"The seal killer," Kajun-sad snapped.

"The *what*? Jonas blinked at the Tlingit man, standing tall and proud in the dark forest. "You know him too?"

"He's the manager of the Alaska Commercial Company," Sacha answered. "They have sole rights from the government to harvest seals on the Pribilof Islands. But they don't just take males or females who are too old to reproduce. They slaughter them by the thousands."

"And the government lets them," Yuri finished. "Because they tax each head that's taken, and all they care about in Washington is money."

Kajun-sad muttered something in his own language, then looked up at him. "In a few more years, there won't be any seals left, just like there aren't any otters."

"We need to get Ilya," Alexei snapped. "We can explain just who Preston Caldwell is later."

Once again, Alexei was right. It was far more important

that they find the boys and arrest the men working the claim than figure out the motives of an enemy he hadn't even realized the Amos family had.

"We're going to spread out and surround the clearing. I'll head up on the left and get as close to the tunnel and campfire as possible, and I'll step from the woods first. The moment I tell the men to put up their hands, I need the three of you to reveal yourselves. Sacha, you take Orville. He's the one with the pony-tail, and I'm pretty sure he's the one who stole Simon Volker's money."

Sacha's eyes widened, but he didn't speak, just gave a firm nod.

"Alexei, you have the man who helped with the search today, and Yuri, you take the short one sitting closest to us. I'll handle Dressner."

"I don't think Dressner is in charge," Alexei muttered. "I think it's that Orville character."

"I agree, but Dressner is the hothead, and if anyone is going to do something unexpected once a gun is aimed at his chest, it's him. Kajun-sad, once we have guns on all the men, I want you to search the cabin, but don't try sneaking in until our suspects are detained. And keep in mind, there could be a guard in the cabin with the boys."

Jonas scanned the group. Everyone had a grim look in their eyes and a determined set to their jaws. They might not be trained lawmen, but they'd probably do a better job at subduing the criminals than half the sheriffs in the country.

"We're ready," Sacha whispered. "Just give the word."

"Good." Jonas gave a firm nod. "Let's spread out."

Jonas turned and crept around the clearing, the crackle of the fire and the voices of the men covering any slight sounds he made. And from what he could tell, the others were quiet as they crept into position too.

Jonas reached the place where the woods gave way to a wall of rock at the edge of the clearing and the entrance to the tunnel was only a few feet away. Then he stopped and waited, giving a few minutes for the others to get into position.

Blood rushed in his ears and his heart thudded against his chest, but that didn't stop him from reaching for his pistol, aiming it at Bruce Dressner's chest, and stepping away from the trees.

"Hands up. You're under arrest!"

The two men on the opposite side of the fire who could easily see him slid their hands up immediately. Dressner turned in his direction, half raising his hands, but Orville slid his hand inside his slicker.

"He said hands up." Sacha stepped from the woods, his pistol aimed straight at Orville. "You reach for that gun, and I'll put a bullet in you."

Orville froze, and Jonas narrowed his gaze at the man, even though his gun was pointing at Dressner. "That's it. Raise your hands nice and slow. Any quick movements, and you'll be buried six feet under." He wouldn't normally be so quick to fire a shot, but the darkness gave him little choice.

Orville's hand was empty when it emerged from his slicker, and he slowly raised both his arms until they were stretched into the air.

"Very good. Yuri, tie them up, hands and feet."

Both Alexei and Yuri had emerged from the woods at the same time as Sacha, surprising all of the men so that no one had much of an inclination to fight.

"Where's Ilya?" Alexei asked.

"In here!" A shout came from the cabin. "Gushklin and I are both here. We're by ourselves, but they have us tied up."

Kajun-sad had already been approaching the cabin, but at

Ilya's declaration, the man burst through the doorway, all sense of caution gone.

Jonas glanced at Alexei, then jutted his chin toward the cabin. "Go see your brother."

Alexei didn't need to be told twice. He holstered his gun and raced across the small clearing, barreling through the open doorway behind Kajun-sad. "Ilya, did they harm you? Are you well? Tell me what happened."

Jonas could imagine the scene unfolding as Alexei untied his brother and Gushklin, then corralled Ilya into a hug that would probably last ten minutes.

Yuri tied Orville, then moved on to the man no one seemed to recognize.

"Sacha, you can go greet your brother."

Sacha darted into the cabin, his stride incredibly quick given his stocky form.

Jonas kept his gun firmly pointed at Dressner while Yuri tied the third man, then offered the length of rope on his belt to Yuri so he could tie Dressner.

The moment Dressner's hands were tied, Yuri looked up. "Can I go see Ilya while you tie his feet?"

Jonas scanned the men, all but Dressner trussed up hand and foot, and all with their mouths clamped shut. "Go on."

Yuri darted into the cabin as well, leaving Jonas to crouch beside Dressner's feet, where he made quick work of tying the man's legs together above his boots.

Then he straightened and looked around the circle, his gun still in his hand. "Who wants to tell me how you ended up kidnapping two boys?"

"It were Snake and Dressner's fault. Dressner was the one who wanted to keep 'em for work, and Snake . . ." The man who had helped with the search glared at Orville.

Something told Jonas this wasn't the man's first run-in with the law.

"Snake, you said? What did he want to do?"

"He's got a boss he works for over in Sitka. He wanted to take the boys there. And Red wanted to kill 'em."

"And what did you want to do with them?"

The man shifted a bit uncomfortably. "I didn't want nothin' to do with 'em, but we didn't have much choice after they found the mine."

So Ilya and Gushklin had found the mine. That had been the main reason for the kidnapping. Not some nefarious plot for revenge, but more of a coincidental accident.

Jonas turned to the man who evidently went by both Orville and Snake. "Tell me about this boss you're working for over in Sitka."

The man raised his chin and leveled a cold glare at Jonas. "He don't know what he's talking about. I ain't got no boss in Sitka."

"Don't believe him," Dressner mumbled. "He's been talking about a fancy boss this whole time."

"He grubstaked us," the man who appeared to be the youngest of the group said. "Lives in Sitka. Has lots of money. Goes by the name of—"

"Mr. Darrow!" Ilya burst from the cabin at a full run, legs pumping as the boy barreled toward him. "I knew you and Alexei would come for me. I knew it this whole time!"

It was all Jonas could do to holster his gun and open his arms in time to catch him. Ilya crashed into his chest, his gangly arms wrapping around his waist.

"Ilya," Jonas rasped, wrapping the boy in a hug and squeezing him tight. Never before had it felt so good to hug another person.

There was still work to be done. The men they'd captured

needed to be transported back to Juneau and questioned further.

But a sense of contentment swept over him, never mind that just a few hours ago, the search had seemed hopeless.

Maybe Kate was right after all. Maybe God really was able to do exceeding abundantly above all he could ask or think.

33

E velina was never going to let her brother go. It didn't matter that everyone else had gone to bed over an hour ago or that she was sitting in Alexei's office with papers from Gushklin's mother spread before her.

It didn't even matter that, at ten, Ilya was far too big for her lap, or that he'd fallen asleep in her arms long ago, or that her own eyes were starting to droop.

The only thing that mattered was her brother was safe. And she intended to keep him in her arms for a full week—maybe longer.

She wasn't sure she'd ever forget the way she'd felt when Ilya had burst into the schoolroom a few hours earlier. She'd been sitting at the back table, studying the map of the search area and trying to decide where they should search first tomorrow. Then Ilya raced inside with Alexei behind him.

Kate had insisted upon giving him a full medical examination, of course, and then proclaimed that she'd head over to the Tlingit village first thing in the morning to examine Gushklin.

But the moment Kate had finished poking and prodding, Ilya had climbed up on her lap, and that's exactly where he'd stayed, first downstairs as the men told Marshal Hibbs whom they'd arrested and why, then upstairs after the Marshal, Alexei, and Jonas had gone back to the jail to question the men again, and everyone else had gone to bed.

"If you ever run off again . . ." she whispered to Ilya's sleeping form, pulling him closer to her chest.

He was dead to the world, and she couldn't blame him after hearing his terrifying story of being kidnapped. In the courtroom on Monday, he and Gushklin had found a map to what looked like a gold vein, and they had decided to check it out for themselves. They'd left Wednesday morning, two days after Jonas had left Juneau, and they hadn't told a single person where they were going.

They couldn't have known that Bruce Dressner had dropped the map, or that Dressner's partner, a man by the name of Orville Jacobs, had connections with Preston Caldwell back in Sitka, and that he may even have murdered Betty Clement.

Oh, there was so very much that no one in their family had known. And it hurt just thinking of it.

A small knock sounded on the door, and Evelina raised her head to find Jonas stepping inside.

He stilled when he saw her, the door halfway open behind him. "I'm sorry. When I saw the light under the door, I thought you were Alexei."

"I believe he went to bed a little while ago, but he might be in the kitchen."

Jonas came farther into the room, his concerned eyes running over Ilya. "Do you need me to carry your brother to his room?"

She repositioned him in her arms, nudging his head farther up until it nestled in the crook between her shoulder and neck. "I'm not ready to give him up just yet."

"I understand." Jonas reached out and stroked a strand of hair away from Ilya's forehead. "But it doesn't look like you're getting much work done with him on your lap."

She sighed, her eyes drifting to the papers spread before her. "I wasn't getting very far anyway, and it's rather depressing."

"What are you working on? A contract for Alexei?"

"If only it were that simple." She nodded toward the desk. "Go on, see that paper in the center? It's a letter from Reverend Jackson. Read it."

Jonas did as instructed, his eyes skimming the words as a furrow formed on his brow. "I must have misread something. It almost sounds as if—"

"Reverend Jackson is claiming that the school has legal custody of Gushklin's older brother, Xetsuwu, and is refusing to send him home like his mother requested? No. You didn't misread anything."

"You can't be serious." Jonas skimmed the letter again. "The man truly thinks he has more rights to a native boy than the boy's own mother?"

"I'm afraid so, and it doesn't seem as though he's going to change his stance outside of court."

Jonas set the letter back on the desk and leaned a hip against it. "Are you going to take the case?"

She looked down at the papers. "There's a part of me that wants to say no, especially for something such as this. It's sure to attract attention, and there won't be any way to keep the Amos name from getting tangled up with the case in the papers. But then . . ."

"You can't say no, can you?" He didn't say it in an

accusatory manner. If anything, his voice seemed to soften as he spoke, and his eyes turned a warmer shade of brown.

"I should talk to Alexei before deciding."

"He just might break a window when he finds out what the reverend is doing."

She smiled. "Maybe I should take him to the beach when I tell him. Then he can throw rocks at the water rather than at anything with glass."

Jonas nodded, then cleared his throat. "I don't, ah . . . suppose that you'll need the new Deputy Marshal for Alaska to testify in court that the reverend is a complete and utter imbecile?"

"Deputy Marshal?" She looked up at him. "When did that happen? And what does it mean?"

"It means the Marshals Service has been looking for a Marshal to live in Juneau for about a year." Jonas leaned on the desk and kicked his feet out in front of him, almost as though intending to settle in for a conversation. "As soon as I brought Ilya and Gushklin back, Marshal Hibbs asked if I would take the job."

"So you'll be a Marshal again?" Was he happy about that? Sad? The lines of fatigue creasing his face gave no indication.

"Of sorts. I'll be under Hibbs, and my technical position will be Deputy Marshal."

"He just might be a worse boss than Reverend Jackson."

Jonas laughed. "I doubt it, but I'm pretty sure I can handle him. I could return to Texas and hire on at my old office. They wanted to promote me to assistant director after we brought down Velez, but I don't want to go back there." He raked a hand through his hair, then sighed. "At the same time, how can I not say yes to working in Juneau? Maintaining any kind of law and order here is next to impossible."

"So you're not worried about being a lawman again in an

official capacity?" It seemed like a big step considering Jonas hadn't even wanted to tell her what his job in Texas had been.

"Perhaps I should be, but when I see all the things not being handled properly in Juneau, I don't feel I can say no."

"That makes sense."

"What about you?" He met her gaze, his brown eyes warm with concern. "Are you worried about representing Gushklin's family in court?"

She swallowed, straightening in her chair despite the weight of her brother. "I'm done turning my back on situations where I know I can help."

"I think we both feel the same way. It wasn't hard to say yes to Marshal Hibbs, seeing as how there are some pretty special people I intend to protect with my new position." Jonas's eyes turned even warmer, holding her there, like a fly to honey, until the desk and walls faded, and it seemed they were the only two people left in the world.

"I can't think of a better man to bring law and order to Juneau," she finally whispered. "But does this mean you won't be managing the trading post?"

Her chest felt a little tight at the notion. She'd still been looking forward to seeing him every day, even if they couldn't be together in the way she wanted.

"I'll work here for a bit, at least until I know how much time being a Deputy Marshal will take, but I'll also look for an apartment to let. Kate's probably ready to have me gone from her examination room."

It made sense. Really, it did. She couldn't expect him to live in the examination room forever. And yet this meant he wouldn't be eating breakfast with them every morning or dinner in the evening. It meant he wouldn't happen upon her at odd times such as this.

"Whether you're at the trading post or have an office down the road, I want you to know that I'll wait for you." She spoke softly, but her words seemed to take up every last bit of space in the room.

Jonas grew still, his throat working for a moment before he opened his mouth and said her name. Just her name. "Evelina . . ."

It came out like a low growl, a sound that was a mixture of frustration and beauty, and she hoped she'd forever remember the way it had sounded on his tongue.

"I know you're not ready for anything more between us now. But one day you might be. I didn't make that clear last night when we spoke, so I wanted to let you know . . . I'll be waiting. For however long it takes."

His shoulders deflated on a sigh. "It's not as simple as merely waiting."

"I'll be here anyway."

"It might take a very long time."

"I'm praying it takes a matter of days."

He groaned, then shoved his hand into his hair. "Don't ask yourself to wait for me. Any man would be lucky to have you right now, this very day."

She wasn't so sure, not considering she was a female lawyer who was about to take on one of the most well-respected people in Alaska. "No one's asking me to wait. I'm volunteering to do it all on my own."

He pushed himself off the desk and came toward her, then reached down and swiped a strand of hair from her face, tucking it behind her ear. "You make me want to kiss you again."

"That sounds like an excellent idea."

But rather than lean down and press his lips to hers, he

dropped his hand from the tender place behind her ear and took a step back. "But not an honorable one, at least not right now. Good night, Evelina. I'll see you in the morning."

And with that he was gone, leaving her to watch as he walked away from her yet again.

34

"You expect the judge to arrive next week?"

"I do, yes." Marshal Hibbs pushed his glasses higher up on his nose. "I want these men to face trial immediately. We can't have prospectors thinking they will go unpunished if they kidnap children they find in the woods. I'm canceling my trip to Wrangell and sending for Judge Lincham so this matter can be handled with all haste."

"That's good." Jonas heaved in a breath, then scrubbed a hand over his face. He'd spent the morning requestioning each of the men alongside the Marshal. As he'd hoped, the man was good at running an interrogation, even if he'd wheezed a couple times when the questioning got intense.

The most interesting turn of events had come when he'd asked the arsonist—who's name turned out to be Harold—why Orville Jacobs had killed Betty Clement. The man's lips had twisted into a scowl, and he'd spat out the entire story about how Miss Clement was sneaking into the office at the trading post when she would pick up and return the Amos's wash. She would do a quick search, looking for any information about

Written on the Mist

shipping contracts she could find, then report them back to Jacobs.

Jacobs had been tasked not just with causing trouble for the Amoses but also with traveling to the different canneries in Southeast Alaska and seeing if they might be willing to switch shipping companies before the season started next year.

Jacobs had been paying Betty for snooping once a week, and she'd been using the extra money to rent a nice apartment for herself. But after Jacobs stole the two hundred dollars, he'd stayed away from Juneau for several weeks, causing Betty to be late paying her rent and the landlord had kicked her out the next day, claiming he had a string of men willing to pay an extra three dollars per month for the apartment.

When Jacobs had finally returned, demanding more information about the Amoses, Betty had been furious, and a fight had broken out.

The other men—all except Jacobs—confirmed Harold's story about Miss Clement, each one of them eager to separate themselves from the murder so they couldn't be charged.

But they would all still go to prison for kidnapping. And as far as Jonas was concerned, the men couldn't be sentenced and transported to a federal penitentiary soon enough.

As for the matter of Preston Caldwell, that was a little murkier. Even though the Amos brothers knew Caldwell had grubstaked the prospectors and offered to pay Orville Jacobs extra money if he could cause their family trouble, no one wanted to pursue any sort of investigation into him, let alone press charges.

It was strange. Earlier, when they'd been questioning Jacobs, Marshal Hibbs had directed the questions away from Caldwell as soon as Jonas had started to ask about him.

Hopefully once the kidnapping trial had been held and the

Marshal left, Jonas would be able to look into the matter in his new capacity as Deputy Marshal.

The door to the jailhouse opened, and a short man with eyes and hair the color of mud stepped inside. "Excuse me. I'm looking for a Mr. Jonas Redding. Or you might know him by the name Jonas Darrow? The man down at the trading post told me he might be here."

Jonas straightened, running his eyes down the thin man with thick glasses. "And you are?"

"You're in luck." The Marshal nodded his direction. "That's Redding right there."

Jonas sighed. Had he just been thinking that Marshal Hibbs was decent at his job?

"Mr. Redding?" The man stepped forward, excitement lighting his eyes. "Did I actually find you? Or wait, do you prefer to be called Mr. Darrow? Either way, I'll have you know you're a rather hard man to track down. Luke Finnigan is the name. I'm a reporter with the *Post*."

The man stuck out his hand, but Jonas only stared at it.

Had the man just said his name was Luke?

And that he was a reporter?

The man kept his hand extended, as though the longer he held it out, the more convinced Jonas might be to take it. "I've been trying to get an interview with you for months. I want to know the details of the Velez case. No, I don't *want* to know them. I *need* to know them. A promotion depends on it, you see. I told my editor I could get an exclusive story with you, and he says that if the interview reveals new information that no other paper has published, he'll consider me for the assistant managing editor position. I came up from Washington, DC to interview you about the Velez case, but am I to understand you just rescued two boys as well?"

"Did you say your name was *Luke* Finnigan?" Just like the

name his sister had written in her letter. *A reporter named Luke . . . wanted to know where you were . . .*

"Yes. Luke Finnigan, senior reporter for the *Washington Post*. Can you tell me what happened with the boys who were recently kidnapped?" Luke pulled a small pad of paper and a pencil stub out of his breast pocket.

"Ah, you might want to talk to Sacha Amos about the rescue. I merely led the search party after Mr. Amos spotted some odd activity on the west side of Douglas Island."

"Yes, but you found the boys, did you not?"

"I did."

"And you brought the men back to the jail?"

"I did."

The man smiled. "This is even better than I hoped."

Jonas's heart thudded against his chest. "Did you, by any chance, pay a visit to my sister in Oklahoma last fall?"

"Yes indeed! She was most delightful, but not all that helpful in tracking you down. Then I got called back to Washington to cover a murder trial. Then there was a money-laundering scandal led by none other than the US Senator from Alabama. Have you heard about that case?"

"No."

"Well, I daresay you can read one of my articles on the subject. I always travel with copies of the *Post*. Comes with the job, you see." The man patted the satchel slung over his shoulder. "But can we do the interview first? Actually, first I want to know if you have any comments on Lucas Crowe being captured and taken back to prison. You were the Marshal who arrested him the first time, correct? What do you think about his escape and most recent arrest?"

"Crowe was arrested?"

The man blinked at him, then gave a solemn nod. "Yes, just last month. Didn't you hear? He was hiding near Lubbock. The sheriff there recognized him from a Wanted poster and arrested him immediately."

And here I was worried that he would try tracking me down. Lucas Crowe had been the biggest threat from his past, the one loose end.

Jonas looked at the clock hanging on the wall. It read quarter after noon. "I know you've searched far and wide for me, but there's something I need to do before I give you any statements. I'll be back, though. I swear it."

And then he was off, racing out the door, down the steps, and through the street, unable to make his legs run to the trading post fast enough. A soft rain was falling outside, but he didn't feel it as he dashed around mud puddles and between horses.

A reporter. The Luke that his sister had written him about really had been a reporter.

All this time, he'd been telling himself that his presence put Evelina at risk. That there were bad men searching for him, and he couldn't guarantee her safety if they were linked by marriage.

But his biggest threat had been apprehended weeks ago.

God has not given us the spirit of fear.

God works all things together for good to them that love him.

God can do exceeding abundantly above all that we ask or think.

The verses that Evelina had shared came back to him, flooding his mind. He'd been too big of a fool to believe a single one of them.

Until now.

Until he saw for himself just how harmless the Luke he'd spent the past two months hiding from truly was.

Jonas burst through the entrance to the trading post at a full run, ignoring Yuri's surprised look and the questioning gazes of customers as he ran toward the schoolroom and flung that door open.

Evelina was standing at the front of the room, her yardstick raised to the chalkboard while the students recited the letters of the alphabet. Every eye turned to him as he stood there, but he didn't care how many people watched.

"Jonas, is something wrong?" Evelina dropped her arm, causing the end of the yardstick to hit the floor.

He strode forward. "Forgive me. I'm such a fool."

"What do you . . . ?"

But he didn't let her finish. He swept her into his arms, then leaned down and kissed her, thoroughly and deeply, never mind the children looking on or the adult voices that filled the room a moment later.

"I love you." He broke the kiss just long enough to whisper in her ear. "I think I've loved you since the first time I heard your voice, even though I was in too much pain to open my eyes and see your face. I'm a fool and an oaf, an absolute imbecile. But if you can forgive me—and be a little patient—I want nothing more than to spend the rest of my life with you."

She peered into his eyes, then reached up and rested a hand against his cheek. "When I told you I'd wait for however long it took, I didn't expect to be in your arms less than twelve hours later."

"The man who was looking for me, Luke, the one from my sister's letter . . . ? He's actually a reporter. Luke Finnigan from the *Washington Post*. He visited my sister in Oklahoma shortly after I left for Juneau. There was never a criminal looking for me, never anything that would put you or any of your family in harm's way. I was just too caught up in my own fear to see it."

"But you see the truth now?"

"I do. And I want nothing more than for you to share a life

with me." He released her, but only so he could slide down onto one knee. "Evelina Amos, will you marry me?"

She pressed a hand over her mouth, her eyes watering. "Yes. I'd be honored to be your wife."

A cheer went up from behind them, and Jonas looked over his shoulder to find not just Yuri standing in the back of the room but the entire Amos family. Every last one of them was smiling—even Alexei.

Jonas stood and took Evelina back into his arms, right where she belonged. "I should also tell you that your sister's right. God is able to do exceeding abundantly above all I ask or think. Because never in a thousand years would I have thought one day I'd be standing here with you in my arms and a bright, happy future in front of me."

A smile filled her face, soft and gentle and kind. "And I desperately want to be part of it." Then she pressed up onto her tiptoes, looped her arms around his neck, and kissed him.

Epilogue

Sacha Amos made his way slowly down the road toward the edge of town. He wasn't quite sure where he was going, only that he needed to get away. The rest of the family might be celebrating Evelina and Jonas's engagement, and Ilya and Gushklin's safe return.

And that was good. Those two things were worth celebrating.

But he wasn't of a mind to celebrate anything, not since he'd learned of the ties between Orville Jacobs and Preston Caldwell.

And to think that Jonas was talking about filing criminal charges against Caldwell. Jonas would need to be talked out of it, made to see reason. No one should have an enemy as powerful as Preston Caldwell.

If only Sacha had learned that lesson for himself a little sooner.

As it was, Alexei and Evelina had spent the morning trying to figure out how many shipping contracts their family had lost for no other reason than Preston Caldwell deciding to ruin them.

Fortunately, no one in his family was asking why the man was so bent on revenge—yet.

But they would eventually, and the thought of it made Sacha want to hop aboard the *Aurora* and sail to a land far, far away.

Because he already knew the reason—and it was entirely his fault.

———

DEAR READERS,

Wow! Just wow! Aren't you glad Jonas finally realized he had the freedom to marry Evelina?

I have to admit, as I was writing Jonas's story, there were times I wondered just how things were going to work out for him. I often give characters in my novels some kind of burden and trial to overcome, but Jonas faced such great loss only a couple months before his story opened, and he was so raw and scarred because of it. But with God, time, and the love of a good woman, he found his way forward again. I don't know about you, but I look forward to seeing just how content he and Evelina will be with each other in future books of this series.

I think my favorite part of this novel is probably the very end, when the reporter walks into the jail, and Jonas realizes just how much of a fool he's been in rejecting Evelina.

So now Jonas and Evelina are getting married, and the entire family is celebrating—or at least, most of the family is celebrating.

Sacha, however, is carrying some pretty big secrets, and those secrets have a lot to do with a certain man in Sitka who isn't very happy about Ilya being found, Evelina being engaged, or the Amos family having an expensive contract to build a ship.

Sacha's going to have a big fight on his hands, with an even bigger enemy. But will he let his family help, or will he insist on handling things on his own? I hope you'll join me for Sacha and Maggie's story, Whispers on the Tide, which releases in the Spring of 2024.

Author's Note

On October 18, 1867, the United States purchased Alaska from Russia. On the top of Castle Hill in Sitka, where a grand governor's mansion then sat, the Russian flag was lowered, the American flag was raised, and over 650,000 square miles was transferred from Russian to American control.

The following years were an absolute disaster.

The United States had no clue what to do with their new land. In fact, the United States didn't even know who to put in charge of Alaska. At first the Army was in charge, then the Navy, then the Department of the Interior, and each entity brought with it a string of generals and governors that barely lasted a year in Alaska.

The ineptitude of the bureaucrats and the inefficiency of having one US Marshal to provide law enforcement for the entirety of Alaska were not made up in *Written on the Mist*. No one knew how to run Alaska, and it left those who stayed behind after the transfer reeling from poor management and stubborn insistence on implementing policies that were never going to work in such a vast, untamed land.

One of the most misguided yet well-intentioned backers of these poor policies was a Presbyterian minister, Rev. Sheldon Jackson. Yes, he was a real historical figure, and he had a sincere desire to "aid" the Alaska Natives. But the methods he used were at best misguided, and at worst horrifying.

Sheldon Jackson did, in fact, become the Minister of Education for Alaska and oversaw education at both day schools and boarding schools. Rev. Jackson was convinced that the only way to help the Alaska Native children was by fully assimilating them into Western culture and forcing them to leave their native culture behind. Most noticeably, this meant students were not permitted to speak in their native tongues at any time or for any reason.

Interestingly, Rev. Jackson was concerned that the assimilation efforts being supported by the US government would lead to his native students losing their tribal cultures. In an effort to preserve these cultures, he began collecting various artifacts for display in a museum.

If you travel to Sitka, Alaska, today, you can visit the Sheldon Jackson Museum. You will find not just one whaling suit, but several, along with whale blubber lamps, hand woven baskets, and other facets of everyday life for the multiple tribes scattered across Alaska.

As hinted at near the end of *Written on the Mist*, Sheldon Jackson was also involved in three court cases where parents sued the Sitka Industrial School for refusing to allow their children to return home after they'd signed a five-year contract agreeing to send their children to the school.

You'll be seeing more about these court cases (and Evelina's fictional role in them) as the series progresses.

Another thing to note historically is that domestic violence was not illegal in the 1800s. It was looked down upon, yes, but it was also considered a private family affair, and not something that others should involve themselves with or the law should interfere in.

Similar to her championing of the Alaska Natives, Evelina is a woman with views well ahead of her time when it comes to her treatment of domestic abuse victims.

I hope you enjoy the small slice of Alaskan history that I was able to include in *Written on the Mist*. I had great fun creating the Amos family, and it seemed only natural for such a family to struggle against the poor management policies that controlled their beloved land. I hope you'll join me for the next installment in the Amos Family's journey, Sacha and Maggie's story, *Whispers on the Tide*. It will release in the spring of 2024.

Acknowledgments

Thank you first and foremost to my Lord and Savior, Jesus Christ, for giving me both the ability and opportunity to write novels for His glory.

As with any novel, an author might come up with a story idea and sit at his or her computer to type the initial words, but it takes an army of people to bring you the book you have today. I'd especially like to thank my editors. Erin Healy's keen insight and ability to understand my characters and their worlds have made my novels shine in ways that I had never thought possible, and I count it a privilege to work with her. Jennifer Lonas is the newest addition to my editing team. Her eye for detail helps me to deliver a polished, professional book to you every single time. And then there's Roseanna White, one of my longest friends and biggest encouragements in this industry. She answers my random emails, helps me brainstorm when I get stuck, and points out so many ways to make my books stronger.

Many thanks to my family for working with my writing schedule and giving me a chance to do two things I love: be a mom and a writer.

Also, many thanks to the hospitable people of Juneau and Sitka, Alaska, especially Rich Mattson with the Juneau-Douglas City

Museum, and Hal Spackman and Nicole Fiorino with Sitka History in Sitka. The three of them answered question after question and provided numerous images and book recommendations to help me bring this small slice of Alaskan history to life.

About the Author

Naomi Rawlings is a *USA Today* bestselling author of over a dozen historical novels, including the Eagle Harbor Series, which has sold more than 450,000 copies. She lives with her husband and three children in Michigan's rugged Upper Peninsula, along the southern shore of Lake Superior, where they get two hundred inches of snow every year, and where people still grow their own vegetables and cut down their own firewood—just like in the historical novels she writes.

For more information about Naomi, please visit her at www.naomirawlings.com or find her on Facebook at www.facebook.com/author.naomirawlings. If you'd like a free novella, sign up for her author newsletter: http://geni.us/35Yn.

Made in the USA
Middletown, DE
16 November 2023

42819092R00250